SOMETIMES

PE**O**PLE

DIE

Also by Simon Stephenson

Set My Heart to Five
Let Not the Waves of the Sea

SOMETIMES

PEPLE

DIE

A NOVEL

SIMON STEPHENSON

HANOVER
SQUARE
PRESS

HANOVER
SQUARE
PRESS™

Recycling programs
for this product may
not exist in your area.

ISBN-13: 978-1-335-42925-4

Sometimes People Die

Hanover Square Press
22 Adelaide St. West, 41st Floor
Toronto, Ontario M5H 4E3, Canada
HanoverSqPress.com
BookClubbish.com

Printed in U.S.A.

SOMETIMES

PEOPLE

DIE

OCCAM'S RAZOR:
the principle, attributed to William of Occam,
that in explaining a thing, no more assumptions
should be made than are necessary.

There was a moment I always loved in the hospital.

It came after your pager had crackled into life to broadcast the disembodied voice of a bored switchboard operator. It came after you had dropped whatever you were doing, rushed down long corridors and pushed your way through minors and into resus. It came after you had pulled on your gloves, drawn up your syringes, and unsheathed your needles. It came, finally, when you and five or six of your colleagues stood silently around the empty trolley and waited for whatever was about to happen.

In that tranquil moment—alone from the time you entered the hospital until you left—there was nowhere more important you should be and nothing else you should be doing. Any second now, this room would be filled with raised voices, blood, electricity, saline, the hissing of gases, perhaps even the splintering of bone. Afterward, when all was said and done, a human life would have been restored or extinguished. For now, though, like a heart in diastole, we waited in silent expectation for the chamber to be filled.

As I sit down to write this, I have that same feeling for the first time *in twenty years: a moment of peaceful anticipation before the doors crash open, and I am once again engulfed in the swirling chaos of blood and life and death and everything else that occurred all those years ago.*

CHAPTER 1

There are many storied hospitals in London, venerated institutions where scientific breakthroughs were made and legendary physicians named unfortunate diseases after themselves. Even the very names of those hospitals—St. Thomas', the Royal London Hospital, The Royal Brompton Heart and Chest Hospital—stir thoughts of centuries of grandeur, prestige, and medical accomplishment.

St. Luke's was not such a place. Built by a tobacco baron in the late 1800s to house the unfashionable lunatics of unfashionable east London, it had stumbled through the next century in the very same style as it had begun: awkward, frowned upon, and teetering perpetually on the verge of bankruptcy. Most of Lord Nicotine's original buildings somehow remained, but over the years a ramshackle series of extensions had been added, including a twelve-story tower block that looked exactly like the neighboring high-rises. Local legend held that this had been constructed by hospital management to encourage the council to purchase the entire hospital and turn the whole place into social housing. The council had not wanted it.

But it would be churlish for me to complain, because I was not the kind of doctor anybody was ever going to name a disease after. I had barely scraped into medical school, and my sole distinction in the entire five years was to have equaled the university's record for the number of retaken exams. Still, I had graduated, and quickly found that I was better suited to life on the wards than in the university. As a medical student, the consultants expected you to be able to reel off a list of seventeen causes of pancreatitis that included organophosphate poisoning and being stung by a scorpion. As a junior doctor, they merely wanted you to do the weary needful: give the patient oxygen, fluids, and analgesia, and call the intensive care unit if they began to look like they might not survive the night.

Even at that, my medical career had taken an unfortunate turn midway through my third year of practice. A dreary year of hearings and rehabilitation later, I had finally been signed off to return to work with the caveat that I attend drug counseling once a week. After everything I'd done, I had known I would have to leave Scotland and start over, and the Senior House Officer job at St. Luke's that I had seen advertised in the back of the *British Medical Journal* had seemed a perfect fit. In some ways that even turned out to be true: not many other hospitals would have employed me, and not many other doctors would have willingly worked at St. Luke's.

My telephone interview gave a new meaning to the word "cursory." There were no clinicians on the call, and the exhausted-sounding HR woman asked only two questions: Was I on the medical register, and when could I begin? I would later discover that St. Luke's was simply in an even worse predicament than I was. Six months previously, the medical department's approval to train junior doctors had been withdrawn by the Department of Health, leaving the hospital short of a dozen junior doctors.

As the pool of candidates that might fill these roles comprised solely of doctors willing to work without prospect of meaningful career advancement, they had never managed to fill more than eight of them.

I confirmed I was on the medical register—albeit with conditions on my practice—and told the HR woman I could start just as soon as I found somewhere to live in London. She reassured me that St. Luke's had an accommodation block on-site that would be perfectly adequate until I got myself settled, and informed me I would start in two days' time. She hung up before I could ask any more questions, and I took the train south the next day.

CHAPTER 2

I got into King's Cross in the evening. It was still summer then, and the day's heat radiated back off the Euston Road and mixed with the diesel fumes of the buses to make the air asphyxiatingly thick. I took a crowded underground train, then an empty overground one, and finally dragged my suitcase through an estate to St. Luke's. It looked like an asylum that a distracted child had constructed from a half dozen unmatched Lego sets.

The accommodation block was a dingy row of condemned terraced houses that even the student nurses had long since abandoned. I had been assigned to share one of these houses with a Dr. Vogel, a locum consultant hematologist from Germany. Nobody had warned Dr. Vogel he was to have a housemate, but he was sporting about it, offering me one of his wheat beers and apologetically informing me that there was no hot water because he had used it all in his bath that morning. I drank his beer, Dr. Vogel talked about motorsport and some recent ad-

vances in platelet science he inexplicably thought would interest me, and I went to bed at the first opportunity.

My first day was a Saturday. Dr. Sudbury, an owlish, fifty-
something rheumatologist who doubled as St. Luke's clinical
director, was the consultant on call. Rheumatologists are often
sticklers for medical tradition—only the truest of believers ever
choose that impossibly complex specialty as a career—and Dr.
Sudbury was no exception. Alone among the senior doctors,
she always donned a pressed white laboratory coat to conduct
her rounds. I remember thinking on that first morning that it
gave her the appearance of a superintendent in an insane asylum;
only now do I understand how prescient that impression was.

Every physician has their own theory of hospital medicine,
and Dr. Sudbury's seemed to be that any patient not visibly dying
should have been sent home an hour ago. After briefly peering
over the top of her half-moon glasses at each new specimen, she
would turn to the junior doctors on her ward round and ask
them only two questions: Why on earth did you admit this patient, and for goodness' sake will you please now discharge them?
She never tired of reminding us of her mantra that "a hospital
is a dangerous place to be." This phrase would come back to
haunt Dr. Sudbury in due course, but her devotion to it meant
she invariably got the round done in under two hours. Many
of the other consultants took until well into the afternoon, and
Professor Wells—an octogenarian research physician who somehow still had an honorary contract for a week of inpatient medicine every six months—had infamously once taken three days.

But even by the time Dr. Sudbury had completed her rapid-
fire ward round on that first day, the accident and emergency
sister had paged me three times to come and see a patient she
suspected had malaria. I had refused to leave the ward round
early, because I had not believed the nurse's diagnosis. An old
medical axiom holds that if you hear hoofbeats, when you look
out the window you will see horses and not zebras. In Scotland,

our patients had indeed mostly been knackered old horses, their diseases the inevitable result of a lifetime of smoking, or drinking, or working in the shipyards.

Of course, when I finally got down to St. Luke's accident and emergency department and pulled back the cubicle curtain, it revealed a Ghanaian man with a temperature of forty degrees. He told me he'd arrived in London three days earlier and when I asked him how he felt, he replied, "The same as every other time I've had malaria." It was only when he said this that I realized that if you hear hoofbeats and look out the window in Ghana, you might be more likely to see zebras than horses.

Sure enough, when I examined him, he had the findings I'd read about in textbooks: mild jaundice and an enlarged liver and spleen. I had no idea how to treat malaria and, even worse, would soon have to face the A+E sister and offer her a treatment plan. Fortunately, the patient himself remembered the name of the drug he'd been given the last time he had malaria, and I was able to pass this off as my own knowledge.

The rest of the shift flashed past in a chaos of patients, X-rays, needles, bloods, and cardiac arrest calls. It was busier than I remembered any hospital in Scotland ever being, but I assumed I was just out of practice. When handover finally arrived at half past eight, I was grateful to turn over the pager to Saz, a cheery doctor from the Midlands who congratulated me on surviving my first shift and promised me it was all downhill from here.

When I got back to the residence, Dr. Vogel was watching a documentary about the history of Formula Three motor racing. He invited me to join him, but I made my excuses and retreated to my room. If you happened to both love the history of motorsport and have leukemia, Dr. Vogel would have been exactly the person you'd want to spend your Saturday evening with. But I did not, and he was not.

I worked the next day too. Sunday shifts in Scotland were always quiet, but if anything St. Luke's seemed even busier than it had the previous day, and I now began to understand that I was not merely out of practice. In a sprawling metropolis like London, patients had diseases I had only ever read about in textbooks, many consultations had to be conducted through a telephone interpreting service, and none of the patients seemed to even have a GP, let alone to have ever seen them.

Each of these things made even simple problems a challenge, and rendered challenging problems fiendishly complex. At lunchtime the Somali interpreter on the Language Line apologized that the highly distressed patient I was seeing spoke a regional dialect called Jiiddu that she herself could not speak, but gave me the number of her cousin who could. When I called the cousin, the cousin's husband answered and said his wife was out at a birthday party, but he himself also spoke Jiiddu and could translate. When I got them on the phone together, the cousin's husband and the patient turned out to have been school classmates in Somalia. Unfortunately, it also now transpired that my patient had attended St. Luke's because she believed magicians had poisoned her; to this, the cousin's husband then added his own diagnosis that my patient was "simply a lunatic" and the further background that "she comes from a family of notorious lunatics." I referred the patient to the psychiatrists, making sure to include the phone number of the Jiiddu-speaking cousin's husband in my notes.

In the late afternoon, I was paged to accident and emergency for a medical standby. A medical standby meant that the incoming patient was moribund yet still breathing and had a heartbeat, so only a single doctor was called. If you got lucky, an A+E nurse might join you.

The patient the paramedics crashed through the doors was an unconscious woman in her forties. She was wearing a long, flowery dress, and her handbag had been placed atop the trolley. On a sunny Sunday afternoon in late summer, she looked like she should have been entering a pub beer garden rather than a resus room. She still had a pulse and a blood pressure, but little more than that: her eyes were closed, she was tolerating the breathing tube in her throat without any sedation, and she did not so much as flinch when I pressed down on the nerve at the upper edge of her eye socket.

The paramedics told me that the woman's husband had noticed her become confused during a wedding anniversary lunch, and shortly after that she had collapsed. A waiter had dialed 999, and by the time the paramedics arrived the patient had already been entirely unresponsive.

"Collapse query cause, Doc," one of the paramedics concluded as they finished their handover. "Good luck, mate."

We both knew I was not the one who needed the luck. "Collapse query cause" was a common and often fixable presentation in the elderly, in whom it could be provoked by anything from dehydration to wearing overly tight socks. In a younger patient, the range of potential causes was far smaller and infinitely deadlier. A problem that arrived as abruptly as this woman's had usually meant a blood vessel had become blocked or ruptured; her coma located that blockage or rupture inside her skull, and her elevated blood pressure was in keeping with such a catastrophe. I scribbled out a request card for a scan of her head, and called a porter to take it to radiology.

Left alone with the patient, I now examined her for any other clues to her sudden collapse. Her heart and lungs sounded perfectly clear, and her abdomen was soft. Her reflexes were intact, but when I used the bottom of the tendon hammer to scratch the soles of her feet, her big toes moved up instead of down. This was an "upgoing plantar response," a sign of serious nervous system dysfunction. I noticed now too that her face was a little red, and when I pulled her eyelids back I saw that her pupils were large. The red face I ascribed to her elevated blood pressure; I didn't have an explanation for her pupils, but it seemed academic given what was surely happening inside her skull.

I checked a quick venous gas, which gave no further clues, and sent some routine bloods to the lab. By the time I had done those things, the porters arrived and took the patient round to the scanner. Twenty minutes later they wheeled her back into the resus room, and I took the notes from her trolley to read the radiologist's hand-scrawled report. It said simply: *CT Head-No abnormality detected.*

This was not the good news it might seem, and likely meant that the scan had simply missed an early clot. Realistically, the only other possible cause for the woman's unexplained collapse was that she had somehow ingested a powerful toxin. That seemed hard to square both with a wedding anniversary lunch and the blood tests that had by now all come back as normal.

Whatever terrible fate had befallen her, my patient was continuing to deteriorate. Her blood pressure had continued to climb, her oxygen saturations had begun to fall, and she had now spiked a fever. A fever often signals infection, but my patient's collapse and normal blood tests meant a more likely explanation was that the mischief afoot in her brain was now interfering with her body's ability even to regulate its own temperature. Nonetheless, an infection was a potentially treatable cause, so I had the nurse set up for a lumbar puncture, wrote the patient up for drugs to control her blood pressure, and called the intensive care unit. The duty anesthetist grumbled that the scan had obviously just missed something and we'd only be delaying the woman's inevitable demise, but grudgingly agreed to come and assess her.

By now the patient's husband had arrived, and I went out to speak to him. He mostly seemed relieved his wife's collapse was not due to an allergic reaction to a banoffee pie he'd insisted they share. It took me some time to communicate how sick she was, and that her problem might not actually be fixable. When I asked if his wife had taken any medicines or other drugs, he shook his head: his wife, he told me, was "a real hippy," and getting her to take even so much as an acetaminophen was a challenge.

I took the man in to see his dying wife, and then went and had the switchboard call Dr. Sudbury at home. She listened in silence as I told her about the woman's stupor, upgoing plantars, red face, and dilated pupils. Only when I had finished speaking did Dr. Sudbury sigh wearily and say that we could not always save everyone. She at least did not ask me why I had admitted the patient, nor instruct me to discharge her.

I was preparing for the lumbar puncture when my new colleague Amelia passed through resus. Amelia was ostensibly my on-call partner for the weekend, but it had been so busy we had barely seen each other. Amelia asked how I was getting on, and I told her I was going to survive the weekend, but I wasn't sure my patient would.

"Her face looks quite red," she remarked.

I mumbled about the woman's blood pressure being up, but instead of reassuring Amelia that I had the situation under control, this information seemed only to intrigue her. She moved closer to the patient, leaned down, and pulled back her eyelids.

"Pupils are large," she said.

"Yes. Her plantars are upgoing too," I replied, irked at the implication that I might have missed those findings. If Amelia caught any shortness in my tone, she ignored it.

"And she feels warm?"

"I'm doing a lumber puncture to rule out infection," I said, by now actively hoping this would end Amelia's interest. I had already provided Dr. Sudbury all this exact same information, and even she—who had decades more experience than Amelia and I combined—had not been able come up with a unifying diagnosis.

"So, high blood pressure, red face, dilated pupils." Amelia continued, "Has she passed urine?"

"I don't know," I admitted, a little embarrassed I'd not had a nurse catheterize the patient yet. Amelia then leaned over the woman and percussed her lower abdomen. The difference between the dull and the resonant notes she elicited reached me across the room.

"Her bladder is full," Amelia said. "Which I suppose means she's 'red as a beet, dry as a bone, blind as a bat, hot as a hare, full as a flask.' I'm sure you already thought of this, but do you think there is any chance this could be anticholinergic syndrome?"

I stopped and looked at Amelia then. She was about the same age as me, and was dressed in a blouse and a skirt that stopped a little above her knees. Her eyes were hazel beneath the thick black-rimmed glasses that were inexplicably fashionable in those days, and her shoulder-length brown hair was held back with an Alice band. A stethoscope hung around her neck in a mirror image of the one around mine, and a reusable torniquet likewise dangled from one of her belt loops. Put another way: Amelia looked just like every other junior doctor working the weekend shift up and down the country, and really had no business presuming to offer such an obscure diagnosis on an equally junior colleague's patient.

Still, I had not considered anticholinergic syndrome and nor, apparently, had Dr. Sudbury. It was a vanishingly rare diagnosis, but the phrase Amelia had just recited was one I too had learned by rote back in medical school, and my patient certainly had all the symptoms. Fortunately, anticholinergic syndrome is caused by overdose, so I had inadvertently already covered myself.

"Her husband says she won't even take acetaminophen," I told Amelia, failing to entirely hide my pleasure at disproving her theory.

"Did you speak to him yourself?" she asked.

"Of course I did," I said. "Poor bastard is in the waiting room."

Amelia nodded and left. I assumed she had gone to get on with her own work, but five minutes later she returned to resus, picked up my patient's handbag, and emptied its contents onto the counter: lipstick, tissues, coins, a purse, and a small glass vial labeled Flower Power. Amelia held the bottle out to me and pointed to the small print words "Active Ingredient—*Atropa Belladonna*." My patient, who would not even take acetaminophen, had inadvertently poisoned herself with belladonna, one of the most powerful anticholinergic drugs on planet Earth.

"Thank you," I said, and actually meant it.

"Just a lucky guess," said Amelia. "It's always easier to be the second pair of eyes."

Now that Amelia had made the diagnosis, the duty anesthetist was only too happy to take the patient to the intensive care unit. He commenced her on a physostigmine infusion and she woke up two hours later, entirely intact but furious at what she called the "unwanted imposition of conventional Western medicine."

After handover that night, I did not return to the residence, but took a bus through the East End to attend the first of my weekly counseling sessions with the Reverend Murdo McKendrick. That he was Scottish like me was merely coincidence, as he had simply been the only counselor on the General Medical Council's approved list who had immediate availability and had been willing to see me in the evening. I soon found out why.

The Reverend McKendrick was in at least his late seventies, had pure white hair and a bright red face, and conducted his business from a one-bedroom flat above a kebab shop in Bethnal Green. He seemed to want me to think this place was merely his "consulting rooms"—he kept referring to it as such—but it was obviously also his home. I had to use the bathroom to provide my urine sample, and his denture-cleaning supplies alone told that story. His rosaceous nose, the spider nevi on his face and the half-drunk bottle of whisky in the bathroom cabinet told another. Much later, I would discover that the Reverend McKendrick had long since been defrocked, and the sessions in which we addressed my previous addiction were his sole means of financing his own current one.

The good news was that he seemed to have even less interest in counseling me than I had in being counseled. That first week—and every week thereafter—he began by making a lot of small talk about the Scottish football I still vaguely followed. I swiftly learned that if I remained perfectly still and silent, the Reverend McKendrick would eventually talk himself into a slumber, his voice slowly quietening like a radio whose batteries were running flat. I would then sit motionless until I could wake him to inform him that our hour was over and thank him for another life-saving session. He got paid enough to keep him in Whyte and Mackay, and I got to remain on the medical register, so the arrangement suited us both.

CHAPTER 3

Rickets. Tuberculosis. Dengue fever. During my first few weeks at St. Luke's, I saw more unusual diseases than I had in my entire career in Scotland. I even diagnosed scurvy, a condition so rare that even Dr. Sudbury briefly seemed impressed, but before I'd finished explaining how I had made my leap of deductive brilliance she was already discharging the next patient.

I could not blame her. The reason the junior doctors had been withdrawn from St. Luke's was that the consultants had simply been far too overworked themselves to ever take much notice of them, and having fewer doctors around had only exacerbated the primary problem. As long as the patients were clerked, and the nurses didn't complain about any of us too much, the consultants were mostly grateful to us simply for being there.

There should have been twelve of us junior doctors in the medicine department, but my arrival had brought the total up to only nine. I got to meet these new colleagues of mine in the resuscitation room, at handover, and in the mess. We each had our reasons for working at St. Luke's, but nobody else's seemed to be that they had been caught stealing opioids in their last job.

Rather, Glen had failed his membership exam and was treading water while he retook it; Saz was locumming to pay the bills while her children were young; Rami had been a neurosurgeon in his native Iraq but the UK had refused to recognize all but the most basic part of his training; Joanne's periodic bouts of psychotic depression had seen her booted out of several more prestigious rotations; Colin was supporting himself while he pursued an improbable alternate career as an opera singer; Kwame seemed simply to have been standing too near a notoriously unfortunate case and had been forever tarred by association; Marianne had been a consultant pediatrician but had decided she hated children so was now retraining. Physicians, heal thyselves.

Only one of our number was not like the rest. Amelia was a Cambridge graduate from somewhere in the home counties, had already passed her membership and could have landed a job at any hospital in the city; she had actually chosen to work St. Luke's, in order to obtain the hands-on experience she would not get at a more prestigious institution. Where else, Amelia had earnestly asked us in the mess one day, would she get the chance to insert chest drains and pacing wires without supervision? The rest of us—who lived in perpetual fear of being paged in the middle of the night to do such terrifying things—only shrugged. Where else indeed?

Amelia had the encyclopedic knowledge of a textbook author, a mind as logical as an algorithm, and the energy of an amphetamine addict. The first part was at least understandable, for Amelia once accidentally let slip that her tutor at Cambridge had been Professor Sir Smithfield of *Smithfield's Textbook of Human Disease* fame. Her knowledge and mind were put to good use at St. Luke's, for Amelia was already such a sharp diagnostician that even the consultants sometimes requested her opinion on difficult cases. Still, it was her energy that was the most unfathomable to us, her supposed peers. After a long day on admissions, Amelia would frequently arrive at handover already in her running gear, ready to head out on a seven-mile run. Even on night shifts, when the rest of us would have long since hidden ourselves away in the on-call room, Amelia actively trawled the wards in search of more work.

It should have made her insufferable, but somehow it all only made her endearing. None of us had ever met anybody with such a passion for medicine. It might have been easy to simply label Amelia a relentless overachiever except for one thing: her motivation in all of this seemed not a once-gifted child's eternal quest for validation, but a genuine love for her patients, and a desire to obtain the best outcome for them.

At lunch one day, I witnessed Amelia diagnose a patient with a rare genetic syndrome by their appearance from across the canteen. If any of the rest of us had spotted it, we would no doubt have politely ignored it; in contrast, Amelia had broken the news, informed the patient of their options and scribbled out for a note for their GP before I'd even finished choosing my sandwich. Amelia wanted to be a neurologist and so her primary job at St. Luke's was on the stroke ward. She nonetheless first planned to work in the developing world, and therefore was studying for a master's degree at the London School of Hygiene and Tropical Medicine on the weekends.

At the other end of the enthusiasm, effort, and prestige scale, my own day job was on Care of the Elderly, the hospital's least glamorous ward. We all did so much on call that we each ended up looking after every medical patient in the hospital at some point anyway, but I had always preferred Care of the Elderly to the fancier specialties, because the old people complained far less than the other patients. Perhaps it was because they had lived through a war, and far preferred to spend their time talking about that.

The Care of the Elderly ward at St. Luke's was even named

The Jack Duckton Ward after a local war hero. A plaque at the entrance stated that Duckton had been part of the British Expeditionary Force that was evacuated at Dunkirk, and he had then fought for Montgomery at El Alamein, where he had been captured by the Nazis. Due to endless bold escape attempts, the Nazis had ultimately sent Jack Duckton to the POW camp at Dachau, where he had dug a network of tunnels that allowed many of the prisoners from the concentration camp next door to escape to freedom.

Jack Duckton himself had long since died—the plaque did not specify if that had happened on his eponymous ward—but his daughter still lived locally and ran a foundation dedicated to raising awareness of her father's heroism. Later, I found out that the proper handling of Eliza Duckton even featured in the induction manual I should have been given. The gist of it was that if she was not regularly invited to be photographed clutching her bony claws around some confused dementia patient or other for a spread in the *Hackney Gazette*, she would create a pretext for a front-page splash that invariably involved accusing St. Luke's of besmirching her father's memory.

Still, Eliza Duckton's protectiveness was understandable, for the story of Jack Duckton's life was the most incredible tale. Indeed, the sole problem with it was that he appeared to have made almost the whole thing up. To have been at both Dunkirk and El Alamein would have required Duckton to have been in two completely separate regiments, and as far I could tell, there had never been a prisoner of war camp at Dachau. Mostly, there was the irreconcilable fact that Jack Duckton had claimed he had rescued hundreds of Jews, and yet not one of them had ever come forward to confirm his account.

If they were aware of any of this, the nurses who staffed Jack Duckton had long ago decided that their energies were better focused on the still-just-about-living rather than the long-since dead. The sister, a Filipino woman called Angela, ran as tight a ship as was possible, and really the ward's only problem was the classic St. Luke's malady: finding and retaining staff. Angela had managed to employ a few of her compatriots, and had attempted to compensate for the remaining shortage by taking on a lot of student nurses. Unlike their medical student counterparts, who were invariably determined to prove the maxim "a little knowledge is a dangerous thing," the student nurses were quietly efficient and generally lacking only in confidence.

The notable exception to this rule was a student nurse called Louise Fisher. I had heard the name and noted an accompanying eye roll a couple of times, but due to our shift patterns not coinciding, I only encountered Louise towards the end of my first month at St. Luke's. She had seemed entirely unremarkable: perhaps twenty-five years old, she wore the same plain tunic as the other student nurses, her pixie-cut hair had been dyed a reddish-brown, and she was perhaps a little overweight. Probably the only remotely striking thing about Louise was that she spoke with a northern accent, but I suspected our colleagues found this easier to decipher than my Scottish one.

Dr. Sudbury had originally asked Amelia to present the belladonna case at our Wednesday teaching session, but when the day arrived she instead announced that, as part of a new initiative aimed at "strengthening interdisciplinary collaboration," the junior doctors' teaching sessions would now be combined with those of the nurses. We all knew this was simply a scheme to reduce the time we were away from the coalface, and it would not have mattered except for Dr. Sudbury's final point: to demonstrate it would truly be a collegiate approach, Louise Fisher would now present the belladonna case to the combined session.

The presentation Louise gave that lunchtime was clinically fascinating, although probably not quite for the reasons she had hoped. Amelia's brilliance in making such an obscure diagnosis had undoubtedly saved my patient's life, but this seemed to have barely registered with Louise, who turned out to have been on secondment to the intensive care unit that day.

According to the presentation she gave, the key learning points of the case had been the IV she herself had managed to site at only the third attempt—the one through which, she repeatedly reminded us, the antidote had been given—the blood sample she had run to the lab in record time, and the phone call she had made to the patient's husband to ask him to bring a change of his clothes for his wife.

At the end of the presentation, when Louise offered to answer any questions, Kwame asked her how it had felt to save a human life. Louise considered this deeply, and then declared that it was a great honor, but really she was simply doing what anybody with her training and expertise would do in that situation. Somehow we all managed not to laugh.

Our lives depend on the expertise of our doctors and nurses, and we sometimes have no choice but to surrender ourselves to their secret mastery of their opaque arts. The notion that a healthcare worker might intentionally harm a patient is therefore a profoundly troubling one.

And yet a hospital is an almost perfect hunting ground for those motivated to end rather than enhance human life. It is, after all, a place filled with the weak and vulnerable, the incapacitated and the mute. It is a place where privacy is prized and secrecy is mandated. It is a place where death is an everyday occurrence.

But why would a healthcare worker ever seek to harm a patient? Apart from the many good reasons no human being should ever harm another, there is an essential paradox in healthcare murder: Why undertake the years of study, and the laborious toil of daily ward work, only to undo all of those efforts with base murder?

Perhaps the answer is simply that, as a group, healthcare workers are no less flawed than anybody else. Certainly, each time a new healthcare killer is apprehended, the professional bodies rush to release statements pointing out the culprit was not a healthcare worker who became a se-rial killer, but a serial killer who became a healthcare worker.

Maybe this is even true, but it seems an unhelpful reflex, for to com-prehend any disease one must surely first study it. For the more common maladies that study can be done with a textbook, but for a pathology as rare as healthcare murder, the best resource will always be the previ-ous cases histories documented in the literature. From such vignettes, attempts can be made to trace the dots between the current case and its forebears, and to perhaps even find some kind of answer to the ques-tion that ultimately haunts all such sicknesses: Why?

CHAPTER 4

That Friday, I started a week of nights by doing what I always had: spending the afternoon at a matinee in the cinema. I could never sleep on the day I began nights, and a long-ago colleague had told me that his own trick was to go to the movies. It was restful, and dark, and a little self-indulgent besides. All those things were necessary before embarking on such a treacherous expedition.

There were always two junior medical doctors on the rota overnight, and that meant that every fourth week we each had to work nights. Nights week began on a Friday evening, and if there is anything more depressing than taking public transport to work as the rest of the city is celebrating the start of their weekend, I never wish to know it.

Actually, I already do know it, because things only ever deteriorated once you arrived at the hospital. At handover, your daytime colleagues would inform you how many were waiting in the emergency department, run through the day's admissions, and tell you about any patients on the wards that seemed liable to cause trouble. And then they would toss you the arrest pagers and hurry away to their own precious weekends of sleep.

For the next twelve hours, the care of the five hundred malfunctioning human bodies currently in the hospital would be down to you and your shift partner. Technically, there should have been a registrar on-site, but they had been withdrawn too and their rota was even barer than ours. On the rare occasions a registrar was listed, they had invariably already worked that day and would work again tomorrow, so they were only available for telephone advice from home. During my entire time at St. Luke's, I never called a registrar once, and nor was I aware of anyone else who had.

Sometimes friends would ask me what a doctor actually does overnight, and the only answer I could come up with was "everything." So we did all our regular daytime work: we saw new patients in accident and emergency, troubleshot sick patients on the wards, put in lines, checked X-rays, took bloods, prescribed fluids and analgesia, ran to cardiac arrests, and—when that had all failed to make any difference—we certified the dead. There was then the extra work because nobody else was doing their regular daytime duties: the phone calls to wake up the laboratory staff when you needed an urgent test; the ECGs you performed yourself because the techs worked only office hours; the patients you ended up wheeling to X-ray because the porters were on their mandatory rest break for another hour.

Finally, beyond these practicalities, there was also the unique mischief darkness visits upon the human body and brain. We all spent a lot of time dealing with its casualties: delirious elderly patients who had convinced themselves somebody was hiding beneath the bed; lungs that creepingly filled with fluid until a patient woke up drowning; anxious minds that decided they didn't like what their own doctor had told them that morning and wanted to self-discharge against medical advice at 3:00 a.m.

Occasionally, in the small hours before the early morning heart attacks started, we'd escape to the mess for half an hour. On one glorious night, Joanne and I had a pizza delivered and even managed to eat a couple of slices before the next cardiac arrest. Mostly, though, it was a straight slog from evening handover until the one the next morning. To this day, the greatest sight I will ever see is a cleaner polishing a hospital floor at six o'clock on a winter's morning. The sun glimpsed rising over the city might tell you when the day has finally arrived, but long before that the first sight of the day staff tells you something far more important: the long night is almost over.

Witness such small miracles seven times in a row, and you would be free. As I made my way home each morning, the number of remaining shifts would repeat in my head like a mantra: four more to go, four more to go, four more to go. Even as I drew the curtains tight against the daylight, put on my eye mask and collapsed into bed, the number would still be whirring around my head: four, four, four.

And yet soon again would come the very worst part: waking up at 5:00 p.m. in a soaking sweat and knowing that you must now do the whole thing all over again. People often spoke about feeling jet-lagged during those weeks of nights, but a week of night shifts was not disorientating in the same way that taking a long-haul flight is. It was disorientating in the same way that taking seven long-haul flights over seven consecutive nights would be. By the time it came to buckle up for the seventh take-off on Thursday evening, I think every one of us would have happily steered the plane straight off the runway if it meant we did not have to endure yet another flight.

I have written so much about the somnambulant horror of a week of nights in the hope that you will understand when I tell you that Mrs. Horsburgh's death barely registered with me. We had come on shift to eight patients waiting and a backlog of sickies needing to be reviewed in the tower, so Saz and I had agreed

I would start in A+E while she cleared the wards. A couple of hours later, I had admitted three, discharged two, and sold one on to the surgeons as a suspected appendicitis. I was about to start seeing the next patient when the arrest page crackled into life to announce a cardiac arrest on level seven of the tower.

In the finest medical schools, doctors are trained not to run to emergencies. The seconds saved have been shown not to improve outcome, and the idea is that by walking the doctor remains calm and can run through their mental checklists to arrive at the scene ready to take decisive action. All well and good in theory, but St. Luke's was so understaffed and sprawled over such a large area that if a doctor had not run to an arrest there would be no point in even going at all, except to certify the patient's death.

And so I ran. In those days it was just about the only exercise I got, and I'd often arrive at a bedside feeling ready to collapse myself. At least on this particular night the lift in the tower block was working and empty, so I did not have to take the stairs. When I got to level seven, the alarm was still flashing outside the patient's room. I entered to find Saz forcing air into the patient's lungs with an Ambu bag, while an agency nurse performed chest compressions. Saz had only arrived a couple of minutes before I had, and the agency nurse knew only that Mrs. Horsburgh had been admitted due to falls and was supposed to be going home tomorrow.

But Mrs. Horsburgh would not be going anywhere now. She was frail and elderly, and the cardiac monitor in the corner was already showing a flat green line. In a cardiac arrest, the shape of the green line on the monitor is the whole game. If it is wildly oscillating, broad and fast, twisting, or even if it looks normal but is not producing a pulse, the patient's heart is still trying and they therefore have a chance. If the green line is flat, the patient's heart has given up, and they barely have a hope.

There are exceptions to everything in medicine, but mostly flat is asystole, and asystole is death.

And yet we carried on with the ballet: fifteen chest compressions to two squeezes of the Ambu bag. Check the rhythm on the monitor every two minutes, and give a shot of adrenalin every three to five minutes. In between, any free pair of hands would work to get a line in, take blood, or relieve the person doing the chest compressions.

When the anesthetist appeared, he swiftly got his breathing tube in and we switched to continuous chest compressions but still took turns to relieve each other. As always, we spoke loudly and performatively over the patient's lifeless body about the possible reasons for their sudden demise. Was this body short of oxygen, blood, heat or potassium? Had a clot formed in the blood vessels that supplied its heart or lungs? Had air leaked into the space between its lungs and chest wall? Could some unknown toxin have done this?

In Mrs. Horsburgh's case the answer to all of the above was no, but it hardly mattered. All that mattered was the green line on the monitor. Each time we paused to look to it, we hoped it had become jagged, or rhythmic, or oscillating. But it remained resolutely flat, and flat is asystole, and asystole is death. After ten minutes, Saz asked if any of us saw any reason to continue attempting resuscitation, and we all agreed it was futile. The anesthetist left without a word. The agency nurse said she would go and call the porters.

Saz had been in the middle of sorting out a sick patient when the arrest call came, so I offered to stay and verify the death, call the family, and write up the notes. A simple favor, one of a thousand in the ebb and flow of a week of nights, and yet it turned out to be a decision that would impact me as significantly as any other I have ever made.

Left alone, I looked around the room. The scene was the same as the aftermath of every failed arrest I had ever attended: the floor littered with used swabs and empty syringes, the oxygen still hissing from the wall supply, the monitor that mockingly showed the flat green line that had not once changed despite all our efforts. And of course, at the very center of this all, a dead elderly woman with broken ribs, puncture marks on her arms, and a useless breathing tube in her throat that by law only the pathologist could now remove.

I turned off the monitor and the oxygen, waited for the room to fall silent, and then set about verifying Mrs. Horsburgh's death. As her demise had been unexpected, the actual death certificate would need to wait until after the postmortem. For now, I simply needed to confirm she was dead, so that the porters would come and take her body to the mortuary.

Smithfield's Textbook of Human Disease wrote about death as if it was any other medical condition, and defined its signs as "the absence of any circulatory, respiratory and cerebral function." In practice, that meant I needed to place my stethoscope over Mrs. Horsburgh's still heart, and then her breathless lungs, and listen to the silence in each place for a full minute. It meant I had to pull back her eyelids to see that her pupils were fully dilated, and that they did not contract when I shone a bright torch into them. It meant I had to touch a wisp of cotton wool to the glassy surface of her cornea and observe that she did not blink. It was a strange process, far less sophisticated than the ballet that had preceded it, and yet at its heart was the most curious fact on our planet: half an hour ago this human being had been alive, and now she no longer was.

When I had finished, I found Mrs. Horsburgh's notes and took a seat at the nurses' station. I wrote up the arrest and concluded my entry in the same way we all did on these occasions: *No breath or cardiac sounds heard, pupils fixed and dilated, absent corneal reflex, time of death 00:34, Rest in Peace.*

I then turned to the front of the file, where the next-of-kin number was a landline for somebody called "Eleanor Wilson."

Whoever had taken down this information had not bothered to write down what relation Eleanor Wilson was to Mrs. Horsburgh, but then why would they have? It would not be them that had to call this number at one o'clock in the morning to wake up a stranger, ask them what relation they were to Mrs. Horsburgh, and then inform them that Mrs. Horsburgh was now dead.

Over and again in medical school we had been taught the correct way to impart bad news: to a prewarned close relative, in a gently lit room, free of interruptions and with a box of tissues strategically placed upon a table. The idea was that you first fired a warning shot, next gently established what the relative already knew, and then finally got down to it. You then gave them space to cry, and after an appropriate pause provided them with the tissues. The tissues, we were painstakingly taught, were crucial to the process, for they served as a metaphor that you could provide the bereaved with the comfort they needed at this tragic time. Finally, you asked the relative if they had any questions, gently broached the subject of organ donation if applicable, and offered them written information about bereavement counseling.

Of course, a telephone unexpectedly ringing in a hallway at one o'clock in the morning renders all of that moot. People know it is not good news, and even as you introduce yourself they usually interrupt to ask if their precious loved one has died. There is therefore no moment for warning shots nor gentle establishment of what they already know; you cannot even offer them tissues, and anyway nobody is thinking about metaphors.

It took Eleanor Wilson a long time to answer the phone, and when she did she sounded irritated, and immediately wanted to know why I was calling her in the middle of the night. Even when I informed her that I was calling from St. Luke's, she asked me if this update about her mother could not have waited until morning. I was glad for the clarification about their relationship, and wondered if her businesslike tone meant that Mrs. Horsburgh's death had actually been expected. That soon proved to have been a false hope: Mrs. Horsburgh dying had simply seemed so far from being any kind of possibility that her daughter had assumed a doctor calling in the middle of the night could mean only that the doctor lacked manners.

Eleanor Wilson was distraught. She actually even screamed, although she had at least been kind enough to drop the phone first. When she eventually picked the receiver up again, she was unable to speak as she was hyperventilating. I asked if anybody was with her, and between gasps she told me that her husband was, but she did not want to wake him up. I gently suggested that he would probably like to know about this, and she reluctantly agreed to go and wake him. Mr. Wilson came on the phone a few moments later and, though clearly also shocked, was able to be more coherent. Naturally, he wanted to know what had happened to Mrs. Horsburgh, and I told him the truth: I had no idea. Her heart had stopped beating, and we did not yet know the reason for that. Mr. Wilson said they would both come to the hospital immediately, and I did not attempt to dissuade him. I asked the nurses to put them in the dayroom when they arrived.

In the meantime, I went back to A+E to see a suspected stroke that turned out to be a migraine. After half an hour, the nurse paged to tell me the Wilsons were waiting in the dayroom.

The Wilsons were middle-aged, and the first thing that struck me was how well-dressed they were, with both of them wearing business suits. This surprised me, both because it was the middle of the night and because St. Luke's was situated in one of the poorest parts of the city. Our other patients did not generally dress like this, and nor did their relatives. I ascribed this odd formality to them wanting to show respect to the late Mrs. Horsburgh, but a more observant physician would no doubt have paid more attention to the fact that Mr. Wilson took notes in shorthand on a legal pad as I spoke. Dr. Sudbury or even Amelia would likely have immediately deduced that the Wilsons were both senior lawyers, and perhaps more specifically that they were barristers. Back then, I barely knew the difference between the two, and the whole thing anyway entirely escaped my notice.

I offered my condolences again, and explained to the Wilsons the little that I knew: Mrs. Horsburgh had been found unresponsive, and despite our best efforts, a team of experienced doctors had been unable to resuscitate her. Mr. Wilson seemed to accept this, but his wife asked me again how this could have possibly happened. I reiterated that her mother's death was unexplained, but reassured her there would be a postmortem that would hopefully provide some answers.

But Mrs. Wilson was not ready to be reassured. Instead, she demanded again to be told exactly what had gone wrong. She was so distressed it was hard to give her the most truthful answer: sometimes people die. Her mother had been eighty-four years old and it was not, as I now pointed out as gently as I could, entirely unheard-of for eighty-four-year-olds to drop dead. Mrs. Wilson countered with the insistence that her mother had been fit and well and had walked five miles every day. Her mother's own consultant had cleared her for discharge, and Mrs. Wilson could therefore only conclude that "something must have gone very badly wrong here."

Again, I explained about the postmortem, and how it would hopefully provide the answers Mrs. Wilson was seeking. Most bereaved families got squeamish at this point, and asked how invasive the procedure needed to be; by contrast, Mrs. Wilson's sole concern was whether the postmortem would be sufficiently thorough. I tried to reassure her that she had nothing to fear in this regard, but Mrs. Wilson was insistent on knowing the details. Eventually, I just had to tell her the gory truth: every single organ in her mother's body would be removed, weighed, measured, and dissected before being put back inside her like a macabre jigsaw puzzle. Mrs. Wilson went quiet for a moment, then nodded her approval. It seemed to be the first thing I'd said that she agreed with.

The Wilsons wanted to see Mrs. Horsburgh's body, and so I warned them of the expected changes: Mrs. Horsburgh would feel cold to the touch, they might notice that her body now felt stiff, and the breathing tube would still be in her throat. They confirmed they understood all of this, and I showed them into the room.

The nurses had tidied up, turned on the bedside lamp, and tucked Mrs. Horsburgh's corpse into bed. I'd hoped that this might help, but when Mrs. Wilson emerged she was only more distraught, and stated that her mother "looks so alive, she should still be alive." Again, she insisted that something must have gone very badly wrong for her mother to have died. For his part, Mr. Wilson wanted only to know the name of the doctor who would be performing the postmortem. When I told him it would be Dr. O'Leary, St. Luke's sole consultant pathologist, he wrote this down on his notepad. Both the Wilsons then gave me their cards, which was when I found out that they were barristers.

The rest of the night shift passed in the usual interminable maelstrom. At morning handover I informed Dr. Shazeen, St. Luke's stroke physician and Mrs. Horsburgh's consultant, of her passing. He reacted to the information in the way that one might to a news report of a distant war: sad, but what could you do? His ears pricked up a little when I mentioned that the family seemed to have concerns, and far more so when I told him Mrs. Horsburgh's daughter and son-in-law were both barristers. Dr. Shazeen said he would have Amelia call them to smooth things over, and I agreed that was a good idea.

Three more to go. Three more to go. Three more to go. I went back to the residence and slept the sleep of the dead, before coming back that evening to do it all again. I made it through to the end of the week in the same way I always had: by vowing this was the last time I would ever do this, and that I'd surely quit before I ever did another week of nights. I never did quit, of course, because almost nobody who becomes a doctor ever quits anything.

CHAPTER 5

I spent the weekend catching up on sleep and avoiding Dr. Vogel's incessant motorsports, and on the Monday I started back on day shifts. At lunchtime, Dr. O'Leary paged me to inform me he had completed the postmortem on Mrs. Horsburgh, and to request I now come and sign the death certificate. Any doctor who had cared for the patient during their admission could do this, but it was ideally supposed to be someone from their own team, so I naturally suggested he call Amelia instead. Dr. O'Leary said he had already tried that, but Amelia was now working her own set of nights. I finished my sandwich and trudged across the parking lot to the pathology lodge.

If that sounds a strange name, the building itself was even odder. A white stone cottage, it was the sole remaining part of the hunting retreat Lord Nicotine had initially built before his Damascene conversion. The thatched roof had long ago been replaced with asphalt, and the interior was replete with the same grubby linoleum and stainless steel as everywhere else in the hospital, but the building's essential function had not changed: it was still the place where dead things were conveyed to be dissected.

Dr. O'Leary let me in, and cheerfully led me past cabinets of refrigerated corpses to the table where Mrs. Horsburgh lay with a white sheet pulled up over her face. Like every pathologist, Dr. O'Leary was singularly untroubled by death, but endlessly courteous to his charges; he even quietly apologized to Mrs. Horsburgh as he pulled back the sheet to show me her face. I took a look and nodded that it was her.

The identification made, Dr. O'Leary passed me the death certificate. He had written that the cause of Mrs. Horsburgh's was a cardiac arrhythmia, an irregular heartbeat that had proved incompatible with life. This, he admitted to me, had largely been a diagnosis of exclusion: his postmortem had revealed a corpse that had until recently been in remarkably rude health, with the only small abnormality being some very slight old scarring around the heart. This scarring, Dr. O'Leary said, could have been enough to trigger an arrhythmia, which in turn could account for the falls Mrs. Horsburgh had been experiencing prior to her admission. He told me he had of course sent the usual samples for toxicology, but those tests would take weeks, so he had spoken to the coroner who had agreed he could release the body so the funeral could take place. I signed my portion of the certificate, Dr. O'Leary shook my hand with an odd formality, and I went back to Jack Duckton to try and prevent any more of my patients from coming his way.

The first recorded healthcare murder may have been committed in AD 54 by the Greek physician Xenophon.

Xenophon was born on the island of Kos and trained there at the Sanctuary of Asclepius, the healing god. Hippocrates himself had studied at Asclepius a few hundred years before Xenophon, but the Father of Medicine's famous exhortation to First Do No Harm does not seem to have formed part of any curriculum Xenophon studied.

After completing his training, Xenophon traveled to Rome, where he eventually rose to the position of personal physician to the Emperor Claudius. In this role, Xenophon became one of the emperor's most trusted advisers, even traveling with him on his military campaigns. In recognition of Xenophon's long service, in AD 54 Claudius granted his home island of Kos immunity from Roman taxation. Although undoubtedly intended as a great honor, this was not necessarily of direct benefit to Xenophon himself, who was widely understood to have a compulsory job for life at his emperor's side in Rome.

A few months later, Claudius abruptly died from what classical sources unanimously agree was an act of poisoning. Claudius' ambi-

tious wife, Agrippina, is said to have obtained toxic mushrooms from a notorious poison-maker and fed them to the emperor at dinner. When the mushrooms failed to dispatch Claudius and instead merely made him unwell, Claudius sent for Xenophon to revive him. Under the guise of provoking purgative vomiting, Xenophon used a feather to introduce yet more poison to Claudius, and thereby complete the deed on behalf of Agrippina.

On Claudius' death, Agrippina's son Nero became emperor of Rome. Xenophon's own motives for participating in the assassination of his only patient are unclear, but perhaps he simply wanted to retire: with Claudius dead, he was able to return to Kos, where he lived out a life of leisure on his now tax-free Roman riches.

CHAPTER 6

Steep as the learning curve at St. Luke's had been, the biggest challenge of my job had increasingly become my accommodation—or, more specifically, Dr. Vogel. He had always been unfailingly polite to my face, but HR accidentally copied me on a reply to a furious letter he had sent them about the "intolerable position" my arrival had put him in, and they had even included with it a copy of his original missive. How, Dr. Vogel had asked them, was he supposed to provide state-of-the-art care to patients with blood cancer when he was kept awake at night by a snoring Scotsman in the next room?

The next day, the woman from HR—seemingly unaware they had sent me Dr. Vogel's letter—paged to ask me how I was finding the accommodation? I told her I had no idea if the snoring was true or not, but a transfer to one of the vacant flats would probably be a good idea all around. The HR woman apologized that she was supposed to keep those vacant in order to entice potential new staff, but promised she would see what she could do.

I did not hear from her again, but two weeks later—right around the time Dr. Vogel began to make a point of using up all the hot water each morning—a handwritten sign appeared on the noticeboard in the mess. It read: *Flatmate wanted- Page 377.*

I paged immediately. A man with the poshest accent I had ever heard rung straight back, and asked me if the patient was already in the anesthetic room?

It took a moment to make him understand that I was phoning about the advert in the mess, but once I did he found the mix-up surprisingly hilarious. He introduced himself as George Williams, one of the orthopedic senior house officers, and I placed him as a hulking figure I had occasionally passed in the corridors. I knew right away that he would make a good flatmate, because orthopods are famously the Labradors of the hospital: pleasant, enthusiastic, and perfectly good at performing their limited range of tricks, but resplendently uncomplicated creatures. George was no exception to this: a keen rugby player, he would later tell me he had wanted to become an orthopedic surgeon in order to fix the broken bones of his fellow rugby players, and "get them back out on the field where they belonged." He seemed entirely oblivious to the fact that a far more effective solution would have been for them all just to cease playing rugby.

George mentioned that an ENT registrar was viewing the room that weekend, so I took the overground to see it the same night. I was desperate to escape from Stalag Motorsport, and who knew when I would next get the chance? Junior doctors move around so much that landlords rarely want to rent to them, and George had only managed to secure the flat by paying a year's rent in advance. I'd assumed he'd simply written a check from a trust fund, but I would later discover he had borrowed this money from the bank.

The place was a two-bedroom apartment in a once-grand

Victorian terrace that the blitz had left marooned amid a sea of estates. It boasted a living room, a kitchen with a breakfast bar, and a single bathroom that was inexplicably en suite to the larger of the two bedrooms. My share of the rent would be four hundred pounds a month; this was an incredible bargain by London standards, which made it daylight robbery by any other measure.

Be that as it may, George seemed inordinately proud of the place, and insisted on giving me a formal tour that included such highlights as the washing machine, the boiler room, and the bin store out the back. He cheerfully described the breakfast bar in the kitchen as "the dining room" and the bathroom arrangement as "unique and fun, sort of like camping." He took perhaps the greatest joy in introducing me to Patrick, an articulated skeleton who hung at attention next to George's desk. On first glance I assumed Patrick was the same model of plastic skeleton many of my classmates had bought in our first year of medical school, but something about the yellowing of his bones drew me in.

"That's right," George enthused. "Old Patrick is as real as they come! And he was probably a murderer, you know—that was who got this treatment in the olden days—but he has paid his debt to society now!"

The sole flaw George would acknowledge with the flat was that the prodigious local street crime meant he had to keep his rusted MG sports car parked at the hospital, and therefore alas could not drive us to work. Still, he added, we were only a few stops away and the trains ran every twenty minutes "like absolute clockwork." Possibly sensing my continued reticence about the bathroom issue, George pointed out that we were both at the hospital so much it would be rare for us to even be home at the same time. This was true and reassuring, but George then went on to say that not only was the arrangement like camping, we were anyway both used to it from the changing rooms at the rugby club. I had never been inside a rugby club, let alone a changing room within one. Still, it was this or Dr. Vogel and his motorsports and platelets. I moved in the next evening.

On my first night, I found out that George had not been kidding about the regularity of trains. I learned this as my room backed onto the tracks; as well as the commuter trains that took us to work, the tracks seemed to bring in every single item sold in London. Luckily, work always left me so exhausted that even endless freight trains passing within inches of my head were never going to keep me awake for long.

It was not until breakfast on my first morning that I discovered George had a surprising third love besides bones and rugby: Amelia. Even more curiously, she apparently loved him back, the two of them having met when they had both worked in a hospital in west London. It seemed a supremely odd combination, and yet in another way it made perfect evolutionary sense: Amelia's brilliant mind coupled with George's bovine strength and affability would give their offspring an incredible survival advantage. George even told me he was looking forward to the two of them going to work in "a refugee camp in a poor country in Africa," where he planned to do something he called "sports orthopedics." He did not appear to care which specific poor African country he went to, but seemed genuinely disappointed when I pointed out that between the malaria and the starvation they probably don't play much rugby in any African refugee camps. In an attempt to cheer him up, I pointed out that Africa has more than its fair share of road traffic accidents, so there would no doubt still be plenty of bones for him to repair. George considered this, and then grinned and reminded me that St. Luke's received a steady stream of trauma victims from accidents on the nearby North Circular road, and so he had plenty of experience in dealing wiith that sort of thing.

CHAPTER 7

By the time autumn arrived, I had begun to experience a feeling so long alien that I at first had barely recognized it: I felt good. It seemed unlikely to have much to do with my weekly counseling with the Reverend McKendrick, for the simple reason that we barely did any counseling. After eight or nine sessions, we were still only at the beginning of Chapter 2 of the photocopied *Cognitive Behavioral Therapy Workbook* he had grudgingly supplied me with at our third meeting.

Instead, I think it was to do with my newfound stability. I now had a job and a home, and perhaps even the beginnings of a career; my boss Dr. Weiden had recently informed me that I had "the makings of a good staff grade geriatrician." This was probably intended as a mild insult: a staff grade doctor was not a consultant, but a competent workhorse who had stepped off the career ladder forever. Still, just a few months ago I had been unemployable, so I took this as excellent progress, and even now signed up for the first part of my membership exam.

I had also started to date someone. Her name was Collette and she was a surgical senior house office from Northern Ireland. She had strawberry blond hair and an athletic build, and her elderly patients were forever telling her that she looked like an actress from an American soap opera that had briefly been popular in the 1970s. She was compassionate and kind, but also as binary and ruthlessly efficient as every other general surgeon in the hospital. Whereas we physicians liked to prevaricate, weigh the evidence and considered time the most useful weapon in our diagnostic armory, general surgeons existed in a black-and-white world of utter immediacy. Their job required it, for nobody wants a surgeon who changes her mind halfway through an operation.

During a weekend on call, I'd been summoned to one of the surgical wards to review an elderly man whose heart was beating too fast following a hernia operation. I'd prescribed him the standard treatment, and it had swiftly resolved the issue. My physician colleagues would no doubt have found fault with this—it was the wrong drug, or the wrong dose, or there was no evidence to suggest that slowing his heart was the correct thing—but as far as Collette was concerned, I had performed an act of black magic.

And so, a week later at a mess party in Hoxton's worst nightclub, she had found me at the bar, pulled me onto the dance floor, waited a requisite thirty seconds and then ordered me to kiss her. She kissed like it was one more surgical procedure—insert tongue, rotate clockwise, rotate anticlockwise, swab roof of mouth, repeat—but who was I to complain? It had been a long time, and it was not as if anybody had ever given me an award for the way I kissed.

George was working nights that week, so Collette came back to the flat. Of course, surgical weekend handover took place at 7:00 a.m. and so by the time we woke up, George was already back home and in bed. I awkwardly explained to Collette that the bathroom was in George's room, but I'd forgotten how practical surgeons are. Collette simply breezed through George's room with a cheery "Good morning," and did her business without any hint of self-consciousness. On her return journey, I even heard her stop to ask George about a patient they had in common, and then briefly chitchat about surgical anatomy.

Medics and surgeons traditionally go together like oil and water, so I had assumed our relationship would be a one-night thing. But that morning Collette insisted we get breakfast in the local greasy spoon, and when we said goodbye she kissed me again. I did not dislike it, and when George woke up that evening I asked him what he knew about her. He assured me that Collette was known for having excellent manual dexterity. That was not any kind of innuendo, but George's way of telling me that Collette was considered a promising surgeon and therefore would no doubt make an excellent girlfriend. When I asked him about her personality, he thought for a moment and then informed me that her suturing was exquisite.

Over the next week, Collette and I exchanged only awkward greetings when we passed each other in the hospital corridors, and I assumed we'd both thought better of it. But on the Thursday she paged me and asked if I had plans for the weekend. Caught off-guard and still over accustomed to making excuses, I reflexively told her that I needed to start revising for the exam I had signed up to take. This was not technically a lie: I did need to start revising for it, I just had not necessarily been planning to do so yet. I felt a little guilty when Collette sighed sadly and said that she understood, because she had her own exam to be studying for too.

Still, that modicum of guilt turned out to be the incentive I needed, and on Saturday I took the train into the British Library, had my photograph taken for a reader's pass, and called up two books to help me study for the first part of the Membership of the Royal College of Physicians. There was *Smith-*

field's Textbook of Human Disease, of course, and the second was called *Sample Questions for the Part 1 Membership*. I found a desk in the reading room, and noticed several other medics around me reading such books as *Pass Your Part 1 First Time!* and *Pearls of the Part 1 MRCP*.

A college membership was the exam you had to pass in order to become a registrar in your chosen specialty. It was split up into three parts and, like most medical exams, bore almost no relation whatsoever to clinical practice. Hardly anybody passed the Part 1 at the first attempt, and it seemed primarily to have been designed to keep the College in application fees and the hospitals in the most junior of doctors. The exam consisted of a hundred multiple choice questions, each of which began with a limited description of a patient and their symptoms; there then followed a selection of five fiendishly possible diagnoses, from which you had to pick the most likely. It was compulsory to answer every question, and the whole thing was negatively marked, which meant that every wrong answer you gave led to you being deducted a mark. In one notorious year, the pass mark had been minus six.

Still, I possessed a secret weapon that my colleagues sitting nearby in the British Library might not. Before I left Scotland, a senior colleague had quietly told me his own shameful pearl of the Part 1 MRCP, which was to ignore the complexities and nuances of the question and view the world as the question-setters undoubtedly saw it. He meant by this that the college faculty were elderly, rich, male, and white, and as horrifically prejudiced a group as you might possibly encounter.

Sure enough, the first ten patients in *Sample Questions for the Part 1 Membership* included a sailor, a man with an earring, and a nurse. The "correct" answers the examiners were looking for in these instances turned out to respectively be: syphilis, HIV, and Munchausen syndrome by proxy. The approach alone would not be enough to pass the exam as sometimes in a given situation—such as the case of an African nurse—it was hard to know exactly which of their prejudices the examiners wished to hear reflected. Still, utterly appalling as it all was, it was an undeniably useful exam technique. I made my way through another twelve questions before I decided I needed a break.

There was a coffee place downstairs. Only after I had entered did I notice that Collette was studying at a table beside the checkout. She was engrossed in whatever bit of surgical anatomy she was memorizing, so I considered ducking out, but even as I weighed this she looked up and enthusiastically waved me over. We talked only briefly, but agreed to meet up when the library closed.

So we worked in our separate parts of the library for the rest of the day, and afterward went to get some food in an Indian place Collette knew behind St. Pancras station. When I pointed out to Collette that we were the only customers, she cheerfully explained she liked the place because it was "always empty" and reassured me that the food hadn't killed her yet. We mostly talked about our exams—the surgical membership seemed to require Collette to know the course of every blood vessel and nerve in the human body—and our future career aspirations.

As I did not have aspirations beyond holding on to my medical license, I really mean that I listened while Collette told me hers: exam by twenty-eight, senior registrar by twenty-nine, married by thirty-one, consultant in a district general hospital by thirty-two, two kids between thirty-three and thirty-five, a move to a teaching hospital by forty, head of department by forty-three. If it sounds like Collette's personal life was inseparable from her career plan, it is because it was: at one point she even mentioned that she would work three days a week until her hypothetical youngest daughter was coping well with nursery school. None of that seemed to be a good match for my record of scraping through medical school and having my license suspended for stealing opioids.

When Collette asked me about my plans, I could only mumble about Dr. Weiden mentioning I had the makings of a good staff grade geriatrician. When this visibly dismayed her, I explained my real dream was to work in a refugee camp in a poor country in Africa. I had stolen this wholesale from George, but it seemed both a little less hopeless and a good way of gently underlining our obvious incompatibility.

But I had again forgotten how ruthlessly pragmatic surgeons are, and if anything my gambit worked only too well. Instead of taking the hint, Collette declared that it sounded like between work, exams, and our "disparate life goals" neither of us were "currently looking for anything particularly serious" from a relationship. We then got quickly drunk in a nearby pub and took the tube back to the house she shared in Acton with a group of antipodean physiotherapists. The bathroom was not en suite to anybody's bedroom, but the various nocturnal comings and goings of Australians and New Zealanders proved worse even than the trains at my place.

And so, to my job and home, I had somehow added a relationship of sorts. Usually one of us was working, or both of us were studying, but occasionally Collette and I found ourselves with a weekend off together. Despite our agreement that our relationship was nothing serious, on these days we found ourselves doing the things that more committed young couples in London do. This mostly involved hungover traipsing through galleries and museums, and once attending something called Doors Open Day where we took two buses to Deptford to see the inside of an old ironworks, which was every bit as riveting as it sounds. One Saturday evening, we even went to the theater to watch a famous film actor murder Hamlet. The show had been playing for months, but he still stumbled over his lines like a schoolboy reading them aloud in English class for the first time. Afterward, Collette described it as "the most stunning thing she had ever seen on the West End stage." She later admitted it was also the only thing she had ever seen on the West End stage.

A few days after that, something genuinely dramatic and moving did actually happen: George came home and announced that he had asked Amelia to marry him. He explained he had planned to propose that summer on holiday in Tuscany, but he had run into Amelia in the X-ray department, decided that the "could not wait one bloody minute longer" and gone down on one knee. When Amelia said yes, the secretaries had all cheered.

It sounded like a scene from a dreadful romantic comedy, and if it had been anyone else I would have thought it a ridiculously performative plea for attention. But it wasn't anybody else, it was George, and his giant frame concealed the purest heart I had ever known. He had even been at pains to explain that he was not planning on changing anything with the flat, and he would probably keep it on while they went to Africa, so I would not be homeless "for at least a good year or two."

That Saturday, they held an engagement party in the back room of a pub in London Fields. Half the hospital seemed to be there, as well as a world cup's worth of rugby players, and an obnoxious group of stockbrokers who called themselves "the posse" and were apparently George's friends from his public school. I avoided all of them, and concentrated on getting drunk.

At some point, George made a speech that was every bit as impromptu as his proposal. He hugely appreciated us all coming tonight, he said, but mostly he was grateful to Amelia for agreeing to spend the rest of her life with him. One of the posse shouted out "At least until the divorce!" but George did not hear this, or if he did he chose to ignore it. We then all toasted George, and finally Amelia made a speech that was about how everybody knew George had the biggest heart of anyone in the hospital, with the possible exception of some very unwell patients on the cardiology ward. We all cheered and endlessly told them how perfect they were for each other, and how much we were looking forward to the wedding. The next day, George told me it had been the greatest night of his life so far.

CHAPTER 8

When Halloween arrived at St. Luke's, it brought with it an unexpected ghoul. I was on nights and when the triage nurse paged to apologize that she had an intravenous drug addict with a fever who needed to come in, I was actually initially pleased. I had seen and treated hundreds of such infections in Scotland, and this was at least one condition for which I wouldn't need to look anything up.

But our drug addicts in Scotland had not been like Felix Smollett. The fact that he was dressed that night as a Ziggy Stardust–era David Bowie was only the smallest part of it. Maybe Scottish heroin addicts didn't generally have the money or inclination to paint a perfect Ziggy Stardust flash on their faces, but more than that they did not have a trio of teenage girls that hung on their every word. None of it made any sense to me until a nurse dressed as a sexy cat whispered that she recognized Smollett from the tabloids and explained he was a musician who was also the son of an admiral. That explained his Mockneyby-Eton accent and just about everything else besides: Smollett was wealthy, privileged, and a little bit famous, so none of the usual rules applied to him. Or at least, he believed they did not.

Certainly, his young entourage did not think the rules applied to him. They somehow deduced I was his doctor from the moment I entered the department, and immediately took turns to pepper me with charm, pleas, insults, and threats. Could I please see Felix now as they were truly very worried about him? Did I ever get any time off, because they could get me into all the best shows in London for free? What was taking me so long? What was my General Medical Council number? Had I heard of one of their fathers, because he was a very important Queen's Counsel who actually specialized in medical negligence? The fact that the girls had all dressed as hippies for Halloween gave the whole thing the appearance of a junior Manson cult.

But it was hard that night to see much appeal in their sickly leader. Even if the sexy cat nurse had not passed me a chart that showed a forty-degree fever, it was clear that Smollett was profoundly septic. Beads of sweat had begun to make his Ziggy Stardust lightning flash run, and every now and then he would erupt in a violent fit of shivering known as a "rigor." He was also pale and unhealthily thin, although that may also have been an aesthetic choice.

When I entered the cubicle, his acolytes did not initially leave at my request but waited for Smollett to nod his approval. Even at that, they clustered outside, listening through the curtain and ignoring the A+E sister's repeated attempts to shoo them away. Smollett himself seemed quite cooperative that evening, although I later learned that was simply because he was too sick to behave otherwise.

Diagnoses are rarely so obvious as they appear in the textbooks, but Felix Smollett had all the signs and symptoms of endocarditis, an infection of the heart itself. He complained of having had fevers for weeks, of night sweats, and of strange red lumps that had appeared on his fingers. When I examined him, I found track marks up his arms, a loud heart murmur, and crackles at the bases of his lungs. The red lumps on his hands were Janeway lesions, something I had only ever previously seen in photographs in *Smithfield's.*

I was still finishing up my examination when Smollett asked me if all this was going to take long, because he was supposed to be playing a show for "some really cool people" later. I told him that he was not going anywhere tonight, or even anytime soon. He had a life-threatening infection of his heart; assuming he survived, he would likely need to be in the hospital for weeks. Such candor turned out to be a mistake, because the Manson Family now burst into tears and rushed in. One of them reassured Felix Smollett that her uncle was a Harley Street cardiologist and would be able to make him better immediately. Yet I think Smollett himself had at least begun to understand the seriousness of his situation, because he sent his young acolytes off to make his apologies to the very cool people.

Hippocrates described diagnosis as "the cornerstone of medicine." Perhaps I'd have believed that too if I hadn't been able to treat anything either. For much of history, a rudimentary diagnosis was indeed all that doctors could offer: your liver is swollen and thus you have "hepatitis," and will soon die; your gallbladder is swollen, and thus you have "cholecystitis," and will soon die; your brain is swollen and thus you have "encephalitis," and will soon die. The lining of your heart is swollen, and thus you have "endocarditis," and will soon die.

Still, Hippocrates was correct in one way, because the key to treating a severe bacterial infection like endocarditis is to accurately diagnose precisely what you are dealing with. A sample of the patient's blood, urine, or whatever else may be infected is sent to the laboratory, there smeared on nutrient-rich plates, and incubated at body temperature in an attempt to grow or "culture" the bacteria in question. If successfully cultured, the offending organism can then be identified by its color, its reaction to hydrogen peroxide, and its microscopic shape: *cocci* are spherical, *bacilli* are rod-shaped, and *spirochetes* corkscrew. The organism is then tested again a range of antibiotics to see which ones prevent it from growing any further. If this all sounds like an old-fashioned, low-tech process, that is because it is: the nutrient rich plates are made of horse blood, the culture process takes a minimum of two days, and the sensitivity testing longer still.

The particular endocarditis that drug users get is classically caused by *staphylococcus aureus*—golden spheres that bubble in the presence of hydrogen peroxide—but to prove that I would need blood, and the track marks on Felix Smollett's arms told me he had long since annihilated all the obvious veins. I therefore did not even bother attempting to collect the blood samples myself, but fell back on a trick I had learned in Scotland. No doctor in the world is remotely as adept as a drug addict at locating their veins, and so I showed Smollett how to use the alcohol wipes to clean his skin, placed the needle and syringe on the bedside table, and pulled the curtain shut behind me. I sat at the nurses' station to write up his notes, and five minutes later he yelled that he had the sample.

I completed the rest of the routine admission tests—a chest X-ray and an ECG—although I did not expect them to show anything. The test Smollett actually needed could not be done in an emergency department at night. Endocarditis can destroy the valves of the heart and so, when it is suspected, an ultrasound scan of the heart must be performed through the chest wall. If that does not provide clear enough information, the probe must then be put down the patient's throat to gain a better view.

But those were headaches for the working day. Tonight's final challenge was to get a line into Smollett in order to give him the broad-spectrum antibiotics that would keep him alive until the culture could identify a specific culprit. Getting an ordinary line in would be impossible for the same reason that obtaining a blood sample had been so difficult. Smollett therefore required central access: a line inserted into one of the large vessels of his neck or groin. Technically, I could do this, but the anesthetists were infinitely better at it. Luckily ICU was quiet when I called and the registrar helpful, so I wrote Smollett up for his antibiotics and fluids and continued on to my next patient, a vampire who was having a heart attack.

The next day, in his cramped little living room above the kebab shop, the Reverend McKendrick asked me if I ever felt tempted to return to my old life. I thought of Felix Smollett then, and told him that the hounds of hell could not possibly drag me back. I even added a lie that from this distance I could no longer understand what had led me to it in the first place, but by the time I finished saying that part Reverend McKendrick was already fast asleep.

If the person who commissions a crime is as culpable as the person who carries it out, Scotland's own Professor Robert Knox has a strong claim to be one of the world's first healthcare serial killers.

In the early 1800s, Edinburgh was a world-leading center for the study of anatomy. As a medical veteran of the Battle of Waterloo who had also studied in Paris, Professor Knox was in great demand as a teacher: he gave public dissections twice daily, and his audience of paying trainee surgeons regularly numbered in the hundreds. It was a highly lucrative business, and Knox relished the social status his local celebrity afforded him.

But regular anatomical demonstrations necessitated a consistent supply of corpses, and the only bodies that could legally be obtained for dissection were those of executed convicts. In Edinburgh, as elsewhere, the solution to the inevitable shortfall had long been grave robbing: "resurrection men" would dig up recently buried bodies and sell them to the anatomy schools, who would turn a blind eye to their provenance. After much public outcry, measures were introduced that effectively thwarted the grave robbers: cemetery night watchmen, iron coffins, and *even ultimately morthouses, in which bodies were thoroughly decomposed prior to burial.*

In the first months of 1828, an itinerant Edinburgh laborer named William Burke and his friend and landlord, William Hare, found an ingenious way to bypass any such possible obstacles: they would simply murder people and sell their victims' corpses to the anatomy schools.

Burke and Hare's sole mitigation might be that their depravities did not commence with murder, but merely with the body of a naturally deceased tenant of Hare's boardinghouse. They used a tea chest to transport this corpse across Edinburgh to the university, where the esteemed Professor Robert Knox personally purchased it from them. As Burke and Hare left, Knox's assistant informed them Knox "would be glad to see them again when they had another to dispose of."

It would prove a fateful comment. Over the next year, Burke and Hare killed at least sixteen people with the sole motive of selling their corpses. Professor Knox paid the two murderers ten pounds per body and repeatedly complimented them on the exquisite freshness of the cadavers they brought him. If there could be any doubt an anatomist as skilled as Knox would know the difference between a body that had been dug up and one that had been freshly murdered, Knox's students even warned him that one of the corpses was the body of a local man who had recently disappeared in mysterious circumstances. Knox simply decapitated the body before publicly dissecting it.

Burke and Hare were only finally caught when another of Hare's lodgers happened upon their most recent victim's body before the two murderers could transport it to the university. Granted immunity in exchange for his testimony, Hare confessed that he and Burke had murdered sixteen people. On the strength of Hare's evidence, Burke was found guilty of murder and sentenced to hanging and public dissection. Hare himself slipped away to Ireland, and was never heard from again.

Professor Robert Knox was not called upon to give evidence at Burke's trial—let alone put on trial himself—but Edinburgh society held him equally responsible for the murders. An effigy of Knox was burned in front of his house, he was expelled from the Royal Society, and temporarily banned from teaching in Scotland. When Knox later applied for a professorship at Edinburgh University, the existing professors voted to abolish the chair rather than give it to a doctor who had resorted to murder in pursuit of wealth and acclaim.

CHAPTER 9

It was a week later, on Guy Fawkes night, that things first began to explode.

An old medical saying holds that "hindsight is twenty-twenty." It means, of course, that the significance of apparently unremarkable things sometimes only becomes obvious in retrospect. And so it was with that week between Halloween and Guy Fawkes: a series of seemingly unrelated and mostly unnoticed occurrences that were nonetheless part of the same lethal whole.

Most obviously, it was the week that winter arrived. Suddenly now it was dark when I left the hospital, and even by six o'clock the encroaching night had fetched with it a thick fog that the dim orange streetlights barely penetrated. It was the Wednesday before I realized that this abrupt darkening was not my imagination, but was due to the fact the clocks had gone back during my night shift week.

Some problem with the track meant that the trains were all off that week, which in turn meant I had to trudge home each

evening as fireworks flashed and echoed around the neighbor-
hood They had started on Halloween itself with a few sporadic
rockets, but over the course of the week the refractory period
between bangs had got ever shorter, as if building to a crescendo.

If this was another harbinger, I had not paid it much attention. No matter what was happening in the darkening world
outside, our work under the fluorescent lights was never-ending,
and St. Luke's was busier than I had ever seen it. There was a
three-day wait for the simplest of scans, and the bed system was
so gridlocked that sick pensioners were now being admitted to
the children's ward, and sick children were being diverted to
another hospital entirely. At the same time, many of my colleagues kept excitedly reassuring me that if I thought this was
bad, I should wait until winter really hit.

And all that chaos was before I even mention the gang war.
St. Luke's catchment area included the epicenter of the UK's
heroin trade, and a turf war had recently erupted between two
rival gangs. The tit-for-tat shootings meant that once a day a
trauma arrest call would come through, and we'd all rush to
resus, don our gloves, and wait for the carnage. Oftentimes the
victims turned out to be surprisingly unhurt—a policeman explained to me this was a combination of "young assassins and old
guns"—but every few days they got their man, and we would
once again perform our futile ballet.

For all this, my biggest issue that whole week was nonetheless a single patient: Felix Smollett. His admission swabs had
shown he had MRSA on his skin, and the only side room available had been on Jack Duckton ward. This still should not have
made him my patient—he was under the care of Saz's boss, Dr.
Zubia, and in every other hospital the nurses would have had
to page her to deal with him—but some longstanding horse-
trading arrangement at St. Luke's meant everybody concurred
he was now my responsibility.

Felix Smollett was as much work as all the gangland assassins and delirious elderly people combined. Yes, his scans needed to be organized and acted upon, but the main problem was that he harangued the nurses with an incessant array of ridiculous inquiries, and they in turn harangued me with the same questions. Could Felix go out on pass this weekend? Could he plug in a small amplifier in the dayroom? Would it be alright for a French news crew to come and film him? Mostly though, again and again: Could he please have more methadone, please?

Methadone is a synthetic opioid, a drug prescribed in hospitals to prevent addicts entering withdrawal, and in the community to help them keep off street heroin. It doesn't get people high, just numbs the edges, stops the cravings and prevents the withdrawal. Nonetheless, we addicts still inevitably want as much of it as we can get.

Back in Scotland, community prescriptions for methadone had originally been dispensed on a daily basis, with the addicts being made to drink it in front of their pharmacist to prevent them from selling it on. When it was discovered that addicts were holding the methadone in their mouths to spit out and sell, they were made to drink a glass of water before leaving the pharmacy. When the addicts responded by inducing vomiting and selling the resulting concoction, there was disgust but also a consensus: if anybody wanted the stuff that badly, they could just have it.

As a recovering addict myself, I was in no position to judge. My own drug of choice had been pethidine, an opioid mainly prescribed for people with gallstones. My descent may have begun with a legitimate need for analgesia—a bicycle accident that fractured my clavicle—but from there it had been as swift and spectacular as any. I'd had far less of an excuse than most of my fellow addicts: no abuse, naivete, or combat-induced PTSD. Instead, I'd had a professional education that had allowed me to witness the devastating effects of such drugs up close. Worse, despite what I had told the Reverend McKendrick, I still yearned for it every day, and wholeheartedly believed that the rest of the world was no more upstanding than I was. All the good citizens who had never been hooked on opioids did not possess better willpower, restraint, or morality than me. They simply had no idea how incredible it felt.

From the first moment I had encountered him, I had recognized this all in Felix Smollett: the same smug sneer, the same certain belief that he knew a secret the straight world was too scared to even ever attempt to comprehend. Every junkie in the world knows this secret, and so does every professional who works with them, but neither side ever speaks it aloud. To do so would be to admit the magnitude of the lies told by both sides: we don't start taking opioids because we are naive, we don't continue taking them because we are searching for some long lost high, and it is not the deathly fear of withdrawal that drives us to absurd lengths to obtain more.

No, the unspeakable truth is this: most of us addicts know both the risks and the benefits, and simply make a clear-eyed choice that the latter outweigh the former. The risks, of course, are well documented: poverty, sickness, prison, and death. If you are not an addict yourself, you are no doubt wondering what benefit could possibly outweigh those horrors? Well, how about this one: the feeling of honey slowly trickling down your spine until nothing else in the world matters.

Most people know that endorphins are the pleasure chemical, the substance released when you feel loved, have sex, run a marathon, or otherwise triumph. But far fewer know that the very word *endorphin* is itself a contraction of the phrase *endogenous morphine*: morphine made by the body. Put another way, every good feeling you have ever known was caused by endorphins, and opioids are those exact same feelings in a handy tablet or liquid form.

That all being so, Felix Smollett's entreaties to me fell on entirely deaf ears. My colleagues would have no doubt refused him on medical or even moral grounds, but my reasoning was more primitive: if I was not getting the good stuff myself, I was not going to give it away to him. One night that week, he even pursued me across the parking lot as I left work, wheeling his IV drip as he begged for an extra ten milliliters. Unlike every other drug-seeking addict I'd ever encountered, his rejected entreaties did not turn to anger, but only to bafflement. He simply seemed genuinely perplexed, and it struck me then that he had probably never been denied anything in his life.

That Friday was Guy Fawkes day, and Dr. Sudbury summoned all the medical and nursing staff to a special lunchtime meeting in the education room. The doctors all thought it was due to the activation of a bed-crisis plan, a shortage of a critical drug, or the announcement that all leave was canceled until further notice. The nurses seemed equally certain that the meeting had to do with congratulating one of their number who had recently given birth to triplets.

The doctors and nurses were both wrong, though, because when Dr. Sudbury arrived, she was accompanied by a ruddy-faced middle-aged man in an ill-fitting suit. My first thought was that he must be a patient she had brought along as an exhibit for an impromptu teaching session on the dangerous effects of alcohol-induced hypertension. Instead, she introduced him as Detective Inspector Glynn Afferson from Highbury police station. That immediately silenced the room.

Dr. Sudbury informed us that she wanted us to hear it from her before we read about it in the *Hackney Gazette*, but an unexpected substance had been found in a deceased patient's blood. No doubt this had a perfectly innocent explanation, she said, but it did necessarily now need to be investigated. Dr. Sudbury thanked us in advance for our cooperation with DI Afferson, and asked us not to speak to the press. DI Afferson then spoke briefly to say he would be in touch directly with everybody he needed to talk to, but would also be grateful for any information anybody else might wish to share. He finished up with an awkward joke about having hated hospitals since he had his appendix removed as a child, and therefore wanting to get this all wrapped up as soon as possible.

It was all very cryptic. Neither Dr. Sudbury nor DI Afferson had even said what the substance was, let alone identified the patient, and they left without offering to answer any questions. After they had gone, we agreed it must be a patient in whom an overdose had been missed. We all saw plenty of overdoses—there'd be a serious one at least a couple of times a week, and that was before you counted the teenage girls who had taken three acetaminophen and hurried downstairs to inform their parents that they hoped they were pleased with themselves because they had really done it this time. Still, we likewise all had experience of another kind of overdose: the hidden one that led to a collapse query cause followed by a dead patient who was only revealed by postmortem toxicology to have intentionally poisoned themselves. These did happen from time to time, and really the only odd part was that Dr. Sudbury and DI Afferson seemed to be taking it all so seriously. Still, nobody thought too much of it, and we all went back to work.

That night, Collette and I went to the fireworks display in Victoria Park, trudging through the mud and fog to huddle around a bonfire. It had been almost four hundred years since Guy Fawkes had failed to blow up the Houses of Parliament, and they still burned his effigy every year. People often say us Scots like to nurse our grudges, but on this evidence the English were just as committed.

We had come straight from work and hadn't had time for dinner, so we bought burgers and beers from a van. I joked that it sounded like a case vignette from my exam: "A twenty-nine-year-old man attends accident and emergency with severe stomach pain. Four hours previously, he had eaten a takeaway hamburger at a fireworks display." Collette did not get the joke, partly because her own exams were not structured like that, but mostly because she was a surgeon: she frowned and said that sometimes food poisoning could be a red herring, and the safest thing would be to take the patient to theater and open him up to check it was not his appendix.

The fireworks started then, the crowd oohing and aahing as the greens and reds exploded above the park. It went on for a long time and the finale was a group of silver Catherine wheels that had been set in the middle of the field. Somebody nearby asked why they were called "Catherine wheels", and the crowd soon decided that such pretty fireworks must have been a favorite of Catherine the Great. I managed not to tell them they were named for St. Catherine, who had been broken upon the wheel,

When the fireworks finished, most people headed for the park gates, but Collette and I took the opportunity to move closer to the fire, where the effigy was still burning. A group of young children were playing on the other side and their parents—not much older than me—seemed to be having a great time as they drank mulled wine while their children ran around.

Maybe it was just the beer, but in that moment—watching somebody on fire, who for once was not me—I wondered if perhaps the ordinary life might still somehow be for me. Despite my innumerable missteps, maybe I too might even be married by thirty-one, with two kids by thirty-five. Collette seemed like she might even be thinking the same thing, because she reached inside my pocket for my hand, and squeezed it. Of course, I remembered then that I had not told her about my past, but I thought then that perhaps one of these days I even might.

CHAPTER 10

I awoke the next morning to a knock on the front door. George was already at work, and Collette had also left early because she spent any free Saturday morning playing hockey for something called London Hospital Doctors United. I'd been puzzled as to how that could work, when all the players surely had regular on-call commitments, but Collette had explained that they simply had a huge squad. She was not lying: I once went to meet her at one of their functions and the entire pub was full, as far as the eye could see, of athletic, ponytailed girls talking loudly over one another.

I pulled on my dressing gown and went to answer it. The door that had been knocked was not the one in the street but the one in the shared hallway that led to our own flat. I therefore expected to see our upstairs neighbor, or perhaps the landlord I had never met. I was not expecting to see a uniformed police officer. He confirmed my name, then asked me if I had half an hour to come down to Highbury police station and help them understand a bit more about what had happened. As this was clearly connected to Dr. Sudbury's meeting the previous day, I said I'd be happy to come, but did not know if I could help as I had no idea even which patient had been involved. The officer reassured me that the detectives would be able to tell me more, but mentioned that I was the doctor who had signed Mrs. Horsburgh's death certificate.

Mrs. Horsburgh. I remembered her, of course: the old woman who Dr. O'Leary had said had died of an arrhythmia. I thought of the arrest on level seven with Saz, the quiet moments I had spent certifying Mrs. Horsburgh, and how I had later sat in a small room while her barrister daughter repeatedly asked me how this could have happened. It seemed now that that Eleanor Wilson might have had a point. Mrs. Horsburgh, after all, had originally been admitted for falls; whatever else the story might turn out to be, she was not an out-of-hospital arrest whose overdose had been missed amid the tumult of an attempted resuscitation.

With hindsight, it was stupid of me to go the police station without a lawyer. I'd surely watched enough police shows to know this was an extraordinarily bad idea, but it did not even occur to me to consider that this was a murder inquiry, let alone that I might ever be considered some kind of suspect. So I got dressed, ate a quick bowl of cereal, and hurried down to the waiting police car. I attempted to get in the passenger seat, but the door would not open, and the officer scrolled his window down to apologize that I needed to ride in the back. I got so many looks from passersby that by the time we reached Highbury corner, even I had begun to assume I must be guilty of something. At the police station, the young officer left me in the waiting room and promised it would not take too long.

The waiting room was much like those in a hospital: dingy and municipal, with posters on the wall for well-meaning but disheartening initiatives. The only difference was that here they were for things like Benefit Fraud Hotline and Knife Amnesty Month, instead of Sepsis Awareness Week and National Dialysis Day. I sat there for half an hour, and with each interminable minute found myself ever more empathic for the hours our patients endured in such dismal surroundings. I was on the point of getting up and leaving when the officer reappeared and buzzed me through the closed door.

My interview under caution, which was what it turned out to be, was conducted by two detectives: Detective Inspector Afferson, and a more junior colleague, Detective Sergeant Newington. DS Newington was about a decade younger than Afferson, and so I was surprised when she spoke first. She began by taking pains to assure me that I was not a suspect, and the only reason for formally reading my rights was that it would allow them to record the interview then refer to it later. The idea that they might even want to refer back to it only made me feel even more uneasy, but I reassured myself that I had nothing to hide. No doubt Guy Fawkes and St. Catherine had taken similar tacks before meeting their own fates.

And then Afferson got down to it. He passed me a photocopy of my entry in Mrs. Horsburgh's notes that verified her death, and asked me to confirm I had written it. I did so, and he then asked me to talk them through my memories of the night. I began by explaining how night shifts have a habit of blending into one, but then told him the small amount I could confidently recall: coming onto a busy shift, seeing patients in A+E, running over to an arrest in the tower, the failed resus, certifying Mrs. Horsburgh, and then my interactions with her family.

They both listened diligently and without interruption, and then Afferson very gently asked me if I had noticed anything at all unusual that night. When I told him that I had not, he nodded and said he understood. We then sat in silence for some awkward moments, until DS Newington asked me if I was really telling them that I did not find there to be anything unusual in a previously healthy woman abruptly and unexpectedly dying without medical explanation.

Irritated both by the insinuation and the transparency of their good cop, bad cop routine, I told her the truth a little shortly: no, I did not find anything unusual in that, because I was a doctor. Any medic in the world could have told them that sometimes people die, and we don't always get to know why. Besides, I said, Dr. O'Leary had concluded it was an arrhythmia, and he was far more of an expert than any of the three of us in this room.

"Yes," Afferson agreed, "that is very true."

I found myself exhaling with relief then, but Afferson was not finished.

"Although I suppose the thing about that," he continued, "is that at the point Dr. O'Leary said Mrs. Horsburgh died from an arrhythmia, he was not aware the toxicology would show a fatal level of pethidine in her blood, now was he?"

Angor amini is a medical symptom that translates as "a sense of impending doom." I'd always assumed it was a melodramatic Victorian way of describing mere panic or anxiety, but I now know better. The reason I know better is that in Highbury police station that Saturday morning I experienced a profound sense of impending doom, and it was caused neither by anxiety nor panic, both of which are defined by their inappropriate excess. In contrast, my own sense of impending doom was entirely justified: in that moment I saw long, vanishing-point corridors, with doors at their distant ends slamming shut forever. If that itself seems melodramatic, consider this: I was being interviewed under caution about the murder of a patient I had certified had died of natural causes, and I had just been informed the cause of death was an overdose of a controlled drug I was on record as having repeatedly stolen and abused.

Somehow, I managed to ask Afferson if Mrs. Horsburgh had been known to be on pethidine, but I already knew what the answer would be. No, Afferson said, Mrs. Horsburgh had not been on pethidine, nor had she ever been prescribed pethidine in the hospital, nor in fact had any other patient on that ward. The two detectives let that information hang there for a moment, and then got down to the questions they had really brought me here to answer. Every sinew in my body was straining to scream for a lawyer, but I did not, because I had the notion that asking for a lawyer might make me look guilty. I of course now know that was ridiculous, because it wasn't even possible for me to look any more guilty than I already did.

They first wanted to know if I had personally given Mrs. Horsburgh any medications. When I confirmed that I had they looked excited, so I hurriedly added that the adrenalin with which I had injected her was a routine part of any resuscitation. Visibly disappointed, they then asked if I had given Mrs. Horsburgh anything else. I told them I had not.

The detectives next asked about my interactions with the Wilsons. DS Newington attempted to conceal them, but I could see over the desk that she was checking my answers against a photocopy of the notes Mr. Wilson had taken on his legal pad during our interview. When I could not remember which Wilson had asked me a particular question, I referred the detectives back to Mr. Wilson's notes. This seemed to annoy them.

After a while, they changed tack and began asking me about the medical specifics of a pethidine overdose, and how a team of doctors could possibly have missed such a thing. I explained that an opioid overdose causes death through respiratory depression. The patient's breath slows, becomes laborious, and then stops; thus deprived of oxygen, the heart itself then ceases after a few more minutes. They asked me if a doctor should have been able to diagnose this, and I told them the truth: that opioids are hard to obtain, so you will usually either know that a patient is on them for some medical reason, or they will look like an addict.

They then asked me if I was sure there was not some other way to tell if a patient had been given opioids, and I understood then that they were asking about Mrs. Horsburgh's pupils. Opioids cause the pupils to constrict, and a patient experiencing an opioid overdose classically has pinpoint pupils. I acknowledged this, and Afferson nodded enthusiastically, as if he thought we were finally now getting somewhere.

"But Mrs. Horsburgh, her pupils were of a normal size, were they?"

I explained that I had not examined her pupils when I arrived, because the whole point of the arrest protocols is to first support life, and worry about the causes later.

"So, nobody looked at poor Mrs. Horsburgh's pupils then?" Afferson asked, sounding deliberately incredulous as he did so.

"Usually the first doctor on scene would do that," I said. This was not actually in the arrest protocols, but I think most of us did it, and I was surprised Saz would have missed this.

They clearly thought the same thing, and now switched their focus to her. Had Saz ever spoken of Mrs. Horsburgh before? What exactly had she been doing when I entered the room? Why had I been the one to write the death certificate, and not Saz? When I had explained all of this, Afferson simply returned to his earlier line of questioning.

"So, just to be clear—you are saying that at no point did you examine Mrs. Horsburgh's pupils?"

"Yes," I said, "I already told you that."

Afferson now played what he thought was his next trump card, by leaning over and circling something on the photocopied sheet in front of me. It was the section of Mrs. Horsburgh's notes where I had written "pupils fixed and dilated." Abruptly, I was back in the little side room on the night in question. I could see Mrs. Horsburgh's eyes as they were after death: the pupils fixed and dilated, the cornea unresponsive, the hazy gray circle of *arcus senilis* around the iris.

"That was after she was dead," I said.

"Obviously, Doctor. But this means you did examine her pupils?"

"Yes, I did at that point."

"And how were they then? Were they pinpoint?"

"No, they were dilated, as it says here."

"But if she'd had a pethidine overdose, wouldn't you expect them to be pinpoint?"

The insinuation seemed to be that I had lied about Mrs. Horsburgh's pupil size to cover up the fact that I had poisoned her with pethidine, but they had got the science wrong.

"No, I wouldn't expect that," I said. "Because pinpoint pupils require the muscles be contracted, and no matter how much pethidine she may have had, everything relaxes after death."

Afferson stared at me for a long time. Eventually, with a new quietness and deliberateness, he asked me if there was anything else pertinent that he and DS Newington should know. I could not tell if he was asking this because he already knew about my pethidine habit, but it was anyway academic. It was a matter of public record, and if he did not know this information already, he surely soon would. Nevertheless, I looked DI Afferson straight in the eye and told him that there was nothing else pertinent that he and DS Newington should know. To this day, I don't know why I did that.

As abruptly as an unexpected knock on the door on a Saturday morning, Afferson and Newington stood up and thanked me for my time. I nodded and got up to leave, but on the way out I turned back around. I told them that the whole thing seemed desperately odd, and that the most likely explanation was a mix-up at the lab. The labs were not infallible, and anytime we doctors got an entirely unexpected result, the first thing we did was to repeat the test to make sure it was accurate. Even as I said this, I immediately regretted it. Who gets interviewed by the police on suspicion of murder and informs them they are simply mistaken, and it was not a murder at all? The murderer, of course. And apparently also me.

The interview rattled me so much that when I got home, I even called the hospital and asked to be put through to Dr. Sudbury, who I knew often spent the weekend in her office catching up on paperwork. The call rang out, and when the operator asked me if I wanted to try her at home, I realized there was nothing Dr. Sudbury could do anyway.

Collette's hockey match was on the south coast so she would be away all day, and when George came home that night I told him the whole story. His main reaction was to express bewilderment that there was a specific toxicology test for pethidine. "Isn't medical science amazing?" he said, and then reassured me there was nothing to worry about as "the blokes at the police station" were no doubt "just doing the needful."

Jane Toppan was a nurse who worked in Massachusetts towards the end of the nineteenth century. Nicknamed Jolly Jane for her cheerful demeanor, Toppan was beloved by her unsuspecting patients who almost universally described her as "an angel." Yet the seemingly sweet Toppan would eventually confess that her driving ambition had been, "to have killed more people—helpless people—than any other man or woman who ever lived."

Toppan may even have held that record in her day, for she murdered an estimated hundred people with morphine, atropine, and strychnine. As well as many of her patients, Toppan's victims included numerous acquaintances and even her own foster sister.

What motivated her to commit such atrocious crimes? Noting that she was in the habit of climbing into bed with her victims and fondling them as they died, the tabloid newspapers of the day sordidly concluded that Toppan obtained a sexual thrill from her killings. Modern psychologists, however, would look closely at her background, and perhaps discern in it the potential seeds of her pathology.

When Jane Toppan was very young, her mother died of tuberculosis. Soon thereafter, her alcoholic father abandoned his six-year-old daughter to the Boston Female Asylum. Two years after that, she was placed as an indentured servant in the home of the wealthy Toppans. The family never formally adopted Jane, but she took their name and continued to work as their servant even after her childhood indenture had ended and she had paid off her "debt".

When old Mrs. Toppan died, Jane Toppan needed a new job and commenced training as a nurse at the Cambridge Hospital. Her mischief there began early: in her first year, Toppan gave a patient by the name of Amelia Phinney a medicine that caused her to lose consciousness. Phinney later awoke with a bizarre memory of the young student nurse climbing into her bed and "kissing her all over her face." At the time, Phinney ascribed this to a fever dream, but years later she read of Toppan's arrest and understood what had really happened. Many others were not so lucky.

Toppan's fourteen year killing spree was ultimately only ended by the deaths of an entire family from whom she had been renting a cottage. Toppan had begun by poisoning matriarch Mattie Davis with a glass of mineral water dosed with morphine. She then moved in with Mattie's widower, and quickly dispatched both him and his adult daughter. This left a final adult daughter, Minnie, as the sole surviving Davis; when Minnie refused to sign off on a debt Toppan owed on the cottage, Toppan dispatched her too. Perplexed by the sudden deaths of an entire and apparently healthy family, Minnie's father-in-law hired a toxicologist, who discovered traces of morphine in Minnie's body.

After her arrest, Jane Toppan readily confessed to the Davis murders, and later to thirty-one others. The only controversy at trial was around Toppan's insistence that she was not insane. Perhaps there was method in Toppan's refutal of madness—a verdict of insanity would remove any possibility of future release—but the gambit anyway failed. Unwilling to believe that a nurse who killed her patients could be any-

thing other than deranged, the jury found Toppan not guilty by reason of insanity, and Jolly Jane spent the rest of her life in the state asylum for the criminally insane.

CHAPTER 11

By Sunday, my sense of impending doom had grown so strong that I could not concentrate long enough to even open my textbooks. Drinking too much coffee unsurprisingly did nothing to improve matters, and so I took the bus into town and ended up trudging around the National Gallery until a macabre portrait of Dr. Crippen sent me scurrying for the exit.

I sought refuge in a Leicester Square cinema, where I picked a Hollywood movie that seemed like it would be sufficiently dumb to distract me for a couple of hours. Of course, I had not read the synopsis properly, and the movie turned out to be about a spy being mercilessly pursued for a crime of which he was entirely innocent. He ultimately triumphed, but only because he could fall back on all his spy training to ingeniously outwit the vast state-level conspiracy he had now uncovered. It did not seem an especially good omen.

That night I called Collette to tell her what had happened with the police. She was appropriately sympathetic, but seemed also to actively distance herself from the issue: she referred to it several times as "your unfortunate problem" and expressed a hope that "the troubles you are experiencing quickly go away."

Dr. Sudbury was not at handover on Monday morning, so I tracked her down in clinic and breathlessly explained that I had been interviewed under caution by the police. She seemed entirely unsurprised, and I found myself asking her if she had known that was their intention. Dr. Sudbury avoided the question, but reassured me that as far as she could see there was nothing whatsoever to worry about. Still, as a general principle, she said that her understanding was that it was usually better to only talk to the police with a lawyer present, and I should do so next time. Next time.

All that morning, I was the talk of the wards and the mess. Maybe George had mentioned it, or perhaps Dr. Sudbury had, but somehow the entire hospital now knew both who the dead patient was, and that I had been interviewed under police caution. A few of my colleagues tentatively broached the subject with me by telling me they remembered Mrs. Horsburgh from her admission; a first year house officer I'd never met before even claimed to have been the one who verified her death. Mostly, they were just desperate to know what the police had asked me, and whether they had mentioned any suspects. When I admitted it had felt like I was the suspect, I had expected sympathy and perhaps even mild outrage on my behalf. Instead, I invariably saw my colleagues process this, and then slightly retreat, as if the suspicion that had fallen on me might be infectious.

Maybe I simply looked the type, but each time this happened I found myself inevitably thinking again about what my life in prison might be like. I did not seem likely to do well there, but consoled myself that perhaps I could ingratiate myself to the other inmates by providing them medical care. Beyond that, the sole upside I could think of was that I would at least no longer have to work nights.

With so much unwanted attention focused on me, it actually came as a relief that I had to accompany Felix Smollett to his appointment at the Brompton that afternoon. The ultrasound of his heart at St. Luke's had not shown anything, and so he now needed the same test but with the probe put down this throat. This was not something that could be done at St. Luke's.

Was it a coincidence that a hospital in wealthy west London was better equipped than St. Luke's? I suppose you could claim that the Brompton had been at the forefront of cardiac research for centuries, and it was therefore only natural it had the best facilities. But west London had likewise been wealthier than the impoverished east for centuries, and even Lord Nicotine himself had died at the Brompton. The official cause of death had been acute gout, which likely meant he had simply lived too well.

A few years ago, a patient making the same crosstown trip Felix and I were now undertaking had collapsed and died in the back of the minicab St. Luke's had sent him in. The ensuing lawsuit meant that all patients now had to be transferred in a blue-light ambulance, and accompanied by a doctor. This was a complete waste of both time and money: the previous patient's aortic valve had ruptured, and the best cardiac surgeon in the world could not have done anything for him whether he had been in a minicab, an ambulance, or a private jet. Still, it was a well-timed afternoon away from the wards, and if the patient had been anyone other than Felix Smollett, it might have even been an enjoyable diversion.

As we drove into town, he insisted on pointing out every squat where he had partied, every pub where he had performed, and every flat where he had once slept on a famous person's couch. Between them all, it seemed to be most addresses in London. I was glad we were in a speeding blue-light ambulance, otherwise he might have noticed even more places to tell me about.

Even at that we still got stuck in gridlocked traffic on Oxford Street, but this seemed to turn Felix somber. Perhaps Debenhams and Marks & Spencer simply offered him nothing to boast about, but he abruptly asked me if it was still possible that he might die from this? I told him the truth: yes, it was absolutely still possible. He then asked how it would happen, the very end? He asked this with a smirk, and so I now informed him why I was escorting him today: the patient with the exact same condition who had dropped dead on this very journey. That finally silenced him, but only as far as Hyde Park Corner.

From there, his memories became those of his childhood, because of course Felix Smollett was a child of west London. Of course his au pair used to take him to the Peter Pan statue where he would hide from her until she cried. Of course he was once brought home in a police car after taking all his clothes off and diving in the Serpentine. And of course his school choir used to sing in the Albert Hall. This led him into a rousing verse of his school hymn, which had me wishing his aortic valve really would rupture. It did not, and he somehow reached the Brompton unscathed.

When the ambulance doors opened, we were immediately greeted by the three junior Manson girls from Halloween. It took me a moment to recognize them, because here on their home turf, the girls were different: their accents were posher, they were far more polite and the school uniforms they were wearing today made them seem at least a decade younger. They had also now been joined by a French boy, who seemed to be some kind of international superfan, because he had a picture of Felix's face on his T-shirt.

The quartet trailed behind us as I escorted Felix to the cardiology suite and checked him in. He seemed surprised when I turned to leave, and asked me how long it would take. I told him that putting the actual probe down his throat took about fifteen minutes, but it was the pre-assessment checks and the sedation that would take the time. One of the junior Mansons burst into tears at that, and said that sedation was too dangerous for someone as vulnerable as Felix, and he should not be exposed to such an ordeal. Her father, she said, would tell us exactly the same thing if he was here. They all then turned to stare expectantly at me, as if the imaginary word of her dad was some irrefutable clinical argument.

I told them that I could not force Felix to do anything, but my own advice was to go ahead with the test, because we needed the information it would provide. Moreover, the ambulance ride alone would have already cost St. Luke's a few hundred pounds, and if Dr. Sudbury found out he'd come all this way only to change his mind, she would probably discharge him on principle.

"How would I get my antibiotics if I am discharged?" Felix asked.

"You wouldn't," I said.

The girls protested that it was not fair, and a breach of the exact kind of human rights legislation one of their mothers regularly prosecuted at The Hague. I ignored them, and Felix grudgingly went and took a seat in the cardiology suite waiting room.

"Will he be alright?" one of the girls then asked me.

"I can't discuss a patient's condition with you," I said.

"You can," Felix shouted back. "I don't care."

"Will he be alright?" she asked again, more plaintively this time.

"I don't know," I said. "He has a very serious illness."

Seeming to take this as a personal affront, the girls all glared at me.

"It's not my fault he's sick," I told them.

"Well, then whose fault is it?" one of them asked.

"It's his own. If he didn't inject that stuff—" I caught myself there, but it was too late, because I had already made another of the girls burst into tears.

"*Quelle domage*," said the French boy, shaking his head at me. I somehow remembered this meant "What a shame," and thought to myself how it was not in fact a shame, but the inevitable consequence of injecting bacteria into your own bloodstream.

I left the Brompton and wandered the nearby streets. In the immediate vicinity of St. Luke's there were three betting shops, a convenience store where the shopkeeper was protected by a wall of Perspex, and a café that was single-handedly responsible for half of the cases of gastroenteritis we saw. The Brompton was surrounded by boutique gift shops, artisan cupcake bakers and high-end delicatessens. Amid these, I eventually found what I was looking for: a bookshop.

I had planned to go to the medical section and look at the membership books, lest the junior doctors of west London even had better textbooks than us. When I got inside, though, I had a better idea: I went to the law section. A nearby postgraduate university meant that this was filled with impossibly complex titles about things like *English Contracting Law in Overseas Jurisdictions*, but eventually, tucked away on a bottom shelf, I located the book I needed: *English Criminal Law for Dummies*.

I took it to the bookshop café, bought a coffee and began to look through. The first chapters were all about the Magna Carta, the *actus rea* and the *mens rea* and so I flicked past them to the chapter entitled "Defenses in English Law." It informed me that the primary defenses available to the accused were: insanity, automatism, mistake, self-defense, duress, and marital coercion. Innocence did not seem to feature anywhere on the list. I wondered if this was because it was considered separately, or because it always failed.

I flicked ahead to the chapter on "Miscarriages of Justice," which did even less to reassure me. It began with the alarming statement that "Miscarriages of justice are inevitable in even the best criminal justice system" and only got worse from there. It went on to say that appeals were occasionally successful, but the process was intentionally designed to take many years, if not decades. I stopped reading then, not just because the book was making everything so much worse, but because I had realized that—much like Smollett's young entourage—I was looking for something that nobody could ever give me: categorical reassurance that my predicament could not possibly have a bad outcome. I finished my coffee, returned the book to the shelf, and walked back to the Brompton.

When I got back to the cardiology department, the receptionist hurried out from behind her desk and told me the doctor had been looking for me. She seemed excited as she led me into the procedure suite.

Procedure suites are more like dental offices than operating theaters, albeit dental offices that have at their center a gurney. Felix Smollett lay, apparently fast asleep, on this gurney, an intravenous drip tricking into the line in his neck. A doctor in his fifties and wearing blue scrubs stood over him, holding an ultrasound probe in Felix's throat. The image this created was playing on a nearby monitor, and it seemed to have mesmerized the doctor. He had not so much as lifted his eyes from the screen at my entrance, but even side-on I could tell that something had delighted him.

"What is it?" I asked.

The doctor turned and looked at me with surprise.

"Vegetations!" he exclaimed with glee. "I have never seen so many vegetations in a single patient! Are you his doctor?"

"I mean, yes," I admitted.

"Then, look! I am recording it," he said, proudly pointing to the monitor, "so you and I can write this case up!"

I looked at the monitor, and once again saw only the snow-storming static of a television without a signal. It reminded me of medical school: a consultant showing you something that was spectacularly obvious to him, but was as invisible to you as a magic eye picture.

"You do see them, don't you?" The cardiologist frowned.

"I'm not sure," I said, using the noncommittal phrasing I had refined in medical school. "Possibly?"

"Then let me get an even better image," he said, and readjusted his probe.

"There! You must see it now! Look, there is the mitral valve, and these glorious things—these are your patient's vegetations!"

Even I could see it now. The mitral valve pulsed open and closed like the mouth of a croaking frog. Clustered on it, and moving with it, were several brilliant white spots.

"Look at those! So many! With this image we should get into the *British Medical Journal*. Maybe we will even have a shot at the *New England Journal of Medicine!*"

As he said this, the cardiologist looked at me and shook his head in disbelief at the sheer triumph of it all.

Vegetations are masses of bacteria and platelets that can form on the valves of the heart in endocarditis, and they are every bit as ominous as they sound, for they make the antibiotic's job far harder. If the vegetations are 10 mm or bigger, cardiac surgery—with all its life-threatening risks and complications—is indicated to attempt to physically remove them.

"How big are they?" I asked.

The expression on the cardiologist's face told me that in his excitement about the glorious journal article we would surely publish together, he had forgotten to measure the vegetations to see if Felix needed an urgent operation. He quickly now did so, using a mouse to control a cursor on the monitor screen.

"Eight millimeters!" The cardiologist cried, making no effort to hide his dismay that Felix Smollett's case was not so immediately life-threatening as to merit open heart surgery.

"And nine millimeters! Goddamn it, nine millimeters! And another one—also nine millimeters!"

If that sounds ghoulish, I entirely understood the cardiologist's desire for an extreme case. In fact, I shared it. Doctors of course want all our individual patients to be well and remain so, even the ones that we can't stand. All the same, we do want to see the extreme cases too, for those are the ones that challenge us and give us things to boast to our colleagues about. Just as detectives no doubt dream of wily serial killers, so doctors dream of stealthily lethal but ultimately curable illnesses.

But I sympathized with the cardiologist for another reason, too: if Felix needed an operation, he would necessarily have to remain here at the Brompton, where the cardiothoracic surgeons were based. That would mean I would not have to endure the ambulance ride back to St. Luke's with him, or even have to argue with him about methadone on Jack Duckton ward ever again. As the cardiologist continued to measure, I found myself rooting for a 10 mm vegetation. But they were all a stubborn millimeter short.

Eventually the cardiologist sighed, set down his probe, and knocked on the glass for the nurse to come and take Felix out to recovery. His disappointment at the size of the vegetations seemed to even have muted his excitement about the article we would publish together. He was nonetheless careful to ensure that we exchanged details, and I still recall that my name seemed to inordinately please him. It is only as I write this that I understand why: his name came before mine in the alphabet, and he would therefore be listed as the more prestigious first author in our paper in the *New England Journal of Medicine*. As things turned out, none of that would ever happen, but neither of us could have known that day. And Felix Smollett certainly could not have.

Half an hour later, Felix and I were back in an ambulance, heading east this time. We had passed his entourage sitting in the foyer as we left, but the girls had been concentrating on plaiting the French boy's hair, and had not noticed us as we went by with the paramedics. Neither Felix nor I had alerted them to our presence.

Felix was still drowsy, and he dozed most of the way across

town. It was only as we neared St. Luke's that he woke up enough to ask me if the test had shown anything. Assuming he would not take it seriously, I told him that it had shown large clumps of bacteria on the valves of his heart. Spoken out loud that sounded harsh even to me, so I reassured him this was not unexpected, and that it did not really change anything apart from the length of time he would need to remain in the hospital. I left out the part that even the cardiologist had never seen such spectacular vegetations.

The news still seemed to affect him deeply. He turned paler than usual, and for a moment he seemed like he might be about to cry. I felt an unexpected empathy for him then. For all his obnoxiousness, he and I both suffered from the exact same sickness. I had just been fortunate enough that my job allowed me to access the feeling we both craved in pill form, whereas he had only been able to find it in a dirty needle.

But my empathy was short-lived. As we turned onto the road that took us to St. Luke's, Felix began to quietly sing, to the tune of "Yesterday" by The Beatles, a new version of his own composition:

"Vegetations…vegetations, all my trouble seemed so far away… but now it seems like they are here to stay… Oh, I believe in vegetations…"

I ignored him and stared out the window, and eventually he stopped.

Back at St. Luke's, I delivered Felix to the nurses on Jack Duckton and went to find Rami to pick up my pager. He told me all my patients had been fine, but there had been a call for me on an outside line. They had refused to give a name, but had left a London number with an unfamiliar area code.

I went to the office on Jack Duckton and locked the door. I still had some faint hope it might be something else—the car-

diologist from the Brompton, or a locum agency—but I think
I already knew who it was going to be. Sure enough, DS Newington answered straightaway.

She thanked me for ringing back, and said that she and DI
Afferson had been hoping they might arrange a follow-up interview to tie up what she termed "a few loose ends." I explained
that I was not off until the weekend; Newington said she already knew that, and they had been hoping I could manage ten
o'clock on Saturday morning. That, of course, made my head
spin: if they knew when I was working, they had either asked Dr.
Sudbury or somehow obtained a copy of my rota. Not knowing
what else to do, I agreed to the interview. As we were hanging
up, I asked DS Newington if I should bring a lawyer.

"If you feel you need one," she said.

That made me feel that I very much did need one. Miscarriages of justice, after all, are quite inevitable in even the best
criminal justice system.

I asked around among my colleagues, but the only lawyers
they knew were the ones they had been to university with who
now worked as juniors on corporate mergers. George tried to
help as always, and said he was sure there were at least a few
brilliant lawyers in his rugby club. He wouldn't be seeing them
until Saturday afternoon though, so he suggested I postpone the
interview. I told him that I didn't think murder investigations
worked like that. This was just as well, as it ultimately turned
out that the brilliant lawyers George was thinking of were all
actually estate agents. Collette had an uncle she offered to ask,
but being a murder suspect did not seem to be the best introduction to her family.

Eventually I went to the accident and emergency waiting
room, picked up one of the flyers for the ambulance chasers,
and left a message on their free-phone hotline. They finally
called me back twenty-four hours later. I had been hoping for
an expert analysis of my case, the outline of an irrefutable de-

fense strategy, and gentle but firm reassurance there was nothing whatsoever to worry about. Instead, I got a bored receptionist who asked for the name of the police station and the time of the interview, and then promised me their duty solicitor would be there. She did not seem to be taking it seriously enough, so I told her that I believed the charge might be murder. She did not react to this, except to wearily reiterate that the duty solicitor would be there.

I spent the rest of that week having anxiety dreams in which DI Afferson pursued me down vanishing point corridors. Each time, right when I seemed on the point of getting away, Dr. Sudbury would emerge from a clinic room and trip me, sending me sprawling. DS Newington would then appear and handcuff me. It did not take a master's degree in dream analysis to understand what those things likely represented.

CHAPTER 12

For the second consecutive Saturday, I found myself in the waiting room at Highbury police station. This time I had eaten a full breakfast and packed my things into my suitcase before leaving home. I did not know if I would be coming back, and did not want the responsibility to fall to George. I still only had the possessions I'd arrived in London with, so there was at least not much, and it would be straightforward enough for him to have it shipped to my parents.

The lawyer did show up as agreed, and to begin with he seemed promising. He was only a little older than me, but he wore a crumpled suit and long coat that made him look the part. Better yet, the desk sergeant seemed to recognize him and perhaps even have a grudging respect for him. The lawyer himself had a confident, almost cocky, manner, and as we waited together, I began to think it was ridiculous I had packed a suitcase. I even started to wonder if I might make it out in time to watch the football in the pub at lunchtime.

That all changed after Afferson and Newington appeared and took us back to the interview room. After the formalities—the introductions, the starting of the tape and video, the reading of my rights—Afferson produced a large brown envelope and asked me to open it. The theatrics were once again so much like a television cop show that I actually began to laugh, but the look my lawyer gave me immediately shut me up. And so I opened the envelope, and took out what I already knew it would contain: a copy of my GMC fitness-to-practice proceedings. A single word had been highlighted in fluorescent yellow marker-pen throughout. The word was *pethidine*.

I felt the familiar sense of doom returning, but now it was no longer impending. It had arrived. I was doomed. The police had a woman who had died of an unexplained pethidine overdose, knew that I was a pethidine addict with a history of stealing the drug, and had me on record as having lied to them about that. I had even suggested to them they were probably mistaken about her death being a murder at all. I asked for a glass of water, realizing as I did so that I too was now playing a role from a bad television cop show: the role of the murderer who is about to confess. I looked to my lawyer for help, but he no longer looked like a lawyer. He looked like an excited schoolboy.

Afferson sent Newington out for my water. We all sat in silence until she returned with it, at which point Afferson reminded me that I'd previously told them there was nothing else pertinent they should know, and asked if there was anything I would like to now tell them. I looked to my lawyer, and he enthusiastically nodded for me to continue.

What could any of it possibly matter now? And so I took a deep breath and told them my whole weary story. The bicycle accident on my way to work in which I had broken my clavicle. The codeine I'd been given afterward. The way those tablets had made me feel. That I had continued taking them, even after the pain had gone. And then the half-empty packet of pethidine left behind in a recently discharged patient's cabinet. The feeling again. The technique I had developed of adding pethidine to a patient's discharge prescription, then swiping it when the prescription arrived on the ward. That I had planned to do this only once, and then twice, and then for a week, and then for a month, until I had been doing it for six months and nobody had noticed. That I had begun to believe the system I had invented was foolproof, right up until the moment it no longer was. The terrible confrontation with Dr. Abernathy and the seething chief pharmacist. The immediate suspension, the at-home detox and the residential treatment. The hearings and the rehearings, and finally the grudging sign-off with conditions. The advertisement in the *British Medical Journal*. The move south for a clean break. The weekly sessions I endured with the Reverend McKendrick in the dreary room above the kebab shop in Bethnal Green. The *angor amini* I had felt when they had mentioned the word *pethidine* the last time I was here. I even told them about consulting *English Criminal Law for Dummies* and that it had stated that miscarriages of justice inevitably occur in even the best systems.

If I'd hoped I might win them over with my honesty, I could not have been more wrong. Afferson was still visibly playing the television detective, and stared at me silently for some time.

"That's all very interesting, Doctor," he eventually said. "All very interesting indeed. But we were actually hoping you could tell us what you know about the murder of Mrs. Horsburgh."

Out of the corner of my eye, I caught my lawyer once again nodding. I did not know if he was expressing his approval of Afferson's performance, or concurring with him that I should just hurry up and confess. It was like a scene from the film I had watched about a spy being falsely accused. But it was not a film, I was the person being falsely accused, and I had no expert knowledge of tradecraft with which to beat the system and clear my name.

I will admit I got a little angry again then. I told Afferson that

I did not know anything about Mrs. Horsburgh's murder, and the reason for that was because I had only even encountered the woman in the course of literally trying to save her life. I told him that I had been working nights, had spent the first part of my shift clearing a busy A+E, and had only even gone to the tower when I got the page, as which point Mrs. Horsburgh was essentially already dead. I was in the middle of explaining to Afferson how routine the arrest had been, when he interrupted me.

"And you have witnesses for that, do you?" he asked. "Witnesses that will confirm you only left the accident and emergency department when you received this call?"

Of course, I did not have witnesses. Dozens of colleagues could no doubt testify to having seen me in accident and emergency that evening, but not one of them could say I had never left the department for ten minutes. It was simply not how it worked.

I attempted to explain this, but even as I spoke I was aware of how I sounded: guilty. The portrait of Dr. Crippen now pushed its way into the front of my mind and silenced me. Eventually I just shrugged and said that there might not be witnesses, but it was definitely what had happened. Even I did not think I sounded particularly convincing.

Afferson asked me if there was anything else that I wanted to say, and informed me that it might harm my defense not to say something that I later relied on in court. My lawyer had apparently now fully changed sides, because when I glanced at him for guidance he impatiently gestured for me to continue. Even DS Newington was alarmed by this, and now took it upon herself to remind me that I had a right to remain silent. That made the lawyer look a little sheepish, and he now hurriedly confirmed that I should indeed be mindful that any disclosures I made could also hurt my case.

I looked around at their expectant faces. There was so much tension in the air that I believe they were waiting for me to confess there and then. But I did not confess. Instead, I told them the truth: yes, I had been a pethidine addict, and in the past I had stolen enough of the stuff to murder a herd of elephants. But here was the thing: somebody who was addicted to pethidine, somebody who was willing to risk their career, life and health for that precious stuff—well, they were hardly likely to squander it killing random patients, were they?

It did not immediately help. The silence that followed was only more pregnant. My lawyer was staring directly at Afferson, and I abruptly understood why: he was waiting for him to charge me with the murder of Mrs. Horsburgh. This was how it happened on television, and this was how it was going to happen for me. I found myself wondering about the practicalities of what happened next: Would I be permitted a phone call, and if so who would I even call? My parents? Collette? A new lawyer? Would I spend the night here in the police cells, or was there still time for them to get me to a prison today? Mostly, I wondered how long my sentence would be. Twenty years? Twenty-five? Thirty? However long it was, my life as I knew it was over.

But Afferson did not charge me. Instead, he looked at Newington and nodded.

"That's good enough for me for now," he said.

"And for me," said Newington.

It was so unexpected that I thought it must just be one more part of the routine, but they stood up and Newington told me I was free to go. It was all I could do not to burst into tears, but I somehow held it together.

Outside on the street, my lawyer congratulated me, and then informed me I owed him two hundred and twenty five pounds, due immediately. He marched me to the cash machine and, as we waited in line, I asked him what he made of it all.

"Fishing trip," he said. "Wouldn't worry about it at all. Do you need a receipt?"

I told him that I did not, gave him the money, and for some

reason even thanked him for all his work. As he walked away, I realized that during the entire interview his sole intervention had been to encourage me to confess to a crime I had not committed. If I ever still do somehow end up in prison over all this, I may have a case for compensation.

I did not go to the pub to watch the football, but straight home, where I knew George would be revising. I needed a sympathetic ear, and George was the kindest person I knew. Sure enough, he did not even raise an eyebrow when I confessed my sordid past to him, and seemed to have no qualms about having an ex-addict for a flatmate.

It turned out that he knew an anesthetist who had developed a fentanyl habit after breaking a leg during a game against a touring French side. What had helped his friend "get it all out of his system," George said, was actually just playing a vast amount of rugby. He suggested if I ever felt the urge again, I simply do the same. He then made the point that I was probably not the only person residing in this flat who'd had an opioid habit. I did not follow this, until George broke out into guffaws of laughter and told me that Patrick had likely been "a laudanum fiend" as "those bloody Victorians were all at it."

But if my previous opioid addiction did not perturb George, my treatment at the police station very much did. He was incensed that the police had questioned me again, and even more so that my lawyer had not stood up for me. He did not have any insights as to why the police had suddenly seemed to change course at the end of the interview, but it actually came as a relief to find this baffled him as much as it did me. We even then went to the pub to catch the late game, George being willing to tolerate football when there was no rugby on.

I did not think until the next day to ask George to keep my second police interview a secret. Work had been difficult enough after my first interview, and everybody knowing that I had been called back for a second interview would surely be far worse.

George admitted he had already told Amelia, but reassured me she was not the type to gossip. Later that week, Amelia found me in the mess and made a point of gently commiserating with me on "everything I had been going through lately." She told me that if ever I needed to talk she'd be here, but equally she understood some things were "simply better left unsaid." She looked at me pointedly as she said that last part; I understood that that was her way of letting me know that my secret was safe with her. I have always been grateful for that, and as far as I know nobody else did ever find out about my second interview.

Dr. Thomas Neil Cream graduated in medicine from Montreal's Mc-Gill University in 1876. He wrote his final year thesis on chloroform, a fitting topic for a doctor who would become internationally infamous as The Lambeth Poisoner, but could equally have been named The Chicago Poisoner or The Montreal Poisoner.

Dr. Cream's first known victim was a young woman in Montreal. She was found next to a chloroform-soaked handkerchief in the alleyway behind his medical office. After first claiming that the young woman had attended his clinic and threatened to kill herself if he did not perform an abortion, Dr. Cream accused a local businessman of her murder in an attempt to extort money from him. When this clumsy scheme backfired, Dr. Cream fled to the United States.

In Chicago, Dr. Cream set up shop as a backstreet abortionist in the city's red light district. At least two of his female patients soon died in suspicious circumstances, but it was the murder of a man named Daniel Stott that led to Dr. Cream being imprisoned for the first time. Stott died immediately after taking an epilepsy "remedy" that Cream had *prescribed for him; Cream then blackmailed the dispensing pharmacist, whom he accused of misreading his prescription. Stott's guilt-ridden wife, however, confessed she was having an affair with Dr. Cream, and that the two of them had intentionally poisoned her husband with strychnine.*

Dr. Cream was convicted of the murder of Daniel Stott and sentenced to life imprisonment in the Illinois State Penitentiary, but after serving less than ten years, he used an inheritance to bribe his way out. He then moved to England and settled in the impoverished London borough of Lambeth.

Two weeks after Dr. Cream's arrival in London, a young prostitute accepted a drink from a stranger and died in agony of what a postmortem would later establish was strychnine poisoning. Dr. Cream then wrote to a well-known businessman, accusing him of the murder, and attempting to blackmail him; Cream also wrote to the coroner, offering to name the murderer in exchange for a large reward.

Those letters went unanswered, but Dr. Cream soon attempted the trick again with another strychnine murder. This time the target of his blackmail was Queen Victoria's personal physician, Sir William Broadbent. The gambit failed once again, and Dr. Cream traveled to Canada to lie low. On his return to London a few months later, the killings began anew and the newspapers erupted with talk of The Lambeth Poisoner. Dr. Cream, who had become so emboldened as to even give a visiting policeman a tour of the murder locations, was soon arrested. A jury took only twelve minutes to find him guilty, and three weeks later he was hung at Newgate Prison.

Dr. Thomas Cream may be one of the most troubling of healthcare killers, because he seems to have had very little in the way of motive. His inept blackmailing appears to have mostly been an afterthought, and there is no evidence it ever worked. Likewise, Dr. Cream had no personal or professional relationship with most of his victims, and sometimes poisoned strangers in public places only for them to die alone hours

later. It therefore seems possible that Dr. Cream's sole motivating ani-
mus was simply that he enjoyed abusing his knowledge to inflict suf-
fering on his fellow humans.

CHAPTER 13

As we stumbled deeper into November, the nights got ever darker, the fog ever thicker, and I continued to put one foot in front of the other and hope that I would not be arrested for murder. I told myself that the silence meant that Afferson must have moved on to new suspects, but at one of our Sunday sessions, the Reverend McKendrick told me that two detectives had been to see him to ask about my progress. The Reverend McKendrick reassured me he had told them I had not shown the slightest hint of sinful temptation, but this did little to calm my nerves.

Collette, George, and I all had exams in early January, and she had begun to take her revision so seriously that we barely saw each other. For a while I wondered if my situation was too much for her, but at lunch in the mess one day she showed me her revision notes. They were painstakingly color coded—a red pen for the word *artery*, a blue pen for the word *vein*, and a green pen for the name of any bacteria—and I understood she had genuinely been working as hard as she claimed. I could not say the same for myself: I had still been traipsing to the British Library most weekends, but instead of revising I would invariably find myself reading books about infamous miscarriages of justice.

Collette's diligence did at least inspire me to buy a set of high-lighters and attempt my own color-coded revision notes, but the results were disastrous. I used the wrong color for a virus in the very first line, and after three more mistakes in the next two lines I abandoned any pretense of a system. Not long thereafter, I gave up writing notes at all, and instead opened another test prep book that Saz had lent me: *Sample Questions for the MRCP.* She had already filled it in, but even I could tell that her answers were almost entirely wrong. Anyway, the main thing I took from the book was reinforcement of the grotesque lesson in prejudice my colleague in Scotland had taught me: a businessman who had visited Swaziland had HIV; a patient from Chile had leprosy; a nightclub singer had syphilis; a nurse with several rare conditions had, once again, Munchausen syndrome.

Work itself was largely unchanged: an unrelenting tide of patients admitted through A+E; an endless ward round on Jack Duckton; ever more X-rays and bloods and discharge prescriptions; ever more arguments with Felix Smollett about his methadone.

He had lately even begun arguing with my colleagues out of hours, in the hope that they might be more generous than I was. He'd had no success, but had managed to provoke a few of them. Marianne had apparently told him that he was worse than the children who had driven her away from pediatrics, and an exasperated Colin may or may not have even challenged him to a fistfight.

The biggest surprise of all, though, was Amelia. None of us had ever witnessed Amelia lose even a drop of her cool in any number of life-or-death situations, but the nurses said they'd almost had to call the police one night because of a screaming match taking place between her and Felix. I couldn't imagine Amelia screaming about anything, so I discreetly asked her about it. She shuddered with embarrassment and admitted it was not her finest hour. If anything, hearing that she did actually possess a single flaw only endeared her to me more.

After Felix, my second largest amount of work was the endless meetings with the relatives of my patients on Jack Duckton ward. These meetings were always requested due to claimed family concerns about some aspect or other of their relative's care, but ultimately boiled down to variations on the themes of either "Yes, but how will the long-term care my relative now requires affect my inheritance?" and "I know it is hard to predict, but can you give me any kind of rough idea of when I will get my inheritance?" At our weekly ward meeting, I suggested that publishing an information sheet on these subjects would free up untold hours each week. Everybody assumed I was joking, and when I assured them I wasn't, they all looked horrified. Even when you are only vaguely suspected of murder, you have to watch what you say.

Still, my ignominy did not last long, because on a Friday in late November Dr. Sudbury called another all-hands meeting. DI Afferson was once again there, and this time DS Newington had come with him. Afferson made another awkward joke, this time about "having to stop meeting like this," but Newington simply glared out at us, as if searching for a guilty party. Perhaps that is exactly what she was doing, for the purpose of the meeting was to inform us that new information had now come to light: Mrs. Horsburgh's unexplained death had promoted an expert review of St. Luke's mortality figures over the past year, and it had concluded that mathematically there had been at least fifteen and perhaps as many as forty-three excess deaths.

DS Newington's stern gaze ensured that nobody laughed out loud, but we were surely all thinking the same thing: excess as compared to *what*? The healthy citizens of west London? Olympic athletes? Our patients were the sickest in the city: they frequently suffered from Victorian ailments, traveled to the farthest corners of the globe to bring home obscure exotic diseases, and sometimes just good old-fashioned shot each other. St. Luke's itself quite obviously did a decent job in a tough spot—Dr. Sudbury and the other consultants saw to that—and so the whole notion seemed ridiculous. Besides, if there genuinely had been fifteen or forty-three excess deaths, what were they actually telling us? That there was some kind of serial killer on the loose at St. Luke's?

As it transpired, Dr. Sudbury and DI Afferson took great pains to say that they were definitely not telling us there was a serial killer on the loose at St. Luke's. They were saying only that a preliminary review of the numbers meant they could not exclude the possibility of something untoward having taken place over the last year. Nonetheless, Dr. Sudbury insisted that it was most likely simply an error, as if tens of human lives might be no more than an unreconciled bank transaction. Still, to ensure full transparency, a team of outside consultants had begun a review of case files, and she hoped this would ultimately provide us all with the reassurance we needed. If this review did show anything untoward, she added, it would allow us to take the necessary next steps. So: there could be a serial killer on the loose at St. Luke's, but hopefully there was not, and anyway the possibility was being properly looked into. Dr. Sudbury then asked us all to reflect on the past year at the hospital, and let her or DI Afferson know if we recalled anything unusual at all.

At some point during this all I caught Newington's eye, and she broke character long enough to give me a brief nod. If anybody else had spotted this, they might have wondered what was going on, but I think Newington was telling me that these excess deaths had saved me from a murder charge. Perhaps she had even argued to Afferson that an addict unwilling to waste pethidine on one patient would hardly have been willing to waste it on fifteen of them, let alone forty-three.

Dr. Sudbury then concluded the meeting by advising us to document every patient encounter, to report anything that seemed remotely unusual and, finally, by reminding us never to forget that hospital was a very dangerous place to be. The last part caused DI Afferson to visibly prick up his ears, and Dr. Sudbury's comical hurry to explain to him that she always said that drew a nervous laugh from the crowd. They were laughing in part because Dr. Sudbury had inadvertently put herself in the frame, but mostly because Afferson's reaction terrified them: if Dr. Sudbury was not above suspicion, neither was anybody else.

Death lurks everywhere in the hospital and, once you begin to look for it, so too does suspicion. That green line between life and death is so precariously thin that the entire system runs on a trust that could be silently and lethally breached at any time. Do the pills that doctor just prescribed interact fatally with a drug the patient is already on? Is the injection that nurse is giving intended to relieve the patient's labored breathing, or to stop him breathing altogether? That cleaner carrying the pillow down the corridor: is she changing it for a clean one, or has she just smothered somebody's elderly relative?

Likewise, Dr. Sudbury had asked us to let them know about anything unusual, but the truth was that everything in medicine was always unusual. Our understanding of the human body is so rudimentary that nothing ever entirely matches the textbooks. Almost every patient we saw had an unexplained symptom or an ill-fitting blood test. Our job was to discern patterns amid the chaos, and if we did not daily ignore small pieces that did not entirely fit, we would rarely have made so much as a single diagnosis.

And yet there was one patient who stuck out for me, a man in his seventies whose name I could not remember and whose notes I could therefore never find. He had been admitted somewhere in the tower with a pneumonia and had been believed to be recovering well. The nurse at the arrest said he had complained of a headache earlier in the day, and she had given him some acetaminophen. She hadn't called for a doctor, because if nurses called for a doctor every time a patient had a headache, nobody would ever get anything done.

I must have been one of the last to arrive, because I was taking the bloods. In an arrested patient, the usual veins in the arms don't give you anything—chest compressions move the blood to the lungs and brain, but little further—and so you have to go for the femorals, the large vessels in the groin. As a medical student, I had learned the mnemonic to remember the relevant anatomy was NAVY: nerve, artery, vein, Y-fronts. What that meant in practice was: don't stick your needle in too far to the outside, or you risk hitting the femoral nerve.

And so I had shoved in alongside my colleagues, timed myself to the pause between compressions, and stuck the patient in his groin. I had been aiming for the vein, but the bright red blood that filled the syringe told me it was oxygenated and I had therefore hit the artery. Whatever. Blood was blood, and an arterial sample would still give me the numbers I needed. The blood was so bright red, I even congratulated my colleagues on their CPR technique; usually after a patient had been down for five minutes, even arterial blood had turned crimson due to a lack of oxygen.

I took the sample to the analyzer on the maternity ward. It wasn't as modern as the one in A+E, but it was nearer and it would give me the results I needed: potassium, glucose, hemoglobin. I decanted the blood to the correct syringe, attached this to the machine, and pressed the button to start it. I watched the machine suck the blood from the syringe, then followed its progress through the narrow tube in which it traversed the solutes and solvents. After a few minutes, the dot matrix printer attached to the machine screeched into life and printed out a reading.

The headline numbers I was interested in were all unremark-able, but there was something odd going on with the others. The analyzer also measured oxygen levels, and the level it showed was so low the sample could only have come from a vein. And yet the blood had been bright red.

I went back and told my colleagues the perplexing results. They had continued with the ballet, but I could tell people were beginning to get bored. Somebody asked how long it had been and the reply came back: nine minutes. It was still too early to call it, and so I stuck the patient's groin again, this time being more careful to go medial enough to be certain I would hit the vein and not the artery.

But I got the same thing: bright red blood. I shifted my body so my colleagues could see where my needle was, and that it was inexplicably filling up with bright red blood. Somebody suggested carbon monoxide poisoning was a cause of artificially red blood, but somebody else said carbon monoxide actually turned the skin red. A debate ensued, but it did not matter: the analyzer had measured the carbon monoxide on the previous sample, and it had been normal.

I took my second bright red sample back to the machine, and got the same result again: an oxygen level that confirmed the sample could only have come from a vein. It was a mystery, yet it did not matter, because by the time I got back to the room they had already called it: time of death, Rest in Peace. It was the middle of a busy shift and nobody else was more than mildly intrigued by the anomaly. I stuck the printout in the notes and went on with my work. If we stopped to investigate everything that did not make perfect sense, nobody would ever get any-thing done.

After the meeting with Dr. Sudbury and DI Afferson, I at-tempted to track down the patient with the bright red blood, but I could not recall his name, and none of the colleagues I asked remembered any more than I did. We all went to so many arrests, it was impossible. No doubt if I had told Dr. Sudbury we could have searched more thoroughly, but how could I tell her I had been involved in another suspicious death? And what even was my suspicion anyway? That somebody had dyed the patient's blood bright red? That they had invented a form of carbon monoxide poisoning that had somehow not shown up on the analyzer? That Dr. O'Leary had then missed whatever had been done to the man?

Some diseases must present themselves. It is another thing doctors tell each other, and it means that time is always the best diagnostician, and will ultimately reveal if the things that do not add up are meaningful or not.

Sure enough, a few years ago I finally came to understand what had happened to the man with the bright red blood. I was up late one night, and found myself watching an episode of an old television show about a cantankerous doctor who solved impossible cases. One of his patients in the intensive care unit had been noted to have bright red blood. Unlike at St. Luke's, his patient was not yet dead, and the doctor had both the time and motivation to find the answer. I had to sit through a whole episode to discover the diagnosis, which turned out to be cyanide poisoning. I looked it up in my old copy of *Smithfield's* and, sure enough, one of the only signs of cyanide poisoning is cherry red blood.

I felt briefly guilty that it had got past me, and that a murder had almost certainly gone undetected, but mostly I felt relief not to have said anything at the time. If I had told Dr. Sudbury or DI Afferson about the patient with the bright red blood, I'd likely still be in prison now.

CHAPTER 14

In the days after the bombshell meeting, we tiptoed around the wards like medical students on our first clinical attachments. Each time we entered a ward, we informed the nurse in charge of our presence; when we left we did the same thing. We showed every drug we prescribed to a pharmacist and had them initial each line on the chart to confirm we were not committing murder but simply treating hypertension. In the accident and emergency department, we took to making loud proof-of-life announcements: "I have just left Cubicle 4 and as you can see she is still alive." Most strikingly, we stopped doing favors for one another, and soon no doctor would so much as write up a bag of fluids for anybody else's patient.

The hospital quickly ground to a halt. Eventually, Dr. Sudbury had to call another meeting to explain that the analysis had not shown anything unusual so far, and it was beginning to look like St. Luke's had simply endured a particularly bad flu season. She therefore asked us to return to our previous collegiate way of doing things, because if we did not there would be far more than fifteen excess deaths the next year.

The relief was palpable. We settled back into our routines, and things really did quiet down for a few days. They might have even stayed that way if Eliza Duckton had not chosen this moment to hold a press conference on the steps of the main building. She declared that her father's good name had been besmirched by the events at St. Luke's, and she would not now rest until she had restored his honor.

Unless Jack Duckton's middle name was St. Luke, none of the press coverage had so much as mentioned him, but Eliza Duckton seemed to consider her father and St. Luke's indistinguishable. Even worse, she had somehow persuaded the Wilsons to attend her press conference; they stood behind her looking miserable while Eliza held up a photograph of Mrs. Horsburgh and announced that she would work tirelessly to ensure that every single victim of this scandal was identified and the perpetrators fully punished, so help her God. Given that the most likely culprit now seemed to be influenza, it was difficult to know exactly what she meant. How could you punish influenza?

It was unclear if any of the crowd that day were actually journalists, or if they were all just clinic patients and passersby, but when the story ran on the cover of the *Hackney Gazette* a week later we got our answer: there had been at least one journalist in attendance. There had been at least one photographer too, because the article was accompanied by a shot of an indignant Eliza Duckton flanked by the dejected Wilsons.

The article itself contained almost no new details beyond what DI Afferson had told us, but those had been spun in such an inflammatory way that I wondered if Eliza herself might have had had a hand in writing it. The mortality figures—described throughout as the "death toll"—had shown "major discrepancies" which opened up "terrifying possibilities." The meeting where Dr. Sudbury had informed us about these figures was described as a "tense closed-door session" wherein "arrogant doctors and furious nurses" had "pushed back" against "any suggestion of error." An accompanying editorial called for an investigation by "Scotland Yard's elite Flying Squad," but even I had seen enough cop shows to know that was not remotely what they did. The *Gazette* might as well have been calling for an investigation by Sherlock Holmes and the Baker Street Irregulars.

Somehow I managed to miss the most interesting part of the article, and saw it only when George mentioned it at home that night. Deep in the piece, it stated that an "unnamed source" had told the *Gazette* that a doctor interviewed in the index case and once "heavily suspected" had now been "all but eliminated from inquiries." This was clearly me—and it was a relief to see it in black-and-white—but the source of the information was a puzzle.

My first thought was it must have come from Afferson or Newington, but they did not seem the type to talk to the press, and especially not the *Hackney Gazette*. Moreover, if the detectives had been the *Gazette*'s generous source, they surely would not have published an accompanying editorial effectively suggesting they were not up to the job. Nonetheless, on closer reading, I noticed a few other details in the story that could only have come from somebody with inside information: a mention of the second meeting at the hospital, and a particular detail about how Mrs. Horsburgh's postmortem had shown a small amount of scarring around her heart. The latter piece of information could have come from the Wilsons, of course, but then they would not have known about the meeting at the hospital.

For a few days, the article was the talk of the mess. A few colleagues admitted they had been contacted by journalists from national newspapers, but they all insisted they had refused to supply any information. The general consensus was that, whatever may have befallen the unfortunate Mrs. Horsburgh, there was no serial killer on the loose at St. Luke's. People die in hospitals, and especially during a bad flu season. We told each other there was nothing for any of us to worry about.

Surprisingly, the person the *Gazette* article had the biggest impact on was Felix Smollett. He became quite obsessed with the whole thing. Every time I passed his side room—which, due its location at the entrance to Jack Duckton ward, was about a hundred times a day—he shouted out some question or other about the different methods by which a patient could be discreetly dispatched: Would a valium overdose be detected at postmortem? What about suffocation? Could you kill a patient simply by giving them too much saline?

I ignored him to begin with, but his questions soon became curiously specific, as if he was conducting an investigation of his own: How many nights in a row did the nursing staff work? Did doctors know how to work the intravenous pumps? What access to drugs did nurses have? Did I know where Angela had worked before she came to St. Luke's? After three days, I paged the bed manager and persuaded her to move him to a distant part of the ward where I would not have to pass him so often.

On a trip to the mortuary to certify another corpse—a hundred-year-old with metastatic cancer, so an entirely expected death—Dr. O'Leary asked me how the morale was among the junior doctors. No other senior doctor had ever asked me such a thing, and so I had to think for a moment before finding the truthful answer: no worse than usual. Dr O'Leary seemed pleased, and told me that was exactly the right attitude: chin up, head held high! It was, he said, an outrage that people were indulging in such lurid speculation when they had no understanding of the incredibly difficult job we did. I was impressed by his collegiate good cheer, until I remembered he was not exactly a neutral observer. If anyone should have noticed a serial killer in St. Luke's, it was surely the doctor whose primary job it was to identify any suspicious deaths.

I did not tell Dr. O'Leary that morale had only remained no

worse than usual because we were coping by using the exact same trick we always did: black humor. After we had got over the initial shock, the idea of there being a serial killer on the loose at St. Luke's had quickly become a hilarious joke in the mess. We even already had a suspect of sorts.

The porters at St. Luke's were, for the most part, the same as at every other hospital in the country: ebullient tattooed older men who daily made the same jokes as they trundled patients back and forth to X-ray, to theaters and to the morgue. One of their number, however, differed from the others in that he always seemed to be spectacularly morose. At lunch the day after the meeting with DI Afferson, Marianne had mentioned how she had noticed this particular porter often seemed to be around when bad things happened: not necessarily deaths, but deteriorations, equipment malfunctions, and lost case notes. Rami and Colin had both confirmed they had also noticed this phenomenon. A consensus briefly built that if there was indeed a St. Luke's serial killer, it must be this porter.

The sole dissenting voice was Kwame. He had pointed out that the porter in question frequently had trouble even locating the laboratory, so it seemed unlikely that he was our cunning murderer. We had therefore settled on the idea that this porter was not the killer, but rather some sort of supernatural harbinger. Somebody inevitably then christened him "The Angel of Death." It wasn't particularly funny or smart or kind, but we were heading into winter in a hospital that might be harboring a murderer, and each one of us was apparently a suspect. We would take our relief where we found it.

And meantime, of course, life continued outside the hospital, or at least insomuch as it ever did. When we weren't at work we were mostly sleeping, and when we weren't sleeping we were studying for our exams. Collette had continued to take hers more seriously than mine, but I was finally getting down to it and making some progress. Meantime, George and Amelia had been enthusiastically planning their wedding. George had even found the place where he wanted them to get married, but he said it was so spectacular he did not want to jinx it by telling me where it was.

Dr. Linda Hazzard *was not a medical doctor, but a homeopath who abused a loophole in Washington state law to describe herself as one. Dr. Hazzard's primary qualifications as a healthcare killer, then, are her crimes themselves.*

Dr. Hazzard styled herself as a "fasting specialist" and her essential con was that starvation was a panacea that could cure any disease. Hazzard wrote about these ideas in books such as Scientific Fasting: The Ancient and Modern Key to Health, *but she did her worst damage at her Wilderness Heights sanatorium in Olalla, Washington. There, she treated her inpatients with a diet of minuscule amounts of tomato or asparagus broth and a "protocol" that included scalding baths and colonic enemas. After they had spent weeks and sometimes months following Dr. Hazzard's regime, dozens of patients died from malnutrition and starvation.*

Astonishingly, Dr. Hazzard's exploits were no secret. After repeatedly encountering skeletal escapees begging for food, unimpressed locals had renamed her establishment "Starvation Heights." One weary headline in the Seattle Daily Times *even simply read* **"'MD' KILLS ANOTHER PATIENT."** *But the authorities were powerless to intervene: the loophole meant that Dr. Hazzard held a valid medical license, and none of her patients had ever complained about her.*

It was the treatment of Claire and Dorothea Williamson, a pair of rich British sisters, that led to Dr Hazzard's downfall. After seeing an advert for Wilderness Heights, the Williamsons had traveled to Olalla to try Dr. Hazzard's starvation cure. It is unclear what, if anything, had been ailing the sisters prior to coming to Washington, but the cure's effects on them were certainly dramatic: after a couple of months, they each weighed less than seventy pounds.

Alerted by a telegram, the sisters' childhood nanny journeyed to Wilderness Heights to check up on them. She arrived to the news that Claire had died, a demise Dr. Hazzard ascribed to a medicine Claire had briefly been given in childhood. Meantime, Dorothea weighed only sixty-three pounds, but was insistent that Dr. Hazzard's cure was "working wonders." The nanny also discovered that Dr. Hazzard had been appointed executor of Claire's estate. The nanny telegrammed the sisters' family, and Dorothea Williamson was only extracted from Dr. Hazzard's clutches when they agreed to pay a "bill" that was effectively a ransom.

Dr. Hazzard was charged with first degree murder in the death of Claire Williamson, but eventually found guilty only of manslaughter. She was stripped of her unearned medical license and sentenced to up to twenty years in prison. After serving only two years, Dr. Hazzard was pardoned by the governor of Washington and released. She then moved to New Zealand, where she would eventually be charged for practicing medicine without a license.

In 1920, Linda Hazzard returned to Washington, and built a new and bigger Starvation Heights. As her medical license had been removed, she called this new establishment a "School of Health" but continued to offer fasting cures to a seemingly endless stream of enthusiastic patients.

All told, Dr. Hazzard is believed to have killed at least eighteen patients and caused vast suffering to hundreds more. Nonetheless, the most troubling part of Dr. Hazzard's story may be its coda. A lifelong advocate for the benefits of the fasting cure on her patients, Dr. Hazzard ultimately commenced a fast of her own and died of starvation in 1938. At her 1911 murder trial, the prosecution had called her a "financial starvationist" and alleged that her whole enterprise was a fraudulent scheme to make money. Dr. Hazzard's own demise suggests the truth about her is even more alarming: Dr. Hazzard truly believed, despite the evidence provided by her own eyes and the emaciated bodies of her dead patients, that her methods worked.

CHAPTER 15

On the first of December the hospital Christmas decorations went up. The centerpiece was a large tree in the main foyer that somebody even went to the trouble of placing fake wrapped presents beneath; empty though these were, they were nonetheless stolen before the end of the day. Artificial snow was sprayed on the windows, and some of the porters even began wearing Santa hats until a killjoy infection control nurse ordered they desist less they somehow give somebody a lethal disease. Everybody endlessly told me the children's ward had the best decorations, and that a walk through would get me right into the Christmas spirit. Against my better judgment, I passed through once when I was nearby. The decorations were indeed beautiful, but the juxtaposition with the sick children did not make me feel festive. It made me feel heartbroken.

But there was no escape. On the same day that the decorations went up, the canteen began insistently serving turkey with cranberry sauce and roast potatoes. The catering staff put up post-

ers—"posters" is generous, they were really just printed pieces
of A4 paper announcing "It's Christmas every day in December at St. Luke's!" One of the cashiers whispered to me that the
canteen manager had accidentally overordered turkey by a factor
of a hundred, and we would all be eating it until mid-January.

Somehow all this enforced seasonal jollity made the idea that
there might be a St. Luke's serial killer seem only more ridiculous. Serial killers—at least the ones in the movies, which was
the only place any of us had ever encountered them—lived quiet,
creepy lives in American apartments where they had covered
the walls with Bible verses they had painstakingly transcribed
by hand. They did not pin tinsel to their uniform, nor string
fairy lights around the nurses' station.

Perhaps it was the absurdity of it all that prompted somebody
to write up odds of likely suspects on the whiteboard in the mess.
The standard odds were 1000 to 1, and that was what most of
us were given. Dr. Sudbury was 100 to 1, whereas Amelia was
a million to 1. The front-runner, of course, was the Angel of
Death, who had been given odds of 1 in 3. Louise Fisher followed swiftly behind at evens. People joked that that the only
reason Louise was not the front-runner was that if she had actually murdered somebody she would not have been able to resist giving a presentation about her accomplishment. I enjoyed
these jokes as much as anyone, until one evening I entered the
mess to see that somebody had changed my odds from 1000 to
1 to evens, the same as Louise's. I did not find any of it funny
anymore, and wiped the whole thing off.

And things only got worse. Hospitals at night are always
creepy—how could crumbling Victorian buildings where untold
thousands of people have died not be?—and St. Luke's now had
more reason to be creepy than any other hospital in the country.
Saz and I did a week of nights at the start of December and at
three o'clock one morning I found myself walking down a long
underground corridor as the Angel of Death came toward me.

He was wheeling the black-covered trolley they used to transport corpses, and as we passed each other he winked at me. I got the feeling then that he knew exactly what we called him, and the idea greatly unnerved me. I was on my way to Jack Duckton to see Felix Smollett who had spiked yet another fever, and when I got there, I found I was actually pleased to see his familiar face.

Of course, if it was creepy for the doctors, it must have been terrifying for the patients. Imagine being admitted to hospital with a heart attack or stroke, and wondering whether the people who are supposed to be taking care of you might actually be trying to kill you. I no longer brought the subject up with the patients, because I'd once attempted to reassure an extremely anxious patient about it, only for them to turn out to not have even heard of any potential murderer and simply be terrified of hospitals.

Sometimes the new admissions did ask about it, and I always reassured them that it was nothing to worry about, that all hospitals experienced a statistical anomaly at some point. Maybe this wasn't entirely true, because Mrs. Horsburgh's death remained unexplained and the pethidine in her bloodstream was only a statistical anomaly in the sense that the level should have been zero. But falsely reassuring them was infinitely better than having them watch everything I did with suspicion; in some patients, simply picking up a stethoscope could now elicit a gasp, as if they expected you to beat them to death with it, right there in the accident and emergency department.

Still, such a ridiculous crime would not have seemed entirely out of place in the ludicrous comedy of errors that is an emergency department during the peak of office Christmas party season, which of course had to occur during my nights week. Our final shift that week was especially absurd, not least because one drunk Santa Claus had broken his foot and fifteen other drunk Santa Clauses had accompanied him to the hospital. For reasons of her own, the A+E sister had decided that the group of them would bring some Christmas cheer to the department, and had permitted them all to enter.

And so they had marauded around, ho-ho-ho-ing and wishing people a Merry Christmas while breaking just about everything in sight. If they hadn't all been fall-down drunk, it might have been festive, but they were, and the party ended abruptly when one of them tumbled into a cubicle where the pediatric registrar was attempting a lumbar puncture on a febrile baby. The sister threw them out after that, but not before they had sung her a final rousing chorus of "We Wish You A Merry Christmas." The song echoed in my head throughout the night and all through the weekend that followed.

On my first day shift back, Jack Duckton ward held a carol service of its own, around the piano in the dayroom at lunchtime. This was apparently an annual tradition, and I'd hoped to create my very own annual tradition of avoiding it. The fact I was on call on a long day had seemed a cast-iron excuse, but at handover that morning Dr. Sudbury had made a point of announcing it was "compulsory, especially for those of you juniors that work on Jack Duckton ward." As I was the only junior doctor there who worked on Jack Duckton, it had been clear who Dr. Sudbury was talking to. I had the strange feeling that she was trying to somehow atone for the two interviews under caution I had endured at Highbury police station, as if a festive sing-along with the patients might somehow wipe the memory of being falsely accused of murder.

I was only a few minutes late to the dayroom but the concert was already in full swing by the time I arrived. A row of Zimmer frames lined the corridor outside, and a few patients loitered in the doorway because the room itself was so crowded. An old man on crutches whose jumper had a picture of Rudolph with a red nose that lit up greeted me with a "Merry Christmas, Doc" and a surprisingly firm handshake. I nodded and smiled, then squeezed past him into the overflowing dayroom.

It was a Christmas miracle. Patients I had not seen out of bed in the five months I had worked at St. Luke's had not only risen from the dead but even had their hair permed for the occasion. Likewise, an old woman whose chest was bad enough that she ordinarily required continuous oxygen was not only breathing air but actually singing. For their own part, the nurses all had antlers or tinsel in their hair, and a table heaved with whatever they eat in the Philippines at Christmas. If that sounds surreal, it would have been no more so than an emergency department full of drunk Santa Clauses, were it not for singing. I do not mean all the voices—for the most part they were the tuneless rabble you would expect—but a single one that was somehow both louder and more melodic than all the rest of the voices combined.

This voice stopped me cold. It was piercing and beautiful enough to reach even my stone-cold heart midway through a twelve-hour shift during which I was carrying three pagers. The carol was "Good King Wenceslas," and whichever nurse this was not only had perfect pitch but the falsetto of a Christmas-tree-top angel. The mass of patients and staff meant I could not initially see who the singer was, and so I maneuvered myself across the room, forcing a parting in the sea of beige and gray as I did. Even at that, I could only get myself close enough to see the back of her head; she was not wearing her uniform, which made it harder still to tell who she was. At that point I gave up trying to identify her, because what did it even matter? This was a rare moment of peace and joy amid the chaos, and I closed my eyes and let the beautiful music wash over me.

Of course, when I opened my eyes again, the singer had turned their head and was now looking directly at me. It was Felix Smollett. He seemed to be smirking at me even as he sung the lyrics:

"Mark my footsteps good my page
Tred thou in them boldly

Thou shall find the winter's rage
Freeze thy blood less coldly."

I picked up some kind of fried meat dumpling from the table, and looked the other way as I bit into it. Dr. Sudbury was sitting near the piano and I made sure she had noticed me, then discreetly set off my own pager. I made a big show of looking at it and shaking my head in weary disappointment, and then left to see if anything was happening in the accident and emergency department.

I was still there a few hours later when a real cardiac arrest call came through from Jack Duckton ward. As I ran there, I wondered which of our old people had been killed by all the excitement. I decided it was probably the woman who was supposed to be on continuous oxygen. I remember feeling bad for Angela, who took such loving care of her patients. Whether it was indeed this oxygen woman, or another patient who had perhaps choked on a dumpling, Angela would not forgive herself for having killed them. It would ruin her Christmas that year, and probably many more too.

The arrest was in the side room I'd only recently had Felix Smollett moved from. I was the first doctor to arrive, but Angela, Louise Fisher, and another nurse I did not recognize had already begun CPR. As I attached the monitor, Angela gave me the quick rundown. The patient's name was Mr. Athole and he was an orthopedic border, four days post knee replacement, who had just begun to mobilize. He had eaten several helpings of leche flan at the party, and an hour ago he had complained of indigestion. A nurse had agreed to bring him some Gaviscon, but she had been waylaid, and by the time she returned he had been slumped over.

The classic cause of a patient collapsing four days after orthopedic surgery was a pulmonary embolism—a blood clot lodging in the artery that carries blood to the lungs—and in this scenario it was almost certain to be fatal. Sometimes the monitor might show a heart still attempting to beat, and occasionally then aggressive CPR could even help dislodge the clot, but the flat green line on the monitor showed Mr. Athole was already in asystole. And asystole meant death.

But we carried on. The anesthetist arrived and got the breathing tube in. Meantime, I took blood via a femoral stab, gave the syringe to Louise to take to the analyzer, and took over the chest compressions. The exhausted nurse I relieved looked surprisingly grateful, but I had not taken over because she was tired. I had taken over because she was not pressing hard enough. I felt two ribs crack with my first compression, but at least the patient's blood would now be moving. I had performed several more compressions before a tinnily electronic "Rudolph the Red Nosed Reindeer" started to emanate from the jumper that had been cut down the middle, and I understood that the body on which I was now working belonged to the congenial man who had shaken my hand so firmly just a few hours earlier.

Louise took so long that I almost called the death while we waited. When she did eventually return, she was excited and breathless. Between gasps, she declared that the analyzer in the maternity had been offline and so she'd then had to go all the way to accident and emergency. En route there, one of her classmates had tried to engage her in a conversation, but Louise had apologized that she had no time to talk. Then, when she reached accident and emergency, a nurse had been about to use their machine. Louise had therefore explained that this was truly a matter of life-and-death and the nurse, whose name was Stephanie, had kindly agreed to let her go first. Louise finally then handed me the printout. The potassium and hemoglobin were fine, and the oxygen numbers were as appropriately bad as anybody else's would be if they had been dead for the past twenty-five minutes. I had begun to call it, when I spotted the line at the bottom: *Glucose 0.1.*

Medical students are endlessly taught to rely on the ABC of resuscitation: Airway, Breathing, Circulation. It is a handy maxim, which prioritizes the tasks in order of importance: a patient without an airway cannot breath, and a patient who isn't breathing has little use for a circulation. Still, there is another part of the mnemonic that is almost equally important, and maybe more so because it is far more likely to actually make a difference: the DEFG of resuscitation is Don't Ever Forget Glucose.

Glucose is sugar, and sugar is life. A human body generally maintains a blood glucose of around four to eight millimoles. Too high a circulating glucose is diabetes; this can lead to serious problems and is therefore kept under control with regular shots of insulin. A more pressing emergency occurs when there is too little glucose in the bloodstream: this is hypoglycemia, and untreated hypoglycemia is fulminant brain damage and rapid death. There is a long list of obscure reasons a human body might manufacture too much insulin and render itself hypoglycemic, but in reality the cause was almost always the same: somebody giving the patient too much insulin. I asked Angela if Mr. Athole was known to be diabetic, and she shook her head with a solemnity that showed she understood this was going to be a problem.

I requested dextrose, and Angela hurried off to get it as we continued CPR. She soon reappeared with it, and I pushed the dextrose in with a flush. Nothing happened. After five minutes I took another blood sample, and Angela gave it to one of the nurses who was not Louise; five minutes later the nurse reappeared with a printout that showed that Mr. Athole's glucose level was now normal. In theory, we had corrected the reversible cause and this would have been an excellent moment for Mr. Athole to wake up, but the green line remained stubbornly flat. We were too late. The damage had been done.

At this point, Dr. Sudbury appeared in the doorway. I ini-

tially assumed this was somehow a coincidence but later realized
that Angela must have told someone to call her when she went
for the dextrose. I recapped the situation for Dr. Sudbury, and
watched in surprise as she rolled up her sleeves and proceeded
to take a blood sample. I warned her that the analyzer in maternity was out, but Dr. Sudbury simply nodded and slipped
the sample into the pocket of her white coat. Only later would
I understand what she had been doing: injected insulin can be
distinguished from that manufactured by the human body because synthetic insulin contains a molecule called a C-peptide.
If this C-peptide is detected, the body did not make the insulin, but it was introduced. Dr. Sudbury, then, was looking for
a murder weapon.

We kept going with the adrenalin, the chest compressions,
the oxygen forced down into Mr. Athole's lungs, but it did not
change anything. At Dr. Sudbury's insistence we continued trying for a further twenty minutes. By the time she eventually
allowed me to call it, those in the room included Dr, Sudbury,
the duty ICU consultant, the anesthetic registrar, the patient's
orthopedic consultant, Louise Fisher, and several nurses. It did
not matter; *no breath or cardiac sounds heard, pupils fixed and dilated,
absent corneal reflex, time of death 15:43, Rest in Peace.*

Immediately after I called it, Dr. Sudbury announced that we
were all to set down everything we were holding and leave the
room. Louise, perhaps assuming Dr. Sudbury had been speaking only to the doctors, began to remove the ECG leads from
the patient's chest. This remains the only time I ever saw Dr.
Sudbury get angry. Louise explained that she was just preparing the body for the porters, and Dr. Sudbury said that was not
what she was doing at all. What she was doing was interfering
with a crime scene.

Sure enough, later that afternoon police officers in white forensic suits came and took photographs inside the side room.
When Afferson and Newington arrived a little later, Felix Smol-

lett immediately cornered them and asked what had happened in his old room. I heard them insist it was "just routine," even as the crime scene photographer's camera flashed behind them.

Dr. O'Leary performed the postmortem the next day, and found no obvious cause of death. Notably, there was no fatal clot in the artery that led to Mr. Athole's lungs, or anywhere else for that matter. Three days later, Mr. Athole's C-peptide came back. It was sky-high. Somebody had injected the friendly old man in the Rudolph the Red Nosed Reindeer jumper with so much insulin that his blood sugar had plummeted until his heart had stopped beating. He had, unquestionably, been murdered.

That night, I had a nightmare that involved Afferson and Newington locking me in a prison cell for the rest of my life. When I asked them why they were doing this, they reassured me that it was "just routine."

CHAPTER 16

I did not go home to Scotland for Christmas. I told my parents that I was needed at work, and told Dr Sudbury that I was available to work. Collette was going skiing with her family, and at one point she had seemed to invite me, but after I admitted I had never actually skied before the idea had not been mentioned again. Anyway, what would I have done, waited around to see people once they'd either injured themselves or simply run out of more enjoyable things to do? That was my job in the hospital, and I at least got paid for doing it there.

Besides, I would not be completely alone in London, for George had volunteered to work the Christmas week too. In fact, he had gone a step further and volunteered to spend the entire thing on nights. He cheerfully admitted he had done this in hope of impressing his boss, but had not realized that she herself was spending December working in a military hospital and would therefore be entirely oblivious to the heroic sacrifice he had made on behalf of his next job reference.

When our medical rota was pinned up, I had been assigned the double-whammy of both the Christmas Day shift and New Year's Eve night. A few colleagues expressed sympathy, but nobody offered to swap one of the shifts. Even if they had, I would not have taken them up on it. What was the point? Everything was closed on Christmas Day, and New Year's Eve is always a disappointment.

The Christmas Day shift should have mostly been fine. None of the infection control nurses were at work, so one of the porters—not, thankfully, the Angel of Death—dressed as Santa Claus and roamed the wards dispensing choking hazard–sized toys to small children, chocolates to diabetics, and no doubt cigarettes to the respiratory patients. Part of his routine was that he gave a potato to everybody who had been "bad," and of course that was every doctor he could find. He came into the accident and emergency cubicle and gave me my potato while I was examining a patient, and even the patient seemed to find that hilarious. I left the unwanted potato he gave me on the counter in the mess. When I returned later, one of the surgical registrars had microwaved it and was now eating it as his Christmas dinner on the grounds that if he so much as saw another plate of turkey he'd have to shoot himself.

Accident and emergency was so quiet all day, it made me wonder if there was much wrong with people on every other day of the year. I saw a few festive-themed cases—an alcohol-induced gastritis, an allergic reaction to a new perfume, a concussion sustained in a fall from a new exercise bicycle—but nothing too troublesome. At one point I even passed through the department to make sure my pager was not broken, and found the nurses all eating mince pies and watching the Queen's speech.

The tower wards that day were just the standard wards: bloods, lines, chest pains, and fevers. The most exciting thing that happened was an arrest call to level nine, but even that turned out to be for a nurse who had choked on a five pence piece her colleague had hidden in a Christmas pudding. By the time I got there a visiting relative had already performed the Heimlich maneuver, the stricken nurse was breathing again, and the five pence piece was sitting on the desk. She offered me a piece of the offending Christmas pudding, but I declined.

Really the only two bad parts of working that Christmas Day were that the train was off so I had to walk half an hour through the snow, and Louise Fisher. For some reason, Jack Duckton ward had a tradition of allowing the most junior member of staff to act up as ward sister on Christmas Day, and my luck meant that it was Louise. Angela was at least working that day too, so she would be present to supervise throughout, but would only intervene if needed. I don't know if this was intended as an educational opportunity, a festive lark, or something in between. Whatever it was, I wished they were doing it on somebody else's Christmas Day.

My pager went endlessly. It began with Louise wanting to know if it was alright for the patients to receive presents, or if that constituted an unacceptable infection control risk? Next she wanted to know if a patient with a chicken allergy could eat turkey, and shortly thereafter the same question but for bacon and sausages. (When I asked Louise what the sausages were made from, she sighed with weary exasperation and explained that sausages are made of *meat*.) At some point she paged to inform me that Mrs. Thadopolos in bed seven was feeling nauseous after drinking a quarter bottle of Baileys Irish Cream that her family had smuggled in; Louise did not think anything needed to be done immediately, but she wanted me to be aware so that I could be on something she called "Emergency Alert." I reassured her that I stood ready to prescribe two acetaminophen and a handful of Tums at the drop of hat. Half an hour later, she called me with breathless excitement to tell me that she had given Mrs. Thadopolos a glass of milk. It had dramatically improved her symptoms, but Louise still could not entirely rule out the possibility that Mrs. Thadopolos was now suffering a silent heart attack. Louise had therefore performed an ECG, which she said "looked a bit funny," and so could I now come and urgently review it in case she really was having a silent heart attack?

That ECG—which was perfectly normal, except Louise had put the leads the wrong way around, so everything was inverted—was the reason I was on Jack Duckton when Felix Smollett's parents arrived. As far as I know, it was one of only two times they ever came to St. Luke's, and I could not blame them; if Felix had been my son, I would not have come to visit him either.

The Smolletts looked exactly how you would expect them to. To this day, Admiral Smollett remains the only man I have ever seen wear a cravat and a blazer while not actually playing the character of a retired naval officer in an amateur dramatic murder mystery. For her part, his wife was dripping in west London wealth and health, her sixty winters having aged her less than forty or fifty often did on this side of town. As a Christmas gift, they had brought their son an embossed set of the complete works of Charles Dickens. I know this because Felix later stopped me in the corridor and asked me if I would be interested in buying an embossed set of the complete works of Charles Dickens for fifty pounds. When that gambit failed, he told me that I could simply have the books if I'd only agree to review his methadone dose "with an open mind and heart."

In the early evening, Eliza Duckton appeared on the ward toting all the mince pies the local supermarket had reduced to clear. She then stood by the nurses' station and made an impromptu speech centered around the football match that had been played on Christmas Day on the Western Front. I was half expecting her to claim that her father had been responsible for that too—perhaps after narrowly failing to avert the assassination of Archduke Ferdinand, but before single-handedly defending the Ypres Salient—but instead her real point was that Christmas was a time for everybody to put aside their differences and come together. Specifically, she said, if there was anybody among us doing harm to other people, that person should definitely stop immediately. I had no idea which of the six of us within earshot Eliza Duckton thought was the notorious St. Luke's serial killer, but she genuinely seemed to believe that a gentle word and a half-price mince pie would forever mend our ways. I cannot speak for the others present, but this only made me give serious consideration to actually becoming a serial killer.

That evening, it was Amelia who appeared at handover to relieve me. It had been Saz's name on the rota, but Amelia explained that she had swapped so that she could spend some time with George. She had packed them turkey and cranberry sandwiches and was planning a kind of midnight Christmas dinner. Somehow this hopeful act of love and optimism—and not the fact that I was alone on Christmas, that I was working, that somebody loved even Felix Smollett enough to bring him an unwanted gift—was the thing that brought home to me just how alone I was. I spent the whole trudge home ruminating about this, and even stopped in at the shop to buy a bottle of whisky. I hardly ever drank whisky in those days, but I was feeling suddenly maudlin and wanted to have a single festive interaction that did not take place at the hospital. The shopkeeper was cocooned behind thick Perspex, but still seemed terrified when I wished him a Merry Christmas.

The whisky did not help much. In fact, it only made things worse. I could not escape the thought that, while I had been swapping my shifts to get out of having to see anybody I knew over the festive period, other humans had people who cared so much about them they would work a Christmas night shift in order to snatch a half hour with them. I proceeded to drink half the bottle of whisky alone on the couch, while watching an Indiana Jones movie on television. At some point I got the idea to call Collette, but the number she had given me went to a Swiss receptionist who scolded me that it was far too late to put a call through.

My attempts to explain that I only wanted to wish my girl-friend a quick Merry Christmas did not help, as the Swiss receptionist responded that I was two days late. It was not yet midnight in the UK, so even accounting for the time difference I knew that I could be at most a day late. The Swiss receptionist and I therefore argued back and forth for several minutes about whether Christmas was yesterday, today, or the day before yesterday, until she ultimately muttered what I assumed was a German expletive and hung up. It was only the next day that I remembered much of Europe celebrates Christmas on the 24th of December.

I continued drinking until Indiana Jones had defeated the Nazis, and then passed out. I woke up on the couch at 4:00 a.m., attempted to answer the page I assumed must have roused me, then crawled through to bed. I was so hung over the next day that I barely even made it to my Boxing Day shift, let alone through it.

I had the weekend between Christmas and New Year's off. Collette was still away and the British Library was closed, so I stayed at home and spent the weekend pretending to revise for my exam, while mostly helping George revise for his. As with everything in life, George conducted his revision in a spirit of joyful enthusiasm that showed up my weary cynicism for what it was. He would cheerily arrive home from his night shift, haul Patrick out of his room, and lay him on the couch.

The game was that I had to make up injuries—"Patrick has sustained a spiral fracture of his femur" or "Patrick has a comminuted dislocation of his shoulder" for which George would then have to then list the relevant blood and nerve supplies, and the most appropriate surgical approaches. I didn't actually know the names of many bones beyond the obvious ones, and so mostly I would just point at a small bone of the foot, and say things like

"This one here has been broken into pieces that look like corn-flakes." George would then express genuine puzzlement and say "But the only thing could do that would be a point-blank shot fired from a small caliber weapon," and I would nod sadly and say that was indeed exactly what had happened to poor Patrick. Obviously I had no idea what I was supposed to be listening for in George's answers, but he seemed to mostly know his stuff. And anytime he did not know the answer, he would immediately give himself away by groaning like a dying rhinoceros.

Sometimes, George would want us to play a different game that did not involve Patrick. In this one—which he described as "a real-world test of situational awareness"—I would simply have to describe a patient brought into accident and emergency, and George would tell me how he would treat them. I'd therefore say things like, "An eighty-two-year-old lady has sustained an injury while bungee jumping, and her left foot now appears to be facing entirely the wrong way."

I was mostly just trying to make him laugh, but George never wavered in his commitment to helping these entirely made-up characters overcome their absurd injuries. He would diligently preface each answer with "I would begin by resuscitating to phys-iological stability" and then hurry on to list the affected bones, their blood and nerve supplies, and the operations he would per-form upon them. Anything that involved a manual reduction—the physical repositioning of a bone—always brought a smile to his face. And he was visibly delighted when I fed him a scenario that involved him being the doctor on call at the Rugby World Cup final when the captain of England emerged from a difficult tackle with a visibly dislocated shoulder.

His delight did not last, because in his enthusiasm, George now forgot to mention the part about ensuring physiological stability, and rushed straight into the reduction. I congratulated him that the shoulder reduction had been successful, but told him I was still very concerned about the patient, who had not been properly resuscitated. Turning visibly pale, George asked me if the captain of England was okay? I shook my head and said that the last blood pressure had been unrecordably low. George asked me if the captain of England had a pulse and I solemnly replied that he did not. Now looking ashen, George told me that he would call the arrest team and commence CPR. I shook my head that it was sadly already too late, and explained that the postmortem would show that the captain of England had sustained not just a dislocated shoulder but had also ruptured his spleen. He had therefore bled out on the table while George was diligently reducing his shoulder. George looked genuinely devastated, and for my own part I felt like I had kicked a puppy. I told myself it was an educational experience, but what can a puppy ever learn from being kicked?

CHAPTER 17

I started back on nights on New Year's Eve, so I went to see a movie that day. I was intending to see the new James Bond, but I got the time wrong and the only thing showing when I arrived was an arthouse French murder-mystery. It turned out to not be a much of a murder-mystery at all, at least in the sense that they did not ultimately reveal who the culprit was. The idea seemed to be that we were all guilty of something—even the audience—and thus so complicit that it did not even matter who had actually committed the crime. Perhaps on some metaphysical level that was true, but nobody was as guilty as the filmmakers who had promised me a story and then not told it. Still, it passed the time.

At work that evening, I took handover from Saz, who gave me a rundown of the highlights of the final day of the year at St. Luke's. It seemed much like every other day: there was a bed shortage, ICU was full, and A+E was on a black alert. A black alert was supposed to mean we were closed to new admissions and the ambulances diverted elsewhere, but as every other hospital in east London was also on black alert, it mainly just gave the *Gazette* their headline for the week. In terms of specific patients, the main thing happening was an outbreak of salmonella from a church buffet at which turkey mayonnaise sandwiches had been served.

Truly, if all my years of studying and practicing medicine have taught me a single lesson about life as a human on planet Earth, it is this: never eat the mayonnaise dish served at a function. Whether it is combined with chicken, tuna, egg or potatoes, and whether it is consumed at a wedding, a funeral, a christening, or a bar mitzvah, the story never changes: everybody is having a good time, and then, the mayonnaise.

Besides those fallen prey to the mayonnaise, Saz mentioned a few further festive casualties I should be aware of: two alcohol withdrawals, one gout flare, and a dialysis patient who should have known better than to eat so much potassium-containing chocolate. The only other thing I should probably at least be aware of, Saz told me, was the newspaper article.

I picked up the copy of the *Gazette* she was pointing to. This week's headline stated **MYSTERY OVER HOSPITAL DEATHS REMAINS UNRESOLVED**. There was a picture of Mrs. Horsburgh looking spry, and one of her barrister daughter and son-in-law looking despondent in front of a Christmas tree. I wondered what kind of Christmas they'd had, with an empty seat at the table, then chastised myself for allowing myself to be manipulated by the picture. The Wilsons had probably spent their Christmas dinner discussing how best to sue me.

The headline itself was only news in the sense that **SKY REMAINS BLUE** would be, so I was not surprised that the article initially seemed to contain no new information. There was the usual stuff about Mrs. Horsburgh's love of walking, the hospital's concerning statistical anomalies, and a robust inquiry being conducted, along with some appropriately reassuring words from

Dr. Sudbury. They so far seemed not to have heard about the unfortunate Mr. Athole. But then, right at the bottom so that it read almost as an afterthought, the article quoted a police source as saying that they expected to make an arrest within the first half of the year.

To begin with, I was delighted. If the police now had a suspect in mind, it could not be me. For one thing, the *Gazette* article had already informed me I had been more or less eliminated from their inquiries. For another, Afferson had previously seemed so close to arresting me that it hardly seemed likely he would wait another six months before doing so.

But yet, who would they actually wait so long to arrest? If Afferson truly thought there was a killer on the loose at St. Luke's, why would he leave them to it for another six months? What did that mean? Occam's razor held that the answer to any puzzle was always the simplest explanation that fitted the facts, but I could think of only one explanation that remotely fitted these facts: the police had no idea who the killer was, and simply hoped that six months would be enough time to catch them. They therefore did not have a suspect in mind. And, far from meaning I was off the hook, that potentially meant that I could soon be very much back on it.

I did not get to discuss the article with Saz, because the wards pager went immediately. It was Jack Duckton, and when I rang them back Louise Fisher immediately answered and told me that I needed to come right away because Felix had "fallen into a coma." I asked her what she meant by this, and she said that he was still breathing, but she could not wake him up. She then added it could also be a stroke, or something she had lately read about called "sleeping sickness." My first thought was that Felix was probably just playing a prank on her, but I hurried over all the same. Even a stopped clock is right twice a day.

The diagnosis was obvious as soon as I got in the room. Felix's breathing was slow and labored, and when I pulled back his eyelids his pupils were pinpoints: he had overdosed on opioids. When I asked for naloxone, Louise's own eyes widened with excitement. She scurried off to get it, and I took the opportunity to examine Felix. He was breathing only six times a minute, and his lips had begun to turn blue, but even in this unconscious and precarious state he still somehow looked inordinately pleased with himself. I put an oxygen mask on him, and watched as the color slowly came back to his lips.

When Louise returned, I gave the naloxone as a push into Felix's neck line. A few minutes later, he blinked himself awake. Taking in me, and Louise, and then the syringe I was holding, he smirked.

"What did you do that for?" he asked. "I was having such a good time."

"Where did you get it?" I asked.

"Get what?"

"The heroin," I said.

"I didn't take any heroin," Felix said. "It must have just been the methadone."

We both knew that methadone would not have done that. I tossed the syringe in the bin and went outside to the nurses' station to write up the notes.

The other nurses were discussing their New Year's resolutions. Mostly they planned to join a gym or not drink alcohol for a month. Louise came out and joined in: her resolution was to get the distinction in her dissertation that would allow her to graduate with honors. They then asked me what my New Year's resolution was, and I told them that I did not have one. That was not really true, because I did have a resolution, and Felix had just reminded me of it: stay clean.

All through the night, the televisions around the hospital showed the new year arriving in various cities. When the bells of London rang out for the start of 1999, I was stood on the top floor of the tower looking out over the city. I could see all the fireworks, exploding over the tall buildings like the prettiest of war zones. This time last year I had been an inpatient in a residential rehab. If nothing else, I had at least come far.

A curious episode in the annals of healthcare killings occurred in the remote Hungarian village of Nagyrév in 1922.

The early twentieth century was an unpleasant time for women in patriarchal rural Hungary: arranged teenage marriages and domestic violence were common, but divorce and abortion illegal. The outbreak of war in 1914 at least provided the women of Nagyrév with some respite, as their brutish husbands were drafted to the front. When captured Allied prisoners of war began to appear in the village, many of the women of Nagyrév took lovers. The prisoners of war treated the women better than their husbands ever had, and by the time war ended, the women of Nagyrév were no longer willing to tolerate their previous mistreatment.

Many of the women therefore turned to Nagyrév's sole local health practitioner, a midwife named Zsuzsanna Fazekas, for advice. Whatever the specifics of a particular problem, Fazekas' simple question to the women who came to her seeking help with a husband was always the same: Why put up with them? Her most frequently prescribed drug now became arsenic, a poison she obtained by boiling strips of flypaper and skimming off the precipitate.

The women dutifully followed Fazekas' prescription and dispatched their husbands. While people today would likely consider the initial actions of these abused women with more understanding than was available at the time, things undeniably escalated. With Fazekas' encouragement, these Angel Makers of Nagyrév began using her arsenic to murder not only their husbands, but also their aged parents and occasionally even their own children. They were collectively so prolific that by 1925, locals had begun to refer to the entire region as "The Murder District" and men in Nagyrév had become notoriously reluctant to get married.

The Angel Makers were able to get away with this for so long in large part because, as Nagyrév's sole medical practitioner, Fazekas was also effectively its coroner. In 1929, government bureaucrats finally noticed the extraordinary number of deaths occurring in Nagyrév and an investigation was launched. Fifty bodies were exhumed from the town's cemetery, and traces of arsenic were found in forty-six of them. Fazekas took a dose of her own medicine and poisoned herself with arsenic before she could be tried, but twenty of her female patients were subsequently found guilty of murder. The case of these Angel Makers of Nagyrév shows both how wider societal factors may set the stage for healthcare murder, and how powerfully corrupting a single aberrant practitioner can be.

CHAPTER 18

On the second weekend in January, I took the train to Birmingham, where my Part 1 exam was being held in the conference suite of an airport hotel. If I'd been annoyed at the notion of having to travel so far, this had lasted only until I found out that George would be going all the way to Aberdeen to sit his own exam.

I stayed the night before the exam at the Holiday Inn Birmingham Airport, eating a microwaved burger in the restaurant and later braving a swim in the hotel's tiny pool. I even almost got into the hot tub, but stopped myself when I realized the whole thing sounded like another case study: "A twenty-nine-year-old business traveler gives a history of relaxing in a hotel hot tub." I then had the disheartening revelation that I could not answer my own question, for while "hotel hot tub" was code for Legionnaires' disease, "business traveler" was also examiner-speak for a man who frequented prostitutes and hence had a terrible STD. I went to bed early in the hope that a good night's sleep would help me achieve a score of zero or whatever the pass mark was.

The hotel had other ideas. The website had boasted rooms with "runway views." This had sounded quirky and fun, but of course it was only once I was in bed that I understood "runway views" also meant "runway noise." I had no idea why anybody should need to fly into Birmingham in the middle of the night in January, but a vast number of people apparently did, with planes seeming to land every ten minutes. I think I probably got about two hours of sleep, but even that could be an exaggeration.

The exam itself was much like the ones we had endlessly endured in medical school: long, straight, rows of desks, stalked by elderly invigilators possessed of the macabre grandiosity of prison guards: *I am just visiting*, their echoing footsteps seemed to tap out, *but you are a wretch who belongs forever in jail*. They made you keep your ID visible on the desk at all times, and if you wanted to go the bathroom you had to raise your hand. They would then studiously ignore you for fully two minutes before pretending to finally see you and magnanimously granting your despicable request.

The morning paper felt disastrous, and the afternoon one even worse. Even using the prejudices of the examiners seemed little help, because the vignettes contained such scant information that most of them invariably ultimately came down to variations on the theme of "Guess which disease we are thinking of?" Even when they did seem to contain sufficient information, the diagnosis I believed they would be looking for never featured as one of the available options. Towards the end of the day, I even thought up my own vignette:

A 29 year-old man fails his important exam. Is this because:

(a) his IQ is insufficient

(b) he slept for only two hours last night because his bed was next to an airport runway

(c) a previous opioid addiction damaged his ability to form new memories

(d) all of the above

As with every other question that day, I could not confidently answer it. I left feeling despondent and took the first train back to London. Maybe train noise is more soporific than airplane noise, or perhaps I was just used to it from the tracks that ran outside my bedroom window, but I slept all the way.

A couple of hours after I got back, George arrived home too. His exam was a clinical one in which he'd had to examine real patients, and it seemed to have gone even worse than mine. Against my advice, he had insisted on taking the train north for the "glorious Scotch views." Even if his train hadn't been delayed it would have been dark by the time he got to Scotland, but leaves on the track outside Doncaster meant that they only even reached the border at eight, and it was gone midnight by the time they pulled into Aberdeen. By then, the elderly and apparently deaf proprietor of the bed-and-breakfast George had booked had locked the place up for the night. Worse, an oil industry conference had meant that all the city center hotels were booked, and so it was not until after two o'clock in the morning that George had found his way to bed in a youth hostel by the docks.

He'd had to be up at six because his own exam started at seven thirty, but he had still got some sleep and had felt confident that nothing else could now go wrong. His examiners had seemed friendly, and the patient they'd assigned him had a straightforward femur fracture of the kind we had been through a hundred times with Patrick. Somehow, though, when it came time for George to present the case, instead of reeling off the blood and nerve supplies the way he'd done a hundred times in our front room, George found that he had completely forgotten the name for the largest bone in the human body. In a desperate panic,

George had therefore blurted out that he would reduce the fibula, which was the other leg bone that started with the letter *f*, and then various combinations of the two words: he would reduce the "fibur," the "femula," the "fibumer." Eventually, the patient herself had taken pity on George and informed him that the word he was searching for was "femur."

George had a return train ticket booked, but he'd flown back on the understandable grounds that he "could not spend ten hours thinking about how he'd forgotten the bloody word *femur*." I reassured him that a single slip up would probably not cost him the exam, but for all I knew it might very well do. And George was in a very different situation than me: being an orthopedic surgeon had been his dream since he first set foot onto a rugby pitch, and this was his fifth attempt at the exam. The Royal College of Orthopedics had already warned him that there would not be a sixth.

George shook his head and said that if he had failed, there would be nothing for it but to leave medicine and become a premiership rugby coach instead. I initially assumed he was joking, but apparently he was not. He did not seem to have realized that becoming a premiership rugby coach had its own high bars to entry, and when I gently pressed him on this he said that he'd just have to find a way to overcome them, as there simply wasn't any other job that he wanted to do. I suggested he might look into becoming a GP and a team doctor for a rugby club. George did not seem to have ever considered this possibility, and the idea visibly cheered him up. He went to the fridge, took out three beers, and hauled Patrick out of his bedroom to sit at the kitchen table with us and discuss which rugby team he'd most like to be the doctor for.

CHAPTER 19

The long winter continued at St. Luke's, and we stumbled our way into February. So many patients. So many arrest calls. The crackle of static, and then the run. Over and again, we performed that hopeless ballet. It didn't matter who you were on with, for each of us knew all the roles by rote: the airway, the chest compressions, the bloods, the electricity. Occasionally we got the result that was supposed to make all the rehearsals worthwhile. But mostly it was always just the rehearsal, the shifting of air and the pumping of blood, long after the heart and lungs had given up. Long after the thin green line had turned flat and the body had taken its final bow.

We had heard nothing more about the investigation, but at some point I was made to attend a meeting about another perplexing issue: Felix Smollett. Any patient being successfully treated with antibiotics should quickly stop having fevers, but Felix had continued to spike a new one every two to three weeks. Each time he did, blood cultures were taken and they invariably showed that some new organism was now infecting his body. Microbiology would then recommend some even more obscure antibiotic, and that would work for a while, and then the fever would spike again, and the cycle would begin anew.

The question was, where was it all coming from? How were new forms of bacteria continuing to get into his bloodstream? We had done all the tests, including even sending him to the dentist to make sure they were not getting in through diseased gums, but none of the investigations had shown any possible cause. The obvious conclusion was that he was still injecting drugs, and was doing so in some grubby way that kept introducing new bacteria. The microbiologist suggested that we give him a supply of clean needles. Dr. Weiden was against this on principle—he asked if we were going to supply the patient with heroin as well—but changed his mind when the microbiologist pointed out it might be the only way to keep Felix Smollett healthy for long enough to be discharged.

The upshot was that I was instructed to speak to Felix, ask if he was still injecting, and offer him a supply of clean needles and syringes if required. He of course entirely denied that he was still injecting, but agreed it would be a good idea for him to have the needles and syringes. These were not for him, he stressed, but for unnamed "friends" of his who might benefit from them. I went and got him a box of twenty insulin needles and syringes from the store cupboard. When he complained that was not enough, I brought him a further box, but warned him they had to last him until he was discharged.

At the start of my counseling session later that night, the Reverend McKendrick asked why the things I must have seen in the hospital had not put me off taking drugs in the first place. On another evening I might have explained to him about the risks and benefits, and the feeling of honey trickling down my spine. Having spent so long that day talking about Felix Smollett's predicament, I simply told him that sometimes I wondered that myself. The Reverend McKendrick did not reply, and I knew before I even looked over at him that he had already fallen asleep.

CHAPTER 20

On a Saturday morning at the start of February two letters dropped onto the mat, one for me and one for George. George was at work, so I placed his on his bed and opened mine. Somehow—and perhaps mostly due to my reliance on the terrible prejudices of the examiners—I had passed the first part of my membership.

I have passed many exams in my life, but none have ever made me feel the way I did that morning. It was not that I had been spared a repeat trip to Birmingham or Aberdeen or wherever else. It was not even that I would not have to endure the clacking of the invigilator's heels as I wrestled again with those two dreadful papers. It was that for all my stumbles, I was unequivocally back on track. I might have only been the cockroach that survives the nuclear fallout, but I had survived.

I cannot now remember exactly what I was thinking, but I assume I must have been delirious with delight. After all, how else to explain the awful thing I did that morning? Because I called St. Luke's, had them page George, and told him that our results had arrived. He first sounded excited, then terrified, and then he quietly asked me to open his letter and read it out. It said simply this:

"*Dear Dr. Williams,*
We regret to inform you that you were unsuccessful in your recent examination. Please note that, as per our previous correspondence, this was your final attempt."

The line went quiet, and stayed that way for some moments. I asked George if he was still there; he did not reply, but I could hear him breathing. Eventually, I heard his pager beep in the background and he apologized that he had to go because he had a patient waiting. I asked if he was alright and he said yes, yes, he was absolutely fine. It was all a bit of blow, he admitted, but it couldn't be helped and maybe he'd just jolly well be a GP and rugby team doctor after all. I asked if there was anything I could do and he told me there was not, but not to worry because he was sure it'd all work out for the best. Just before I hung up, George asked me how I had done in my exam. I admitted that I had passed, and he congratulated me with such a note of genuine triumph in his voice that it made me feel only worse for him.

Still, by the time he got home that night, George seemed to be more or less his usual self. He insisted on celebrating my success by bringing in an Indian takeaway and beer, and once again brought Patrick out to sit at the table with us on the grounds that he had "been through all this stuff with us."

George endlessly toasted my achievement, and repeatedly told me that I would be the next Dr. Sudbury. This was a monumental step up from what Dr. Weiden had told me about having the makings of a reliable staff grade, but I suspect Dr. Sudbury was the only physician whose name George knew. In anybody else

I might have considered such enthusiasm for my career in the face of the loss of his own a sign that something was wrong, but George really was a Labrador. At one point he even made a joke that there was certainly something "humerus" about an orthopedic surgeon who could not name one of the largest bones in the human body.

George's Saturday shift had been a single day swap, and when I got up the next morning he was still in bed. He'd stayed up later than me to drink the rest of the beer, and I saw he'd been circling adverts in the *British Medical Journal* for General Practice training programs in places like Sheffield and the Outer Hebrides. Whoever it was that said the unexamined life was not worth living had never met George.

After the elation of passing my exam had worn off, I trudged on through my own overly examined life. There was no news from Afferson, no more articles in the *Gazette*, and no sign of any arrest. I kept up my sessions with the Reverend McKendrick, and probably the most alarming development in my life was that Collette—who had inevitably passed her own exam with distinction—had increasingly begun to talk of the need for me to meet her parents. In less complicated news, the clean needles seemed to have helped Felix Smollett, as he had now not spiked a fever in a full three weeks. Dr. Weiden had asked me to arrange another scan at the Brompton, and if it showed Felix's vegetations were gone, we would then "kick him out."

George seemed to have completely got over his failed exam, and had even taken to saying that he was glad he wouldn't be an "old sawbones" anymore, and could not wait to become a GP. This seemed to largely be because somebody had told him GPs only worked four days a week. "Imagine it," he'd tell me. "Every weekend a bank holiday! And no more bloody on call!" Being George, he'd then invariably temper this with a brief paean to the heroic importance of my own on-call work, which he thought must be "a whole lot more rewarding than fixing damn bones all day."

George and Amelia had also found their poor country in Africa. One of the radiologists had a connection to a hospital at a place called Mbala in northern Zambia, and she had told Amelia they were in desperate need of staff. The place was so remote that there were a lot of communication delays, but at some point Amelia managed to get through on the phone, and it was agreed that they would go there in the summer, immediately after their wedding. Amelia would be the physician in charge, and George—who would defer his GP training for a year— would be an honorary GP who could also set up and coach a rugby team if he could provide the necessary equipment. Their visas would need to be approved by the minister of health, but this could certainly be done by the summer.

With their trip to Zambia set, the two of them had now begun to redouble their efforts to plan their wedding. A crate of champagne arrived for George to test, and our fridge had begun to fill with sample starters and cakes. And then, on an otherwise ordinary rainy Wednesday night toward the end of February, it happened.

CHAPTER 21

At breakfast that day, George had been his usual cheery self. The *Telegraph* he got delivered each morning—our baffled newsagent had told him he was the only subscriber in the entire borough—contained a report about a dramatic rugby match in the southern hemisphere, and he insisted on reading it aloud. If it had been anybody else, I'd have found it infuriating, but with George it was charming in the same way that he was still desperate to please his boss, despite the fact that her specialty had no use for him. When he had finished reading about the Springboks or the All Blacks or whoever it was, he asked me if I thought Antibiotic Use in Joint Replacement Surgery would be a good audit for him to do. I told him it would be if he planned to pursue a career in orthopedics, but otherwise seemed like a thankless waste of precious time, and he laughed heartily.

I believe that was the very last time I saw him, yet I cannot be sure. I have searched my recollections of that day so many times that I no longer know what was real and what was not.

Had I passed George in the corridor, the canteen, the mess? I do not think so, but how could I ever really know? One day at the hospital was much like any other, and they swiftly blurred into each other.

The inquest would later establish that George had undertaken his ward round in the morning, completed his jobs with his usual good humor, and had gone to the canteen for lunch at quarter past twelve. There, thanks to the generosity of one of the canteen staff who had a soft spot for him, he had eaten an extra large portion of beef Wellington.

The orthopedic juniors liked to go to theater in the afternoon, and George's boss had expected him to scrub in for the afternoon list. But George had not appeared, and so his boss had simply assumed George had got busy on the ward and had the scrub nurse hold the retractors instead. By 5:00 p.m., George had reappeared—surgeons do two ward rounds a day, which is perfectly possible if each consultation consists solely of making sure the patients are neither visibly infected nor actively bleeding to death—and everybody who encountered him then said he had been his normal happy-go-lucky self.

Where had George gone during that missing afternoon? That question haunted me for so long that I once assumed it would haunt me forever. I wasn't just searching for the answer to the obvious question—how can a loud-voiced, rosy-cheeked, 225-pound rugby player disappear in a busy hospital for three hours—but to the far deeper one contained within it: Why? In the aftermath, Amelia and I went over it so many times together, and neither of us could come up with a remotely satisfactory explanation.

We had both worked long days that Wednesday, and were halfway through evening handover when the cardiac arrest pager crackled into life and summoned us to the hospital parking lot. Technically, it was the night team that should have answered the call, and maybe if we had known what awaited us we would have sent them. We'd just handed over a dozen waiting patients, though, and it seemed that sorting this was the least we could do, so it was Amelia and I who ran out into the rainy night.

It was one of the physiotherapists who had found him. Later, we discovered that George's last entry in a patient's notes had been at 7:00 p.m., so he must have finished writing—*Plan: review tomorrow with repeat X-ray of hip*—and then gone straight outside and got into his car.

It had clearly taken him a few attempts to find his own vein—fucking orthopods—but George had got there in the end. By the time the physiotherapist saw him slumped against the driver's side door at seven thirty, he had likely already been dead for twenty minutes. George had made the mistake of not locking the door, and when she opened it he had slumped out onto the ground. The physiotherapist had started CPR, while screaming at a passing nurse to get help. The nurse had run back inside and put out the arrest call, and meantime the physiotherapist had found the syringe that was still hanging out of George's arm. It was on her return that the nurse had noticed the empty vial of potassium that had fallen out of the car with him.

It was dark outside, but the parking lot was almost empty, so Amelia and I saw them as soon as we got outside: the physiotherapist, the nurse, and the anesthetist who for once had beaten us there. They were crouched down next to George's car, and as we ran I remember thinking it would be a funny story to tell him. As we got closer, I began to wonder, but I put the thought out of my mind until Amelia suddenly stopped running. I turned and looked at her. The expression on her face had already told me everything, but then I turned back and now saw what she had seen. Our cardiac arrest was George.

If I am completely honest about what I felt in that moment, it was this: nothing. People on television who manage to do their jobs in extreme situations are forever claiming "the training just kicked in" and I now believe they are right. The collapsed patient was not George, because he was not anybody except a thirty-two-year-old male who had undergone a cardiorespiratory arrest. The job now was therefore the same as it always was: to convince a heart to start beating, and perhaps the muscles of a diaphragm to start contracting. Even the latter was not entirely necessary, for there were machines that could do the work of breathing if required. But the heart. For now, the heart and the heart alone was the thing.

As we arrived, they were already completing the first cycle, and had paused to look at the rhythm on the portable monitor the anesthetist had attached. It showed only the flat green line that almost certainly meant death in the resus room, but in a dark and wet hospital parking lot there was no "almost" about it.

Resuscitation doctrine holds that you should never interrupt CPR to move a patient. But two porters were already arriving with a gurney, and we could see the lights of the emergency department with all of its drugs and electricity no more than twenty seconds away. And so, without even discussing it, we got George up on the trolley and rushed him to resus where we restarted the familiar ballet.

I began on chest compressions, which was good because it meant I did not have to think. One hand placed atop the other, fingers interlaced, and the heel of the lower hand positioned in the midline over the patient's sternum, a thumb's width from its base. Thrusts aimed at applying thirty pounds of pressure to compress the patient's chest by a depth of two inches, and thereby increasing the thoracic pressure by the twenty millimeters of mercury required to force blood from the heart to the lungs and the brain. A hundred of such compressions per minute. In medical school we had learned that the best way to ensure this rate was to perform the compressions to the tune of "Nellie the Elephant" or "Stayin' Alive." Those things had stopped being funny years ago, but tonight seemed like simple mockery.

The anesthetist took the airway, of course, and got the breathing tube in faster than I have ever seen anyone do before or since. I found out later that he had frequently worked with George. Likewise, I have never seen so many accident and emergency nurses around a single patient: they took bloods from arteries and veins, inserted lines, and somebody even taped George's eyes closed, apparently in the hope he would not be shocked by what he saw if he did somehow wake up. It was an absurdly futile gesture, and yet I understood the rationale. The rationale was that they loved George.

As for Amelia, she led the arrest. It was not remotely fair, for her to be charged with saving her fiancé's life, and yet nobody attempted to take over. Amelia was the best doctor among us, and we all knew she represented George's best chance at life. And so she shouted for all of the things that could conceivably help to lower potassium—bicarbonate, insulin-dextrose, nebulized salbutamol—and these were each immediately and without question given.

None of them worked. We attacked George's lifeless body for an hour, far longer than we would have done for anybody else, and still the flat green line did not shift. Somebody must have called Dr. Sudbury because she now appeared in a maroon velour tracksuit; apparently she had been at her badminton club. Dr. Sudbury likely had not led a cardiac arrest in twenty-five years, but she still knew exactly what to do: she informed Amelia she was taking over, and then immediately called it. Amelia burst into tears, and one of the nurses put her arm around her, and led her to the relatives' room.

The resus room emptied. There was no training to kick in for this part, no mnemonic for what to do when the dead body on the trolley is your flatmate. There was no algorithm that explained how George could have been laughing about rugby players and audits over breakfast this morning but now be cold on the table in front of you. There was no procedure for when you had failed to save him, for the sudden quiet and emptiness that would haunt you forever. So I simply listened to the silence of his heart and lungs, removed the tape, stared into his wide, dead eyes, and wrote the usual in the notes: *no breath or cardiac sounds heard, pupils fixed and dilated, absent corneal reflex, time of death 21:47, Rest in Peace.*

As I finished, one of the nurses came in and told me that Dr. Sudbury would like to see me in her office. I nodded, but the nurse lingered in the doorway.

"We all always said he was our favorite doctor," she told me.

I tried to acknowledge her, but I could not. He had been my favorite doctor too.

Dr. Sudbury was on the phone when I got to her office, but she waved me in. She had put her white coat on over her track-suit, and I remember thinking that she looked only more ridiculous. I'd assumed the call she was on must be to do with George, but it turned out she was making arrangements for the recovery of her badminton racket. When she got off the phone she told me she was sorry for my loss, and that she knew it must be especially hard given that George and I were flatmates.

I was surprised that Dr. Sudbury had even known who George was, let alone that we were flatmates, but I later worked out that DI Afferson had likely previously told her this. She then wanted to know if George had been depressed, and I instinctively said he had not. Dr. Sudbury reminded me how skilled people can be at hiding such things, and I found myself flashing back to all the times I had said this very same thing to the baffled relatives of people who had killed themselves. They were always insistent that there had been no warning signs whatsoever, and I had always nodded sympathetically while silently assuming they had simply not picked up on the signs the way I would have. But I then recalled the months I had spent strung out on opioids, during which none of the doctors or nurses I worked with had apparently noticed. Was it possible that George had been concealing some desperate sadness? I really did not think so, but medicine had long ago taught me that no human can ever claim to fully know the heart of another.

Dr. Sudbury asked me about George's parents. I had never met or spoken to them, but I knew their number would be printed on our phone bill, because George called home for an hour every Wednesday night. Dr. Sudbury said she would be happy to call them if I could get her the number, but I told her that I would do it. It seemed like the least I could do for George.

Dr. Sudbury nodded that she was sure George's parents would appreciate that. She then sighed, spoke wistfully about a talented classmate of hers who had killed herself when they were juniors, and then about several other colleagues who had met the same end over the years.

It is not uncommon for doctors to kill themselves, but so far I had been mercifully untouched by it. Anesthetists and psychiatrists always top those grim tables—the former have the drugs to do it effectively, the latter know best how to conceal their intentions—but our collective war against disease is one of attrition, and suicide is an occupational hazard for us all. How could it not be, when we take an unusually conscientious and empathic group of people, blur their boundaries between life and death daily, then work them to exhaustion in a culture so binary it can admit only complete success or abject failure? Sometimes, the strangest part to me is simply that more of us don't meet this same sad end.

When she had finished eulogizing her late classmates and colleagues, Dr. Sudbury apologized that there was something else she needed to ask me, because people were going to ask her. Was there—at least, did I think there might conceivably be— any way that George might have had knowledge of some of the things that had potentially happened at St. Luke's? Was there even any possibility that he might somehow bear some responsibility for any of them?

I did not pause before I told Dr. Sudbury there was no possible way whatsoever. She looked at me then in the same way I had seen her look at patients whose symptoms did not add up, trying to puzzle out whether I was naive, misguided or somehow complicit in the situation. Dr. Sudbury had not known George, so there was no point in trying to explain to her that he could not have been involved simply because he was George, and so I instead reminded her of the other reason: he was an orthopod. If somebody had really been cunning enough to kill fifteen or forty-three patients such that each and every one of them had got past Dr. O'Leary, that person was not George. It was true that Mr. Athole had been an orthopedic patient, but I doubted George would have even known how much insulin would have been required to reliably dispatch him.

Perhaps I was still in some kind of shock, because I even told Dr. Sudbury that if any orthopod ever become a serial killer, their modus operandi would probably have been to bludgeon people to death with an orthopedic mallet. Dr. Sudbury looked at me, a little concerned, but then actually laughed and said yes, indeed, that was no doubt right. She asked me if I needed any time off, and I told her I did not, and I would be back at work the next day. Dr. Sudbury then thanked me for my dedication, but I wasn't being selfless. I was already dreading going home, and the thought of spending days sat around with only Patrick for company made me nauseous.

George's car keys had found their way onto Dr. Sudbury's desk, and as I departed she gave them to me. I put them in my bag, and forgot about them for months. I got home a little before eleven that night and called George's parents, but their number rang out. I assumed they had gone to bed early and were heavy sleepers, but it turned out Amelia had already spoken to them. They appeared on my doorstep at six o'clock in the morning, a small, humble, and broken couple from the north of England who had driven through the night and then waited outside in their car for a few hours so as not to disturb me.

For a moment, it was hard to believe they were truly George's parents. I had always assumed George had been born in a castle as the most recent in a long line of George Williamses, but his parents seemed like extras in a National Coal Board documentary from the 1970s, right down to his dad's cloth cap. Amelia would later tell me that George had gone to his boarding school on a scholarship, and she'd always thought his accent and adoration of rugby were his way of cementing his escape from the red brick terraces he had grown up in. His parents wanted only to sit in George's room, to be among his things. They did not weep, but just sat there silently. It was the saddest thing I had ever seen.

I left George's parents in the flat when I went to work. Halfway through the morning Amelia paged me and asked me to meet her in the hospital chapel. This surprised me as I had not known that Amelia was religious, but it turned out she was not. It was simply the only quiet place in the hospital where she could be sure we would not be bothered by patients or colleagues.

I had been writing a discharge on a nearby ward, and so got there first. The hospital chapel was a small, carpeted room with some cheap patio furniture arranged around a lectern inscribed with a cross, a Star of David, and a crescent moon. Large pipes ran along the ceiling from its previous incarnation as some kind of plant room, but these had at least been painted off-white and it was still the most serene place in the hospital. As I sat and waited, I wondered what I could possibly say to Amelia that might make her feel better.

Of course, when she arrived Amelia was not looking for any support for herself, but seeking to support me. Had I slept? Had I eaten? Did I have somebody to talk to? This was classic Amelia: twelve hours ago she had lost her fiancé in the cruelest way imaginable, and here she was asking me if I was okay. I saw now why she and George had been such a perfect match: it was not, after all, their complementary strengths, but rather the ineffable goodness of their paired hearts.

Still, for all her kindnesses, Amelia looked pale, and dark rings I had never glimpsed during a week of night shifts had appeared under her eyes. I thanked her, reassured her that I was okay, and said that I had actually been more worried about her. Amelia admitted it probably had not properly sunk in yet—though God, she said, the phone call with his parents had been tough—and it would no doubt fully hit her in the next few days. She promised to come and talk to me when it eventually did. Our pagers both sounded then, and we both returned to the jobs we so often complained were all-consuming, but now desperately needed to distract us from having to think at all.

When I got home that evening, an upstairs neighbor I had seen but never before spoken to stopped me on the communal stair. She had heard about George—it had apparently been on the local news—and wanted to pass on her condolences. I thanked her and tried to carry on, but she continued talking.

I assumed she was just prying, but it turned out she especially wanted to offer her sympathy for the fact that it had happened in the flat. She was entirely wrong, of course, but I still had no intention of telling her that it had ended for George in a shitty hospital parking lot. So I told her only that he had not died in the flat, and she seemed genuinely surprised. I of course then asked her why she had believed it had happened there, and she said she had been home yesterday afternoon and thought she'd heard loud banging coming from our flat. She quickly admitted that she must have been mistaken about where the noise was coming from, but it did make me wonder: Was there any possible way George had actually come home that missing afternoon? And if so, what had he been banging?

Inside the flat, I went and stood in George's room. Aside from placing a photo of the three of them on his nightstand, George's parents did not seem to have touched a single thing. It was all still there: his well-thumbed textbook of orthopedics, a signed photo of the England rugby team, a pristinely untouched copy of *Smithfield's* and, of course, Patrick. It was as if George would come back to us all any minute with his ebullient, "Good evening!"

I knew that George had kept a diary hidden under his mattress, and I took it out and read a few pages in hope of finding some answers. Immediately I wished I had not, and understood that it anyway would not tell me anything. It contained only entries that detailed the weather, the amount of time he had spent operating, and any rugby scores. The day before he died was no exception:

Cloudy but no rain, 3 hours in theater
(1 x appendix, 1 x gallbladder), Saracens 32-London Irish 18.

The day he had died was left blank. It was as if there had been no weather, operations nor rugby that day, nor would there ever be again. I replaced the diary, sat on his bed, and wept.

I think that was one of only two moments I cried during the aftermath. The other was when I saw that somebody had pinned up George's funeral notice from the *Telegraph* in the mess. It was not an obituary, just an announcement: *Dr. George Williams. Suddenly and unexpectedly. Family flowers only.* It was so concise, and it did not do justice to my large and garrulous friend, who filled any room he entered. Still, it was in the *Telegraph*, and I knew that would have delighted George. In death he had finally ascended to the world in which he had always wanted to belong.

George was the talk of the hospital, of course, and therefore so was I. Once again, I felt all eyes on me when I walked onto a strange ward, and heard conversations abruptly stop whenever I entered the mess or the canteen. Even Felix Smollett approached me and asked if it was true that the doctor who had died had been my housemate. I grudgingly acknowledged it was, and

Felix shocked me by saying he was tremendously sorry to hear that. He even asked about "the other doctor, his girlfriend." This too surprised me, but then I remembered the infamous shouting match he'd had with Amelia.

Felix seemed to be quite genuinely upset by the whole business, but it made a certain sense. Perhaps George's death reminded him of his own mortality, and how precariously close he had come to dying, or maybe he had even discerned that the two of them were a curious reflection of one another. George had forsaken his humble origins for an upper-class life that was mostly invention, and Felix had done the inverse. It had not helped either of them, although Felix now at last seemed to be on the upswing. His fever had remained in abeyance, and we were still just waiting on the scan at the Brompton that would let us kick him out.

CHAPTER 22

If the day George died was the worst of my life, the day of his funeral came a very close second. It was held at the place where George and Amelia had planned to marry, which turned out to be the church of St. Clement Danes in the Strand. At George's insistence they had not announced that, for fear of jinxing it.

I could understand why. It is hard to convey in words just how grand a place St. Clement Danes is, but it was designed by Sir Christopher Wren, sits stoically unmoved on its own island amid the rushing traffic of the Strand, and is the St. Clements of "Oranges and Lemons" fame.

But even this grandeur had not been what had initially attracted George to St. Clements: he had first visited the church to pay homage to its former rector, William Webb Ellis, the inventor of rugby. St. Clements doubled as the church of the Royal Air Force, and strictly speaking only RAF pilots were permitted to get married there, but somehow George and Amelia had charmed the rector. When Amelia had called him to inform him the wedding would not now be going ahead, he had offered to host George's funeral instead.

It got off to an impressive start. The grand exterior of St. Clements was matched only by the simple beauty of its interior. The floor was white marble and the pews black ash, whitewashed walls supported a high vaulted ceiling, and twenty-foot-high windows flooded the entire place with springtime light. A giant pipe organ stood on a balcony above the entrance; at the opposite end of the room, a huge stained-glass window of Jesus tending the little children stretched from just above the altar to the ceiling.

More than anything, though, there was the sheer abundance of people. I arrived early, when the church was still empty, and sat at the front with George's parents, Amelia, and Collette; it was only when the casket arrived that I finally turned around and saw the entire church had filled. There was George's rugby team in their ill-fitting blazers, and the boorish school friends called "the posse" that I recognized from the engagement party, but mostly there was just about the entire staff of St. Luke's. I noticed, too, several people on crutches and sporting various forms of external fixators; these had to have been George's orthopedic patients. I remember thinking that if I had died, I'd have been lucky to have Collette there, and possibly Amelia and Saz. The stage really was set to give George the send-off he deserved.

But the service was an unmitigated disaster. The rector appeared to have untreated Parkinson's disease, and a glance at the expression on Dr. Zubia's face during the stuttering homily showed I was not alone in this assessment. A second cousin that George had never once mentioned had written a fifteen-verse poem that she read aloud. Unfortunately, the only words that rhymed with George were *forge* and *gorge*, and she had managed to work each of them in several times. George's father then attempted to give the eulogy, but got only as far as saying "My boy, George—" before breaking down. For an awful moment it looked like the rector was going to attempt to read his speech for him, but George's father then blurted out a much truncated version, which boiled down to him saying he loved George, and would forever miss him, and God was an utter bastard for having taken him. For reasons known only to herself, it was Louise Fisher who got up from her seat in the rear and rushed down the aisle to comfort him. "I'm a student nurse!" she stage-whispered as she went, as if that explained anything.

The only redemptive thing about the whole ceremony was Amelia. She gave a short eulogy that was heartfelt but eloquent, and she finished by reading a poem by Auden that did not rhyme, but allowed everybody to weep cathartic tears. As she finished, I turned around and spotted Afferson and Newington for the first time. They had clearly only come to look for clues, but even so DS Newington dabbed a tissue at her eye.

There was no burial, as George's parents had arranged for that to happen privately near their home in Yorkshire. Instead, there was a reception in the function room of a hotel behind the Strand. Amelia had intended this to be a way for George's various friends to meet, and for us all to comfort his parents. But his parents did not come, and the friends all sat resolutely with the groups they had arrived in.

In our group from the hospital, we went over it all once again. Every one of us had sat with enough stunned families in enough small rooms to know that nobody ever expects it. But usually, at least with hindsight, there are signs: a history of depression, a previous attempt, a relative who had gone the same way. With George there was none of that. He had not only not been depressed, he had seemed as constitutionally incapable of depression as a puppy.

That left only his failed exam, which several colleagues had concluded was the only possible explanation. Even Amelia seemed to cling to this idea, although she must have known better. Doctors are often lifelong overachievers who know far too much about the seeking of validation through academic success, but George had been the opposite of all that. He had even once told me that he viewed exams the same way other people viewed birthdays: they happened about once a year, some were good and others were not so good, but whatever happened there would no doubt be another one along before too long.

When the hotel threw us out, we went to a pub, and another after that, and then another still. We all drank so much that at one o'clock in the morning we found ourselves singing karaoke in a Chinese restaurant off Leicester Square. It was undoubtedly what George would have wanted, but I was on call the next day and only survived by locking myself in the office and giving myself a fast bag of intravenous fluids.

CHAPTER 23

After George died, it felt like everything changed.

My home life was of course infinitely different: with nobody to sing public school hymns as he washed up his muesli bowl each morning, or to loudly announce that Patrick had just whispered to him that it was time for a beer, our flat fell eerily quiet. Even at night, with no gentle snoring or southern hemisphere rugby games on the radio coming through the thin walls, the silence that filled the gaps between the rumbling trains was too stark. And everywhere, of course, were reminders of him: his toothbrush above the sink, his crate of wedding champagne in the cupboard, the bedroom I had to walk through to get to the bathroom. After two weeks, the ever-pragmatic Collette insisted on tidying George's room—making his bed, and throwing out anything perishable—and I made no attempt to stop her. I had told George's parents I could move out at any time, but he had paid the year upfront and they assured me they were in no hurry. I therefore simply continued paying my rent into the bank account they had not yet got around to closing, but I could not bring myself to move into the bedroom where his earnest diary still lay beneath the mattress.

For all that, the biggest change was at work, where the endless parade of sick and dying strangers took on a new meaning. There is a kind of confidence trick that happens when you work in a hospital. Each day we put on our smart clothes, our stethoscopes, and our badges, but atop them all we don a cloak of invincibility to protect us from the traumas and maladies that life has visited upon our patients. The patients had heart attacks and strokes, and injured themselves falling from scaffolds or simply crossing the road. We, the doctors, did not. We weaved our path slightly above all that, untouched by such sorrows.

On some level, we had long since ceased thinking of our patients as people, but rather merely as bodies: a museum display case of plumbed-together hearts, brains, lungs, livers, and spleens. No doubt they each thought of themselves as grandparents and siblings, teachers, artists, and poets, but once they came through the hospital doors, they were something else to us: a shadow on an X-ray, a run of irregular heartbeats, or an asterisked number in a column of blood results to discuss with the boss on the ward round. Perhaps that was inevitable. How else to otherwise get through our days that routinely involved that flat green line?

George dying pulled out the magic rug that lay beneath all of that. He had been one of us: the bold, the invulnerable, the untouchable—and now he was dead. And if a 225-pound prop forward's life could be extinguished by a vial of potassium chloride, what chance was there for any of the rest of us? We walked so often among so much tragedy, that we had long ago begun to believe that we must surely be immune. And now we had discovered we were not immune, not one bit immune, not any of us.

We each sought solace where we could. For George's surgical colleagues, this took the form of running a half marathon in his memory. No doubt he would have preferred a rugby tournament, but I did not tell them that, and instead dutifully filled in each sponsorship form that came my way. Amelia had decided she would still go to Zambia and now threw herself into the preparations; it might have been unthinkably lonely to anybody else, but to Amelia it was the greatest tribute she could ever pay George. For my own part, I sought solace in the one place I knew I was guaranteed to find it.

It was as easy as it had always been. An elderly patient I admitted arrived from a nursing home with a carrier bag full of medicines that I had to sort through. There was the usual stuff—an antidepressant, aspirin, something for blood pressure, something for cholesterol—but at the bottom of the bag was a single strip of pethidine. Twelve small tablets, two years out-of-date, and long since forgotten by both the patient herself and whoever had prescribed them. I slipped them into my pocket.

As a teenager, Marcel Petiot was expelled from several schools for committing petty theft. He subsequently volunteered in the French army in the First World War, but was court-martialed for stealing supplies. After serving his sentence and being returned to the front line, Petiot intentionally injured his own foot with a grenade in order to secure his discharge.

Despite this history of serial dishonesty, Petiot was admitted to an accelerated medical school program after the war, and gained his medical license in a little over a year. He set up his first practice in the small town of Villeneuve-Sur-Yonne in the north of France, and quickly developed a reputation for financial impropriety. He may also have committed his first murder there: a young woman with whom Petiot was having an affair mysteriously vanished, and neighbors would later report having seen Petiot loading a suspiciously large trunk into his car around the time of her disappearance.

Having eventually been run out of Villeneuve-Sur-Yonne due to numerous allegations of theft, Dr. Marcel Petiot moved on to Paris in 1935. There, he quickly built a thriving practice by over-prescribing narcotics, but it was when the city fell to the Nazis in 1940 that Petiot hit upon a scheme more wickedly depraved than anything he had previously attempted.

Posing under the name "Dr. Eugene," Petiot put the word out that he commanded a network that could provide safe passage to South America for resistance fighters and Jews for the price of twenty-five thousand francs. When his desperate victims arrived at his office, Petiot took their money then, using the pretext that Argentina required its immigrants to be inoculated, injected them with a fatal dose of cyanide.

Dr. Petiot initially disposed of his victims' bodies in the Seine, but eventually grew lazy and started simply burning them in the furnace of his central Paris house. The thick black smoke drew the attention of the gendarmes, who discovered the remains of dozens of bodies, as well as a quicklime pit in the back garden. Dr. Petiot nonethless escaped and spent almost a year on the run, including several months during which he had the audacity to pose as a resistance leader. He was eventually caught, tried and found guilty of twenty-six murders, and beheaded by guillotine in May 1946.

Even in the grim annals of healthcare killings, Dr. Petiot's crimes seem strikingly heinous. A doctor who abused his position to murder the most desperate of people, his motivation was seemingly nothing more psychologically complex than the same dishonest greed that had characterized his youth.

CHAPTER 24

On April Fools' Day, I arrived at work to find the hospital besieged with reporters. My first thought was to wonder what new scandal Eliza Duckton had manufactured, but the scale visibly dwarfed even her lofty ambitions. This was not merely the *Hackney Gazette*, but reporters from the national papers, and even a television truck with a satellite dish on its roof. The nurses on Jack Duckton told me there was going to be a press conference at eleven o'clock. They did not know who was giving it or what it was about, only that the BBC would be carrying it live.

I hurried through the ward round that morning to be done by eleven o'clock. The patients were all as distracted as I was, and the only person to give me any trouble was Felix Smollett, who peppered me with questions. These had nothing to do with his condition, or even the fevers he had started to experience yet again. Instead, he wanted to know only about the press conference. If nothing else, it made a change from having to argue with him about methadone.

I got to the mess just before eleven. I had never seen it so busy, and had to push my way in to reach the corner where my own colleagues were. I squeezed onto one of the falling-apart couches between Kwame and Marianne, and as I sat down the BBC cut to a live feed from St. Luke's.

A long table had been set up in the corner of the canteen, and sitting at it were Dr. Sudbury, DI Afferson, DS Newington, Eliza Duckton, and a man none of us had ever seen before whose placard said he was the chief executive of St Luke's. Behind them all, a large banner bore the words **OPERATION NIGHTINGALE**, flanked on each side by the logo of the Metropolitan Police.

DI Afferson began, and I can only guess that Dr. Sudbury had given him a primer in breaking bad news, because he hit all the correct notes: an introduction, a warning shot, an establishment of facts, and then the reveal. The reveal was this: having now completed their inquiries, the police were confident that at least twelve of the unexplained deaths that had occurred at St. Luke's during the period in question had been murders.

The mess fell silent as on-screen the cameras flashed. Afferson had repeatedly attempted to achieve a Hollywood moment in our interviews, and now he finally had one, live on television for the whole country to see. He seemed to briefly pause and bask in the moment's glow before stating that he would now hand over to his colleague, DS Newington, to announce what he described as the "operational details." Newington thanked him, and said a full-scale investigation was being launched into what the evidence now strongly suggested was a serial killer. For reasons of their own, the police had named this Operation Nightingale. Afferson then took a few questions from journalists, who mainly wanted to know if there could be more victims, and whether or not they had a suspect. Citing the ongoing Operation Nightingale—he seemed to savor the phrase as he said it—Afferson stated that he would not be drawn on either subject, and then handed over to Dr. Sudbury.

Dr. Sudbury had clearly undergone her own media training, for she looked directly into the camera and said she now wished to directly address the local community. Speaking in deliberately calm and slow tones, she did her best to reassure our patients and their family members that St. Luke's was both safe and open for business. Of course, with a serial killer on the loose, only one of those things could be true. One of the anesthetics registrars shouted that Dr. Sudbury was the mayor in *Jaws,* insisting they keep the beaches open; the whole mess erupted, first with people cheering, and then with others shushing them so we could hear what Dr. Sudbury was saying. When she finished speaking, Afferson handed over to Eliza Duckton who reassured the public that the killer would undoubtedly soon be caught, as this was certainly not the kind of thing her father had fought a world war for.

And then it was over. The anchor introduced a new segment about the bombing in Kosovo, and we all trudged back to work. The second I got back onto Jack Duckton ward, Felix accosted me wanting to know if I had any inside information. I told him I had just watched the same press conference he had, and knew no more than he did. Angela must have ordered the nurses not to talk about it, because nobody on the nursing staff spoke about it at all. Well, nobody except Louise Fisher, who I overheard ask Angela if they now needed to do anything differently. Angela understandably took affront to this, and told Louise that unless she had been murdering people, she should continue on exactly as before.

At four o'clock, Dr. Sudbury called a meeting for the doctors. Unlike the previous meetings, the nurses were not invited, and we speculated this meant suspicion had fallen on one of them. In fact, it turned out to be the opposite: Dr. Sudbury said the nurses' union had intervened to stop them from attending meetings with us, on the grounds that they did not wish their members to seem "guilty by association." Dr. Sudbury seemed to have called the meeting primarily to insist that she personally remained convinced it was all simply a great big misunderstanding. Nonetheless, she reminded us all to document everything, and to never lose sight of the fact that hospital was a dangerous place to be.

Operation Nightingale clearly intended to keep their machinations secret, but as they swiftly interviewed just about the entire nursing staff, enough information about their questions trickled out that we were able to begin to piece things together. By the week after the press conference, some wag had turned the whiteboard in the mess into the kind of "murder wall" you see in movies. This had initially again been a joke that named such notorious medical killers as Dr. Crippen and Harold Shipman as suspects, but at some point somebody wiped it clean and started over in earnest.

On one side were the cases we knew the police were looking at: Mrs. Horsburgh, Mr. Athole, and a Mr. Singh, a patient who two of the nurses said they had been asked about. In the middle of the whiteboard were the substances believed to have been used, and on the far side was a column marked "suspects." It contained the following names: the Angel of Death, Dr. Sudbury, Louise Fisher, and DI Afferson.

Maybe this all seems disrespectful, or even macabre. But being disrespectful and macabre in the mess was the only way we got through even the routine horrors of our job. If we did not have a place to decompress with our fellow sufferers, there is no way any of us would have been able to keep it together through the rivers of pus and blood we spent our days and nights wading through. The mess itself was not much—a large yet dingy room containing a few threadbare couches and a grotesque microwave—but it was our place of refuge. At some point a misguided dermatology registrar had bought some house plants in an attempt to cheer it up, but nobody had watered them after she rotated out, and they had soon died. Saz had then brought in a small potted cactus, on the basis that it was at least unlikely to die of neglect.

For a couple of weeks, the mess whiteboard even brought me a more personal relief from the stresses of Operation Nightingale, as Mr. Singh's death predated my own time at St. Luke's. Initially, too, the drugs the police were asking about provided comfort, for the simple reason that they were not pethidine. Instead, the nurses reported having been asked about a wide range of complex and obscure things: flecainide in combination with a beta-blocker, an old antidepressant, the rare immunosuppressant mycophenolate.

But as more details emerged, I began to feel the old claustrophobia returning. As the list of patients on the whiteboard grew, the killer seemed to have had a clear predilection for Jack Duckton ward. Moreover, the drugs the police were asking about were not substances that the Angel of Death nor any visiting stranger would have realistically known about. These were drugs only a clinician—a doctor, a pharmacist, perhaps a nurse—would have known to use.

The night after the word *co-danthramer* appeared on the board—a rare drug that I alone of my colleagues sometimes used in the terminally ill elderly—I had another nightmare. In it, Afferson came to St. Luke's and arrested me on Jack Duckton ward, and my lawyer—the same one from my interview at Highbury police station—quit on the first day of my trial, but not before loudly proclaiming that he could not possibly defend someone so obviously guilty. As I began to make my own now-hopeless case to the judge, she impatiently removed her wig to reveal herself to be Eliza Duckton.

I was not alone in letting my imagination run wild. With Operation Nightingale issuing no formal statements, the newspapers simply published whatever they could: something-creepy-

happened-when-I-worked-at-St.-Luke's stories from former
staff members, gut-wrenching interviews with relatives who
had already grieved their loved ones' deaths once and now had
to grieve their murders anew, and a yellow-wrist-bands-for-
awareness campaign led by Eliza Duckton. My nightmare not-
withstanding, I actually found myself feeling sorry for her: she
had dedicated her life to making Jack Duckton the best known
Care of the Elderly ward in the country. That had finally now
happened, but not for the reasons she had always hoped.

But the worst of it was reserved for poor old Dr. O'Leary.
He was crucified by the tabloid press, who managed to ambush
him into locking himself out of his own house, took pictures of
him frantically searching for his keys then calling his wife from
a pay phone, and used the ensuing article to christen him "Dr.
Bungle." Even the short statement the British Medical Association had released about not rushing to judgment regarding the
complex situation at St. Luke's had taken the time to severely
criticize Dr. O'Leary for his failure to notice these deaths. The
Royal College of Pathologists subsequently put out a statement
in his defense that declared he had been doing "a difficult job in
challenging circumstances," but none of the papers even mentioned it, let alone published it. Dr. O'Leary resorted to pinning
it up on noticeboards around the hospital, and even handing it
out to the journalists who now loitered by the hospital entrance
interviewing the smoking patients to add color to their stories.

Of course, I had other things on my mind, or more specifically one particular thing. In medical school, I had learned about
the phenomenon of "reinstatement," which was a fancy way of
saying that addicts frequently start right back up where they had
left off. It had seemed to me improbable, and yet here I was, already back to taking eight tablets of pethidine a day. That would
have been more than enough to dispatch an elderly and opiate-
naive patient like Mrs. Horsburgh, but to a reinstated addict like
me, it was already merely what I needed to get through the day.

It probably did not help that it was so easy to get hold of the damn stuff. Everybody was so focused on events inside the hospital that nobody took much notice of the medicines we gave our patients to take home. As soon as I had got through that first strip of pethidine, I had discovered that my old scam worked as reliably at St. Luke's as it had once done back in Scotland.

Of course, each Wednesday night, I still had to traipse across the borough to see the Reverend McKendrick. Fortunately, he had by now abandoned even any pretense of interest in my cognitive behavioral therapy, and he now only ever wanted to know if I had any news about developments at St. Luke's. I never did, but sometimes I made up things to stop him thinking too deeply about the urine samples I still needed to provide each week.

How I got around those was that at the end of my shift I'd ask one of my patients to provide a sample on some pretext, and then I'd make my journey with a stranger's warm piss in my pocket. Even worse, the Reverend McKendrick always insisted that I provide the sample at the end, so I'd spend the whole session with my hand in my pocket trying to keep the stranger's piss warm while telling him that suspicion had this week fallen on a radiographer or canteen worker.

The main reason I had nothing to tell the Reverend McKendrick was that none of us doctors had even been interviewed yet. Some of my colleagues seemed puzzled by this, but it made a terrible kind of sense to me. It was like what happens when you diagnose a patient with a terminal illness: after the trauma of diagnosis there is a lull. The first time you see the patient back in clinic, they tell you that dying of whatever you diagnosed them with really isn't as bad as they imagined it would be. You smile and nod, and it is only a few months later that they sit in the same chair and tell you their particular illness is the worst thing on God's good earth and beg you to just end it for them.

And so, like our condemned patients, we waited. We knew

something bad was coming for us, but just not what, or when. And then our interviews began.

The police had already interviewed everyone else—the nurses, the cleaners, even the tea-room volunteers—and were clearly making a point of keeping the doctors until last. Ever the optimist, Amelia maintained it was simply because they knew we were so busy, but that was the same kind of magical thinking that led patients with advanced cancer to believe they could be cured by eating nothing but spinach. No, there could only be one reason the police had delayed our interviews, and it was because we ourselves were the primary suspects. Detectives on cop shows talk about means, opportunity, and motive. Nobody had the means and opportunity that we did, and as for motive—well, what motive beyond simple wickedness could anybody possibly have to kill twelve entirely unrelated patients?

CHAPTER 25

Over the course of the next two weeks we were all interviewed under oath at Highbury police station. A few of my colleagues took union reps with them, and a couple even brought lawyers, but I did neither. I was not in the union, did not have another two hundred and twenty five pounds to spare, and anyway I had done far better without a lawyer.

The interview was held in the same room, but it had been updated with new furniture and voice-activated video recording equipment. DS Newington described this makeover as a perk of having a big inquiry. It seemed to perhaps be the only one, because she looked weary, and Afferson himself seemed almost broken. I supposed I might have been that way too, if I had found myself in charge of a high profile and potentially career-making case that I could not solve.

Still, Afferson's questions to me were another surprise. He began by asking me if I had managed to stay off the pethidine; for a moment I wondered if he was about to produce a sheaf of incriminating discharge prescriptions. Thankfully he did not, and I reassured him I had indeed managed to stay off it. That seemed to placate him, because he then apologized that he understood it might be upsetting, but he was now going to have to ask me about George. Specifically, they had noticed the extra needle marks around his vein, and wanted to know if I thought they signified the involvement of somebody else in George's death.

I can only guess that they imagined an unidentified assailant had somehow overpowered George, taken several attempts to find a vein, and then injected him with enough potassium chloride to kill him; they also seemed to believe the attacker had done this in the middle of a busy parking lot, without being seen or heard. I told them that was ridiculous: a determined ninety-year-old woman can stop you from ever hitting a vein, and George was a hulking rugby player. If he had wanted to stop someone injecting him, he could have certainly done so. I reassured them that three failed attempts to find the easiest vein in the body made it almost certainly the handiwork of an orthopod.

I'd thought that would be the end of the questions about George, but the detectives then asked me if I had noticed anything strange about his behavior. I began to explain that I had not, but that was not so unusual. I was telling them how doctors actually kill themselves more than most other professions, when Newington interrupted.

"Anesthetists and psychiatrists, yes, we know that. But that is not what we are asking here."

There was something unexpected in her tone, and I looked at Afferson.

"What we are seeking to establish," he said, "is whether there is any way your late friend George might have been our killer?"

I don't think I actually laughed out loud, but the expression on my face must have been the next best thing. Certainly, the looks on Afferson's and Newington's faces showed that they believed I had insulted them. Good, I thought, because that was the least they deserved for insulting George's memory.

I proceeded to lay out for them some of the great many reasons why an orthopod, and especially George, could not possibly be their killer. These included that orthopods rarely left their natural environment of their own wards and the operating theater, and would therefore have been noticed on the other wards; that orthopods weren't even very good at accurately diagnosing death, let alone causing it; that an orthopod like George had almost certainly never even heard of a drug like flecainide, and would definitely have no idea of its fatal interaction with beta-blockers; and most of all that they were all simple creatures who mainly liked contact sports and fast cars and repairing the injuries those things inevitably created.

I even made the mistake of mentioning George's diary. The two detectives pricked up their ears at this, and asked if they could see it. I told them I did not think George would have appreciated that, but anyway there was nothing in it apart from weather, operations, and rugby scores. Newington suggested those things might be code for something, but the idea was so preposterous I found myself involuntarily rolling my eyes. Afferson seemed profoundly irritated by both Newington's suggestion and my response.

They changed tack again after that, Afferson sighing and Newington shaking her head. It was as if a high school drama teacher has asked them to pantomime "hopelessness" in an attempt to elicit sympathy. It was almost comical, even more so when Afferson then exhaled and casually asked me—as if it has just occurred to him—whether I perhaps had any suspicions about anybody myself.

The thing was, I actually did not. None of it made any sense. Why would anyone kill what presumably were strangers, let alone strangers who mostly only had a few good years of life left? What was even the point?

Moreover, just about everything I knew about crime came from television and movies. Killers were generally spouses or lovers or hitmen hired by shady corporations; serial killers were invariably creepy men who lived alone and liked to dress up as their mothers. None of it seemed to fit with whatever had happened at St. Luke's. I realize in hindsight that I was up against the exact same issues as Afferson and Newington, as they too seemed to have also learned much of their police work from television. I told them, truthfully, that I had no idea who the culprit could have been, and asked if I could now leave.

But Afferson and Newington were not yet done. In fact, the dejection and request for help had been another ruse, perhaps aimed at getting me to state on the record that I had no suspicions. Because Newington now brought out another of their trademark envelopes. I tensed myself for it to be my discharge prescriptions. It was not, but the contents were still shocking: the envelope contained photographs of our "murder wall" in the mess.

I felt almost violated. The mess was supposed to be our sanctuary, but somehow the police had managed to get in there and take a photograph without anybody noticing. There was always at least one doctor in there, and it puzzled me as to how they could possibly have done this without us knowing. I realized later that one of my colleagues must have taken the photograph and supplied it to them.

I began to explain about our black humor, but Newington interrupted me and told me they did not care about that. Afferson added that if I thought medical humor was dark, I should hear what was said in their own break room. I asked him what they said about us, and Afferson only smirked. Newington then explained that cops weren't traditionally fond of doctors, as they never found us very helpful when they had to bring a suspect to the emergency department. I countered that we were absolutely helpful, but to our sick patients rather than their captors who seemed to believe that the cure for every disease was a pair of handcuffs and a night in the cells. This seemed to irk Afferson, who asked me if I thought we were all playing on the same team, which I countered by asking him if he did. He considered this for a moment before replying that he did "sometimes." I told him that seemed about right to me.

Newington pointed to the photograph of the mess whiteboard, and asked me what I could tell her about the first name on the list. Who, they wanted to know, was the Angel of Death? I glibly replied that the Angel of Death was Joseph Mengele. They looked at each other meaningfully, and Newington began to write the name down as if it might be the clue that cracked the whole case. Only when she frowned and asked me to spell it did I explain that Mengele was a Nazi doctor who had performed hideous experiments on people in concentration camps. I saw Newington frown and write the word *Nazi?* in her notes, but Afferson now understood and was visibly irritated.

"And could it refer to anybody else?" he asked.

I acknowledged that in this context it referred to one of the St. Luke's porters. Their body language told me that they already knew this story, but I ran through it again: a few of us had noticed a particular porter seemed to be around when bad things happened; that had originally led us to speculate he might be the killer, but we had quickly decided that could not be the case. If an orthopod would not know that flecainide and a beta-blocker were a deadly combination, a porter certainly wouldn't. We had therefore decided he was not the murderer but rather some sort of harbinger. Afferson asked what a "harbinger" was, and Newington explained it was an "avatar." I had clearly already annoyed them enough for one day, so I did not correct her.

They then moved on to the next name on the list: *Cat.* This one had been a more recent addition, and they obviously had no idea of its significance, as they asked me whether it was short for Catherine or Catriona. Fortunately, I had been present in the mess when this name had been added, and I knew it referred to a recent news story: workers at a nursing home in the north of England had noticed that a resident cat had an uncanny habit of sleeping on the bed of elderly patients before they died, and had therefore ascribed powers of premonition to it.

"And you think this same cat is killing the patients at St. Luke's, do you?" Afferson asked, now seemingly on the point of fury.

I shook my head. "No, it was just a joke. We decided the cat must sense some chemical given off by the dying."

"And is that correct? That people who are dying give of some kind of chemical?"

"I don't know," I said, "But I can't think of any other explanation."

Newington diligently wrote *No other explanation for cat?* beneath *Nazi?*

Finally, Afferson asked me about the third name on the whiteboard: Louise Fisher. They already knew exactly who she was, and wanted to know why the doctors considered a mere student nurse one of the prime suspects. I told them that this too was a joke.

"A joke like a cat, or a joke like a Nazi scientist?" asked Afferson.

"Not exactly like either," I said.

"Yes," said Afferson, "because neither of those work at St. Luke's, now do they? Whereas Nurse Fisher very much does."

Afferson stared at me, seemingly daring me to contradict what appeared to be his new theory: that the vainglorious Louise Fisher was the murderer of St. Luke's.

"She does work there," I said, "but she is only on the board as a joke."

"And do you think it is a funny joke?"

"It seemed sort of funny at the time," I said. "I'm not so sure now."

"The thing is," said Afferson, "DS Newington and I just don't get this particular joke. So perhaps you could explain it to us, and then we might have a chance at finding it funny too. That way, we could all have a laugh together, eh?"

Afferson was not looking for a laugh, but a clue or, better yet, a slipup. Still, I explained the joke to him: how student nurses were usually shrinking violets, long on kindness and rote-learned knowledge yet short on confidence, but Louise was the exact opposite of all of that. I mentioned the presentation she had given about Amelia's case, and the Christmas Day shift I'd spent answering her every whim. Afferson and Newington let me keep talking without interruption, and when I finally got through, they let the silence hang in the air.

"And so, you think she did it then, do you?" Afferson asked. "Your honest opinion?"

I told him, truthfully, that I did not think she had done it. Louise Fisher undoubtedly liked to place herself at the center of events, but like an odd-looking porter or a nursing home cat, she seemed unlikely to possess the technical knowledge to fool an experienced pathologist like Dr. O'Leary.

"That's all fair enough," said Afferson, "but do you maybe find her just a little strange?"

"Because we find her a little strange," Newington added.

It seemed an odd intimacy for two detectives to confide to an interviewee. I felt like a patient to whom a doctor had just gossiped about another patient. I told them that hospitals were full of strange people, and it did not make them murderers. That seemed to placate them, and I thought they were about to end the interview. Instead, Afferson now asked the question he had apparently spent the whole morning building up to.

"And did your friend George ever talk about Louise Fisher?" he asked.

It was a troubling question. I had no idea what the actual answer was, but that did not matter. What mattered was why

Afferson should be asking such a curious thing. I recognized in myself the feeling I sometimes saw in patients when I asked them if they had ever been exposed to asbestos or industrial dyes; even if you did not know what the question signified, it obviously portended something ominous.

I told them that, as far as I recalled, George had never once mentioned Louise Fisher. When that drew only a nod and an expectant silence, I found myself continuing to talk. I explained how separate hospital wards often are, that George's and Louise's paths would have had very little reason to cross, and that I did not think I had ever even seen George on Jack Duckton. I told them it was definitely not impossible that George had been called in to see a referral there at some point, an old lady with a frozen shoulder or an elderly man with hip pain, but it would have been a brief visit.

"So what would you say," asked Afferson, now in full *Columbo* mode, "if I told you that Nurse Fisher had begun her training on the orthopedic ward, and would have been working there when George started at St. Luke's? Would that change things at all?"

This did surprise me, but it at least made Louise's sprint up the aisle at George's funeral a little less performative. I acknowledged to Afferson that it would change things slightly, but it did not alter the fact that George had never spoken of her. Neither Afferson nor Newington responded to that, and I abruptly had the sense that there was another piece of information they were withholding from me.

"What makes you think they knew each other?" I asked.

Newington looked to Afferson, and he nodded at her.

"What?" I asked. "What is it?"

"The potassium that George used," Newington said. "He got it from Jack Duckton ward."

My first thought was about how guilty this made me look. My flatmate had killed himself with potassium obtained from

the ward I worked on. It seemed to explain why they had asked
me about the extra marks on George's arms.

"You think that I—I gave it to him?"

"No, Louise Fisher has admitted she supplied it to him," Afferson said.

I briefly felt relief, and then confusion, and then anger. The
relief was that I was not in the frame for giving George the potassium; images of having to explain accusation this to Amelia
or George's parents had flashed before my eyes. The confusion
was as to why it had happened at all: Why had George needed
to obtain potassium from Jack Duckton when he could have got
it from his own surgical ward? Was it just that he didn't want to
get his own nurses into trouble? And of all the damn nurses in
the hospital, why had it been Louise Fisher? This last was the
anger: Louise had overstepped her boundaries once again, and
now my friend was dead.

"I don't understand. Why would George have even asked
her?" I said. "And why would she have given it to him?"

Even as I said that, I began to wonder if Louise might have
actually done no such thing. It would not have been the first
time she had inserted herself into a story that barely involved her.

"George told Louise he had a patient with low potassium, and
that his own ward had run out," Afferson explained.

That part was more believable, and I experienced a brief pang
of sympathy for Louise Fisher. As we had discovered in the aftermath of the second meeting with Afferson and Dr. Sudbury,
hospitals run on small favors every day. No doubt in a folder
somewhere there was a written protocol that detailed the correct procedure for obtaining potassium when your own ward
had run out, and it probably involved sending a fax to the dep-
uty compounding pharmacist, who would fax the ward back
within two business days to confirm when the potassium was
available for pickup. Of course, if the patient went that long
without potassium they would have long since died, and so we

all did favors for colleagues when they asked us. If ever our actions were investigated—as now—they would look like inex-
cusably dangerous breaches of protocol, but thousands of them
needed to happen every day simply to keep the hospital running and the patients alive.

"I don't understand," I said. "What was George even doing
on Jack Duckton?"

"Louise told us that he was looking for you. She said she offered to page you, but George declined and asked for the potassium."

"And you are sure this was all on the day he died?" I asked.

"Yes. It was a little after 2:00 p.m.," said Newington.

This seemed like it might be an important clue as to where
George had spent his missing afternoon, but it also created a
whole new and far more pressing mystery: Why had George
been looking for me? And if he had actually wanted to find me,
why not just page me when Louise offered? Or why not just
page me himself? I felt another surge of anger inside me. Louise and I had crossed paths on Jack Duckton a thousand times
since George's death, and she had never mentioned a word of
this to me.

"When did she tell you this?"

"A few weeks ago," said Afferson. "When we interviewed
her."

"She has never told me any of this," I said.

"She hadn't come forward because she was afraid of getting
into trouble. That's probably why she didn't tell you either."

Afferson and Newington abruptly stood up then, to signal
our interview was over. A few moments later, I was back out
on the street once more. None of it had made any sense. I even
found myself wishing I had brought a lawyer, if only so I could
have asked him what on earth was going on. I would have gladly
paid another two hundred and twenty-five pounds to have even
the slightest inkling.

CHAPTER 26

At work the next day, I saw Louise sitting alone at the nurses' station on Jack Duckton. I leaned over her to use the phone to page someone, then sat down beside her, as if waiting for them to ring back. They wouldn't be ringing back, because I had deliberately paged the night porters.

"Bed three wants more methadone," Louise said when she eventually noticed me.

"And I want a holiday in the Maldives," I said. "But it's also not going to happen."

"I'll tell Felix I asked you," she whispered conspiratorially. "That means I did my part."

I nodded. I had planned to play it cool, to sidle into the subject without making allegations, but I could not help myself.

"Did you see George on the day he died?" I asked.

If Louise understood the accusation inherent in this, she ignored it.

"I did!" She leaned in, as if we were co-conspirators. "And he was looking for you."

"Why was he looking for me?" I asked.

"He didn't say. He seemed kind of stressed. I offered to page you, of course, but—"

"What kind of stressed?"

"You know, just stressed. Like, a little frantic."

But I did not know, because I had never seen George remotely stressed or frantic in my life. In Amelia's eulogy she had described him as "the most laidback man she'd ever met" and the whole of St. Clement Danes had laughed with recognition.

"But what was he even doing on the ward?" I asked. "Had he just come here looking for me—"

"I think he had been in seeing bed three," said Louise.

"What?" I asked. "George was seeing Felix Smollett? Why?"

"Don't you remember? He'd been complaining of a sore hip."

Now that Louise had mentioned this, I did remember it. Felix Smollett had gone through a predictable phase of trying to get more opioids by inventing sicknesses. He had feigned appendicitis, and when I pointed out the scar that told me his appendix had already been removed, he had instead begun to complain of a pain deep in his hip. I had been sure he had been faking that too, but Dr. Weiden had insisted we get an X-ray and have orthopedics look him over. It had not been George on call when I paged with the referral, but it could easily have been passed on to him.

I pulled Felix's notes from the trolley. Every day on the ward round I opened them and every day I wrote a variation on the same thing:

Stable.

No change.

Antibiotics per microbiology.

★Do not prescribe more opioids★

I flicked back through dozens of these to the day in question

in February, where I found only my regular entry. I replaced
the notes in the trolley and headed to the side room.

"Do you want me to come and get you if they ring you back?"
Louise shouted after me.

I ignored her. Nobody would be ringing back.

It was not visiting hours, but Felix's teenage entourage was
in his room. I asked them to leave and they did, albeit grudgingly and with the usual complaints about how desperately unfair it all was.

"Did Lou tell you that I need more methadone?" he asked,
as soon as they had left. Of course he would have an overly familiar nickname for his nurse.

"She mentioned it, but you don't need any. How's your hip?"

"What? My hips are great. Always have been!" Felix said,
and then caught himself. "I mean, right at this moment they
are fine. But one usually gets sore a few hours after my methadone. That's why I think I need more. I mean, it's one of the
reasons. The others are—"

"Did an orthopedic doctor ever come to see you about your
hip?"

"Today? No."

"No. Not today. February the sixth."

"I mean, maybe? It'd be in my notes, wouldn't it?"

"It's not in your notes," I said, "but the doctor that would
have come to see you was George, my friend that died."

Felix seemed genuinely puzzled by this.

"No, no, definitely not," he said. "I would have remembered
that."

I was already on my way out of the room when he said something that stopped me in my tracks.

"What about some pethidine, Doc? Could I at least maybe
have some pethidine?"

I turned and stared at him. He smirked a little, or at least I
thought he did.

"If I can't have any more methadone, could I have some peth-idine?" he said. "I've heard it's very similar."

"You don't need any," I said, and walked out.

For an awful moment I wondered if Felix had somehow cot-toned onto my scam, but then I remembered his mother was a GP. No doubt she had looked me up in the medical register, dug out the report, and mentioned it to him. Felix Smollett might be a shit, but he at least only knew about my former pethidine habit, and not my current one. I went to get lunch.

Even as I approached, I could hear that the canteen was awash with excited chitter-chatter. I was relieved that it did not evap-orate when I entered, but from the snatches of conversation I overheard I could discern only that the buzz had something to do with a development in Operation Nightingale. The only people who did not appear to be excited by the news were a table of porters. They seemed to be seething.

When I got to the mess with my sandwich, the television was tuned to a breaking news story on the BBC. A police source was said to have leaked the name of a suspect in the murders at St. Luke's to the press: Albert Grenslow. I did not recognize the name and would have had no idea who that was, but the newscasters were also already referring to him by the macabre nickname they said all the other St. Luke's staff knew him by: The Angel of Death.

When we think of healthcare serial killers, we think first of nurses and doctors. But hospitals employ many kinds of workers, and the green line between life and death is so precariously thin that numerous employees have both the means and opportunity to kill.

When the nuns that ran Kentucky's Marymount Hospital noticed eighteen-year-old Donald Harvey visiting his grandfather on their wards, they offered him a job as an orderly. Harvey took them up, and would later confess that during his first full year of employment he smothered two patients with pillows and dispatched ten others by connecting their breathing tubes to near-empty oxygen cylinders. Over the next two decades, Harvey expanded his repertoire to include poisoning with arsenic and cyanide. All told, he would murder some eighty-seven people in the various hospitals he worked in.

Harvey was only finally caught when a sharp-nosed pathologist noticed the bitter almond smell of cyanide during what he'd thought was a routine postmortem. A subsequent investigation identified Harvey as the likely culprit, and a police search of his home turned up a diary in which Harvey had written a detailed account of the murder. When this news broke, other staff members began to come forward with long-held concerns, and the full scale of Harvey's crimes was revealed.

Why did Donald Harvey do it? He initially claimed that his crimes were "mercy killings," performed solely to relieve his patients' suffering, but his excuse lasted only until his conviction. After being sentenced to eight life terms, Harvey admitted his true motives to a reporter from the Columbia Dispatch: "I controlled other people's lives, whether they lived or died... I thought it was my right. I appointed myself judge, prosecutor and jury. So I played God."

CHAPTER 27

Collette and I both had the May bank holiday off, and she insisted we go on a romantic mini break. She had been keen to go to Paris or Bruges, but I had been keener to not cross an international border where the opioids I'd need to take with me might be discovered. I therefore surprised her by booking us a long weekend at a country house hotel in the Cotswolds. If Collette was disappointed, she was polite enough not to show it.

A weekend without drugs would not have killed me. The whole notion of opioid withdrawal being intolerable is largely a myth created by us addicts in order to keep us in drugs. Sure, I would yawn and maybe shiver, I'd be more irritable than usual, and I might have to run to the bathroom a few times. But opioid withdrawal was nothing like in the movies, and usually little worse than a bad hangover. Still, even the yawning and shivering and occasional desperate shitting would not have made for an ideal mini break in Paris or Bruges, and so a trip to the

Cotswolds—with all the drugs I could carry—seemed a better proposition.

We left after work on the Friday and took the train to Acton, where we picked up Collette's car. The seats had plastic covers on them to keep them pristine, and the CD player had been preloaded with five CDs. Four of them were audiobooks about the history of surgery, and the fifth was an entirely unseasonal Christmas album by George Michael.

It being rush hour on the Friday evening of a bank holiday weekend, it took us forever to get out of London. We crawled out past Heathrow Airport, where even the planes circling overhead seemed to be stuck in traffic. After that, the motorway began to clear a little, and we passed exits for towns and villages with the kind of names that only the English could have said with a straight face: Wooburn Green, Kingston Blount, Aston Rowant. As we passed Oxford, Collette cheerfully announced we were "nearly there." Alas, this proved premature as we still had to traverse Ducklington, Stanton Harcourt, Upper Windrush and Minster Lovell. Finally, though, we passed through Duntisbourne Abbots and Perrots Brook, before taking the turning just outside the village of Birdlip, which led us to our hotel.

Covington Manor was the ancestral home of a family of erstwhile slave-owning aristocrats, a grim heritage awkwardly referenced in a cocktail menu whose drinks were named after various Caribbean ports. The slavers' descendants had fallen on harder times than their more efficiently cruel forebears, and so now lived in what had once been the estate workers' cottages and supported themselves by giving weekending Londoners a taste of what their website described as "the rural high life."

The package I had booked was called "The Lovers' Getaway." It included a bottle of champagne on arrival, a "couple's massage" and a dinner in something called the Jamaica Room. I had chosen it solely because it worked out as the cheapest way to get a room for three nights, but I had forgotten to mention this to Collette. She seemed so thrilled by the whole thing that the person checking us in even felt the need to quietly apologize that the "champagne" was actually prosecco.

Our room was on the first floor, at the far end of a corridor painted in bright staphylococcal yellow. The rooms were all named after types of horses, and ours was called Clydesdale. If I was meant to find this evocative, I did, but not for the reasons the proprietors intended: back in Scotland the Clydesdale was the bank beloved of pensioners, and I could not hear the name without remembering my grandmother arguing with the teller about whether or not her pension was in.

Inside, our room contained a four-poster bed, a television, an en suite bathroom, and an improbable number of framed prints of horses. We drank our prosecco, then each took showers to wash off the day's hospital grime, and went down for dinner in the Jamaica Room.

There were four other couples dining in the Jamaica Room that night, and they all seemed depressingly similar to us: about the same age, weekending from London, comfortable enough to stay here but economical enough to have to do it on the package. We never learned a single one of their names, but referred to each couple in the same way the staff did, which was by the types of horses the rooms they were staying in were named after: the Friesians, the Appaloosas, the Westphalians, and the Percherons. We, of course, were known to all as the Clydesdales.

The menu described itself as a "Chef's Tasting Menu," which I quickly learned meant that it was not a menu at all, but simply a list of food you were going to be served, whether you wanted it or not. It was all edible enough in a retro-boarding-school-dinner kind of way: a prawn cocktail, followed by a thimbleful of what I thought was Bovril but was apparently oxtail soup, followed by an English garden salad, followed by a steak and kidney pie, followed by something called an "inverted rhubarb crumble," which seemed just to be a regular rhubarb crumble served upside down. I was making this point to Collette, when she nodded across the room to where the Percheron stallion had got down on one knee in order to propose. When the Percheron mare said yes, almost the whole Jamaica Room cheered the Percherons. I noticed that the Westphalian mare was looking glum; I was about to remark on this to Collette, but I realized that she was also looking somewhat morose, and so I bit my tongue.

After breakfast in the Pantry the next morning, we had our couple's massage. We had joked about how awkwardly sexual it sounded, but in fact it could not have been more frigid, for a "couple's massage" meant simply that each of us was entitled to a standard individual massage from the resident masseuse. Collette went down first, and when she came back she told me it was good, but I could tell she had not really enjoyed it. When I got down to the massage suite, I quickly understood why: the masseuse was Lady Covington herself, and this was clearly not a part of her job she enjoyed. Even having taken two pethidine I lasted only five minutes before I made up an excuse about sciatica and left. Lady Covington did not seem remotely disappointed.

That afternoon, Collette and I set out to explore the Cotswolds, starting with Kelmscott Manor, the one-time home of William Morris. I had no idea who William Morris was, but Collette had found a leaflet in our room that had described his one-time home as "a must for pre-Raphaelite aficionados." I was not a pre-Raphaelite aficionado—I was not an aficionado of anything except pethidine—but Collette was keen and even insisted that we take the guided tour. I learned far more about William Morris than I could ever have hoped to know.

Eventually we escaped to a tearoom in a nearby village. From there, Collette insisted we visit a place called Copse Hill Road that had been selected as "the most romantic street in Britain." With its tranquil river, tall trees, and old stone buildings it was undeniably charming, but it seemed to me that the judging panel had been overly generous in its willingness to ignore the village's name, which was "Lower Slaughter."

Not for the first time in life, I found myself wondering if it was just me. Collette seemed to be enjoying our mini break, as were all our stablemates, and none of them seemed to remotely mind how ridiculous it all was. Maybe it was my addiction, or simply my job, but I couldn't talk about how picturesque a village called Lower Slaughter was without laughing out loud at the incongruity of its name. This understandably irked Collette, and we drove back to the hotel in silence.

Things only got worse at the hotel. Perhaps I had truly left them in plain sight, as she later claimed, or perhaps she had noticed my pinpoint pupils and gone looking, but it did not matter: Collette found the pethidine in my toiletry bag. She emerged from the bathroom, handed the box to me, and asked me to explain myself.

I could not. The most routine use of pethidine was in a patient with gallstones, and as a general surgeon Collette knew perfectly well that I had no such thing. Worse, I had been stupid enough to bring the box, and it still had the label featuring the name of the patient for whom I'd first prescribed them, then stolen them from.

And so I told her the truth. The whole weary story, but this time with an added coda: after the bike accident, the prescriptions, the rehab, there was now George. I had been perfectly clean for over a year, but I had turned back to the opioids after George's tragic death. Was that true? Perhaps. I didn't know anymore. There was an undeniable temporal relationship, but in medicine correlation does not mean causality. If you looked at it empirically, my first bout with the opioids had begun long before I even met George, so it was hard to blame my current addiction on him.

Collette was quiet for a long time, and then told me that I had to get help. The most awkward part of the whole thing was having to admit to her that I already was getting help. That for as long as we had known each other I had been trotting off to Bethnal Green once a week to have my counseling with the Reverend McKendrick. Even at that, I could not bring myself to tell her that I lied to him each week, and especially not that I regularly smuggled a stranger's piss across town. Instead, I told her that the Reverend McKendrick was aware I had relapsed, and that we were working through it together.

Collette seemed relieved to hear that, and I understood why. She was not merely glad that I was getting help—though that was no doubt part of it—but that it got her off the hook from having to turn me in. Doctors have a duty of candor to report colleagues who are breaking the law, but the fact that a professional was already aware of the issue and was working to resolve it gave her cover. I did not tell her that the GMC did not know about my relapse, and she did not ask. Instead, she asked me what the Reverend McKendrick's plan was, and I told her we had agreed on a weaning dose, and that the pethidine I had brought to the Cotswolds was part of that undertaking.

We had planned to venture out into the village that night, but neither of us now felt like it, and so we ate at Covington's bar from the most jingoistic menu I have ever seen. Collette had something called a "Good Old-Fashioned English Shepherds Pie" and I had "Churchill's Favorite Bangers and Mash." This time, we did not get halfway through our meal before news of a proposal came, the barman informing us that the Appaloosas had got engaged that afternoon. I made a joke about hoping it was not contagious, and immediately regretted it—initially because it was just stupid, but even more when Collette burst into tears.

The barman began to busily polish his glasses, and I felt envious that he had such an easy out. In our entire time together, Collette had barely expressed a single feeling, and when she had done, it was only ever to remind us both that, while we clearly were having a good time, our relationship was definitely just temporary. Before I could think of anything to say, she told me not to read anything into her tears, that she was just hormonal, and ordered us two beers and two shots. We got blackout drunk, then went upstairs and passed out.

But there was no escaping ourselves the next day. We woke up with terrible hangovers to a torrential rain outside that seemed to sink the entire hotel into a quagmire of gloom. Even the pethidine I discreetly took did little to lift my own spirits, and when the Friesians proposed to each other at breakfast and then turned expectantly to the room, not even the Westphalians applauded. It was hard to believe we still had another entire night of this to endure.

Collette had chosen a place called Woodchester Mansion for that day's outing. Unlike the dozen other stately homes nearby, Woodchester Mansion had been designed in the Gothic style, but abandoned late during construction. A hundred years later, it remained unfinished. I doubt Collette intended it as a metaphor—she was a surgeon—but it might as well have been.

From the outside, it appeared complete: three stories high, its windows were reminiscent of the imposing facade of the Houses of Parliament, and its roof rose to three stately battlements. Step through the door, though, and nothing was as it should be: the whole thing was incomplete, with floors, ceilings, and sometimes even entire rooms missing. That is: it looked the part from the outside, but crucial elements were absent. If there was a better way to describe myself, my career, or our temporary relationship, I had not encountered it.

There was no guide, and so we trudged through the rooms ourselves, doing our best to avoid the puddles, while half-heartedly attempting to guess the intended purpose of each empty room. At one point we sat on a bench in what a plaque told us was supposed to have been the ballroom, but was now simply a drafty expanse.

"What are we even doing?" Collette asked.

I did not have an answer. This was probably just as well, as it turned out to have been a rhetorical question.

"You know, since we lost George," she said, "sometimes I feel like I just don't know you at all."

There was nothing I could say to that, because Collette was right: she did not know me at all. Maybe she never had done, but certainly since George had gone and I had started back on the pethidine she did not. Perhaps there was not much left to know anymore, for I no longer felt like a normal human. All my synapses were currently wired for one single thing, and that thing was pethidine.

I desperately wanted then to say something to comfort her, to apologize for dragging her into my misery, to reassure her that it truly was not her but all just me. I wanted to explain to her that a few months ago I had almost been sent to prison for the rest of my life, my best friend had died and I had relapsed into an addiction that the statistics said would now most likely kill me. That between all those things, not much remained of myself and I was sorry for any hurt I had caused her. Instead, I reminded Collette that we had agreed our relationship was not meant to be anything serious. She got up then, and told me we should really be getting back to London because we both had our next exams to revise for.

We had paid to stay another night at Covington Manor, but Collette was right—what was even the point? We went back to the hotel only for the time it took to pack and wish the Westphalians—who were gleefully recounting the story of their proposal that morning—our best. We sat in silence all the way to Reading, and when we finally did begin to talk it was only mundane details about work and medicine. Collette offered to drive me home but I declined, and when we got to Acton I have never been so happy to see a tube station in my life.

I still had the next day off work, but the British Library was closed for the bank holiday, so I spent the morning studying in my room. At lunchtime I phoned Collette to apologize again and ask if he she was okay. The Australian who answered the phone told me that she was out playing hockey, but I could hear her in the background.

At work the next day, Collette broke up with me. She had paged me to do this, but I was seeing a patient and by the time I managed to ring back Collette was already scrubbed. Nonetheless, she had the theater nurse who answered for her relay the message that "it would be better for you two not to see each other again." Not knowing what else to do, I asked the nurse to let Collette know that I entirely understood.

Emotions are the hardest thing to recall, but I believe that in that moment I felt exactly the same thing I had for months: nothing. Perhaps it was the opioids, perhaps it was George's death, perhaps I was morbidly depressed and did not know it. But the breakup's initial sole effect on me was its simple binary fact: I'd had a girlfriend the day before, and now I no longer did. It provoked no more feeling than the fact it was Monday, and yesterday had been Sunday.

Nonetheless, at my counseling appointment with the Reverend McKendrick later that week something peculiar did happen: I burst into tears. The reverend seemed as embarrassed as any human I have ever encountered. It took him fully five minutes to even acknowledge that I was crying, and another five to inquire why. I told him I was crying because Collette had broken up with me, but that was only part of the truth. I was also crying because George had died, and because I was an addict and had once again built for myself the exact same prison that I'd had to work so hard to escape. We sat silently for a while, and then Reverend McKendrick quietly said that I might find great comfort in the church. I don't think he actually meant it, but I thanked him all the same.

CHAPTER 28

It was a week later that the Angel of Death himself died.

I should not call him that. He did nothing whatsoever to deserve that name, nor the fate it seemed to inexorably lead him to. His name was Albert Grenslow. He was sixty-seven years old when he died, and he was even briefly my patient.

I was on call for admissions the day he died, and when they paged with the referral I was in seeing Felix Smollett on my morning round in Jack Duckton. Felix was taking great delight in showing me the front cover of that day's *Mirror*: a headline that said "**FIRST PHOTOGRAPHS OF ANGEL OF DEATH**" that was accompanied by two photographs of an oblivious Albert Grenslow smoking behind the hospital.

As I left the room to answer my page, Felix asked me if I thought the Angel of Death was the St. Luke's killer. I told him I absolutely did not, but when he asked me how I could be so sure, I just carried on walking. I did not want to have to admit the truth to Felix nor anybody else: I could be so sure

Grenslow was not the culprit because the only reason the paper was even writing about him was that our bad joke had got far enough out of hand to elevate an undoubtedly innocent man to national infamy.

I should have known something was up from the atmosphere in the accident and emergency department. It was often quiet in the morning, but on this particular day there was a palpable tension beneath the calm. The usually friendly admissions nurse seemed oddly curt when she told me my patient was in the negative pressure room, and that his notes were in there with him.

The negative pressure room was set a little away from the shop floor, on a lonely corridor that led away from the accident and emergency department. It was meant to be used for patients with transmissible infectious diseases, but of course patients rarely knew they had such a disease when they arrived. Instead, the room was mostly used for situations where its geographical isolation would be an advantage: disruptive young patients, elderly patients who needed somewhere quiet to die, and staff member patients who merited more privacy than the shop floor afforded. To the latter end, I had previously examined an oncology nurse with a deep vein thrombosis and a physiotherapist having a panic attack here. If I had stopped to think, I probably could have put it all together before I even entered the room.

But I did not stop to think, and so instead I cheerily opened the door to reveal the Angel of Death. It took me a moment to recognize him because he was wearing a hospital gown, had an oxygen mask over his mouth, and a nitrate infusion was running into his arm. Out of his uniform, and lying atop the trolley I saw Albert Grenslow as he really was: old, vulnerable, sick, and apparently utterly alone in this world.

"Good morning," I said.

He nodded at me. He seemed scared.

"I hear you've been having some chest pain?" I asked.

Mr. Grenslow nodded, closing his eyes as he did so to signal that he remained in pain. I picked up the notes and flicked through to the ECGs that had been stapled to the back. They did not show the permanent damage of a heart attack, but the first one showed that not enough blood had been getting to his heart. The second ECG was better, but was not yet anything like normal.

"The pain you are having is what we call angina," I said. "Have you ever had this before?"

Mr. Grenslow shook his head, but when I ran through the risk factors he nodded at them all: a family history, high blood pressure, high cholesterol, smoking. The final risk factor tripped off my tongue by rote.

"Have you been under a lot of stress lately?" I asked, wishing even as I spoke the words that I hadn't done so.

Mr. Grenslow nodded, and motioned to a copy of the *Mirror* protruding from the clinical waste bin.

"I'm sorry they printed that," I said.

Mr. Grenslow nodded, but we both knew I had far more than that to apologize for.

"And I'm also sorry we ever called you that," I added. "It was just supposed to be a joke, but it wasn't ever funny and it went too far."

"It's alright, Doc," he managed to whisper. He began to say something else, but the pain became too much, and he instead gave me a thumbs-up. I knew I didn't remotely deserve his forgiveness.

"I'm going to get you some morphine to make you more comfortable. They've started you on a treatment to open up your arteries," I said, "and we are going to keep a close eye on your heart tracing. It looks like things are settling down, and as long as that continues and the pain goes away we can get you home today, and in a week or so we'll get you on the treadmill and see where we are. Does that sound okay?"

Mr. Grenslow nodded and extended his hand for me to shake.

I did so and then hurriedly left the room, feeling once again like the terrible shit I was. I found his nurse and told her to give him more morphine, but this did nothing to assuage my guilt.

I returned to Jack Duckton to finish my ward round. Louise Fisher asked me if it was true that the Angel of Death had been admitted. I told her that if any patients were to be transferred under her care I was sure the bed manager would be in touch, but beyond that any and all medical information was confidential. I don't think she even understood I was scolding her, because she simply looked puzzled.

I did the rest of the ward round, and then stopped by accident and emergency again on my way to lunch. I could not face having to shake Mr. Grenslow's hand again, so I did not go to the negative pressure room, but simply reviewed his repeat ECG at the nurses' station. Perhaps it had been the nitrate infusion, or simply the few hours distance since the newspaper story had been published, but the ECG was back to normal, and the nurse reported that Mr. Grenslow was now pain free. I told her to keep the nitrate going for another hour, at which point they could begin to wean it down before sending him home. It was a situation we had all dealt with hundreds of times before, so I did not anticipate hearing any more about Mr. Grenslow.

The arrest call came in the middle of the afternoon, while I was seeing a boarder in the tower. Somehow, even as I heard the switchboard operator say "Accident and Emergency," I knew that the next three words out of her mouth were going to be "Negative pressure room." I dropped the boarder's chart, and ran all the way there.

But there turned out to have been little need for my hurry. For once, the accident and emergency doctors had involved themselves in an arrest call, and between them and the two anesthetists who had also shown up, the room was already awash in green and blue scrubs. I took my turn doing chest compressions, but the line on the monitor remained flat, and flat was asystole, and asystole was death. We called it after thirty minutes. When we finally emerged from the room, the other porters were lining the corridor in a sort of grief-struck honor guard. I could not look a single one of them in the eye.

An hour later, Dr. Sudbury paged me, to ask if I had any concerns about the passing of Mr. Grenslow. I told her only of my clinical concern, that he had seemed to be improving, and I was unclear why he had suddenly deteriorated again. I made no mention of what Dr. Sudbury must already have known, that the nickname we had given him had been responsible for the onset of his sickness and likely his relapse too. Sure enough, the next day, every national newspaper in the country led with the news that the Angel of Death had died. The funeral took place a week later, and—temporarily devoid of its entire staff of porters—for those few hours the hospital fell briefly but spectacularly apart.

When Dr. O'Leary's postmortem findings were released, the papers all reported them as showing that the Angel of Death had died of a heart attack brought on by increased levels of adrenalin occurring as a result of stress. In fact, the postmortem itself had shown at least one part, and perhaps both parts, of that statement to be untrue.

The part about Mr. Grenslow having died from a heart attack was certainly untrue, because people generally understand a heart attack to mean the sudden blockage of a coronary artery. By contrast, Dr. O'Leary had found that Mr. Grenslow's arteries were all surprisingly patent, with no significant narrowing or clot. No, the thing that had changed in Mr. Grenslow's case was the very shape of his heart itself: when Dr. O'Leary had cut open his chest, he had found a heart that ballooned out at its apex around the left ventricle. The Japanese call this condition Takotsubo syndrome, because the physical appearance of the heart resembles their octopus trap of that name. In English, we do not call the condition after the physical appearance of the heart, but after the event that usually provokes it. We call it Broken Heart syndrome.

People are often surprised to learn that Broken Heart syndrome is a medical condition as real as any other. In response to severe emotional or physical stress, the human body releases vast amounts of adrenalin, and this can cause the left ventricle of the heart to undergo drastic remodeling. This remodeling was what killed Mr. Grenslow, who therefore died not of a heart attack, but of something far worse: a broken heart.

But was it brought on by stress, as the papers stated? That depends on where you believe the vast amounts of adrenalin that Dr. O'Leary's tests found in Mr. Grenslow's bloodstream had come from. A national newspaper accusing a person of being a serial killer would certainly seem a stressful enough event to cause the release of a lot of adrenalin. But Broken Heart syndrome classically occurs immediately after the stressful event, and Mr. Grenslow did not fall sick until hours later, at a time when he seemed to be recovering. Perhaps, then, there could be more to it: if a surfeit of the body's own adrenalin supply can cause the heart to reshape itself, surely a surfeit of the hospital's adrenalin might do the exact same thing?

I am not saying that this happened. But what I do know is that Mr. Grenslow's room was on an isolated and little-traveled corridor, and from almost the moment he was admitted the entire hospital seemed to know he was there. There was not a permanent or even regular staff presence at his room, and if the St. Luke's killer had wished to dispatch Mr. Grenslow, it would have been straightforward enough. Moreover, doing so by injecting him with adrenalin—a drug which he would receive a large amount of during any attempted resuscitation—would have been effectively untraceable.

Dr. Sudbury seemed to have this same thought, because the next day I noticed the nurses on Jack Duckton checking the resuscitation cart. When I asked Angela about it, she told me Dr.

Sudbury had ordered an audit of all the adrenalin supplies in the hospital. A week later, Angela whispered to me the overall count had come up eight short. Things were always going missing in the hospital, so perhaps this was just the cost of doing business, but eight prefilled adrenalin syringes were more than would have been needed to dispatch poor old Mr. Grenslow.

I waited for the call from Afferson asking me to come down to Highbury police station for a "little chat," but it never came. He must have known about Albert Grenslow's demise and also that I had been his final doctor. His lack of interest puzzled me for a while, but I assumed Dr. O'Leary's report had convinced him there was no evidence of foul play, and perhaps he was anyway embarrassed by his own earlier credulous interest in the Angel of Death as a suspect.

CHAPTER 29

Amelia's work authorization from the health minister of Zambia had come through in early May. The hospital at Mbala had wanted her to start immediately, but being Amelia she had diligently worked her two-week notice at St. Luke's. She might as well not have bothered, because it was only delaying the inevitable. It was unlikely St. Luke's would be able to recruit even any doctor to take her place, and Amelia was not any doctor.

We had a farewell meal at an Indian restaurant in Brick Lane. Dr. Sudbury even came, and she told us that her own first boss had taught her that a consultant's most important duties were to pay for the meal and then leave. And so she did, but not before we toasted her with a drunken round of "She's a Jolly Good Fellow." It was the only time I ever saw her flustered. After she left, Rami made a joke about Dr. Sudbury taking her own advice and sending herself home at the earliest opportunity. We were all already so drunk it was the funniest thing any of us had ever heard.

It got more drunken still. Somebody made a toast to George, somebody else made another one, and soon we were all drowning in a boozy sea of toasts to our beloved George. We kept telling each other how he would have adored this, and how proud he would have been of Amelia for going anyway, but none of this could mask the devastating truth: there should have been two of them going to Zambia, and now there was only one. We ended up in a karaoke bar in Shoreditch, singing endless repetitions of Toto's "Africa." I think it was the drunkest I have ever been.

I was on call the next day and only got through the shift thanks to an arrest call to the pediatric oncology ward for a visiting grandparent who had collapsed. Grandad turned out to only be having a panic attack, but in the mayhem I was able to pocket a fentanyl lollipop from the kid's bedside cabinet.

It was not my finest hour, but the day Amelia actually departed was awful in an entirely different way. I had done the first of a week of night shifts, and arrived home in the morning to find her waiting for me on the doorstep. She told me that she had come to say goodbye to me, but I knew what she really wanted to do was sit once more in George's room. We had already packed up most of his stuff, but had not known what to do with it; his parents had said they wanted it, yet had made no arrangements to collect it, and his sports car likewise still languished in the hospital parking lot. Eventually, I would offer to hire a van and drive George's belongings up to them, but at that point they would ask me to simply find them a good home, and I would end up taking everything the charity shop. Well, everything except Patrick, who now sits by my desk and looks at me as I write this.

That Saturday morning, though, the boxes of George's things all remained in his room. Combined with Patrick and the framed photograph of the England rugby team that I hadn't had the heart to take down, it still felt like George might yet walk through the door at any moment. I made two cups of tea, and took them into George's room.

Amelia was sitting on the edge of his bed. She looked up and smiled as I entered, but this movement sent the tears that had welled in her eyes streaking down her cheeks. For once, I did not fetch tissues, because what use could any metaphor be when a true love was dead? Instead, I sat down beside Amelia and put my arm around her. She sunk her head into my shoulder and began to sob, the depth of her grief causing the very muscles of her diaphragm to spasm each time she took a breath. It was as if her body itself was protesting the sheer outrage of having to go on living.

I do not know how long we sat together, but I remember deciding that I would not move until Amelia did. I had not known how to offer her any solace since George died but now, finally, here I was: a literal shoulder to cry on. It seemed the very least I could do. After fifteen minutes, or perhaps an hour, I felt her begin to stir. And then she did something that took me entirely by surprise: she pulled my head to hers and kissed me.

I have thought so many times about what happened that morning, that sometimes I have even wondered if I simply imagined the whole thing in a somnambulant and grief-stricken fog. But alas, no, it happened.

I know it happened because Amelia kissed me with an urgency I can still sometimes feel. In the moment this surprised me as passion, and I even briefly flattered myself to think it might have had something to do with me. But it was not passion at all, but rather a kind of desperation and fury, a raging at the gaping void. Desperation that a life so large could be extinguished by a few drops of clear liquid, fury that hers had been ripped asunder by those same few drops. And rage at all of it, and all of us besides.

Perhaps Amelia had the excuse that she was somehow getting

her revenge on George for abandoning her. Or maybe being perfect is a near-impossible task at the best of times, and the exquisitely unfair arrival of such profound tragedy had simply brought her down to the same level as the rest of us. I have no such excuses for what occurred on my dead friend's bed that day, among all his sad things and with Patrick looking on. It was urgent and primal and it was over quickly, but even as it happened I knew that in a lifetime of wrongs it would forever stand out as the worst thing I had ever done.

When it was over, we fell asleep together, intertwined in our shame, or at least I thought we did. When I woke up it was six o'clock and dark, and Amelia would have already been halfway to Africa.

I felt terrible. That was not even unusual, for the circadian disturbances combined with the thought of having to work all night always made me feel rotten when I awoke ahead of a shift. Nonetheless, this particular evening was different, and I felt far worse than usual. I felt bereft.

No doubt what we had done was a large part of it, but it was not just that, nor was it even Amelia leaving, nor what had happened to George, nor with Collette, nor my own dismal situation. It was that everything felt like it had gone wrong, for everyone. Each one of us had been the top of his or her class all the way through primary school and high school, and just five or so years ago we had graduated from our universities and felt like we had the world at our feet. And now where were each of us? Behind in the life schedule we had mapped out, strung out on opioids, alone on a plane to Africa, or dead. The job was brutal and it brutalized each and every one of us. Many of our colleagues and classmates had begun to find solace in partners and weddings and homes, and the idea that they would have their own top-of-the-class kids someday soon, so no doubt some of us were lonelier than others. But all of us were lonely. Why?

Because of course we were. For many of us, the loneliness was what had brought us to medicine in the first place.

I stuck on a quarter of a buprenorphine patch I had taken from a patient with prostate cancer I'd seen on the urology ward, and went to work. It was Saturday night now, and the train was full of revelers: Londoners off to their drinks and their movies and their Chinese and Italian dinners with their dates, their spouses, their lovers. And here was me: alone at the back of the carriage, carrying the dismal peanut-butter sandwiches I probably wouldn't get time to eat until morning handover. Other people had lives and families and loved ones, and my job was to patch them up and send them back to those people and things. I did this at nights, on weekends and bank holidays.

At work that night, I had the distinct feeling the entire hospital was falling apart. Perhaps it really was coincidence that this happened as Amelia departed, but perhaps it was not. Amelia had been one doctor among dozens of us, but she was always so meticulously efficient that I wondered if the unnoticed things she did—the thorough clerkings, the endless rounding on her own patients, the "while you are here, Doctor" ward work that the nurses invariably asked her to do because she was the most approachable of all of us—had actually been the grease that kept the entire machine spinning.

Either way, I had never had a run of nights like it. It was not especially busy in terms of admissions, but the entire hospital seemed to be engulfed in a whirling chaos. A patient with a penicillin allergy was given a large intravenous dose of the drug, and I spent hours on Saturday night trying to stabilize him before a bed became available in the intensive care unit. Somehow the entire Sunday day shift then passed without anybody noticing the phlebotomist had not turned up for work, and that meant I had to begin my shift by bleeding what seemed like half the patients in the hospital. Even worse, at 10:00 p.m. on Monday night I walked into the Jack Duckton relatives' room to discover a group of adult siblings who had been waiting in there since before evening visiting; nobody had yet told them their grandmother had died several hours earlier.

More than anything, though, there was the paperwork: that week of nights was an endless paper trail of fluid charts, drug charts, and discharge summaries. Was it possible Amelia had single-handedly been doing all this work in addition to her own work? Yes, I realized as I wrote up yet another drug chart, it was more than possible. It was almost certain. Zambia was incredibly lucky to have her, but they had probably already worked that out by now. I only hoped that they would treat her more kindly and more carefully than George, London and even I had done.

CHAPTER 30

I somehow survived most of the week, and as we reached the end of Thursday evening's handover I began to think I might actually make it through to Friday morning. And then Colin got to the last patient on his list: Felix Smollett.

Even just hearing his name gave me a sinking feeling. The Jack Duckton nurses had been so embarrassed after grandmother-gate that I'd barely been called there all week, and I hadn't even thought of Felix. So when Colin mentioned him, I assumed the nurses had got bored arguing with him and wanted me to come and tell him he was not allowed any more methadone. That would have been bad enough, but Colin now informed me that Felix had spiked another fever.

Fever means something particular to medical people. I have heard non-doctor friends ascribe a fever to jet lag, eating spicy food, summer, being in a warm room, being in a cold room, and even having recently cleaned one's teeth. But they believe such things only because they do not comprehend just how spectacular the human body is at maintaining physiological homeostasis. Thirty-six point nine degrees Celsius is the correct temperature for the human body; a temperature even half a degree higher means that something is likely amiss, and another three and a half degrees beyond that is incompatible with human life. To a doctor, then, a fever is a check-engine light that guarantees something is afoot under the bonnet. Colin had taken cultures from Felix, so at least for now there was not much more to do. If he spiked again, it'd be for discussion with microbiology, but they would not have changed his antibiotics on the basis of a single fever.

So I did not immediately go to Jack Duckton ward. For all I knew, Felix's fever might simply represent an ordinary virus rather than a relapse in his endocarditis. Besides, there was a multiple sclerosis flare waiting in accident and emergency, and a chest pain in the tower. I went and sorted out the chest pain patient first, and was about to start in on the multiple sclerosis, when I was paged from Jack Duckton.

I rang back and Louise Fisher breathlessly answered, and told me that Felix had spiked another fever and urgently needed blood cultures taken. I reassured her Colin had done them earlier and another set showing the same thing would not change anything, but Louise replied that she had Felix's notes open in front of her, and the consultant microbiologist had quite clearly written that he was to have cultures each and every time he spiked. I hung up and headed out and across the parking lot.

When I got to his side room, I was surprised at how unwell Felix seemed. He looked as bad as he had on the night I had admitted him, and the lack of Ziggy Stardust makeup only made this more apparent. He was always pale, but this shade was no longer heroin chic but mortuary chic. He was sweating profusely, and as I stood in the doorway he erupted into a shivering rigor. The nurses had hooked him up to the monitors, and each one of these confirmed the dismal picture: his pulse was fast, his blood pressure was down to double digits, and his oxygen saturation was far short of what it should be. I suspect if I had listened closely, I'd probably have been able to hear his heart murmur from the doorway.

When he noticed me, Felix still somehow managed to muster a smirk and mumble something about his "brother in arms," which I assumed was a reference to our shared addiction. I cannot say if he said any more, because by then I was already back at the nurses' station and on the phone to the intensive care unit. The anesthetic registrar agreed that it sounded like Felix needed to be admitted, but apologized that there simply were not any beds. He promised to come and "take a look" as soon as he could, but we both knew there would be little he could possibly add on Jack Duckton ward.

I went back and examined Felix. His fever was thirty-nine point five, his murmur was much louder, and he was visibly short of breath. He declined to take his own blood now, and so I somehow found a femoral vein in his groin. I noticed several recent puncture marks there, but when I asked whether he had at least used the clean needles when injecting himself, he ignored me. I wrote him up for fast fluids, called for an X-ray, and asked Louise to give him acetaminophen for his fever. I told her I'd be back to review him when his bloods were in, but to call me if his blood pressure dropped any further.

Sometimes I wonder if I should have fought harder for the intensive care admission, but the registrar could not have simply conjured up a bed. Besides, I think deep down I knew there was nothing the intensive care unit could do for Felix, and the reason for that was there was nothing anybody could do for him. His infection had visibly become life-threatening, and there are only two treatments for that: remove the source, or hit it hard with antibiotics. Felix's infection was in his heart itself—so removing that would clearly come with its own issues—and he was already on antibiotics so broad and powerful that the pharmacy had to have them specially shipped in from Public Health England. Maybe in intensive care they could have supported his organ systems, but without a way to treat his infection it would realistically have only prolonged things.

I had just finished seeing the chest pain when the lab paged to tell me that Felix's white blood cell count had skyrocketed, a result that confirmed his infection was spiraling out of control. Some new bacteria had indeed been introduced, no doubt when he had been injecting himself. I called the microbiologist, and she confirmed Felix was already on absolutely everything she and her colleagues had been able to think of. She said I could always take another set of cultures, but the information would not be back in time to help him. Just about the only thing left to do, she said, was pray.

Even by the time I got back to Jack Duckton ward, Felix had deteriorated further. He was so drowsy that there was no smirking or even mumbling this time. I strapped a non-rebreathing oxygen mask around his mouth and nose, and turned the wall supply up until the little plastic ball was rammed to the top of the gauge. I wanted to know how dehydrated he was, so I asked the nurse to attach a manometer to his neck line in order that I could measure the filling pressure of his heart; when she looked at me blankly, I had Felix reclined at a forty-five-degree angle and got the nurse to hold his head to the left while I looked for the venous pulsations in his neck. When I could not see them, I gently pushed on his liver and the rising wave in his neck vein now confirmed that he was indeed dehydrated. We then gradually filled him up with fluid, checking the waveform in the veins on his neck every fifteen minutes to ensure I was not overfilling him. When this did not sufficiently raise his blood pressure, I started him on an adrenalin infusion. My pager kept going, and I kept ignoring it. Whatever else those calls might have been, they were not a young person actively dying. Felix quickly become unresponsive, and after half an hour Louise excitedly declared he had fallen into another coma.

At some point amid all this, I telephoned Felix's parents. I had been hoping his father would answer and I could get off the phone with a simple instruction for them to come to the hospital, but of course his mother picked up. I began with the usual spiel—that I was sorry to wake her, but I was calling from St. Luke's hospital—and Dr. Smollett immediately cut me off and demanded to know what her son's numbers were. I got as far as telling her his systolic blood pressure before she said they were on their way and hung up.

No doubt it was a temporary rally caused by the adrenalin, the oxygen and the fluids, but Felix briefly regained consciousness around 2:00 a.m. He seemed genuinely surprised to still be alive, and looked at me, struggled to place me, and then nodded with what I initially thought was recognition of me.

"I'm going to die tonight, amn't I?" he said.

I could only nod back. Felix had an untreatable infection and he was being kept alive with drugs that increased his blood pressure at the expense of his fingers and toes, and a toxic concentration of oxygen his lungs would not tolerate for more than a few hours. He seemed to accept the news that he was not long for this world with equanimity. He smiled faintly, and then asked me a peculiar question.

"Have you ever been to Prague, Doc?" he asked me.

I wasn't sure if I had heard him correctly, so I waited, and he repeated it.

"I asked if you've ever been to Prague?"

"No," I said, "I can't say I have."

"Well, you should. It's a very interesting place, Prague."

And then he smiled and closed his eyes, and after that he did not open them again.

I did not think much about the Prague stuff. The movies have taught us that people's last words are perfectly chosen epithets, but I have stood over enough death beds to know they are mostly nonsense. Yes, a few people want you to tell their families they love them, but mostly people's last words are as fallibly human as the lives that preceded them: sad, angry, lonely and—perhaps more than anything in a hospital like St. Luke's—simply confused. Too many times I have told families that Grandpa passed peacefully, when in fact he spent his last breaths screaming that he was being eaten alive by bats or crocodiles.

The anesthetist had been waylaid by a trauma case in theater, and arrived a little after 2:30 a.m., when Felix's blood pressure had already begun its final descent. Twenty minutes later his heart ceased beating, and we put the call out. He was young so he got the works—adrenalin every three minutes, bicarb every five, electricity because it could hardly make things worse—but it did not matter. His heart was filled with a pus that even our chest compressions simply pumped out around the rest of his body. At some point the anesthetist's boss—one of the few senior doctors in the hospital overnight—joined us. He was the one who called it at 3:20 a.m., but he left me to verify death: no breath or cardiac sounds heard, pupils fixed and dilated, absent corneal reflex, time of death, Rest in Peace.

By now, Felix's parents had arrived and were waiting in the relatives' room. I took a deep breath and went in to break the bad news, but Dr. Smollett ran our whole consultation. A glimpse through a half-closed door of the arrest team in her son's hospital room had told her everything she needed to know, and by the time I joined them she had already broken the bad news to his father. He sat in shocked silence, and Dr. Smollett simply wanted to know all the medical details: observations, doses, cycles, joules.

At the time I assumed she was looking for fault, but with hindsight I think it was simply her only way of making sense of it. Her son was twenty-eight years old and had been endlessly tipped for greatness, so his death was utterly unfathomable. By contrast, the death of a patient with endocarditis who had a systolic blood pressure in the fifties, and had not responded to eight doses of adrenalin or multiple attempts at defibrillation made a perfect if awful sense. The meeting lasted about ten minutes and concluded with Dr. Smollett saying they did not want to see their son looking "ghastly," and would much prefer to remember him as the handsome young man he had been.

Since the launch of Operation Nightingale, Dr. Sudbury had introduced a new policy that she was to be immediately informed of all unexpected deaths, and so I now called her. She initially seemed cross, first at being woken on a night when she was not on call, and then at the news of the unexpected death of a young person. When she heard it was a patient with endocarditis, and that he had been overwhelmingly septic, however, she seemed frankly pleased.

"They at least can't claim this one is a murder," Dr. Sudbury said, before catching herself. "I'll need to talk to the coroner to see if we can spare the family a postmortem, so don't write a death certificate just yet."

By morning handover Dr Sudbury had already spoken to the coroner, and the news was in that DI Afferson had insisted on a postmortem. I would have done the same thing in his position, and when I called Dr. Smollett to let her know, she seemed surprised we had thought there was any possibility Felix might be spared one. She asked me what I thought had killed her son, and I told her the truth: overwhelming sepsis. He had a fever, his white cell count was through the roof, his murmur was louder than it had been before, and the lack of other localizing symptoms seemed to seal the diagnosis.

"Yes," she said. "Yes, I do agree with all of that, of course. It was definitely sepsis from his heart. But why now? Why now when he had finally been getting better? Do you have any thoughts on that? I've never heard of a bacteria suddenly becoming resistant like that. Have you?"

Confidentiality rules dictated I should not have said anything to her, and yet she was a mother grieving her son. More than that, she was a colleague of sorts.

"I think he was still injecting," I said, "and maybe some new bacteria got in."

Dr. Smollett sounded surprised. "Really? I thought he was past all that. He was on methadone, but of course you know that. What makes you think he was still injecting?"

"There was an incident at New Year," I said. "The nurses noticed Felix was drowsy. He had pinpoint pupils and woke up with naloxone. And when I took blood from him last night, there were puncture wounds in his groin."

"Yes," Dr. Smollett sighed. "Yes, that would all make sense, I suppose."

"I'm sorry for your loss," I said.

"Thank you," she said. "But it's not your fault. You were the one who first diagnosed him, so you probably saved his life at that point. I mean, for all the good it did. But you tried. And I'm all the more impressed, given that you clearly didn't like him very much."

She hung up before I could protest, and I found that I was relieved she had. It would have been a lie, and she would have known it.

Dr. O'Leary—still expected to do his job, despite the public opprobrium heaped upon him—performed the postmortem. He found what we all knew he would: florid vegetations on Felix Smollett's valves, a heart that contained several small abscesses, and telltale track marks in the groin. He listed the cause of death as overwhelming sepsis secondary to infectious endocarditis, secondary to intravenous drug use.

When I went to the pathology lodge to sign my part of the death certificate, Dr. O'Leary led me to the body as usual. His respectful manner was unchanged, but he seemed to also feel paternal toward Felix Smollett. "He was so young," he lamented, "and so tremendously talented. It is a terrible shame. I hope the poor boy is at peace now." I had never heard Dr. O'Leary say such things about any other patient, and he closed his impromptu homily by telling me "Whom the gods love they take early." I did not believe in any gods, but still could not agree that they would particularly love Felix Smollett, unless those gods happened to be impressionable sixth form girls.

Even Dr. O'Leary's death certificate was not quite the end of the story, though, because DI Afferson now insisted on a second postmortem by a Home Office pathologist. Again, with the dead body of a semi-famous young person to account for, it was hard to blame him. The Home Office pathologist concurred with Dr. O'Leary's findings, but did now also have an additional piece of information: the blood cultures Colin had sent the night Felix Smollett died had grown a rare species of *clostridium* that was most commonly found in desert soil.

As this was an entirely different bacteria from the *staphylococcus* that had originally been grown, or any of the many others that had followed, the obvious explanation—and the one both pathologists concurred on—was that Felix had introduced the bacteria when he was injecting himself. Quite how he could end up with such a dirty needle when I had given him two boxes of clean ones was a puzzle, but not enough of a puzzle for anyone to investigate further. Likewise, the relative rarity of the bacteria was worthy of little more than a raised eyebrow and a puzzled shrug. Sometimes people die.

Healthcare murder is such a heinous crime that we tend to look only for the most powerful motives: greed, lust, love, severe psychological damage. But we overlook pettier concerns at our peril.

In 1965, surgical patients at Riverdell Hospital in New Jersey began to die unexpectedly in the post-operative period. One recently hired surgeon, Dr. Stanley Harris, lost five patients including Nancy Savino, a four-year-old girl who died after a routine appendix operation. Dr. Harris investigated the deaths, and quickly noted the similarities: the patients had all died of a sudden respiratory arrest, they all had intravenous access, and the head of the surgical department, Dr. Mario Jascalevich, had been in the immediate vicinity of all the patients shortly before they died.

Dr. Jascalevich had worked at Riverdell Hospital for twenty years. He was highly respected for his surgical skill, but his colleagues considered him abrasive, and he was known to have strongly disapproved of the hospital's recent expansion. One colleague described Dr. Jascalevich as "not the kind of person you'd go for a beer with."

Dr. Harris' investigation into the deaths at Riverdell led him and hospital management to Dr. Jascalevich's locker. There, they found what seemed a smoking gun: eighteen mostly empty vials of curare, a powerful anesthetic drug. Utilized correctly, curare paralyzes the respiratory muscles in order to allow a mechanical ventilator to take over the work of breathing; used without a ventilator, a single dose of curare can cause a respiratory arrest of the kind the Riverdell patients had all died from.

Dr. Jascalevich admitted the curare belonged to him, but claimed it was for a program of experiments he had been conducting. He provided no other context or supporting evidence for this independent research program, but was neither arrested nor charged. Dr. Jascalevich left Riverdell soon after, and the unexplained deaths immediately ceased.

A decade later, a tip-off led to the New York Times publishing a story about the Riverdell deaths, and New Jersey prosecutors subsequently ordered an investigation. Five bodies were exhumed and traces of curare were found in three of them, including that of Nancy Savino.

Dr. Jascalevich's trial was the longest in the history of the state of New Jersey. At its heart was an unspeakably gruesome notion: the prosecution charged that Dr. Jascalevich had murdered twenty-five patients merely to make his recently hired colleagues look incompetent, and thereby demonstrate that he had been correct in opposing the hospital's expansion.

The trial was hampered by the years that had passed, the complexity of the evidence, and a sideshow around the jailing of the New York Times journalist who had received the tip-off. Dr. Jascalevich was ultimately acquitted, but the court of public opinion found him guilty: the State Board of Medical Examiners withdrew his license, and the negative publicity quickly bankrupted Riverdell.

CHAPTER 31

When news of Felix Smollett's death broke, it made the national news. The BBC called him **"THE MOST PROMISING SONGWRITER OF HIS GENERATION."** There was talk of a tribute album, and possibly even a statue outside a squat where he had debuted his best-known song.

Even that all seemed a little much to me, and yet it was merely the beginning. On the following Friday, I left work to find over two hundred people holding a candlelit vigil in the hospital parking lot. There were the usual sixth form girls, of course, but others too: students, older couples, a few faces I recognized from television, Felix's parents, and even a Buddhist monk.

Eliza Duckton made an improbable but inevitable speech about how Felix and her war hero father were undoubtedly now united in heaven. Mrs. Horsburgh was not mentioned, having now apparently been usurped by the arrival in the afterlife of a more newsworthy companion. The Buddhist monk then gave some kind of blessing that a translator explained "would permit

Felix's beautiful soul to soar free"; I don't know how accurate that was, because I saw the monk frown when the translator said this. Finally, the crowd lit candles in the daylight then united in murdering John Lennon's "Imagine." The whole thing left me feeling more wretched than I had in quite a while. George had been the best human I had known, and the wider world had not given a single shit when he died. Now, within sight of the car inside which he had departed this life, perfect strangers were lighting incense in memory of an obnoxious young man who had only ever thought of himself.

And so I went home, ran a hot bath, lit my own candles, took double my usual dose of pethidine, and got in. As the hot water encased my body from the outside, so the pethidine warmed me from within. As the candles flickered around me, I decided it was the fire and I was water, or I was the fire and it was the water. Whatever it was, it consumed me in the exact way I needed it to, and I slunk down into it all, grateful for the release.

I awoke at 4:00 a.m., shivering in cold water in the dark. It took me a moment to realize what had happened, and I chided myself for having been so stupid. Nobody would have found me for a long time. If I had been trying to die, there were certainly far better ways of ending it all, ways that would not result in a tabloid headline that said **"MURDER INQUIRY DOC LAY DEAD IN BATH FOR DAYS."** I dried myself off, crawled into bed, and slept until the afternoon.

When I woke, I walked around the flat and, as I increasingly did, found myself back in George's room. I wondered again why it had been him and not me, but mostly I marveled at the wreckage of my own life. Was it the shift work and the endless disease and death that had made me an addict and an outcast? Or had I chosen this life because—somewhere deep down—I had always known that I was such a person? I asked Patrick, but he of course had no more of an idea than I did, and he still had not forgiven me for what had happened with Amelia. I did not blame him, for I had not forgiven myself either.

Whichever way around it had happened, I fell ever faster and harder. I no longer had to answer to Collette—she had stopped even acknowledging me when we passed in the corridors—and George and Amelia were both forever lost to me, but somehow it seemed to be the death of Felix Smollett that had broken this camel's back. While he was alive I could not stand the guy, and yet he was undeniably another young person gone, another heart and lungs silent over two minutes. Perhaps too, we had also been more alike than either of us had cared to admit. Perhaps we really had been brothers in arms.

And that being so, maybe it was because I no longer encountered the Ghost of Christmas Future on the ward round each morning that I began to take risks I would not have considered even a few weeks earlier. I got careless with the discharge prescription scam, sometimes performing it multiple times a day. Worse, I even found a new grift on it: I noted any patients I encountered who were legitimately on an opioid, and when it came time to discharge them, helped myself to half of their take-home medication. This was especially dangerous, because I was no longer stealing opioids from patients who had no idea they had been prescribed them. I was stealing opioids from patients who knew exactly what they were entitled to, and were likely every bit as addicted as me.

Increasingly, too, I used at work. One afternoon in clinic I even nodded off as I was examining an elderly patient, but when she gently woke me she only sympathized about the terrible hours we were made to work. More or less the same thing happened at my counseling, but fortunately the Reverend Mc-Kendrick was himself already asleep and I still woke before him. Even when I was not actively falling asleep, I did the same tell-tale things all addicts do: I was late, I lied, I forgot to eat, and I yawned and sneezed far more than any normal human should. I worked daily among people trained to spot exactly these things, but nobody ever did. Maybe nobody was looking, or maybe they simply did not want to see.

But it did not matter, because I could not stop. Each morning when I woke I shuddered at the spiral I was in, and vowed that one day soon I would fix it all. But a few minutes later, once the pill was in my mouth, I had forgotten everything again. The world was golden. I was submerged in a warm candlelit bath, even on the ward or the admission unit. Morphine is endorphins, and endorphins are morphine. It is not rocket science. And neither is what happened next.

Every addict starts out saying we will never inject. It is the one line that must never be crossed, and the very fact that it is so utterly unbreachable renders everything this side of it safe: if you only don't cross the line, then the worst consequences can never befall you. Yet the more time you spend in the golden state, the more that line begins to look thin, and then blurred, and then faded, until some day you wake up and realize that there is no line, there never has been a line. There is only the blissful feeling, and more of it exists just on the other side of wherever you once imagined that line to be.

For me, it was nothing more than pragmatism that finally obliterated the line. An irate pharmacist had paged me to ask why a patient who had been admitted with a mild pneumonia was now going home with a two-week supply of pethidine? I had played dumb, and told her that the patient had told me they took it for back pain. The pharmacist retorted that she had contacted the GP, who had confirmed the patient had never once been prescribed pethidine. She scolded me that I had to be more careful, and that I should never simply take a patient at their word where opioids were concerned. I had got away with it that time, but I knew she would be looking out for the word "pethidine," and that supply would now be closed to me, at least for a while.

When I was down to my last strip of pills, I grew desperate, but then made a discovery: perhaps due to the fact they have fewer addicts in London than in Glasgow, the staff at St. Luke's were far less protective of the controlled drugs than their northern cousins. In Scotland, the nurses had guarded the keys to the controlled drug cabinet like precious jewels. If ever you needed morphine, they would grudgingly fetch it for you only having first ascertained which patient it was for, and the nurse had better already have heard them screaming in agony. By contrast, when you asked for morphine at St. Luke's, the nurse simply tossed you the keys and told you to make sure you locked the cupboard afterward.

The first time I injected was in a cubicle in the staff toilets of level nine of the tower. I did not want to do so, but what choice did I have? The vial was in liquid form; drinking it was spectacularly inefficient, and I needed to get as much of it into my body as quickly as I could. And so, to my veins. It was not like I was not already good at it: I made it up in a 10 ml syringe, tightened the same tourniquet I used on my patients around my own upper arm, and swabbed the inner crease of my elbow with alcohol until the veins stood out like drainpipes.

That first time I was cautious, pushing the morphine in at a milliliter a minute over ten minutes. I didn't feel much for the first thirty seconds, but as soon as it reached my heart and started its journey around the body I understood why people injected. The hit was infinitely stronger and better than I could have ever imagined. Whereas previously I'd felt pethidine as honey trickling down my spine, injecting morphine was a whole other level. It was as if my spine was now honey. Or I was honey. Or everything was honey.

When I was finished, I gathered up every piece of wrapping, even the needle sheath, and deposited them in a sharps bin several floors away. I quickly got more careless, and soon it became open season. When a nurse made a joke about all the opioids I had been giving my patients, I changed up and began taking my samples to the blood-gas machine in the theater suite so that I could swipe vials from unattended anesthetic rooms. I did something similar in the oncology wards, and once or twice even in the pediatric wards. Really, I am surprised I lasted as long as I did.

When the end came, on a stiflingly warm Friday in June, it was spectacular. I was on call that day and had not managed to score in over twenty-four hours. I was therefore withdrawing while also admitting an unseasonal number of patients. As evening handover approached, I had resigned myself to not getting hold of any opioids that day, but then an arrest call went out for a major trauma involving a pedestrian and a motorcyclist. The pedestrian had already been down for forty-five minutes when she arrived in the department and so we quickly called it, but in the next bed the surgeons were reducing the motorcyclist's fractures before taking him to theater. He weighed 280 pounds, and was going through morphine like it was water. I palmed two vials into my pocket as I left the department.

At handover I could feel the cold glass against my leg, and ran through the patient list as quickly as I could. Kwame asked why I was rushing, and I mumbled something about it having been a long day and also expecting a phone call at home that night. It was an excuse too many, and I could tell that he knew I was lying, but it was still better than admitting I was desperate to get home so that I could inject myself with the opioids I had just stolen.

Home was twenty minutes away if I got lucky with the trains, but up to forty if I didn't. Even that seemed too long to wait, and as I hurried across the parking lot I realized I still had George's car keys in my bag. I walked over to his car, unlocked the door, and got into the driver's seat, the same place where George had sat to end it all.

I had left my tourniquet in my locker, so I took the belt from my trousers and drew it tight around my arm. I looked for a vein, but it was dusk and the shadows made it hard to see. I chided myself: years ago, I had been taught that locating a vein was never about the look, but about the feel. Sure enough, I used my fingers and found the bounce of my houseman's vein. Unlike George, I hit it first time: I felt a give as the needle breached the skin, and then a second one as it entered the vein. I felt them so clearly that I would not even have needed to see the flashback of blood into the chamber of the syringe, but I did see it. Even in the half-light I saw it. And then I pushed in the whole 10 mls.

Soon everything was honey. I was alive. It did not matter. It was better than did not matter. It was hilarious. Everything was wonderful. Collette was doing fine, wherever the hell she was. George might be dead and Amelia gone to save the world, but none of that mattered. I found myself thinking of the Percherons and the Westphalians and laughed out loud. Why was I laughing? Why would I not? I was the greatest physician who had ever lived, for I had found the cure to what ailed me. Everything was golden and would be forever. The only thing was, I really needed to drive this car. It was what George would have wanted, to keep the engine turning over. Things failed if they were not regularly used, and what harm could it possibly do?

Out of the parking lot, and on to the street. It was years since I had driven any car, and even George had frequently complained how awkward his little sports car was to handle. But it was all okay, because the morphine had made me a natural. I took side streets and high streets, and each half mile and mile I traveled was more golden than the last as the glorious morphine saturated every receptor in my brain. The bookmakers and launderettes were a painting of which the great William Morris could only have dreamed. Or maybe even Blake himself. Yes, they were melancholic, but they were also beautiful, and then the rain started and turned them and the rest of the city into an impressionist's painting: *Night at the Kebab Shop; Bingo Palace Rhapsody; The Eternal Service Station.*

I cannot say where I went, or for exactly how long I drove. I know only that it got dark, and at some point I found my way onto the North Circular. For the past year I had done what I could for its pilgrims and victims, filling them with blood and fluids and adrenalin while the orthopods worked out how to piece them back together. So I knew its dangers as well as anyone, but I also knew that this road would not hurt me. How could it, when we were so intimately connected? We understood each other, the road and I, and anyway I was invincible, and anyway none of it even mattered, for it was all golden, it was all honey.

I wove in and out of traffic like the race-car driver I should have been, the fast lane to the slow lane, and back across once more. And all the time I felt my foot pressed hard against the floor. At some point I rolled down the window and let the air and the summer rain at me. I felt the cobwebs of the dead blow away, and the rain baptize me into my new and born-again life. I told myself it was what George would have wanted. I turned on the stereo and discovered that George—never not the cliché—had been listening to Bruce Springsteen. Soon I was no longer simply a race-car driver winning yet another Grand Prix. I was an American, driving on a lonesome highway toward a sultry woman who waited somewhere on a porch where a screen door banged in the breeze. I cranked up the volume further, and that is the last thing I remember.

The police's primary witness was the driver of the dairy tanker I overtook shortly before I clipped the crash barrier at the side of the road. He reported seeing the sparks, and then the MG leaving the ground and flipping several times through the air but somehow ultimately landing right side up before plowing straight into the central reservation. Meantime, he himself had braked so abruptly that the forward momentum of his load tore it from its coupling and his cargo now overtook him and skidded down the urban motorway. It was painted black and white like a Friesian cow, and it must have been quite the sight: a giant mechanical cow hurtling through the night, spraying milk all over the North Circular as it pursued a wrecked little sports car. If I had not already been unconscious, I am sure I would have appreciated it.

A minicab driver was the first to reach George's car, and he reported it was such a wreck that he initially assumed the driver was dead until he heard me snoring. He reached in, shook me and shouted, but later told the police that I seemed to simply be fast asleep. The helicopter doctors arrived on scene within fifteen minutes, and it was one of them who noticed my pinpoint pupils and informed the arriving police, who arrested me even while the firemen were cutting me out of George's car. I had a punctured lung, which did not really need to be tubed but the helicopter team must have wanted the practice because they did so anyway. They even gave me naloxone to reverse the opioids. Given the fact that my fractured fibula was visibly poking through my skin, I can only imagine they did that out of spite. Spite may also be why they sent me to St. Luke's in an ambulance rather than taking me to the Royal London in their helicopter; I was still wearing my ID badge, so they certainly knew where I had come from.

By the time we reached accident and emergency the naloxone had kicked in, and I was wide awake. I asked the policeman who was sat with me to draw the curtain around the cubicle so that my passing colleagues could not see that I was handcuffed to the bed. He obliged, but of course it did not matter. Everybody already knew what had happened.

The A+E registrar treating me was at least a locum I had not met before. He examined me thoroughly, sent me for X-rays and scans, then pronounced the damage: three broken ribs and a fractured fibula that looked to him like it might need to be pinned, but the orthopods would decide that. I called it a "femular," but the locum registrar didn't laugh. He at least agreed the chest tube was unnecessary, and took it out then and there.

Saz was working nights and she stopped in. I could tell that she had been crying, and I found myself surprisingly moved by that, but she then told me that if ever I wanted to talk about George I could. That made me feel like a shit, because of course I did not want to talk about George. What I had done had not even been remotely about George. At least, at the time I did not think it had been about George. At this distance, I view things a little differently.

The orthopods concluded I did not require an operation, just reduction, a cast, pain control, and mobilization. Nonetheless, I spent a week on the orthopedic ward, I suspect because nobody felt comfortable sending me home with the opioids I legitimately needed for pain control. For the first few days the nurses treated me with the cool professional distaste I myself had once reserved for patients with entirely self-inflicted injuries, but once word got around I was George's grieving friend they started to be nice to me and even moved me to a side room. I was not above playing up to this by asking each new nurse if she had known George. I stopped doing this when one of the younger nurses burst into tears, and I felt like a shit once again.

A few colleagues from the medical team came to see me, but most of them did not, and I was grateful to them for saving us both the embarrassment. On the second day, Dr. Sudbury came in and encouraged me to walk around: the sooner I did that, she said, the sooner I could be discharged. She sympathetically asked if I was bored and when I admitted I was, she offered to bring me some discharge summaries to audit. Later that day, I woke from a nap to find Collette stood at the end of my bed. I awkwardly thanked her for coming, but she informed me in clipped tones that she was only there because my bruised spleen made me a surgical patient. She took my charts and must have left them at the nurses' station when she was finished with them, because she did not reappear.

On the third day, I received a surprise visitor: the Reverend McKendrick. For the first time since I had begun seeing him, I was actually somewhat interested in what he might say. I had been doing a lot of thinking as I started at the ceiling, and it was abundantly clear that I desperately needed somebody's help.

But the Reverend McKendrick had not come to offer me support, nor even to reassure me he would be praying for me. No, he had taken the bus to the hospital solely to scold me for lying to him. He told me that my relapse would look terrible on his appraisal, and it was unspeakably selfish of me not to have considered that factor when I "indulged myself." I turned the other cheek—by which I mean I closed my eyes and pretended to be asleep—and waited for him to leave. He soon fell silent, and for a moment I worried I'd horribly miscalculated as it seemed like he might have fallen asleep too. After a few minutes, I heard him sigh and get up and leave.

I must have actually fallen asleep soon thereafter, because when I woke up DI Afferson was sat in the chair by my bed. I was surprised to see him, but even more so by the feeling his presence gave me: relief. Afferson was like Sherlock Holmes compared to the traffic cops who had taken my statement, and I wanted to ask him what neither they nor anybody else had so far been able or willing to tell me: Just how much trouble was I now in?

Afferson shocked me by announcing that he'd "had a word" and got my charges "knocked down" as far as he could. I had clearly been guilty of driving without insurance and there was nothing he could do about the automatic fine and points on my license, but as he put it "Nobody had been killed." The drugs, of course, were another thing entirely, but that was between me and the General Medical Council. None of any of that, he said, was a matter for Operation Nightingale.

Operation Nightingale. In all the excitement I had barely thought about the danger lurking at St. Luke's. Belatedly, I realized I should have been paying more attention to the medicines I was being given each day, lest I became the next victim. Mostly, though, I wondered if Afferson had reverted to believing I was the culprit, and simply did not want any traffic offenses delaying the murder conviction he was still planning to get me. Even with all the wishful thinking in the world, I could not think of any more convincing reason for him to have intervened on my behalf.

Still, I played along. Afferson told me that he had come to ask me about George again, and he hoped that the good faith he had shown by helping me might now be reciprocated. Specifically he thought that perhaps me driving George's car—well, maybe there was some significance in that? I told him the truth: I'd discovered the keys in my pocket as I left work, and my late flatmate's beloved sports car had simply been a convenient place to shoot up.

We sat in silence for a moment and then Afferson cut to the chase: What could I tell him about George's final afternoon? He told me they knew that George had returned to the flat we shared, but nobody—not Amelia, nor George's boss, nor his parents—had any idea why he would have done such a thing in the middle of the working day. I briefly wondered why they had not asked me about this sooner when they had clearly spoken to everyone else about it, but Occam's razor provided the answer: they had still thought I might be involved, and had not wanted to tip me off. I asked Afferson why they had not searched the flat and Afferson, seemingly caught off guard, admitted it was because they had not been able to obtain a warrant.

I then asked him why they even believed George had gone home. I explained that if they were relying on the word of a neighbor who merely thought she heard some undefined banging, that was probably not the best idea. Afferson acknowledged they had interviewed the neighbor, but said they had not been relying on her evidence. Instead, they had tracked George's movements using CCTV, and he had indeed gone back to the flat that afternooon.

This took me by surprise: both that George had definitely returned home, and even more so that Afferson had gone to the trouble of having the CCTV checked to establish this. Operation Nightingale was supposed to be about catching a serial killer, not establishing the minutiae of the last moments of a suicidal junior doctor. I felt the old claustrophobia recur, then, and asked Afferson why he was so interested in this.

Afferson mumbled something vague about "dotting every i and crossing every t." He did this so convincingly that I might have even believed him if he had not then begun to talk about the potassium George had used. It troubled him, he said, that George had obtained it from Jack Duckton ward. Why had he not just obtained it from his own ward? I said I did not know, and acknowledged that this was a question that still kept me awake at night too.

But Afferson seemed to have given the subject more consideration than even I had. As George had not obtained the potassium before leaving the orthopedic ward, Afferson had concluded that George had not been intending to kill himself at that point. His decision to kill himself must logically therefore have been made sometime between leaving level six and asking Louise Fisher for the potassium on Jack Duckton ward.

George had gone to the canteen to eat lunch during this period, but Afferson thought it unlikely anything untoward had happened there. After all, George had been given an extra large portion of beef Wellington, and the colleagues that ate with him that day had reported that he seemed to be in his usual good spirits. He had then set off and, as far as they could tell, he had proceeded straight from the canteen to Jack Duckton ward to see a referral.

And that was where they had drawn a blank. Louise believed George may have seen Felix Smollett, but Felix himself had denied this and George had not written anything in the notes, so it seemed likely he had not. Likewise, beyond the fact that he had asked for potassium, there seemed to be nothing untoward about George's conversation with Louise. The most critical time period, according to Afferson's hypothesis, had therefore occurred between George leaving the canteen and arriving on Jack Duckton ward. What had happened during that time to make George not only kill himself, but first go home and then return to the hospital to do so?

I didn't have any idea. I told Afferson that as far as I knew I had not even encountered George at the hospital that day. He nodded and asked me what I made of George going home. I speculated that it may have been an abortive attempt: perhaps George had planned to kill himself at home that afternoon, but when he got there had been unable to go through with it? Finding himself still alive at 4:00 p.m., his sense of duty had kicked in, and he had returned to the hospital to do the afternoon ward round. Afterward, he had decided to get the thing done then and there.

Occam would not have approved of this explanation, and Afferson, who now took his leave, was clearly equally unimpressed by it. It required several separate things to be true—that George had first planned to kill himself at home, that he had thought better of it, that he had felt compelled to return to do the ward round, that he had then decided to do it at the hospital after all—and that is not how good diagnoses work. I had the feeling that there was some crucial piece of information that I was missing, and if only I could deduce it then—like an elusive unifying diagnosis—everything would fall into place.

CHAPTER 32

Ihad a lot of time to ponder my missing unifying diagnosis, because instead of being discharged home I was transferred without explanation to something called The Healing Place, for a month of drug rehabilitation. Despite its bohemian name, The Healing Place turned out to be a rundown sanatorium on the windswept Norfolk coast. For most of its existence it had been known as the Royal Benevolent Home for Sick Physicians, but it had recently undergone a rebrand, at least on its stationery. The old name remained emblazoned across the building, and the patients and our collective hopelessness did not seem to have changed much either.

There were a dozen of us sick physicians, nine of whom were alcoholics. The remaining three were a gynecologist with an eating disorder, a general practitioner with a gambling addiction, and myself, a junior doctor with a pethidine habit. We each got our own room, which I suppose was a small mercy.

During office hours, The Healing Place was run by a disinterested matron, with a local psychiatrist visiting on Mondays and every second Friday. The rest of the time we had the drafty old building to ourselves. There was a compulsory group therapy session every Tuesday, and an optional one every Thursday. I only ever went to the Tuesday one and it was quite dire enough, with all twelve of us enthusiastically formulating treatment plans for each other while showing no interest whatsoever in helping ourselves. Only the gynecologist and the general practitioner regularly attended the voluntary session; in my last week it became clear why, when they announced their plans to leave their respective spouses and open a pub together.

I spent most of my time walking on the nearby beach and sheltering in the café where the local teenagers met to smoke cigarettes. For the first week I still had my leg cast on, but after a trip to Norfolk Hospital to remove it, I started to go farther and farther. Midway through my second week I discovered a pub in a village four miles away, and this became a daily pilgrimage. When the matron found out I had been going there, she asked me not to tell the others there was a pub nearby, but told me she was pleased at how much I was walking.

But I was not walking so far out of a commitment to my rehabilitation, or at least not consciously. There was no possible way for me to obtain opioids, and I was walking so far because the two pints I allowed myself were the only thing that even briefly took away my yearning. The walk itself also gave me time to think about George.

Over and again, I returned to his afternoon trip home to our flat. Why had he made it? He had not mentioned meeting a tradesman, and as far as I knew the landlord had not even visited the flat when George moved in. The planned-for-home-then-completed-at-work suicide seemed absurd, and so what was left? George was endlessly pragmatic, so it was not impossible he had discovered some bit of administration that needed doing before he departed forever, but our phone bill showed no outgoing calls, and Afferson had told me George's bank account showed no transactions that day. Could there, then, have been some physical reason for George to have gone home before ending it all? Some object he had either needed to collect from or deposit at the house? I wondered about his car keys, but George had always kept them, along with his house keys, clipped to his ID badge. Moreover, there had been nothing unusual on him when he died, and I had packed up his room and not even found so much as a hidden pornographic magazine.

One smaller mystery was at least solved when the psychiatrist told that me at my exit interview that my stay at The Healing Place had been funded by St. Luke's. It made a certain kind of sense, because the whole notion of an asylum specifically for sick doctors was so antiquated that only somebody like Dr. Sudbury, who was old enough to remember the good old days, would even have known such a place existed.

The psychiatrist had apologized that she'd had little else to add, but what even could she have? She was as well-intentioned and hopelessly overworked and under-resourced as the rest of us. She gave me the usual recommendations—cognitive behavioral therapy, a support group, hypnotherapy, exercise—and offered to prescribe me an antidepressant if I thought it would help. I declined and she agreed it probably would not help much, because my primary problem was not depression, but something more intractable. She then told me the most honest thing I'd ever heard from a doctor: life was hard, and the trick was just to stay alive however you could, because sometimes you got a run where the good days outnumbered the bad.

Still, there was at least one tangible benefit to my stay at The Healing Place. It was the only facility in the country specifically approved for treatment of sick doctors, and my sojourn there meant that I had not been summarily struck off the medical register. That would still happen in a month or two at my delayed General Medical Council hearing, but it at least meant that I would be able to earn a little money and work out what on earth I was going to do with my life now.

CHAPTER 33

I had only been back at work for two weeks when they made the arrest. Up until that point, my return to St. Luke's had all gone surprisingly smoothly: nobody had so much as made a single joke, and even the sympathetic and inquisitive glances I had initially caught in the canteen and mess had quickly tailed off.

I was working in a cubicle on Jack Duckton, wrestling a catheter into an elderly man with a prostate the size of a tennis ball. It was only when I finally got the damn thing in that I noticed the ward had fallen strangely silent. I finished up the job and pulled the curtains back to reveal DI Afferson, DS Newington, Dr. Sudbury and two uniformed police officers. One of the uniforms already had his handcuffs out.

Afferson and I stared at each other. Contrary to what people often say, in that brief moment I did not see my life flash before my eyes. I saw it disappear. For all the bad things I had actually done, it seemed absurd that I was now going to spend the rest of my life in prison for things I hadn't.

But something was wrong. The policeman with handcuffs did not move toward me, and somehow they all seemed as surprised to see me as I was to see them.

"Oh, for fuck's sake!" Afferson eventually said.

It turned out they were not here to arrest me, but somebody else they mistakenly thought had been behind the curtains. I did not get the chance to ask who they had actually been waiting for, because right then Louise Fisher emerged from the break room, and DI Afferson arrested her on suspicion of twelve counts of murder.

DS Newington then began to read her rights, and Louise fainted right there in the ward. One of the uniforms half caught her, and reflexively tried to hold her up, when the whole point of fainting is that evolution designed it to allow the prostrate body to restore blood flow to the head. Dr. Sudbury therefore attempted to wrestle the policeman off Louise, and all three of them fell to the ground in an ungainly heap.

Nobody was seriously hurt, and Dr. Sudbury and the policeman swiftly both got to their feet. With the blood flow to her brain now restored, Louise quickly regained consciousness, although she no doubt wished that she hadn't. Afferson asked me if Nurse Fisher was medically cleared to be taken to the police station, but before I could reply that I would need to examine her and run some tests, Dr. Sudbury stated that Louise was absolutely cleared, adding that she was sure that Louise would go with them quietly, as there was no need to create any more of a scene. Apparently relieved to have been told what to do, Louise offered up her wrists, was handcuffed, and was escorted off the ward.

From the live pictures that every television in the ward soon cut to, it was clear that a scrum of journalists and television crews were waiting outside the hospital. Later, people would talk about how they had immediately known Louise Fisher was guilty because she did not seem remotely surprised in that footage. I somehow even remembered it that way for a long time too. But I recently found some of it online and it is true that Louise did not look surprised as she was led out from St. Luke's that day. She looked terrified.

Afferson would later insist that the police had not tipped off the press, but realistically nobody else could have done it. He also just happened to have a statement prepared, which he read aloud while his colleagues put Louise in the car. It was all about how it had been a long and fiendishly complex investigation, but the Metropolitan Police, and specifically the expert team at Operation Nightingale, hoped this arrest would reassure the public. And while he was sure that everybody would understand there was a limit to what he was able to say, he could certainly state with confidence that they were not looking for anybody else in connection with the heinous crimes that had taken place at St. Luke's.

CHAPTER 34

Predictably, the tabloids christened Louise Fisher "The Angel of Death." The previous Angel of Death, the late Albert Grenslow, was not even mentioned as a footnote. No doubt he would have preferred it that way.

The story dominated the headlines for weeks: Louise's lawyer said she was denying all charges and looked forward to clearing her name; a High Court judge granted a further forty-eight hours for questioning; Louise's original lawyer asked to be removed from the case; an infamous barrister took her case; Louise was then charged and remanded in custody; bail was denied due to the gravity of the offenses; Louise had been transferred to remand at Durham Prison, where many of the country's worst female killers were housed.

Meantime, reporters and television news crews from all around the world lay siege to St. Luke's. Dr. Sudbury had her hair cut in a surprisingly fashionable bob, put on lipstick, and gave numerous interviews. She claimed this was all in the interests of reassuring the local community, but quite how many East London pensioners she imagined would see a live interview on a South Korean twenty-four-hour news channel was unclear. Anyway, our patients seemed to have little need for reassurance: accident and emergency reported twice as many attendances as in the preceding weeks.

But it was not just the patients. Every time I went to review a patient on another ward, a member of staff would ask me if I had known Louise Fisher. When I acknowledged I had, they asked me if with hindsight there had been any clues. Over and again, I told them about the Christmas Day I had spent answering her incessant pages, and the presentation she had given about the belladonna woman.

A week after the arrest, I did a weekend of long days and spent my lunch looking through that day's papers in the mess. The *Mail* had an interview with a woman who had been Louise's teacher in primary school, and now claimed she had always known that she was "a wrong 'un who would come to a sticky end." Someone who had apparently been a childhood friend told the *Daily Record* a troubling story about Louise dismembering dolls. The *Mirror* reported that the Angel of Death was being held in solitary confinement for her own safety; the *Sun* countered with the information that Louise had in fact made herself popular by providing medical advice to her fellow inmates. The *Guardian* ran a think piece on why women kill and who the men responsible are. Most interesting, though, was the *Telegraph*: their legal expert had spotted something in the court filings that implied that the two sides were negotiating a plea deal for Louise Fisher.

Diverting as all this was, I still had my own legal woes to worry about. In late July, my fitness to practice hearing was held at the General Medical Council's offices in a Georgian terrace opposite Regent's Park. The grand building and its stuffy atmosphere were a world away from the ramshackle facilities and sellotape-and-string service we ran at St. Luke's. It did not seem a good omen.

A summary of my last hearing was read out—the one in Scotland, where I had earnestly pledged never to stray again—and then a retired senior pharmacist from St. Elsewhere's testified to the 427 tablets of pethidine I had stolen at St. Luke's. The real number was actually far higher, because they had somehow not caught me helping myself to any legitimate prescriptions, nor had they realized I had been taking vials to inject, because the syringe I had used had mercifully been destroyed in the wreckage of George's car.

But it hardly mattered. If I had arrived harboring any delusions that they might show mercy, I had known I was toast from the moment I walked into the room. At all my previous hearings, the panel had been reassuringly courteous and had made a point of addressing me as "Doctor." Now none of them so much as made eye contact, and it was obvious they were planning to throw the book at me.

I briefly wondered again what I would do, but came to the same conclusion as always: there was not much to wonder about, for there are not many career options open to a disbarred doctor. Even if this somehow did manage to stay out of the papers, the only thing I was remotely qualified to do was work in a hospital, but after my registration was permanently erased I would not have been able to get a job washing the dishes in the kitchen.

The evidence was undisputed, and even included a statement from the Reverend McKendrick describing me as "the most duplicitous and Satan-touched soul he had encountered in a half century of pastoral work." The hearing therefore did not take long.

As the Chair of the panel prepared to pass sentence, I half expected him to place a piece of black cloth atop his head. Instead, an administrator entered and whispered in his ear. The Chair seemed surprised and a little irritated by what he had heard, but announced that another witness had arrived and had requested to give evidence. I wondered who might have had enough of a vendetta against me to drag themselves into town to declaim me when the result was already a foregone conclusion. The thought made me shudder: the Wilsons, Dr. O'Leary, Eliza Duckton, perhaps even Collette; the list was long, and the appearance of any one of them would make it only ever more likely that it would soon be my turn for the tabloid headlines.

But the witness was Dr. Sudbury, dressed in the smart suit she'd had no use for since the camera trucks departed St. Luke's. To begin with, I assumed she had come simply to put some clear blue water between St. Luke's and me, and to reassure the panel—and no doubt the tabloid press—that robust systems had now been put in place to prevent anybody ever repeating my wickedness. I could not blame her. She was just doing her job, and in her position I would have done exactly the same thing.

But as Dr. Sudbury began to speak, I quickly understood that she was not there to condemn me. Instead, she described an extraordinarily competent young doctor, who had joined St. Luke's at a time of great strain and had played an invaluable role in the care of countless patients. I briefly wondered if she was even speaking about me. Maybe Dr. Sudbury sensed this, or simply understood she was going overboard, because at this point she turned to look at me and nodded as she spoke. I found myself choking back tears.

When Dr. Sudbury had finished, the Chair of the panel cleared his throat and asked if I was truly contrite. I said I was, and for once I think I may even have meant it. The Chair then announced that, given what were clearly exceptional circumstances and the faith shown in me by a senior physician, I would be permitted to return to supervised practice with the proviso that I now attend counseling twice a week. I could not believe I had got off so lightly, and it soon turned out I hadn't: another panel member intervened to recommend I commence a methadone maintenance program, and the Chair declared this "an excellent idea."

I had been opioid-free since the crash, so starting me on methadone at this point would simply be readdicting me. I began to explain this, but Dr. Sudbury shook her head at me not to push it, and so I did not. Taking methadone would not be as life-wrecking as losing my registration.

Outside, I thanked Dr. Sudbury profusely, and promised her that I would never let her down again. She seemed genuinely puzzled. I realized later that she had not attended the hearing and said those things for my benefit, and quite probably she did not think I was any kind of exemplary doctor. Nonetheless, she knew I was an available doctor, and that was all that had mattered to her.

My hearing was mentioned only in the *Mirror*, and there merely as a small item at the bottom of page eight. Thanks to the intervention of Dr. Sudbury—who the article described as "St. Luke's steely and forthright leader"—it was framed as an example of the terrible stresses the Angel of Death's murderous spree had wrought on her unfortunate colleagues, even driving one of them to addiction. Inevitably, Eliza Duckton had supplied a quote saying it was not the sort of thing her father had fought a world war for, but then perhaps nothing was. It was, after all, quite unclear that her father had ever fought a world war.

The worst parts, then, were the counseling and the methadone. The Reverend McKendrick was so thrilled to have doubled his income that he seemed to have forgotten all about our previous sessions, his visit to St. Luke's, and even the letter he had written to the panel. He enthusiastically embarked on a new course of CBT, and even stayed awake for the first two sessions. By the third session he was back to falling asleep twenty minutes in. It was almost as if nothing had changed at all.

The methadone was an even worse idea, but the fortnightly urine tests I now had to undergo at a drug clinic in Muswell

Hill meant I had no choice but to take it. Unlike with the reverend, there a nurse actually came with you into the bathroom and watched you piss into the bottle. It was degrading, but I could hardly argue with the necessity; even if I had, they would not have listened. They had at least still trusted me enough to prescribe a weekly supply of methadone, and so each morning and night I measured out and drank the mandated five milliliters of the bitter red liquid.

It did not get me high, but simply left me sluggish, and I continually had the feeling that I had just woken from a nap and could very much do with drifting back into one. And so I fell into a somnambulant routine that was little different from the same one I had always followed: work, sleep, work, sleep, and every four weeks this alternated briefly into sleep, work, sleep, work. And repeat.

CHAPTER 35

All through that languid August, Louise Fisher drifted in and out of the news. She had saved a fellow inmate from choking by performing the Heimlich maneuver, or she was being moved to a different wing for her own safety, or she had been caught attempting to sell her version of events to a tabloid newspaper. The stories they ran rarely now even mentioned St. Luke's, or the fact that Louise had not yet been found guilty of a single crime. Sometimes they did not even mention her actual name. Her infamy transcended all that; she was become the Angel of Death.

At St. Luke's, it seemed like we had quickly begun to forget about her, but perhaps we just had more than enough to be getting on with. There were the usual strokes, heart attacks, and infections, and the local gangs had once again begun shooting each other. There was also the granny-dumping: on the Friday preceding each summer bank holiday weekend, two dozen old ladies were abandoned in accident and emergency by relatives who claimed they were worried about Grandma's chest pain.

When Grandma inevitably protested that she had no such pain, the relatives would sigh and explain Grandma was also confused, but they would be happy to pick her up on Tuesday.

And of course, beyond our work at the hospital itself, we all had our own concerns. I sat and passed the second part of my membership exam in Manchester. This was not much of an accomplishment, for everyone knew that the first and last parts were the difficult ones, and the second part simply a way for the college to make yet more money. Still, it was a welcome relief, and the exam had started late enough that I had not needed to spend an uncomfortable night in an airport hotel.

Around the middle of the month, I received a postcard from Amelia. She had completed her induction training in Lusaka, and would soon be moving to her hospital in Mbala, so this would be her last chance to write for a while. She said she had been learning to identify different types of malaria under the microscope, and had now delivered the ten babies that would make her the most qualified obstetrician in the district. She made no mention of what had happened between us on the day she left, and I understood that she was as keen as I was to never think of it again. She signed off by asking me to wish her new patients luck, but of course none of them needed luck, because with Amelia as their doctor they had something far better.

A few days after that, our estate agent sent a letter addressed to George, even though he knew perfectly well that George was dead. It stated that the landlord planned to renovate the entire building, but the upstairs tenants had another ten months to run on their lease. The upshot was that I could remain living at the flat on a month-to-month basis. I'd have to cover George's rent too, so it was far too expensive for me, but the thought of looking for another place—or worse, moving back in with Dr. Vogel—filled me with dread, and so I stayed on.

Finally, on the late August bank holiday weekend, I arrived at work to find the parking lot once again swarming with television crews. I went straight to the mess, where my colleagues were crowded around the television, which was covering the day's breaking news with all the frenzied excitement of a terrorist outrage: Louise Fisher had confessed to the murders at St. Luke's. Every channel had interrupted their regular programming to broadcast the story, but none of them had much information to impart beyond the very basic facts.

The plea agreement involved Louise formally admitting only to injecting Mr. Athole with a fatal overdose of insulin, yet having the eleven other cases taken into account. In return, she would be sentenced to life in prison, and would not be eligible for parole for at least twenty years. The television pundits all agreed that Louise would actually never get out; the only Home Secretary who would ever sign off on her release would be one who believed more in the power of redemption than in the power of their own career. It seemed a strange bargain for Louise to have struck, for it was one that she did not appear to have got anything from. The pundits agreed Louise was probably simply glad to avoid the attention of a trial, but of course none of them had been there for her presentation about Amelia's belladonna patient. I watched the news loop for ten minutes, and then went to get on with the ward round.

*We tend to assume that healthcare killers work alone. The case of the
Death Angels of Lainz shows us that may be a fatal assumption.*

*Nurse's Assistant Waltraud Wagner was twenty-four years old when
she first killed a patient at Pavilion 5 of Vienna's Lainz Hospital. An
elderly lady had begged Wagner to help end her suffering, and Wagner
obliged by giving her a fatal overdose of morphine. If that killing might
somehow be considered a warped act of mercy, none of the many that
followed can possibly be.*

*Wagner had enjoyed her first killing so much that she now recruited
three of her night shift colleagues to join in what they all seemed to consider a kind of game. Wagner taught her colleagues to give their elderly
patients fatal overdoses of morphine, insulin, and tranquilizers. She
even taught them to perform something she called the "water cure": a
method of drowning an elderly patient with water while holding their
nose closed and depressing their tongue. As fluid in the lungs is common among the elderly, this finding would not be been considered a sign
of foul play at postmortem.*

The gang's elderly victims were murdered for such minor transgres-

sions as snoring, bedwetting, or even simply having the temerity to use the call button. Wagner would later state that the patients who got on her nerves "were dispatched directly to a free bed with the good Lord." Wagner's deeper motivation seems to have been the sense of power that killing gave her: "Of course the patients resisted, but we were stronger," she boasted at her trial. "We could decide whether these old fogies lived or died."

It was this entitled braggadocio that eventually brought down the Death Angels of Lainz. Rumors of something amiss in Pavilion 5 had circulated for years, but unnatural deaths of elderly patients are hard to identify and harder still to prove, especially when those deaths are caused by the patients' carers. The four nurses' assistants were out drinking in a local bar when a local doctor overheard them laughing together about a patient they had recently given a water cure. The doctor went to the police and the women were arrested. The gang subsequently confessed to killing at least forty-nine of their patients, but authorities believe the true number of victims to be over three hundred.

CHAPTER 36

Autumn soon fell once again on St. Luke's: the same darkness, the same fog, the same fireworks crackling over the nearby estate each night. A year had passed since I first arrived and everything had changed, and yet nothing had. George and Amelia were gone, Collette had rotated onto another hospital but there I still was, trudging around my patients on Jack Duckton ward each morning: this one for social services, that one for X-ray, this one's relatives want a meeting about their inheritance, that one's general practitioner needs to talk to you about their diabetes. On and on it went, the names and the faces of the patients changing but their circumstances never much altering.

Still, there was at least some hope on the horizon for me. I only had one more part of my membership exam to get, and once I obtained it I would be able to work as a registrar, to attend clinics and regional training days rather than endlessly battling the ward nurses and radiology secretaries. I would also theoretically be much more employable, although my recent history with the General Medical Council might yet make that moot.

In any case, the only route out of my daily trudge around Jack Duckton was to pass my exam. The application form for the September sitting had stated that the college took into account how far candidates had been required to travel for the first two parts of the exam, and so I felt confident that I would be assigned a hospital in London. I got the Belfast Royal Infirmary.

I flew there, and arrived in the city a day early. For as long as I have been taking exams, people had warned me not to revise the day before an exam, so after checking into my hotel I went to the arthouse cinema across the street. The matinee happened to be an old movie about a heroin addict. At the end of the movie he got clean, and said "The straight life, it's not all that bad. I actually wake up some mornings and I feel like, 'Somethin' good is gonna happen today.'" It occurred to me that I never woke up feeling like anything remotely good might happen, but then the methadone I was compelled to take meant I was not really clean.

Fearful of another night like the one I had experienced at the Birmingham Airport Holiday Inn, I took a sleeping pill before I went to bed. The phenomenon of a drug having the opposite effect of its intended one is called a "paradoxical reaction" and of course I now experienced my first one. Instead of sending me to sleep, the sleeping pill made me wired. I lay awake all through the night with my thoughts racing: thoughts about George, about the Reverend McKendrick, about Collette, Amelia, Dr. Sudbury and even Louise Fisher. By the time I heard somebody leave that morning's newspaper outside my door, I had not slept for a single minute. It was not great preparation for the exam, but I reassured myself that I was entirely used to seeing patients when I had barely slept.

This final part of the exam was a clinical exam. It involved the candidate being taken to see a series of patients in clinic rooms, examining them, and then informing the examiner of the correct diagnosis and a suggested treatment plan.

As always, we gamed the system as much as we could. There were ten cases, and we knew that two of them would be respiratory, two gastrointestinal, two cardiovascular, two neurological, and two would be wild cards. It was also known that only patients with clinical signs—abnormalities that could be consistently found on examination—were good subjects, and every hospital inevitably had a limited pool of such patients. That being so, if you knew what a particular hospital specialized in, you could take a guess at what at least one of the cases would be. Belfast Royal Infirmary was best known for the treatment of cystic fibrosis, so it seemed a good bet my exam would include one such case.

My first nine patients were a weird admixture of bad and good luck. The neurological patients were traditionally the most difficult, but I got an old stroke and a Parkinson's disease, both of which I'd had abundant practice diagnosing on Jack Duckton. The cardiac cases were far harder—an unusual murmur and a half-treated arrhythmia—and the first wild card had been an Ehlers-Danlos syndrome that I'd got only half right. Surprisingly, the two respiratory patients had not included a cystic fibrosis, and so by the time I got to the tenth and final patient, I knew it was the remaining wild card and would almost certainly be my missing case of cystic fibrosis. I had also caught a glimpse of the examiner's mark sheet, and knew I was sitting exactly on the borderline of passing and failing. I took a deep breath and followed him into the clinic room.

The patient, a young woman in her twenties, was already lying on the couch. She was not thin like many people with cystic fibrosis can be, nor was she on oxygen, nor attached to any other medical paraphernalia. I did briefly wonder if she might have some other disease, but there were not so many conditions that well-looking young people with clinical signs might secretly be harboring. I introduced myself, and examined her.

As I proceeded, I grew a little flustered. I was not eliciting any signs. In an adult patient with cystic fibrosis I expected to at least hear crackles at the bases of her lungs, but these were absent. Likewise her fingers had not shown the trademark clubbing, nor did she bear the scars of the lung transplant that might have resolved those signs. And so I stopped, took a deep breath, and re-evaluated.

The young woman looked well enough not to be a patient at all, but simply a medical secretary or off-duty nurse drafted in to fill a gap. I knew that this happened occasionally. It was hard for any hospital to find ten patients with reliable signs who were willing to spend the day being poked and prodded for the sole purpose of advancing a stranger's career. And even if they did agree to attend, it was not uncommon for these chronically ill people to have to cancel at short notice. Belfast Royal Infirmary had, I concluded, run out of patients and given me a ringer.

I finished my examination, turned to the examiner and triumphantly reported my findings: a completely normal clinical examination, with no evidence of any medical condition whatsoever. The examiner stared at me in horror, and so did the patient.

"Is there anything else you would like to do?" the examiner asked.

I looked at the patient again, and followed her gaze to the scales in the corner of the room. I had been primed to state that I would weigh and measure every patient I saw, but after the first couple the examiner had started to sigh each time I said it, and so I'd stopped repeating it.

"I'd weigh and measure the patient?" I said.

"Go on, then," said the examiner.

I'd never heard of a candidate actually having to weigh and measure the patient, but I did as he suggested and asked the patient to walk over to the scales. There was something a little unusual about the way she began to get up from the couch, and it made me briefly wonder if I was missing something rheumatological, an early-onset arthritis or a Still's disease. Of course, once she was standing up I saw the issue: the patient, who came up to about the height of the examiner's chest, had dwarfism. My sleep-deprived brain had been so focused on the idea of cystic fibrosis I had not noticed.

I must have let out a groan then, because the examiner nodded. He did so again when I measured the patient to be a little under four and a half feet tall, and informed him that I would like to correct my diagnosis, as I now suspected the patient had a form of dwarfism. The examiner nodded and wrote something down on his paper that I could not see.

A week later, the letter came in the mail. The examiner must have taken pity on me, because somehow I had passed the final part of my membership of the Royal College of Physicians.

CHAPTER 37

The human brain has many amazing capabilities, but none is so amazing as its capacity for forgetting. I have encountered patients with diseases that make you forget something as bizarre as the correct words for your fingers or as devastating as the faces of your entire family. And yet it is even in good health that we forget the most: lovers, feelings, the events that have had the most powerful impact on our lives. I make this point to say that by the time October rolled around, I had already all but forgotten about Louise Fisher. And then I received her letter.

It came addressed to me "Care of the Doctors' Mess, St. Luke's," so God knows how long it had languished among my old pay stubs and nagging circulars from infection control before I checked my pigeonhole. Louise Fisher had the handwriting of a child, and her short note simply asked me to please come and visit her at Durham Prison, because she had a very important matter to discuss. She had underlined the word *very* several times.

Even now, I am not sure why I went, except that it was some

interplay of boredom and convenience. I had plans to go to
Scotland for a week at the beginning of November and had already booked my ticket. The return journey would anyway pass
through Durham and the ticket allowed me to break my journey, so I could spend the afternoon visiting Louise and still be
back home in London before midnight.

I had not even realized the significance of the dates when I
booked it, but I took the train north on Halloween. To mark the
occasion, the train staff had all dressed up in costume. No doubt
it had seemed a good idea at the time, but the train in front of us
broke down outside Coventry and we ended up being delayed
by three hours and having to take on all the passengers from the
broken-down train. By the time we arrived in Glasgow, I had
never seen a more fed-up set of witches and warlocks in my life.

I spent a quiet week in Scotland, visiting with my parents and
catching up with friends. Most of them now had spouses or kids
to show off; my only claim to fame was that I had worked with
the Angel of Death. Still, it was a big claim. Everybody wanted
to know about Louise Fisher, and I quickly learned to tell them
only what they wanted to hear: that she was an obvious mon-
ster, and she had given me chills each time I spoke to her. Any
time I told people the real story—that she was mundanely ordinary, and it was hard to believe she'd even had the imagination
to kill anyone, let alone the technical knowledge—they were
visibly disappointed. I kept my methadone hidden at the bottom
of my bag and measured out my spoonful each morning and
evening. At the end of my stay, my parents told me how proud
they were that I had got clean, especially given everything that
had been going on.

I did not tell them that I would be visiting Louise. A few
weeks previously Louise's uncle had visited her in prison, and
the photographs had been in all the papers. I dreaded seeing a
similar photograph of myself, but by now I was too intrigued to

hear what *very* important information Britain's worst living serial killer could possibly have to tell me to even consider not going.

When I called ahead to make sure I would be able to visit, the telephonist at the prison sighed wearily and said that Inmate Fisher was not accepting visits from the press. I told her that I was Louise's friend, which was a stretch, but "former colleague" made me sound far too much like an accomplice. There was a silence, and the telephonist then stated that visiting was 2:00 p.m. until 4:00 p.m., to bring identification, and it would be entirely up to the inmate if she wished to see me.

I took the train south on the Sunday. In Glasgow's Central Station, a four-foot-high picture of DI Afferson's face in a shop window caught my eye. It was like something from one of my nightmares, but I at least understood why it was there. The day after Louise's plea bargain had been announced, Afferson had announced a deal of his own: he would be publishing a book about the case called *Catching the Angel*, and it would hit shelves the very next week.

The book had been an overnight bestseller. Afferson had appeared on all the television chat shows, and for a few weeks he was almost as famous as Louise herself. One national newspaper described him as being "the Sherlock Holmes to the Angel of Death's Professor Moriarty," which I suppose could have been true if Sherlock Holmes had been of average intelligence, and Moriarty just a little less bright.

I had avoided reading Afferson's book because it had seemed so ghoulish and inappropriate. But now here I was, en route to visit the Angel of Death herself, and with a few hours to kill on the train. I went in and bought a copy. The person at the counter told me it was the best book she had ever read, and then physically shuddered at the very thought of Louise Fisher.

"She's evil, that one," she said, "pure evil. They should throw away the key."

They already had thrown away the key, and I found myself

feeling something unexpected for Louise then: sympathy. She had been many things, including irritating and self-aggrandizing, but evil seemed a stretch. And yes, she had killed twelve people, but something had been troubling me about that, and it was almost too awkward to say out loud. It wasn't any question of her guilt—Louise had confessed, after all—but a more complex issue about the depth of that guilt.

The question was this: Was murder committed in the hospital at least somewhat different from other kinds of murder? In the eyes of the law and to upstanding citizens everywhere, murder was rightly always murder. But most serial killers have to go to extraordinary lengths to find their victims, commit their crimes, cover them up, and continue getting away with it. As far as I could tell, Louise Fisher had nonchalantly committed her crimes during her coffee breaks, and to begin with the deaths had been so unremarkable that nobody had even realized any of her victims had been murdered. Many of the patients hadn't had long to live anyway; clearly, killing twelve sick inpatients was not remotely okay, but was it the same as killing twelve perfectly healthy people?

As the train pulled out of Central Station, I opened Afferson's book. The first pages were a pompous prologue wherein he thanked his publishers, his family, and his high school English teacher as if he were accepting the Nobel Prize for Literature rather than flogging a cash-in account of being in the right place at the right time. He then rambled on for an abundance of paragraphs about how tough the job of a modern detective was, before finally thanking the one very special person who had believed in him "through thick and thin." This was not his wife, nor even a colleague, but the literary agent who he could not possibly have known for more than a few months.

I began to flick ahead. Fully the first half of the book consisted of filler about Afferson's childhood in Wales. It was like reading *Under Milk Wood*, if it had been ghostwritten by an airport crime novelist. Here is a sample passage:

> *That April our humble little home was burgled and my beloved grandfather's beloved VCR, upon which he unfailingly recorded his beloved One Man and His Dog, stolen; the local Constable disinterestedly stated there was simply nothing he could do, as the thieves likely hailed from Monmouth or Llewyeln, or perhaps even somewhere further west. Indeed, they may have also come from the east, or south, but yet not the north because that way there lay only the beaches of Rhyl, where as a child my other beloved grandfather had once taken me. Anyway, later that day, I felt something change in me.*

On and on it went. As he told it, Afferson's childhood seemed to be nothing but a series of unfortunate minor criminal incidents, each one of which became a powerful motivator for his subsequent career in mid-ranking law enforcement. As well as his grandfather's beloved VCR, his cousin's beloved bicycle was tragically stolen, and what seemed to be two further beloved grandfathers suffered entirely unavenged crimes committed upon their beloved motorcars. Afferson also painstakingly shoehorned in endless visits to an elderly aunt who had once worked as a medical receptionist, apparently to show how uniquely qualified he was to track down the St. Luke's killer. Unsurprisingly, his other main formative influence was every cop show that had ever played on television, and he wrote at length about his favorite episodes of *Bergerac* and *Taggart*.

But none of that was even the worst of it. The worst of it was that Afferson alternated these clunking autobiographical passages with brief sections that contrived to imagine Louise Fisher's point of view. This was done through the prose of an omniscient narrator, who only ever referred to Louise in the third person as "she":

She was seven years old now, and already knew she was different from the other girls. Whereas they cherished kittens and puppies, she pulled their tails and dreamed about putting their eyes out.

A little later, Afferson had his omniscient narrator speculate on "her" chosen career:

She was now twelve, and was hospitalized to have her tonsils removed, such as was the fashion in those bygone days. Did she then look at the pretty nurses in their starched uniforms and think that someday too she would be just like them? Or did she see something else that those young women possessed that she yet craved: Power? Did that innocent-looking schoolgirl look around at her fellow patients and simply see yet more unfortunate cats and dogs whose tails she might pull? As the detective in charge of Operation Nightingale, it was my job to find out—and given that I knew only too well what it was to be a victim of crime, I fully intended to.

As we passed through Edinburgh, I flicked past endless chapters about Afferson's salad days at police college and the first arrest he made, to where he finally began to write about St. Luke's. Maybe nobody had told him that St. Luke's academic credentials had long since been withdrawn, or perhaps he was simply advancing his boyo-from-the-valleys-against-the-ivory-towers-of-the-medical-establishment narrative, but he kept incorrectly referring to it as a "teaching hospital."

Dr. Sudbury was described as "matronly," which seemed unfair when there was nothing remotely matronly about her. If anything, she was avuncular: reliable when you asked for her help, but otherwise happy to let you make your own mistakes, as long as you sorted them out yourself too. Afferson even described her as possessing a "self-incriminating turn of phrase," which sounded far more suspicious than it was. What Dr. Sudbury had, of course, was a single catchphrase about hospital being a dangerous place. She would have been using those words since Louise Fisher was an innocent-looking schoolgirl having her tonsils removed, such as was the fashion in those bygone days. I flicked on another few pages, and came to this passage:

Early on in the investigation, my interest was piqued by a particular clique of doctors: two male flatmates, and the girlfriend of one of them. They appeared to be hiding something, and to this day I am not sure that they are not. Nevertheless, I am now certain that whatever it was had nothing to do with these particular deaths.

I had been sort of enjoying how atrociously written the book was until then, but even the fact that Afferson had accidentally rhymed "piqued" with "clique" did not make those lines any more forgivable. I did not care that Afferson suspected me of something, but it was unfair on Amelia and a rotten way to speak of the dead.

Still, I carried on reading, because Afferson had the good sense to end the wretched chapter with a cliffhanger: a promise to reveal the key breakthrough that had led to the arrest. Over the page, he immediately kept his word and revealed this coup: his team had discovered that Louise Fisher had falsified medical records, often writing her notes at the end of her shift, when everybody knew that medical records were meant to be contemporaneous.

That made me laugh out loud. Afferson had considered the fact Louise wrote up her notes at the end of the shift a smoking gun, but if that made her guilty then every nurse I had ever worked with should be in prison alongside her. Nurses are always so run off their feet that they only ever finally get time to fill in their notes at the end of their shift as they hand over. It always drove me nuts when I went to find out what had been happening to a patient and there was nothing from that day written in the nursing notes, but it did not make any of them killers.

Still, Afferson's misunderstanding had led to Louise's arrest, and it was the arrest that had led to a confession. I now read that, even as she was being driven from St. Luke's to Highbury police station, Louise had admitted to having injected Mr. Athole with insulin. She had subsequently claimed that this was an honest mistake, and she must have simply been looking at the wrong drug chart, but Afferson did not buy that because no other patient on the ward had been on insulin. When this had been put to her, Louise had suggested that perhaps Mr. Athole's drug chart had been altered by persons unknown. Conveniently, the drug chart had never been found.

When we reached Durham, I deposited my bag in the left luggage at the station and set out across town for the prison. It was a crisp autumn day, with a clear blue sky and a frost on the ground. As I made the fifteen-minute walk from the station to the prison, I could hear the cathedral bells chiming noon and the plainsong of choristers drifting over the river. Compared to the grimy urban surroundings of St. Luke's, the whole place seemed absurdly pastoral, though of course that probably did not count for much if you were incarcerated in the country's most notorious women's prison.

Visiting would not commence for another hour, so I sat in a nearby pub and read a little more of DI Afferson's book. The barman spotted this and nodded approvingly before informing me that his cousin worked at the prison, and had told him that the Angel was "as bad as they come." For the first time, I began to wonder if visiting Louise Fisher might actually be a mistake.

I turned back to the book, but there was not much left worth reading. Despite having seemingly only just got to the important stuff, Afferson now declared that "operational reasons" meant that he could not go into specifics about any details of the murders, or even Louise's formal interviews. Instead, he circled back in time and wrote about the pranks his classmates played at the police training college, his first job as a constable standing outside the Houses of Parliament, and why he would be proud if his children someday grew up to be police officers, although he would prefer they took the graduate entry route.

By the time I left the pub, I felt like I actually knew less about Louise and the events at St. Luke's than I had to begin with. I threw *Catching the Angel* in a bin in the street. This was primarily a pragmatic gesture, because I could not turn up to visit Louise clutching a copy of a lurid book about her. Nonetheless, I enjoyed putting Afferson's book where it belonged.

Outside the high walls of the prison, I joined a long queue of visitors. Mostly, they were prematurely middle-aged women: mothers who had once had their own struggles and now could only watch as their daughters played them out once more. One of these women tapped me on the shoulder and politely told me that lawyers did not have to wait in the general visiting line. She seemed baffled when I reassured her that I was not a lawyer, so I repeated my half lie that I was visiting a friend.

A little after one o'clock, a grim-faced guard opened the gate and we filed inside. We signed a register, passed through a metal detector, underwent a pat-down, and then took seats in a waiting area. Every now and again, a receptionist would call the name of a particular prisoner and a number, and that person's visitors would stand up and proceed to the visiting room. As I waited, I heard the names of some notorious female criminals, but we all simply looked down and pretended not to recognize them. Nonetheless, when Louise Fisher's name was called, my fellow visitors stared at me with open bafflement and hostility.

The visiting room felt like a school canteen, with orange plastic chairs, checked linoleum on the floor, and a faint smell of disinfectant mixed with boiled cabbage. Were it not for the number six hanging above the table she was sitting at, I might not have recognized Louise at all. Partly that was because I had only ever seen her wearing a nurse's uniform and she was now wearing a prison uniform, but mostly it was because she looked so much better than she ever had at St. Luke's.

I am not joking. Louise had lost a little weight, but more strikingly, she seemed to sit up straighter, make more eye contact, and be more alert. It took me a moment to figure it out, but the major difference was this: Louise Fisher was now quite clearly far happier than she had ever been at St. Luke's. What kind of a person is happier in prison than being free in the outside world? I wondered if the woman in the newsagent and the barman had both been right. Maybe it was indeed for the best that they had all but thrown away the key.

Louise seemed delighted to see me. She thanked me for coming all this way, and asked how my journey had been. I told her it had been fine, and that I had actually been on my way back from Scotland anyway. I had been trying to telegraph that my visit was not a big deal, and she should not read too much into it, but of course that failed.

"I didn't know you still had family in Scotland!" she enthused.

I could only shrug, because there was no reason for her to have known anything like that about me; we had been colleagues for barely a year, and had anyway hardly known each other. It also occurred to me that perhaps it was for the best that one of Britain's most notorious serial killers did not know where my family lived.

"My own folks live in Macclesfield," Louise then announced, as if her parents had not given an interview from their front room that I and the entire rest of the country had watched. Her mother had been entirely adamant that Louise was innocent, but her father had been more circumspect. When asked directly, he had quoted what he said was his favorite verse from the Bible: "Let he who is without sin cast the first stone." It might have been a valid point, except for the obvious fact that while none of us watching were without sin, most of us watching could be reasonably confident that we had not murdered twelve people.

There were vending machines in the corner of the room. Other visitors were buying their prisoners food and drink, and I noticed Louise's eyes drift across to them.

"Would you like something?" I asked Louise.

"A cup of tomato soup, please. And, if you wouldn't mind, some mint imperials?"

I got up and walked over to the vending machine, aware of the eyes of the prison officers upon me as I did so. I got myself a coffee, and Louise her tomato soup and her mints. She put a mint in her mouth and then immediately started to sip her tomato soup.

"So, how is everything at work?" she asked.

I remember being surprised she still called it "work," but I don't know what else I expected her to call it—maybe "the scene of the crime"? I shrugged and told her the truth: St. Luke's was exactly the same. There were still far too many patients, and never enough hours in the day, and Dr. Sudbury still discharged everyone as swiftly as she could. At this, Louise nodded and got an expression on her face that I can only describe as wistful. I found myself wondering if she was wistful for our patients and the monotony of our daily ward rounds, or for all the killing.

"Do people there still talk about me much?" Louise asked, and there I thought was my answer: the thing she was wistful for was the attention.

"At first you were all anybody talked about," I said, truthfully, "but not so much now."

She nodded, and I saw her bottom lip quiver a little. The idea that people no longer talked about her seemed to have saddened her far more than the fact that she would be in prison for the rest of her life, or even the thought of her broken-hearted parents sitting in their front room in Macclesfield.

"I got your letter," I said.

"I know you did," she said, "and I'm so grateful to you for coming. You're the only one who has."

"Did you write to other people?" I asked, realizing even as I did that of course she had written to other people.

"I wrote to all the doctors," she said. "Just Amelia and Dr. Sudbury at first, but later you, and everyone else whose names I could remember."

Somehow, I felt cheated. "I didn't know you knew Amelia," I said.

"I didn't," said Louise, "not really. But everyone always said she was the best doctor."

For the first time since I had arrived, Louise looked like she might feel some guilt about something, and hurriedly added, "But we all thought you were a good doctor too."

A confessed serial killer was trying to help me feel better about myself, and was doing so because she thought I did not know that Amelia was a far better doctor than I'd ever be. Had my previous nadirs not all been so appalling, it would have been a new low.

"Your letter said that you had some important information?" I said.

Louise nodded, glanced around the room, then leaned in closer to me.

"I didn't do it," she whispered. "I didn't kill them."

The buildup had been so earnest that I almost laughed out loud. I had broken my journey south, plodded through Afferson's interminable book, trudged across Durham, sat in an empty pub, lined up in the cold and been searched simply to hear the information that a confessed serial killer now disputed her conviction.

"But you confessed?" I said, making no effort to hide my irritation at the ridiculousness of it all.

Louise seemed hurt by this.

"Only to Mr. Athole," she said. "I never confessed to the others. We just agreed they would be taken into account."

"But you did kill Mr. Athole?"

"It was an accident. I gave him insulin, but only because it was written in his chart."

"Was it?" I asked.

"Yes!" she insisted. "Twenty-two units in the morning, and sixteen units in the evening. I don't know who wrote it, but I can still see it. I'm supposed to give them what the chart says. I was just doing my job."

"So where is the chart now?" I asked.

"If I knew that I wouldn't be in here," she said. "But those charts go missing all the time. You know that."

The thing was, I did know that. The daily chaos of hospital life meant that charts and notes were forever going missing. Mostly they reappeared, but occasionally they did not. The latter generally did not result in a murder conviction.

"But why would insulin have been written up on his chart if he wasn't diabetic?" I asked.

"I don't know," she said. "Maybe somebody wrote it on the wrong chart?"

This, too, was horribly plausible. There isn't a doctor alive who has not accidentally prescribed something on the wrong chart. Usually such a mistake gets swiftly picked up by an eagle-eyed nurse or pharmacist, and corrected before any harm can be done. Usually.

Louise was staring at me. She seemed to be imploring me to believe her.

"But at the arrest, when we found out that his glucose was low, you didn't tell us you'd given him insulin," I said.

"Because I was scared!" she said. "And then I wasn't at work for a few days, and when I came back everybody was already saying it was one of the murders, so how could I tell them then?"

My mind flashed to the patient with the mysterious cherry red blood that I had chosen not to mention to anybody, lest I somehow incriminate myself.

"I thought they would know about the insulin, anyway,"

Louise continued, "because they should have had his chart. My lawyer says that if I hadn't told them I'd given Mr Athole the insulin, they wouldn't have even had a case against me."

My head was swimming. I had come to Durham hoping to have some things confirmed and answered, and instead I now had to question everything I'd thought I had known about the events at St. Luke's.

"Look, I appreciate you telling me all this," I said, "but I don't see what you think I can actually do."

"But that wasn't what I wanted to tell you," said Louise. "I mean, it is part of it, of course. But I also wanted to tell you something about your friend George."

"I'm listening," I said.

"The day that he died, I was making up my IVs in the stockroom. George came in and asked for some potassium for a patient upstairs, so I gave it to him and—"

Louise caught herself and stopped speaking. I knew exactly why: in our previous conversation, she had been careful to avoid any mention of the role she had played in George's death.

"I already knew you gave him the potassium," I said, "and it's alright. It wasn't your fault that he died."

Inside, I was still certain that whatever else she may or may not be guilty of, George's death was almost entirely Louise Fisher's stupid fault, but I needed her to continue talking.

"He showed me a photograph," she said.

"A photograph of what?"

"I don't know," she said.

"What do you mean, you don't know? If he showed you a photograph, then—"

"I mean, I saw it," she interrupted, "I just didn't know what it signified. It was two young people. George asked me if I recognized them, and I told him the truth, that I didn't. And then he put it in his pocket and went away. But he seemed very upset."

"But if he seemed so upset," I said, now unable to help myself, "then why did you give him the potassium?"

I regretted saying that even before I saw Louise's bottom lip spring back into action and the tears start to well in her eyes. Only an hour earlier, I might have considered making Britain's most notorious serial killer cry a small victory on behalf of all the murdered patients of St. Luke's. But now I was not even sure Louise Fisher was any kind of killer at all, and I felt terrible. I apologized, and told her that George's death was not remotely her fault, that anybody in her position would have done exactly same thing. Louise tearfully asked me if I really believed that, and I reassured her I did. She then asked me if she had been a good nurse, and I found myself telling her that she had been one of the best nurses I had ever worked with. It was not remotely true, but it somehow seemed the least I could do.

There was still an hour of visiting left, but I suddenly felt an urgent need to get out of there. If there was a possibility that Louise actually was innocent—well, then it could easily have been me sitting on the other side of the table. I could have been the one wrongly labeled the Angel of Death, and it could have been the very mention of my name that prompted newsagents and barmen to shiver. It could have been my parents being interviewed in their own little front room and indignantly telling a skeptical news anchor that I had never shown any hint of being the murdering type.

I mumbled something about having to catch the next train and stood up to go. Louise seemed disappointed, but what could she do? As I left, I asked her to let me know if she remembered anything else about George. She enthusiastically promised that she would, and asked me to stop in and see her next time that I was traveling to Scotland. I agreed, although I think we both knew that I would not.

I don't even remember the walk back to the station, and my head spun all the way home to London. It was Guy Fawkes

night once again, and I watched bonfires being built and effi-
gies laid upon them. As darkness began to fall, the pyres were
lit and soon there were orange glows in every village and town
we passed. It was as if the whole country was united in a cel-
ebration; well, the whole country except me, who as usual was
back to watching it all unfold from behind a pane of thick glass.

As the miles passed, I ruminated on what I had just heard.
What to make of any of it? Was Louise Fisher—the notorious
Angel of Death—truly innocent of everything apart from ac-
cidental bad luck? But if so, then who had murdered all those
patients? And more importantly than anything—at least as far
as I concerned—why on earth would George have shown her a
photograph? And who had the people in the photograph been? It
was all so bizarre and yet more than ever now it had that feeling
not of a stream of unrelated coincidences, but of a constellation
of related symptoms that a unifying diagnosis, a single piece of
information that explained everything, would tie together, if
only I could find it.

But I could not find it. Occam's razor held the simplest explanation to be that Louise Fisher was a lying and murdering
psychopath, but I simply could not square that with the person
who had sat opposite me and begged to be told she had been a
good nurse, nor with what seemed the almost complete lack of
evidence upon which she had been convicted. Apart from her
confession about Mr. Athole—which truly did seem the kind of
there-but-for-the-grace-of-God event every doctor and nurse
has nightmares about—there was less evidence against her than
there had ever been against me.

When I got home that night, I went through George's boxed-
up things once more, but there was no photograph, just as I
had known there was not. There was only Patrick, staring at
me. Still, I noticed one smaller emptiness alongside the greater
one: George's diary was missing. I could only guess that Amelia had taken it, and I felt churlish for never having thought to
offer it to her.

François "Papa Doc" Duvalier is not traditionally considered a health-care killer. Still, as a trained physician who was responsible for tens of thousands of deaths, his case and motives merit consideration.

Duvalier was born in 1907 and graduated in medicine from the University of Haiti. In 1944 he joined a US-sponsored campaign aimed at fighting the deadly tropical diseases that plagued his homeland. It was during this tireless work with rural communities that Duvalier's patients first nicknamed him Papa Doc, in honor of both his compassion and expertise. Two years later, Duvalier was appointed director of Haiti's National Public Health Service, and subsequently became the country's minister of health and labor.

After he was elected president in 1957, Duvalier's first acts included exiling his opponents and installing his own loyalists to run the army. He also set up the organization that would become his personal secret police, the Tonton Macoute. It therefore seems reasonable to say that the Duvalier era was unlikely to ever be a bastion of liberal democracy.

But something else happened, too. Two years after his election, Duvalier suffered what was reported at the time to have been a massive heart attack. He lay unconscious for nine hours, until he was reportedly revived by a glucose injection. As Duvalier was a diabetic and glucose injections do not treat heart attacks but low blood sugar, the episode seems more likely to have represented a hypoglycemic coma caused by an insulin overdose than a heart attack.

It is of course understandable that Duvalier's physicians may not have wished to admit their president's sickness was the result of medical error. It would not matter much, except for what came next: Duvalier underwent a dramatic change in personality. After his "heart attack," he became erratic, paranoid, and obsessed with his wicked voodoo alter ego, Baron Samedi.

Heart attacks do not generally cause personality change, but the neurological damage caused by prolonged hypoglycemia can, and the transformation in Duvalier drove the subsequent devastation of his country. Over the next months and years, Duvalier personally participated in torture, publicly displayed the corpses of his innumerable victims, and even ordered the head of a slain enemy brought to him on ice so that he might commune with the dead man's soul.

Papa Doc's descent to becoming one of the twentieth century's worst despots represented an astonishing fall from the earnest young doctor who had once tirelessly defended rural communities against the scourges of dengue and malaria. Is it possible, then, that we are all no more than a single period of prolonged hypoglycemia away from such incorrigible wickedness? Modern scanning techniques increasingly demonstrate disruptions in the brain architecture of our worst killers, but the cause rarely seems as clear-cut as in the case of Papa Doc. Perhaps someday the precise biological mechanisms of extreme psychopathology will be fully elucidated, but in the meantime, Papa Doc provides another reason why even a healthcare worker might become a killer, and serves as a terrible reminder to always remember the DEFG of resuscitation: Don't Ever Forget Glucose.

CHAPTER 38

Iwrote to Amelia to tell her about my visit to Louise, and to ask if the photograph might mean anything to her. She had gone to Zambia in large part to get away from George's death and so I felt guilty for doing so, especially given what had occurred between us.

Still, she was the only person who might know the significance of the photograph, and also the best diagnostician I knew. If anybody could find the unifying diagnosis, it would be Amelia. When I went to mail the letter, the woman at the post office said she had never sent anything to Zambia before, and seemed to find the whole business unspeakably exciting.

In early December, somebody pinned up a flyer in the mess at St. Luke's advertising a reading DI Afferson was giving at the large Waterstones on Piccadilly. It had no doubt been put up as a joke, and sure enough it only took a day before somebody marker-penned a Sherlock Holmes–style deerstalker and pipe onto his plummy face. For my part, I could not resist making the trip into town to hear what he had to say.

To this day, I do not know what I was hoping for. I had already read his book, and there was nothing of interest in it. Perhaps I thought Afferson might say something during the event, let slip a crucial fact that unlocked the whole thing. Or maybe I was hoping he would describe some incontrovertible evidence of Louise Fisher's guilt that would let me forget the whole thing forever. Maybe I just wanted him to acknowledge some uncertainty that would tell me that he too sometimes lay awake and wondered about it all.

Of course, none of those things happened. The event, held in a five-hundred-seat auditorium filled almost entirely with middle-aged women, consisted of Afferson reading aloud the section about his beloved grandfather's beloved VCR, then several of the third-person sections about Louise, and then a question-and-answer session. Afferson looked different now: he wore an expensive-looking sports jacket, the ruddiness from his cheeks was mostly gone, and his teeth glistened an unnatural shade of white. He showed no emotion during the readings, but seemed to speak with a far heavier Welsh accent than he ordinarily did, as if he had been listening to Richard Burton records on repeat or some savvy publicist had convinced him that sounding as Welsh as possible could be an important part of his brand.

If anything, the question-and-answer session was only less illuminating. The questions had all been submitted beforehand, apparently to allow the publishers to select only the most sycophantic of them. I thus had to endure an hour of Afferson pontificating over just what made him such a good detective, whether all nurses and doctors were latent psychopaths, and whether crimes as serious as Louise Fisher's meant we should have an overdue national conversation about the merits of bringing back hanging. One of the questioners even forsook her approved question to ask Afferson if he would go on a date with her. Afferson seemed to make sure to get a good look at the woman before responding that he was happily married, so a date was alas out of the question.

The event finished with a standing ovation, and an announcement that Afferson would be signing copies of his book downstairs, although due to overwhelming demand he would unfortunately only be able to sign books purchased that night. Even though many of the audience had brought along their own well-thumbed copies of Catching the Angel, and they all already clearly knew the book by heart, this did not deter them. I do not know what the collective noun for a group of obsessive true crime fans is, but from the rush to the door that evening, the best candidate might be the word stampede.

By the time I got downstairs, the line was already snaking through biography, past romantic fiction and even reached as far as the greeting card section. I had come intending to keep entirely out of Afferson's sight, but I now decided that I needed to see him myself. What if he really did hold some precious final clue, and this was my last and best chance to elicit it? So I picked up a copy of Catching the Angel from the table, and took my place in line. I was dead last, and it took over an hour for me to reach him.

"And who should I make this one out to?" Afferson asked, now such a professional he no longer even looked up as he did this.

"To the doctor who might be hiding something," I said.

This did made him look up, and he uttered a "Fuck's sake" under his breath, before curtly asking what I wanted. I realized then that I had no idea what I actually wanted. I mean, I wanted answers, but even if Afferson actually knew them he was not likely to volunteer them, and especially not in front of his publicist. So I told him I was here because I had some things I wanted to talk to him about, and that I needed to do so privately. He stared at me, then told me to wait for him in a nearby pub called The Three Crowns, and said he'd be there when he could.

Afferson joined me there an hour later. When he arrived, he complained bitterly about the endless boxes of books they had made him sign, but calmed down as he began to drink his pint. To begin with, he seemed strangely interested in what I thought of *Catching the Angel*, and particularly whether or not it possessed what he called "literary merit." I told him I was really no judge of that, which was entirely true, but that I nonetheless believed it did, which was not. Afferson then lamented that he had got a lot of things wrong with the book, particularly the sections about Louise. It would have been far better, he said, for those to have been written in the second person—*"You have just had your tonsils out, as was the fashion in those bygone days"*—but he had made the mistake of listening to his editor.

Still, Afferson said, his next book would be the one to show people what he could do. Yes, *Catching the Angel* had sold by the trolley-load, but he had even bigger ambitions for the follow-up. It was about the Aberystwyth Milkman, an obscure Welsh serial killer who had terrorized the mining villages in the 1940s and 1950s. This new book, he said, would undeniably have literary merit, as this time he would simply not be rushed into having it hit the shelves, but would take a full month or two to write it.

Afferson then asked me how things were at the hospital. He particularly wanted to know about Dr. Sudbury, who he described as "one of my favorite characters." I wasn't sure if he meant that the real-life Dr. Sudbury had a personality that he appreciated, or that he was pleased with the way he had depicted her in the book. Perhaps it was both. Either way, now that the pleasantries were done, he turned his attention to me, and asked me whether I had indeed been hiding something.

I told him that he already knew all my secrets, except one: I had recently been to visit Louise Fisher in Durham Prison, and she had been adamant she had killed only Mr. Athole, and that it had been an accident. Afferson visibly bristled at this, but as ever he knew better than to interrupt a speaker and halt the flow of information he might later use against them. And that was how I also found myself telling Afferson about the photograph that Louise claimed George had shown her on the day he died. Afferson had not mentioned anything about a photograph in his book, so I was unsure whether he knew about it or not.

Afferson took a large drink of his pint, and then stared at me. His gaze was so direct and unnerving that I felt like I was back in Highbury police station. I found myself overexplaining my actions, telling him that the mystery around George's death had haunted me, and I'd felt compelled to visit Louise in case she could shed any light upon it.

When I finally managed to stop talking, Afferson allowed another of his trademark pauses to build between us. For a moment I thought he was going to get up and walk right out, but instead he began to quietly lecture me. He told me I had to understand that this was exactly what sociopathic murderers did when they began to feel the walls closing in on them: they lied, and they cheated, and they did whatever they could to obfuscate. The photograph, he said, had just been one more such gambit from Louise Fisher.

"Then she did tell you about the photograph?" I asked.

"Of course she did," said Afferson, "and we looked into it. But it did not make any sense. What photograph would your friend George—who, I understand, was at most an acquaintance of her's—possibly have wanted to show her?"

Besides, Afferson continued, where was this mysterious photograph now? It had not been found on George or in his car, and if it had been at the flat I would presumably now be waving it in his face. Moreover, where was George even supposed to have obtained this photograph from? His parents had not known anything about a meaningful photograph, and even Amelia had seemed oblivious to it when they had asked her about it.

That last part made me curse the letter I had sent Amelia. I'd only written to her to find out if the photograph meant anything to her; if I'd known she had already informed Afferson it did not, I could have saved her the heartache of having to think over it all again. I found myself hoping the woman in the post office had messed something up, and that my letter had not reached Amelia in Zambia.

Afferson lit a cigarette, sighed, and told me that he had been around many deaths like George's, and the photograph was meaningless in the grand scheme of things. Even if it had ever existed, he said, it had not killed George. George's death—which, he reminded me, was categorically by his own hand—was nothing like any of the others, and Louise was only trying to drag him into her case to muddy the waters. Afferson drained his pint and left the pub.

Of course, our conversation did not resolve anything for me. An incorrect diagnosis is like having a pebble in your shoe: you can go a certain distance with it by reassuring yourself that you are simply imagining the unease you feel, but deep down you know it is wrong, and at some point it will need to be addressed. That was how I felt about both George's death and whatever it was that had happened at St. Luke's. So much of it did not make sense, but that one part now stuck out above all else: the photograph. Of course, Afferson's explanation—that there had never been a photograph—would have perfectly answered that, except for one thing: I believed Louise. Working in medicine gives you a sense for when people are lying, and I could not shake the belief that Louise Fisher had been telling the truth in Durham Prison that day.

As I rode the bus home that night, I worked myself into a logical frenzy. The afternoon he died, George had returned home for reasons that still remained unknown. According to Louise, he had been in possession of a photograph he found distressing. No photograph had been found on his body or in his car. Putting all those things together, it was clear that—unless George had simply thrown the photograph away, which seemed unlikely given its apparent importance—the only place the crucial photograph was now likely to be was inside our flat.

When I reached home that night, I went to George's room to search for the photograph again. This time I was unrestrained by decorum or any desire to preserve the belongings that nobody had a use for now anyway. And so I did not just reverently look though George's things for the hundredth time. This time, I took them apart.

I first took down the framed photograph of the England rugby team and wrenched the back from it to make sure there was nothing hiding inside. I stripped his bedclothes and searched under the mattress. I tore the soles out of the running shoes he wore to trudge around Victoria Park, lest he had secreted it in there. I pulled out all the inlay booklets in the box of CDs that were the final testimony to his improbable love of reggae music. I emptied out a shoebox full of cards and letters from Amelia. I looked everywhere, and came up as empty-handed as I always did. Exhausted and already feeling ashamed of myself, I gave up and lay on George's bare bed.

I felt the weight of Patrick's eyes on me. He was as inscrutable as ever, but I knew he would not have approved, because I knew George himself would not have approved. When I had told George about my opioid addiction, he had not asked me even a single question. I had understood this was not because he did not wish to know, but rather that he felt that my right to privacy was more important than his desire for information. Here, I had just done the exact opposite to him. Maybe ransacking his room was not as bad as reading his diary or sleeping with his girlfriend, but it was still another indignity.

"Come on, Patrick," I said. "Where the fuck did he put it?"

Patrick, of course, only continued to stare at me. But then, as I stared back at him, something occurred to me.

An inch below the top of Patrick's head, a near-imperceptible line ran around the circumference of his skull. George had once cheerily informed me it was where they had opened Patrick's skull "to scoop out his brains like a boiled egg," and then insisted I inspect the quality of work.

"And that wasn't even done with a power tool, you know," George had boasted, seemingly proud of both his anatomist forebear and perhaps even of Patrick for sitting so still. I had then made the mistake of attempting to lift off the top of Patrick's skull, at which point George had delightedly pointed out several tiny brass screws that held it in place.

"Very resistant to infection, brass," George had assured me. "Not that it matters to old Patrick anymore, of course."

That had been the end of it, but tonight as I stared at Patrick I realized that the interior of his skull cavity was just about the only place in our flat that I had not yet searched.

The problem lay with getting the top off Patrick's skull. George had owned a toolbox, but with typical surgical pragmatism he had decided that the best place to store it was in the small space behind the boiler. The day I moved in, he had shown me this ingenuity with great pride, and said something about it all being part of the fun of sharing a small flat. He admitted he did not know how he would ever get the toolbox out again, but cheerfully declared we would cross that bridge when we came to it.

I had now come to that bridge. It took me fully twenty minutes of twisting, reaching, and cursing, before I got the wretched thing out on to the hall floor. As I finished, the upstairs neighbor began banging on our ceiling at all the noise I was making. Assuming this was the same noise she had heard during George's missing afternoon, I seemed to be on the right track.

I received another good omen when I opened the toolbox, for at the very top lay a tiny hospital-issue orthopedic screwdriver. Sure enough, when I laid Patrick out flat on George's bed, it fit perfectly into the brass screws of his skull. The only catch was that whoever had tightened the screws had been strong and determined, and it took me another twenty minutes to get the five of them out. When I did, I lifted off the top of Patrick's skull, and was met with only disappointment. There was nothing there.

Rather: when I looked inside there was nothing there. But medicine has taught me to check everything in as many ways as possible—to first look, and then to feel—so I ran my fingers around the inside edge of Patrick's skull, and stopped when I came to something rougher than the smooth polished bone.

I angled Patrick's skull so that the inside was illuminated by George's desk lamp, and now saw what I had felt: the back of a photograph that had been placed against the temporal bone, its discolored backing almost indistinguishable from Patrick's yellowed bones. I fished it out as delicately as if I were performing actual brain surgery, and turned it over beneath the lamp.

The photograph seemed to have been taken about a decade before, and it showed a young man and woman, both of whom were in their late teens or early twenties. They were stood on a medieval-looking bridge in a city where old stone buildings crowded the background. The two people looked to be lovers or at least very close friends, for they had their arms around one another. I assumed the city must be Cambridge, but that was only because of the identity of the young woman. She was younger, her hair was short, and she was not wearing her glasses, but it was unmistakably Amelia. The young man took me far longer to recognize, because I had never seen him look so vital and healthy, let alone with hair down to his chin. It was Felix Smollett.

I went to the kitchen, poured myself a large glass of whisky, and sat down at the breakfast bar that George had insisted on referring to as "the dining room." I tried to piece it all together, but it did not make any sense. Amelia and Felix were not meant to have known each other, let alone to have been the good friends or even lovers this picture suggested. And how had George got hold of it? If he had truly seen Felix on the ward that day, had Felix given him the photograph? But why?

And, more than anything, why had Amelia and Felix concealed the fact that they had once known each other? When I had asked Amelia about their spectacular argument, she had made no mention of any shared history. I likewise remembered that after George had died, Felix had expressly asked me about "the other doctor, his girlfriend." If he hadn't been deliberately hiding the fact that he knew Amelia, he would have used her name.

So: Felix Smollett and Amelia had known each other, and they had sought to keep that fact secret. But George had discovered it, and a short time later he had killed himself. It was perplexing and important new information, and yet it still was not my unifying diagnosis. If anything, it was another set of symptoms that made a diagnosis even more elusive. For one thing, it gave more credence to Louise's claim of innocence, because if she had been telling the truth about the photograph, she may well have been telling the truth about everything else. Even more importantly from my perspective, it deepened the mystery around George's death: Why had a photograph of Amelia and Felix been so devastating to him? Even the obvious explanation did not explain much: if I discovered my girlfriend had ever dated Felix Smollett, I'd have been horrified too, but I wouldn't then have killed myself a few hours later. At least, I didn't think I would have.

Even with the whisky I did not sleep much that night. At work the next day, I asked the nurses on Jack Duckton if they remembered ever seeing Felix Smollett with Amelia, but they mostly looked at me blankly. Almost a whole year of patients had come and gone, and our endless war of attrition meant that many of the staff had changed too. Only Angela properly remembered them both, and she said she could not recall them ever interacting beyond the shouting match we'd all heard about.

My medical colleagues were little better: most of them remembered me grumbling about Felix, but none of them could recall Amelia ever talking about him. I even went down to medical records to dig out his notes, but a card left in their place told me that Operation Nightingale had taken them, and instructed me to contact DS Newington with any inquiries.

By now, Saz had given up even attempting her exam and moved on to a new job in accident and emergency at a hospital in South London. I called the switchboard and had them page her. She was in the middle of a busy shift and sounded stressed, but even after she had told me that she did not remember anything beyond the famous argument, she had seemed in no rush to hang up. I could tell that this new information troubled her too.

We speculated as to how Amelia and Felix might have known each other, and Saz asked me if it was possible they had studied together. I initially said no, because Amelia had gone to Cambridge, but realized as I said it that it was not entirely impossible he had also studied there. He'd never have finished the course, but the chance to have a Cambridge degree was exactly the kind of opportunity Felix would have been gifted and then squandered. A trauma call had begun to go off insistently in the background, but before she rang off, Saz reminded me that we at least knew which Cambridge college Amelia had gone to, because she had told us that Professor Sir Smithfield of *Smithfield's Textbook of Human Disease* fame had been her tutor. I went immediately to the hospital library, found a copy of *Smithfield's*, and read that the legendary classifier of disease was provost and dean of Cambridge's Magdalene College.

I had that Friday off because I was starting nights. For once, I did not go to the movies, but took the train to Cambridge.

CHAPTER 39

Magdalene College was across town from the train station, and in December the whole of Cambridge had a festive feel. It reminded me a lot of my sojourn in Durham, except I hadn't had to spend the train journey reading Afferson's book. Perhaps I should have been reading *Smithfield's*, but like every other doctor of my generation I already mostly knew it by heart.

I gained admittance to Magdalene by telling the ancient and sclerotic-looking porter that I was here to visit the college's Samuel Pepys museum. He grudgingly let me in, showed me into a gloomy seventeenth century library and admonished me not to touch anything, as every item was priceless. This seemed likely to be true only in the sense that a lot of the items did not have a price. For instance, one of the exhibits on most prominent display was Pepys' handkerchief; if anybody was willing to buy a used handkerchief from the chronicler of one of the deadliest plagues known to man, well, that person was not me.

I watched out of the window as the porter returned to his

gatehouse, waited for him to disappear inside, and then I set out to find Professor Sir Smithfield. I was still young enough to pass for a postgraduate student, so it was easy enough to fit in. I wandered until I eventually found a stairwell with the words *Academic Physiology* chiseled into its masonry, and a brass plaque that said *Dr. Smithfield-Fourth Floor.* Even the plaque must have been at least a decade old, because he had been properly known as Professor Sir Smithfield since the publication of the edition of the textbook I had used in medical school.

I climbed the winding stone staircase to the fourth floor, where a studded wooden door barred any further progress. It was so old and elvish-looking that I half expected it to creak open and reveal Tolkien himself tucked beside it. Instead, I knocked, heard a loud sigh and an irritated "Come!", and entered.

Professor Sir Smithfield was sitting behind a grand desk piled high with journals, books, and papers, but what immediately struck me was how tiny and wizened-looking he was. He had loomed over our profession like a colossus for decades, but in life he cannot have had much on a hobbit. I thought immediately of the casual cruelty of his turn of phrase—physical appearances in his textbook were frequently described as "unappealing" or "grotesque"—and I briefly wondered if his apparent intolerance for imperfection might have something to do with his own physique. I did not follow this line of thought, because he immediately and with some irritation demanded to know what it was that I wanted. I told him I was hoping I could ask him some questions about Amelia Bowen.

It would require a more accomplished anatomist than me to describe what the mere mention of Amelia's name did to the musculature of the esteemed professor's face. Certainly, I saw the *orbicularis oculi* contract, and for the briefest of moments I assumed he was smiling at the memory of what must have been his greatest ever student. But then his *corrugator supercilii* knitted his brow into a frown, his *nasalis* flared and his *procerus* pulled his eyebrows down. For a moment he seemed as angry as I have ever seen any other human get, and then he quietly and firmly asked me which newspaper I was from. It was a surprising question, and no doubt I hesitated a moment too long before claiming the *Observer*, because Professor Sir Smithfield stood up and ordered me to leave at once.

I began to explain that I was actually a fellow doctor and a longtime student of his textbook, but this only further enraged him. He loudly shouted that he was summoning security, and then undermined this threat by tinkling a delicate handbell on his desk. After that, we stared at each other until we heard a stomping and panting on the stairs. Eventually, the old porter hurried in, pausing only briefly to puff on his nitrate spray, before he frog-marched me down the stairs, across the quadrangle and out into the street. He then went back inside, locked the gates behind him, and threatened to call the police if I didn't "disperse."

Jesus Green was nearby, and I went and sat on a bench there to try and puzzle it all out. As ever, the new information I had obtained only added more confusion. Professor Sir Smithfield may have just been a cantankerous old curmudgeon who did not tolerate interruptions, but the mention of Amelia's name seemed undeniably to have enraged him.

This was in diametric opposition to the normal way of things. Once at St. Luke's, when the nurses had reported a new admission as being irritable, Dr. Sudbury had requested Amelia go and speak to him. Her rationale was that if the patient could be short even with Amelia, there must be something going wrong inside his skull. The patient was indeed curt with Amelia, and sure enough the scan this earned him showed he had suffered a small bleed on the brain.

I could not use my return train ticket for another two hours, and so I killed some time at the Fitzwilliam Museum. I'd been enticed in by posters for an exhibition about polar exploration, but once I got inside I found myself inexorably drawn to the museum's collection of Egyptian mummies. The dedication and respect with which the Egyptians had preserved their dead rulers seemed to be matched only by the enthusiasm with which the British had plundered them. Remembering the paternal care Dr. O'Leary took of his charges, I told myself that we at least generally treated our own dead better now.

But then a memory, of myself as a medical student. In my second year, I still harbored a vague but absurd notion of becoming some kind of brain surgeon, and had signed up for a module in head and neck anatomy, which turned out to utilize the leftover heads from the cadavers whose torsos were currently being enthusiastically dismembered by the first years. There were thirty of us in this class, and on the first morning each of us was issued a head to dissect, a process that we would commence by cleaving it in two on a bandsaw. And so we waited in line to do so, casually chatting about our hangovers and plans for the next weekend while each holding a decapitated human head in our hands. It does something to you, medicine, it really does.

An hour later, as I waited on the station platform, I spotted Professor Sir Smithfield hurrying toward me in the company of an equally determined and furious-looking young woman. She introduced herself as the college press officer and handed me a printed piece of paper that began with today's date and the angry salutation, "To Whomever It May Concern." It stated that the University of Cambridge had no record of an Amelia Bowen ever graduating, and had retained no further information relating to any period of study or incidents therein. If the *Observer* or any other publication intended to assert otherwise, they must first contact the college's solicitors or risk a libel suit.

Not for the first time that year, I found myself baffled and traveling on a train. I stared at the piece of paper all the way back to London. What did they mean, that she had never graduated? Was it somehow possible that Amelia had not actually qualified

as a doctor? The idea seemed preposterous, and yet there it was
on the paper in front of me:

THE UNIVERSITY OF CAMBRIDGE POSSESSES NO RECORD OF THIS PERSON EVER HAVING GRADUATED.

My train came back into St. Pancras, and so I went next door
to the British Library to look Amelia up on the medical register.
Nowadays the medical register is online, but back then it was still
a large hardbound book, and I had previously noticed that they
kept a copy of it in the reading room. I began by looking myself
up. I told myself I was simply making sure it was a new enough
edition that contained our peer group, but I think I just wasn't
quite ready to find out Amelia had never actually graduated.

My own entry was there—albeit with an asterix that meant I
had conditions on my practice—and so with trepidation I turned
to the Bs. I exhaled with relief when I saw Amelia's name, but
caught my breath again as I read to the end of the line:

Amelia Bowen MB BS (with Honors) Registered. Prague 1995.

Prague. In all the time we had known each other, Amelia
had never once mentioned Prague, let alone that she had gone
to medical school there. The word on the page seemed so alien
and unexpected in this context that I might even have assumed
it was a misprint. But Felix had mentioned Prague with almost
his dying breath, and I anyway already knew all about the medical school there. After all, I had nearly transferred there myself
during the academic nadir of my own third year.

Nowadays it is a far more revered institution, but twenty years
ago Prague was best-known as a second-chance medical school.
It was the place that medical students went to finish their courses
after other universities had kicked them out, or failed applicants
with the richest parents went to commence them.

It was impossible to believe that Amelia had ever failed anything in her life, but I now took out the photograph and saw
what I had previously missed. The medieval bridge was not in
Cambridge, nor were the nearby buildings the colleges I had
first presumed. One ancient city looks much like another, but
in the far background there was a block of what I now saw was
brutalist Soviet architecture. The picture of Amelia and Felix
with their arms around each other had not been taken in Cambridge. It had been taken in Prague.

I looked around the reading room, as if I might somehow be
caught in my discoveries, and that in turn might make them ir-
reversibly real. Some diseases must present themselves, but I did
not like the way this one was shaping up. Whatever the answer
might be—and however it might relate to George's death—
Amelia seemed to be ever more intimately caught up in it.

When Dr. Sudbury could not make a diagnosis, she had a
habit of focusing on only the patient's most unusual symptom.
An unusual rash or intractable hiccups might have twenty or
thirty possible causes, but one of those was indubitably the answer to the entire case. This, then, was the approach I decided
to take with the mystery that had begun to envelop Amelia.

The most unusual part of the whole thing was a student as
obviously gifted as Amelia commencing her studies in Cambridge, but graduating from Prague. And yet she had clearly
begun at Cambridge, so what had gone wrong there? How had
she ended up in Prague? I could only imagine that something
very bad indeed had occurred at Cambridge; Dr. Smithfield's
assumption that I was from a newspaper, and the alacrity with
which he had subsequently summoned the press officer, seemed
to suggest it may even have been newsworthy.

The microfiche librarian helped me locate the *Cambridge Advertiser*, and I began to dig. I started with 1990, the year Amelia
would have commenced university if she'd graduated in 1995.
By now it was already 6:00 p.m. and I'd have to leave by seven

thirty to make handover, so even though the *Advertiser* was only weekly I did not hold out much hope. An hour of scrolling through endless pages of local news about controversial planning decisions, record-setting jumble sales and rained-off fun days seemed to confirm that I would not get far. But then, just after 7:00 p.m., I spotted a headline entitled **INCIDENT AT MAGDA-LENE**. It provided no details, except that two ambulances had been called to the college.

The following week's issue contained more information about the incident, which included the fact that a second year student had died of an ecstasy overdose during a night out. The drug had apparently been supplied by a fellow student, and the college was now conducting an urgent investigation. There was nothing in the next week, but one more week after that the college had put out a statement that the student who had supplied the drug had been expelled. It did not mention her by name, but it stated that she had been studying medicine on the college's most prestigious scholarship. It was therefore undoubtedly Amelia.

I sat back and exhaled a sigh of relief. It was tragic that a young student had died, but it explained Dr. Smithfield's reaction to the mention of Amelia's name, why she had ended up in Prague, and why she had felt obliged to keep this part of her history a secret. I chastised myself for the darker thoughts I had begun to entertain, about whether Amelia might have somehow had some involvement in the events at St. Luke's.

Of course, the articles I had found did not explain how Amelia and Felix Smollett had known each other, nor did any of this explain why George had killed himself. The greater malady remained undiagnosed, and I spent my week of nights summoning up the courage to do something so unconscionable it still makes me shudder even to think of it: I paid a visit to the grieving Smolletts to see if I could wrangle any more information out of them.

The "hero killer" might be the most recognizable type of healthcare murderer. There have been many examples, but German intensive care nurse Niels Hogel is one of the most striking.

Due to the frequent cardiac arrests that occurred during Hogel's shifts and his undeniable skill at saving those patients, Hogel's colleagues dubbed him Resuscitation Rambo and even fashioned him a necklace out of used adrenalin syringes. There was only one small problem: Hogel was himself deliberately causing the cardiac arrests by injecting his patients with powerful drugs such as lidocaine and amiodarone.

Hogel had commenced working in the intensive care unit in Oldenburg Clinic at the age of twenty-one. Two years after he joined the department, hospital administrators noticed an unusual spike in resuscitations and deaths, and Hogel was transferred to the anesthesiology department under a cloud of suspicion. His new supervisors quickly grew uneasy about the number of emergent situations he continued to find himself in, but the hospital still did not fire Hogel. Instead, they paid him severance and gave him a reference that noted his ability to act "prudently and in an objectively correct manner in critical situations."

This reference enabled Hogel to obtain a new job at a clinic in nearby Delmenhorst, where he was again soon noted to be involved in more emergencies and fatalities than he should have been. All the same, in the absence of clear-cut evidence, hospital administrators once again failed to act definitively. It would be several more years before a colleague finally caught Hogel standing over a dying patient with four empty vials of unprescribed medication nearby.

The ensuing police investigation noted that deaths had almost doubled since Hogel's arrival at Delmenhorst, and he was ultimately convicted of eighty-five counts of murder. The true number of victims is believed to be higher still, and many of the deaths could undoubtedly have been avoided if the hospitals who employed Hogel had acted on their first suspicions.

Why did Niels Hogel do it? Like many so-called "hero killers," his primary motivation seems not to have been to harm the patients under his care, but rather to impress his colleagues with his skill in saving them; the fact that the patients he poisoned often did die seems to have merely been the cost of doing business.

CHAPTER 40

It might well be one of the worst things I have ever done, but I at least called ahead. Fortunately this time it was Admiral Smollett who answered the phone, and he was too polite to decline my request. And that was how I found myself standing nervously outside a town house in Chelsea at eleven o'clock on a Saturday morning. I took a deep breath, and knocked on the door.

It was Dr. Smollett who opened the door. If she was perturbed by my visit, she did not show it, and ushered me into a front room straight out of *Town & Country* magazine, all pinks and purples and watercolor paintings of Norfolk landscapes on the wall. One of them was of the beach I used to walk on near The Healing Place, but it seemed best not to mention this.

Admiral Smollett brought through tea and biscuits on a tray, and we all sat in silence while he poured it. He then asked about my journey, and I told him it had been fine and offered them both my condolences again. Dr. Smollett nodded politely, and then asked me why I was there, and what was it that I wanted from them?

There was no point in lying to Dr. Smollett. She knew the way my mind worked, because hers worked in exactly the same way. Moreover, having been one herself, she knew full well that junior doctors didn't pay home visits to the bereaved parents of deceased patients, and especially not months after those patients had died.

And so I told the Smolletts the truth, or at least a version of it. I told them I was here because my colleague and housemate George had killed himself, and I still did not understand why. I was here because it seemed likely that shortly before George died, Felix had given him a photograph, and this photograph seemed to have distressed George greatly and may have even played a role in what followed. I was here because I hoped they might somehow be able to shed some light on all of this.

The Smolletts seemed chagrined, but not entirely surprised, and for a moment I let myself hope they might be about to give me my unifying diagnosis. As it turned out, they were merely accustomed to their late son causing mischief.

"Unfortunately, that does sound rather like something Felix might have done," Admiral Smollett said. "He did have a habit of, well, enjoying getting a reaction from people."

"You've brought the photograph, I assume?" said Dr. Smollett.

I took it out and passed it over to them.

"He's so young there," said Admiral Smollett.

"Where was this taken?" asked Dr. Smollett.

"I believe it's Prague," I said. "He mentioned something to me about it once. And there are those buildings in the back."

"He loved it in Prague," Admiral Smollett nodded. "And we were so happy he was having a good time. He'd got himself in a bit of a trouble here in London, and so he went out there to teach English. Of course, that turned out to be where he first got into the really bad stuff."

"Oh?" I asked.

"He never injected before he went to Prague," Dr. Smollett said. "Not that that wouldn't have happened elsewhere. It's a common enough trajectory, as you do know."

Her husband had not clocked this, but I knew that Dr. Smollett was not referring to my professional experience, but telling me that she knew about my own struggles.

"I wondered if either of you might recognize the girl?" I said.

Both Smolletts looked closely at Amelia, and then shook their heads.

"He wouldn't tell us much," said Admiral Smollett, "but I know he did meet a girl out there. He was besotted with her for a while, but that ended abruptly, and we did not hear more after that."

As Admiral Smollett spoke, I noticed that Dr. Smollett was studying me.

"Do you know the girl?" she asked me.

"No," I said, "I don't think that I do." Even I thought I sounded entirely unconvincing, and I realized then that Dr. Smollett would have known all about the second chance medical school in Prague.

"Then I don't see how this all ties in with your dead friend," she said.

"Me either," I said. "It might not. I just—I'm trying to find all the information I can."

"Maybe you need to find out who the girl is?" Admiral Smollett suggested.

"I think I do," I agreed. "Anyway, I've taken up enough of your time."

I stood up to go, but my hosts remained seated. They were not done with me.

"We were actually also hoping you might give us some information," said Admiral Smollett.

I sat back down, feeling my heart sink as I did so.

"We never really got to the bottom of Felix dying," explained Dr Smollett. "I mean, I've never even heard of a patient who keeps getting recurrent endocarditis with different organisms. Have you?"

It was true I had not heard of such a thing either but, equally, most patients do not continue to inject themselves after they have been diagnosed with a life-threatening disease. Dr. Smollett already knew what I was thinking.

"We've been told you gave him clean needles, so it wasn't those," she said. "It must have been the stuff itself. It must have been contaminated. So, the key to all those infections is going to be where on earth he was still getting it from."

I had also wondered where Felix was getting his heroin from, but I'd assumed his young acolytes brought it in for him. The only other possible explanation was that he was obtaining it from somewhere in the hospital, but that had been difficult enough for me to do.

"Where do you think he was getting it from?" I asked.

"I don't know," said Dr. Smollett, "but something doesn't feel right, you know? For it to be that consistently contaminated—it seems, well, tremendously unfortunate. That doesn't happen to most people who do this. And that's before we even talk about whatever that absurd bacteria that killed him was. It apparently lives in the desert, you know."

I could only nod. Dr. Smollett was right: most people who injected heroin did not repeatedly contract endocarditis, let alone multiple obscure forms of it. And yet we both knew it was academic, for finding out where their son had obtained his dirty heroin from would not bring him back. There was a sad and empty silence, and this time when I got up neither of them tried to stop me.

I worked a new shift that afternoon, an invention of Dr. Sudbury's that ran from two o'clock in the afternoon until midnight. Our numbers had recently been swollen by half a dozen doctors

Dr. Sudbury had managed to recruit from Romania. Even as we finally had enough bodies to staff the normal rota, she had instead spotted some efficiency savings. If only one junior was on the morning round on Saturday, that would free up several hours that Dr. Sudbury believed could be more effectively utilized in the busier evening.

The idea almost provoked a mutiny and so did not last long, but it was the reason I found myself having dinner in an empty mess at 8:00 p.m. As always, I was going over it all once again—Dr. and Admiral Smollett, Prague, the repeatedly contaminated heroin—and vaguely watching the news, when I noticed the plant on top of the television. It was a cactus, the one that Saz had brought in after all the other mess plants had died because nobody had bothered to water them.

CHAPTER 41

The Romanians were all remaining in London and so had been happy to work through the holidays. Even better, Dr. Sudbury had somehow recalled that I had worked Christmas and New Year's the previous year, and had given me the whole thing off apart from Christmas Eve. That being so, I flew to Prague on Christmas Day.

The flight was almost entirely empty, my only fellow travelers a group of Czech soldiers, an elderly man, and a school party of young women in headscarves. The flight attendants tried to make the best of it by wearing tinsel in their hair as they served us dehydrated turkey and watery cranberry sauce, but it was like a Christmas Day shift in the emergency department: none of us wanted to be there, and we each knew that somewhere along the line every one of us had made a wrong choice.

I had bought a Prague guidebook at Stansted Airport, but passed the flight in the same way that I now spent just about all of my time: running through the signs and symptoms in search of the mystical unifying diagnosis. With hindsight, I can see myself now as one of those patients who comes to clinic having turned bright yellow, lost forty-two pounds in weight and found a craggy lump in their abdomen but is still genuinely shocked by their diagnosis. Some diseases must present themselves, but perhaps some are so obviously lethal that we enter denial and can only finally come to the diagnosis when the time is right. Somewhere over Germany I gave up trying to solve it and fell asleep. A stewardess wearing faux-fur antlers woke me to put my seat belt on as we came into land.

The airport in Prague was almost empty. Somebody had made a half-hearted attempt to decorate it for Christmas, but this had only made it look even sadder. Perhaps he was just unhappy at having to work Christmas, or maybe it was because I was the last one off the plane and easily the most suspicious-looking among us, but the border guard barked endless questions about where I was going and why. When I eventually asked him how long this was all likely to take, he smirked and informed me that I had now been selected for a random search. He emerged from his cubicle and led me to an anteroom, where three of his equally irritated colleagues awaited me.

Which, of course, was where they found my methadone. I had brought my prescription, so it was legal both for me to possess it and to enter the Czech Republic with it. The border guards did not care about that, and instead took the opportunity to treat me as if I was Pablo Escobar. A sniffer dog was produced, I was aggressively searched, and finally a more senior officer appeared. He had obviously been dragged away from a family meal, and was equally obviously furious about it, and gave me two options: I could dispose of the methadone in front of them, or I could retain it but be held in an airport cell until the next plane departed back to London at nine o'clock that same night. I therefore watched as he poured my red comfort down the sink, and then his colleague—the one who had started this whole thing—stamped my passport, smirked once more, and wished me a merry Christmas and a pleasant stay in the Czech Republic.

My guidebook had warned me the airport taxis were a scam, so I took the bus into town. Or I at least tried to: I boarded the wrong bus, ended up miles away, and had to take a taxi to the Hostel Czech anyway. Prague was now the third in the triumvirate of medieval cities I had visited in the past few months, and as we drove through it I saw the center of town was bustling with tourists, primarily marauding packs of American college students. Disneyland is famously open every day of the year, and I suppose Prague is too.

My guidebook had described the Hostel Czech as a "no-nonsense budget option," which seemed about right. The check-in woman was friendly and spoke English. She asked about my journey and when I told her that the border guards had given me a hard time, she shrugged and said "Yes, fuck them, of course." I appreciated the "of course," and the implication that it went without saying. If nothing else, the guidebook had been right about the hostel being no-nonsense.

The room she assigned me was near the end of a long corridor. It was cramped, with a single bed, a cheap TV angled on a stand in one corner, and a tiny sink. The rooms on either side were identical, except each one was occupied by what seemed to be a dozen Australian backpackers. I encountered one of them in the corridor on my way to the shared bathroom. He invited me to join them at a Christmas party, but I declined and explained that I planned to get an early night. Back in my room, I waited for them to go out to their party, but as it crept toward ten I realized I had misunderstood: the party was being held in their rooms, and also outside in the corridor that ran between them. I fashioned some earplugs from paper towel and fell asleep to uneasy dreams haunted by antipodeans shrieking in stereo. It reminded me of the nights I had spent at Collette's place.

In Britain, the day after Christmas is Boxing Day, and it is a time for hangovers, bad television, and self-loathing. In middle Europe it is St. Stephen's Day, the feast day of the Christian martyr who was stoned to death for merely suggesting that God did not dwell solely in the temple. In that perspective, even if she was innocent of all but one unintentional murder, Louise Fisher had got off lightly. Such were my thoughts as I ate my continental breakfast and read my guidebook.

I was trying not to think very much about the day ahead. I had come to Prague in the hope of finding out more about Amelia's time here, and perhaps even her relationship to Felix Smollett. But I had two problems. One was that, without my methadone, I would shortly be going into withdrawal. The other was that I simply had no idea where to begin my investigations. If it weren't Christmas I might have tried the university, but it would be closed for the holidays, and anyway I did not even have a name like I'd had with Professor Smithfield.

The sole thing I had was the photograph. When I had showed it to the receptionist at the Hostel Czech, her face had lit up with recognition. At first I could not believe my luck, and it soon turned out I was right not to. The receptionist had not recognized the people in the picture, but rather the bridge itself: she told me it was the Charles Bridge, the most popular tourist attraction in the Czech Republic. This did not seem to bode well.

With no better leads to follow, I went there. It was an ordinary medieval bridge over a wide river, but it currently played host to a Christmas market. If this sounds picturesque, it was, but you also have to understand that Prague was anyway more or less one giant Christmas market. Here on the Charles Bridge, as everywhere else, none of the tourists seemed to actually be buying anything, just half-heartedly lifting up items to look at, then quickly putting them back down when the stallholders got too interested.

After a couple of missteps, I located the spot where the pic-

ture had been taken. The buildings all lined up immaculately,
but what did it really matter? There had not been a Christmas
market when Amelia and Felix had stood here on some summer's day a decade or so earlier, so it was not like the stallholders selling handcrafted wooden birdhouses would remember
them. Anyway, one of the people in the picture was dead, and
the other was in Zambia, so what was I even doing here? Not
for the first time, the thought occurred to me that telling me to
go to Prague might just have been another piece of Felix Smollett's mischief.

I sat on the edge of the bridge and took out my guidebook. If
I had come all this way for nothing, I might as well see some of
the sights. The top recommendation was the Prague Zoo, but if
I'd wanted to spend my time looking at creatures perplexed to
have been removed from their natural habitat and imprisoned
for observation, I'd have been at work on the admissions ward.
Instead, I chose the nearby Alchemical Museum.

It was housed in the basement of a medieval tenement. Once
you purchased your ticket you passed beneath a dragon that
guarded the stairwell to the secret laboratory beneath. The fact
that to modern eyes the "dragon" was obviously a badly taxi-
dermied crocodile hardly mattered, because a seventeenth-
century visitor would not have known the difference, and I anyway respected the confidence trick. We did much the same thing
at the hospital with our stethoscopes, our white coats, and our
impenetrable language. The important thing was not that we
knew everything there was to know about the human body, it
was that our patients believed we did. And, like a stuffed crocodile masquerading as a dragon, the trinkets of our trade contributed to the performance.

Likewise, after I had descended the stairs into the "secret laboratory" that was really a dank stone basement, who was I to
question the guide's absurd claim that in this very room lead had

once been turned into gold? After all, here were the very burettes, the scales, the flasks that the long-ago alchemists had used.

Still, as the guide lectured us on the miracle of alchemy, I found myself thinking that these medieval Czechs had been going about it all wrong. If I was to devote my life to transmogrifying one substance into another, I would not bother messing around with lead and gold, or even wine and the blood of Christ. No, I would perfect the art of transforming water into morphine. All the riches and salvation in the world were not worth two minutes of the precious bliss. Besides, if you could make morphine from water, you would very quickly end up with all the gold anyway, and you would have done more to alleviate the sorrows and suffering of this world than even Jesus himself.

On and on the guide droned, and the more he spoke about alchemy the more I thought about my own personal gold. It had felt cold when we descended and now it was hot. Far too hot. I could feel the sweat trickling down my back and chest. I felt nauseous too, and then I noticed that the room had begun to spin. It was almost imperceptible at first, a slight rocking from side to side, but within a minute or two it was all I could do to remain standing.

I was going into withdrawal. I turned and hurried upstairs, underneath the stuffed crocodile and out onto the street, where I puked up the remains of my breakfast onto the cobbles. Nobody walking past so much as batted an eyelid. Tourists puking in the street seemed to just be a normal part of everyday life in Prague.

I knew that opioid withdrawal would not kill me. Still, this one felt far worse than I had experienced before, and I realized then I had been on the methadone for five months. In the distance I spotted the flashing green cross of a pharmacy, and I stumbled down the street to it and bought every medicine I could think of that might help in any way: dramamine, acetaminophen, ibuprofen, even Gaviscon.

I then entered the nearest café, ordered a beetroot soup that I did not touch, and took all the pills instead. Ten minutes later, I went to the bathroom and threw them all up. My bowels then decided to get in on the act and I spent half an hour alternately cramping and shitting. Somebody knocked on the door and shouted in Czech, but there was nothing I could do. When it was over, I caught sight of myself in the mirror. I looked like Felix Smollett had on the night he died.

But I would not die. I gave myself the same lecture I had given to so many hundreds of addicts over the years: it was not my job to make them feel good, it was my job to make sure they did not die. And *Smithfield's Textbook of Human Disease* categorically said that opioid withdrawal would not kill them.

The lecture worked about as well on myself as it did on them. By that I mean I got into a taxi, gave the driver what I thought was the equivalent of ten pounds but later discovered was a hundred, and asked him to take me to the nearest emergency department. He did not need telling twice, and was even good enough to stop to let me puke again on the way.

I knew that if I booked in with withdrawal symptoms and told the truth, the advice would be the same in Prague as it would be anywhere else in the world: GTFO. That being so, I booked myself in as a suspected appendicitis.

In those bygone days before CT scans became routinely available, suspected appendicitis was one of the few diagnoses that would earn you an automatic hospital admission anywhere in the world. If as a patient you turned up at the emergency department, told the doctor you had a pain that had begun in the center of your abdomen and moved to its lower right side, then the only way they could be sure it was not appendicitis was by admitting you and observing you for twenty-four hours. If you deteriorated during this time, you would be taken to theater and your appendix whipped out; if you didn't deteriorate, you could then be sent home with a shrug and a packet of acetaminophen. Many professional hypochondriacs were aware of this, and often pulled the stunt a few times until somebody went ahead and removed their appendix, either mistakenly or simply to stop them coming back.

To begin with, it worked like a charm. The surgical resident who saw me first had been well-trained, and knew to watch the response on my face as he palpated my abdomen; being equally well-trained, I flinched and grimaced at all the appropriate moments. When he had finished his examination, he said that he could not rule out this being appendicitis, and apologized that he would now need to take bloods and keep me in for admission. I nodded that I understood, flinched again for good measure, and asked if there might be something I could have for the pain? Ten minutes later, a nurse appeared and shot me up with something intravenous that immediately alchemized my pain into bliss.

I lay there for a few hours, observing the controlled chaos around me. Emergency departments really are the same all over the world: the many impatient patients, the few genuinely sick ones, the harried and weary staff tending to them all. The lab codes sellotaped to the computer. The many gray telephones and the single red one. The passive-aggressive printed notices. The chipped coffee mug with a slogan that even in Czech I knew must say, "You don't have to be mad to work here, but it helps."

I did not know which particular opioid the doctor had given me, but I had decided that I would keep up the ruse for as long as I could. Major abdominal surgery and even the removal of a surplus body part seemed a small price to pay for several more doses of the good stuff. When everything was honey, nothing else mattered.

At midnight, a more senior surgeon snapped back the curtains, her junior colleague from earlier trailing in her wake. The senior surgeon was also well-trained, but had the added benefit of both experience and a little more information. My bloods had come back normal, which did not entirely exclude appendicitis, but

did not support it either, and I likewise had not spiked a fever
since arriving. She therefore tried several things in an attempt to
catch me out: having me cough; pressing down on the left side
of my abdomen, but releasing quickly enough the pain would
have been felt on the right; asking me if I would like something
to eat. I flinched appropriately for the first two, and assured her
that I'd be happy to never eat again. She nodded, and said she
was now fairly certain that I did have appendicitis, but the only
way to confirm the diagnosis was to do a rectal examination. I
had not considered that, and the mention of it must have made
me flinch in a telling way, because she now nodded for her junior colleague to leave.

"You're medical, aren't you?" she said once he had gone, and
I knew it was over.

"I'm a physician in London," I admitted.

"It seems like a lot of work to go to for some morphine,"
she said.

"I'm usually on methadone. They took it from me at the airport. I started to withdraw."

"So why not just ask us for some? Why this—" she searched
for the English word, and seemed to relish it when she found
it "—*charade*?"

"Because you wouldn't have given it to me otherwise," I said.

She nodded. This was undeniably true.

"But why are you here on the day after Christmas at all, drug-
seeking in a Czech emergency room?"

I don't know if it was the opioid, or the relief of no longer
being in withdrawal, or simply having somebody to talk to, but
I told her. I told her the whole story: that I worked at St. Luke's,
the hospital she had probably heard about this year; that they
had initially thought I was the one responsible for the deaths;
that my friend had died; that a nurse I worked with had been
found responsible for the deaths; that there was something troubling about the whole thing, and it seemed to somehow involve

a young patient of mine who had died, and a colleague who now worked in Zambia.

The photograph had found its way onto the cabinet beside my bed with the rest of the contents of my pockets, and the surgeon now picked it up and studied it.

"This is your friend who killed himself?"

"No," I said, "not the man. But the woman is my colleague. Her name is Amelia."

"Yes, I recognize her," she said. "She went to medical school with us."

If my first reaction was shock to have got so lucky, my second was to kick myself for not having done so sooner. Of course the most likely place to find a doctor who had studied medicine with Amelia in Prague was the city's biggest hospital. This surgeon was about my age, and my first action that morning should have been to come to the hospital and search for somebody like her to show the photograph. Still, she could not tell me much. She explained that by the time they graduated—the numbers swollen each year by an influx of medical students from abroad—each year group at Prague University consisted of upward of five hundred students, and she had only known Amelia as an acquaintance.

"Is there anyone else that I could talk to?" I asked. "Somebody who might have known her better?"

The surgeon thought for a moment, and then told me that the guy Amelia had been closest friends with was a Dr. Stepien who she believed now worked at the National American Clinic in Karlov Vary. Her pager went then, and she told me to wait for my discharge paperwork. I did so, but what arrived instead was a nurse with a box containing enough pethidine to get me through the next few days. I could have wept with gratitude, but as it was I simply asked the nurse to thank the doctor for me. I got dressed and hurried back to the Hostel Czech, where I slept fitfully until six o'clock in the morning, wolfed down my breakfast and two pethidine, and headed to the station.

CHAPTER 42

The train out to Karlov Vary would take two hours. Seen from a carriage window, the urban sprawl outside Prague looked a lot like the central Scotland of my youth: housing estates and industrial parks, factory farms, and graffitied children's playgrounds. I quickly fell asleep.

I awoke as we approached Karlov Vary. Something new had appeared in the landscape: billboards in English that touted the benefits of all kinds of medical and surgical procedures. Nineteenth-century travelers had once visited European spa towns to take their restorative waters, but nowadays they came for liposuction, nose jobs and colonoscopies. It was at least a better class of tourist than the marauding packs of puking exchange students that roamed Prague.

It was easy to find the National American Clinic, because a giant billboard in the station proclaimed I should turn left out the doors, and I would reach it in under three minutes. The bigger challenge was navigating the insistent throngs of hawkers who seemed to all make a beeline for me. Maybe I still looked pale after yesterday's events, but they clearly considered me the traveler in most urgent need of expensive private medical care, and eagerly pressed flyers into my hands while asking what I was looking for. When I did not reply, they listed the services they could provide and the discounts they could obtain: endoscopy at 10 percent off, three sessions of cryotherapy for the price of two, as much liposuction as I could tolerate for five hundred euros. I smiled politely and continued out of the station.

Apart from a tired-looking Stars and Stripes that hung outside the National American Clinic and a price list in dollars, there was nothing American about the place beyond its bombastic name. Be that as it may, the marketing strategy seemed to have worked because the waiting room—which, with its marble floors and fresh flowers, was more like the lobby of an upmarket hotel than any hospital I have ever worked in—was packed. Mostly, the would-be patients seemed to be German, although I overheard some speaking in French and also what I think was Russian. Nobody looked particularly sick, but nobody looked entirely well either.

The receptionist was wearing a nurse's uniform, but she wasn't really a nurse. If she had been, she'd have known that the MRI scan of the customer in front of me had been canceled because the internal pacemaker circled on his intake form meant that going ahead with the scan risked blowing up the entire building. As it was, she apologized for the inconvenience and said she would speak to the radiologist and see if the patient could be squeezed in today.

When it came my turn, I requested to see Dr. Stepien. The pretend nurse asked if I had an appointment. When I told her it was a personal matter, she told me firmly that the doctors did not see personal callers. I therefore asked her if Dr. Stepien had availability; when she acknowledged he had some later that morning, I requested an appointment for Botox, which the billboard outside had told me was the cheapest service available at a hundred and fifty US dollars. The pretend nurse seemed to consider arguing, but a queue was forming behind me and she told me my appointment would be in half an hour. I passed the time reading various health magazines, most of which seemed to concur that the secret of a long and enjoyable life was to have regular enemas, preferably of the lilac and cucumber variety.

When the pretend nurse called my name, a real nurse led me into a clinic room that was more like a penthouse suite. Here, she measured and weighed me, and performed an entirely unnecessary ECG. Five minutes later, Dr. Stepien appeared. He was about the same age as me, and this caused him to do a double take.

"You are not here for Botox," he said, not as a question but as a statement of fact.

For the second time in less than twelve hours, I found myself confessing to a Czech doctor that I was seeking healthcare under false pretenses. I told Dr. Stepien about my encounter with his surgical colleague in the emergency room in Prague, though I of course omitted the part about having gone there because I was withdrawing from opioids. Instead, I took the photograph out to show him.

He stared at it for a moment and then sat down and took his glasses off.

"You paid a hundred and fifty dollars to ask me about this, so I suppose you must have a good reason?"

"I do," I said.

I left that to hang, and after a moment he began to talk. Maybe I had learned something from DI Afferson, after all.

Dr. Stepien told me that he had met Amelia on the day she arrived in Prague, as she had been assigned the room next door to him in the residences. She had only completed a year and a half of study in England, but they had fast-tracked her into the third year of the curriculum, which was his class. The two of them had quickly become close friends, and he had acted as her guide to Prague. He spontaneously told me they had never been lovers, which made me think he probably wished they had.

The most striking thing about Amelia, he said, had been her brain. He had never met anybody with a mind like hers. She had seemed to require to only hear a fact once to forever retain it, but more than that she was the most logical thinker and best diagnostician he had ever met. Their professors had noticed this too; Amelia had won every academic prize going, and had even been granted her degree with honors. This was a once-in-a-decade distinction at Prague University, and consequently Amelia had been offered her pick of residencies.

Stepien caught himself then, and asked me if I had heard everything I needed to. I hadn't, of course, and he must have known that I'd hardly have traveled from London simply to hear him reminisce about the academic achievements of our mutual friend. Nonetheless, I had the feeling that if I pushed too hard for more information on Amelia, he would end our consultation. So instead I pointed to the photograph.

"And do you recognize him?" I asked.

Stepien looked again at the photograph, and nodded.

"This is Felix," he said. "They dated briefly. He wasn't around for long, and he was a drug addict."

I nodded. "Felix was my patient," I said. "He died of endocarditis."

This visibly surprised Stepien. He studied me now, trying to figure me out, and I saw something soften in his face. It appalls me to write it now, but in that moment it felt true: I think he'd decided that any doctor who had killed Felix Smollett could not be all bad.

"And Felix, he was Amelia's patient too?" Stepien asked.

"No. But she worked in the same hospital. It's complicated but, look, I was mainly wondering if you had ever practiced with her?"

"Yes. We did our residency together for a year."

"And how was that?" I asked.

"Our residency? The same as yours, I suppose. Brutal. Sick patients. No sleep. I think it is the same everywhere, no?"

"But how was Amelia, as a colleague?" I asked.

Stepien looked at me then, and I had the feeling that he knew for the first time what I was really asking, and why.

"In our first six months, she was the best resident in the hospital," he said.

"And the second?"

Stepien sighed. "Well, in the second job, we can say that Amelia had a lot of bad luck."

"What kind of bad luck did she have?"

"I mean, not her personally. But her patients. The patients always seemed to have bad luck—complicated illnesses, strange drug reactions, and just many unexplained events. She was the very best at fixing them, of course, and to begin with we were always relieved that she was there."

"To begin with?"

"It happened too often. Nobody should be that unlucky."

Stepien did not say anything more. He did not need to.

"But there wasn't an investigation?" I asked.

"It's a hospital," he said. "Sometimes people die."

Sometimes people die. I knew that, of course, just like I knew and understood exactly what Stepien was telling me.

"I have to go now," he said. "I have another patient who does actually want Botox. I hope you got your money's worth here."

"I did," I said.

When doctors give our patients bad news, we sometimes leave them alone in the room for as long as they need. I sat there in the fancy room in the National American Clinic for a long time, finally contemplating the truth that I should have worked out long ago. I had my unifying diagnosis, and it had been right in front of me all along. The single piece of information that made everything fit was Amelia.

Of all people, George the orthopod had been the doctor to make the diagnosis first. Perhaps he had put it all together himself, or maybe he had got most or even all of it from Felix Smollett. However he had come to learn about it, George had known, and had seen no route out for himself but to end it all: he adored Amelia and could not possibly have lived without her, and yet he now had to either send her to prison forever or break his sacred oath and turn a blind eye to murder. A logical and binary surgeon to the end, George had chosen the only pragmatic solution: he had killed himself. Likewise, he had hidden the photograph in the most secret place he knew not because he had ever intended me or anybody else to ever find it, but because his training had endlessly taught him he must never destroy an important record.

Felix, of course, had possessed no such scruples. When they had happened to cross paths again at St. Luke's, he'd used whatever he had known about Amelia's past to blackmail her into supplying him with the opioids he craved. This was no doubt the real subject of the argument that had nearly caused the nurses to call the police; it had indeed been about methadone, but we had all entirely underestimated Felix's leverage.

Even at that, it is possible Felix's hold over Amelia was merely the knowledge that she had not graduated from Cambridge, but—recalling Felix's fascination with every morbid detail of Operation Nightingale—I suspected it was far more than that. Amelia had reciprocated by giving him his opioids, but making sure they were contaminated. She had finally managed to dispatch him with a speck of the cactus soil from the mess that had brewed its lethal badness inside Felix even as she flew to Zambia.

As for the others, well, they had all been Amelia too. Mrs. Horsburgh, who had died of an opioid overdose that nobody had spotted—along with the opioid, Amelia had also given her belladonna to dilate her pupils, hadn't she? And Mr. Singh, and the patient with the flecainide and beta-blocker, and my patient with the bright red blood, and who even knew how many more than twelve her real final total had been?

It was still not impossible that Louise Fisher had killed Mr. Athole, but it seemed a great coincidence; the more likely explanation was that Amelia had written up the insulin on Mr. Athole's drug chart, and then removed it once the deed was done. Louise had taken the credit for Amelia's belladonna diagnosis at her case presentation; Amelia then ensuring Louise also took the credit for one of her murders seemed to have a perfect symmetry to it that must have appealed to Amelia's fastidious side. We would never know the truth about Mr. Grenslow, but Occam's razor held that he died by the same hand that all the others had.

And who knew what had happened in Cambridge? The most generous version was that the trauma of accidentally causing the death of her friend had somehow contributed to Amelia's actions. But something in Smithfield's reaction—his fury at the mention of Amelia's name, his instinct to involve the press officer—told me that he had long known that she was capable of unspeakable things. Likewise, what had occurred between Amelia and I in George's room—and the diary that had gone missing thereafter—now took on an entirely new meaning.

On the train back to Prague, I did something I had not done in months: I cried. I cried for myself, for Mrs. Horsburgh, the Wilsons, Mr. Grenslow, and Mr. Athole and his firm handshake and Rudolph the Red-Nosed Reindeer sweater. I cried for Louise Fisher, in prison and condemned as evil for crimes she had not committed. I even cried for Felix Smollett and his parents. Mostly, I cried for poor old George. I'd always hoped that finding out why he had killed himself might bring me some relief, but this brought only anguish. My friend had not left this world because he had failed an exam or lacked enough serotonin to make it through the dark February days. He had left this world because he had discovered that the person he loved more than life itself was a murderess.

CHAPTER 43

Back in in London, I waited until after New Year to call DI Afferson. The approaching millennium had rendered the whole city hysterical, and I wanted to ensure I had his full attention. For my own part, I marked the passing of a thousand years in suitably anticlimactic fashion, by taking an extra dose of methadone and getting an early night.

The officer who answered Afferson's extension on the third of January told me Afferson was on sabbatical, writing his next book. The inflection in her voice told me that she did not approve of this. I then asked to speak to DS Newington, and was surprised to be put through to something called the Community Safety Initiative. It seemed like the kind of place a detective would be sent as a punishment in the movies. I never found out if that was what had happened, because Newington seemed irritated to hear from me, and even more so when I told her I was calling with important information about the events at St. Luke's. She scolded me that the case was closed, but said she would pass the message on to DI Afferson. Three days later, Afferson paged me at work, and we agreed to meet in a pub in Euston.

It transpired he had wanted to meet in Euston because it was near the British Library, where he had been working on his Aberystwyth Milkman book. When I got to the pub, Afferson was already sitting at a table with a pint in front of him, and made a show of getting up and buying me one.

"Now then," he said as he sat back down. "Just what was it you wanted to talk to me about?"

"It wasn't Louise Fisher," I said.

"What wasn't Louise Fisher?" he asked.

"Any of it," I said. "She didn't do it."

Unsurprisingly, Afferson seemed irritated by this.

"I've got a confession and a conviction that says otherwise. Are you saying you know something that a High Court judge doesn't?"

"I suppose I am, yes."

"Well, fine. Who was it then? Because unless you are here to confess I don't think you actually know what you are talking about."

"Amelia," I said. "It was Amelia Bowen."

"Your flatmate's girlfriend? No, it wasn't her. We looked at her. I even wrote about it in my book."

"Well, you didn't look at her hard enough."

I thought Afferson might get up and leave then, but he didn't. And that alone told me what I had been looking for that night in Piccadilly: he wasn't entirely convinced it was Louise Fisher, and this thought still nagged at him like a pebble in his shoe.

Afferson did not speak again, but waited for me to talk. I did, but this time it was not because I was incriminating myself. It was because I knew a great many things that he did not.

And so there, in The Euston Flyer while commuters drank pints, a drunk man in a suit played the slots, and trains arrived from and departed for Scotland, I laid it all out for the detective who had become nationally famous on the strength of a false conviction. Afferson did not interrupt, and when I finished speaking, I took out the photograph and placed it on the table. He stared at it.

"So where did you get that from?" he asked.

"It was hidden in George's room all along."

"That's quite a story," he eventually said. "Maybe you should write a book."

I was about to say something, but he cut me off.

"Leave this with me," he said. "I'll look into it."

Afferson lifted up the photograph and walked out of the pub, turning his collar against the January rain as he went. He had hardly touched his pint.

A week went by. And then another, and then another. I called the police station and asked to be put through to Newington again but her extension rang out, and the next time I tried they refused to put me through. I even called Afferson's literary agent and publishers, but neither would relay a message.

Louise Fisher's lawyer was at least willing to talk to me on the phone. He listened to about half of my story and then cut me off and told me that what I was suggesting was "incredibly damaging" to his client. Once a person had been convicted, he told me, innocence and guilt no longer mattered, only legal procedure. The police would never willingly reopen Louise's case, and nobody ever got off by demonstrating actual innocence, or if they did it invariably took decades. No, Louise's best chance at winning her freedom now lay with a legal technicality he was pursuing around her confession having been made before she had been informed of her rights. Claims of actual innocence would jeopardize this, so he asked me not to talk to any reporters, and not to tell Louise about any of this either. I ignored this and wrote her a letter, telling her I had new information, and that I would come to see her in Durham as soon as I could, but there was something I needed to do first.

CHAPTER 44

The thing I needed to do first was go to Zambia.

I was not planning to make some kind of citizen's arrest, and I did not expect to find any new evidence. If anything, telling Amelia what I knew would realistically only make it harder for her to ever be brought to justice. I had no doubt that if she ever chose to disappear, she would likely be able to.

But I needed to know for certain that she was guilty. I mean, I already knew, but I needed to have the diagnosis confirmed. In medicine, making the diagnosis is the important thing, but the true satisfaction lies in performing the test that confirms it: the microscopic confirmation of an elusive parasite, the laboratory identification of a hormone secreted by a rare tumor, the glowing uptake of an isotope on a bone scan. These findings are rarely good news for the patient, but for the doctor they are reassurance that a puzzle has been finally and forever solved.

So I wanted to confirm to myself that I was right. But, perhaps just as much, I wanted Amelia to know that I had caught her. That she might have outsmarted everybody in Cambridge, and Prague, and London, and no doubt Zambia too. But she had not outsmarted me. I had seen her. I knew who she was, and I knew what she was. I knew what she had done to George.

Getting to Zambia itself turned out to be surprisingly easy. I had always imagined Africa as an impossibly distant continent, but the truth was that Zambia was only two plane rides from London and almost even in the same time zone. I would legally need only a yellow fever vaccination, and a clinic in central London did the needful and gave me a prescription for malarone, an antimalarial. When I asked them what to do about my methadone, the nurse said nobody would be remotely interested. This would prove to be correct.

Truly, the malarone was the only difficult part about the whole thing. I could not travel until I had been taking it for two weeks, and it gave me a headache and made me restless. Still, I had worked at St. Luke's for long enough that I knew malaria would give me a worse headache and perhaps also kill me, so it seemed worth it.

I landed first in Cairo, where the international airport was crowded but had the same duty-free stores and ATMs as those I had just left behind in London. It was only on my next flight, aboard the plane to Lusaka, that I began to feel like I had reached another continent.

This plane was much smaller, and half-empty. I was seated beside a garrulous Irish oil worker, who insisted on giving me the benefit of his expertise as a self-styled "old Africa hand." The golden rule, he insisted, was never to catch malaria. But he said none of the drugs worked, and the thing to do was to drink copious amounts of the local beer, which would undoubtedly protect me. I pointedly took a malarone and yawned loudly, but neither of these things deterred him. He proceeded to tell me a long story about once having been aboard a plane that had begun making desperate maneuvers while passing over Uganda. The passengers all assumed some technical malfunction had doomed them, but after twenty minutes the pilot came on the radio and apologized that Idi Amin had spotted them in the sky and demanded an air show. Soon, I really did fall asleep.

We landed at Lusaka a little after seven in the morning. Even inside the tiny terminal it was already far too hot, and only more so when I got outside. Worse, it was almost impossible to find a driver willing to take me to Mbala. They all shook their heads, and mumbled about Mbala being in the Northern Province, and the rainy season making the roads up there too treacherous. Eventually, I found a driver called Jacob who warned me it would take two days but said he would do it for fifty dollars plus expenses. I knew I was supposed to haggle, but I'd recently spent a hundred and fifty dollars on Botox that I didn't even get, so it seemed a bargain.

Like seemingly every other vehicle in Zambia, Jacob's car was a beaten-up four-wheel drive. The red dirt streets around the airport were crowded with people and motorbikes and seemed to my green eyes like a scene from a movie about Africa. At one point Jacob even had to do an emergency stop to avoid hitting a donkey that had wandered out into the street. I was not wearing my seat belt, because there weren't any, and I only narrowly avoided hitting my head on the windscreen.

When Jacob found out I had come from London, he proceeded to talk about Arsenal for the next three hours. I didn't know the names of many of the players, but that did not matter, for Jacob only needed me to agree at certain points and condemn the depravity of Tottenham Hotspur at others. Eventually, he asked me why I was going to Mbala, and I told him that I was visiting an old friend who worked at the clinic there. Jacob nodded, and said Mbala was an excellent place to have a clinic, because it was truly riddled with sickness.

As we got deeper into the countryside, Zambia looked only ever more like African countries did in Hollywood movies. I

quickly ticked off every cliché I knew: minibuses overloaded
with people, potholed roads lined with stalls, children playing
by the roadside, and every third person wearing a premiership
football shirt. I had made the mistake of claiming to support
Chelsea in the hope it might stop Jacob talking about Arsenal
and Tottenham Hotspur, but instead every time he saw someone in a Chelsea shirt he now honked his horn and grinned
back at me in delight.

As evening fell, the air got cooler and soon the sun began to
set. Jacob said he knew a good hotel—five stars, he said, Mi-
chelin guide—and drove us to what turned out to be an abandoned youth hostel. We reclined our seats and slept in the car.
When I woke up it was 5:00 a.m., and the sun was already beginning to rise. We drove north through the morning until,
only fifteen miles from Mbala, Jacob insisted on stopping at a
roadside restaurant to use the bathroom. He was in there for so
long I was worried he was going to require medical assistance,
but when he came out he restarted the car as if nothing had
happened. We reached Mbala a little after noon, just as an approaching storm began to darken the skies.

The hospital at Mbala was unlike any I had seen before or
since. It consisted of little more than a large tent and several
run-down shacks, outside one of which hung a hand-painted
sign that said "ICU." As we approached, I became dimly aware
of a curious keening sound. It sounded like the mating call of
some tropical bird.

The most striking thing, though, was the sheer number of
people. Initially I assumed they were patients or relatives, but
as we got closer I saw that they were mostly gathered around
a small stage, upon which a man was stood. He seemed to be
a preacher of some sort, not from how he was dressed—he too
wore a football shirt—but from the words he spoke: "in my father's house there are many rooms; if it is not so, I would have
told you." I understood then that the keening sound was ema-

nating from the crowd; it was the sound of a great number of
people wailing.

We had happened upon a funeral. Seeming to have realized
this at the same moment as me, Jacob quickly shut off the engine, got out of the car, and stood at respectful attention. I followed suit. The preacher continued his homily, which was all
about how many rooms there were, so many rooms in his father's house. So many rooms that you couldn't imagine. So many
rooms that you could not even conceive of this many rooms.
So many rooms that even God and Jesus and the Holy Spirit
themselves could not keep track of them all. And if even they
could not keep track of them, who were we to ever question
that our almighty Father had a plan and indeed a room for each
and every one of us?

Of course, I wasn't wondering about God's plan for me. I was
wondering who had died, and I felt a little sick thinking the deceased might be yet another of Amelia's victims. I noticed now
that the coffin itself stood off to the side. It was gaudily white
with faux gold handles, the kind of thing you saw on the news
when a pop star had died; some of the red mud had inevitably
got onto it and it looked only even more preposterous. As the
preacher continued, I wondered about the ways a patient might
have died here that were not caused by Amelia. If they had been
a case in my exam, a patient at Mbala would have died from
tuberculosis, HIV, schistosomiasis, or malaria, but of course
Africans have ordinary sicknesses too, so it could just as easily
have been a pneumonia, a bleeding stomach ulcer, a leukemia.
I was still wondering this when I thought I heard the preacher
say, "Dr. Amelia."

I listened more intently, and it came again: Dr. Amelia. The
preacher seemed to be exhorting the crowd to do what Dr.
Amelia would have wanted. And what Dr. Amelia would have
wanted was for them to live healthy and productive lives. To eat
fruit and vegetables. To not smoke cigarettes or drink liquor.

And to exercise regularly, the way she did on the evening runs they had all seen her taking.

The running. That was when I knew I was not mishearing things. Sure enough, the preacher now turned to talking about safety on the road, that God had a plan but he needed each of us to do our part too, and that included always wearing our brightest clothes when we went out running, especially if it was dark. If we did not do this, he said, God could not be responsible for what befell us. I understood then what had happened to Amelia: she had been knocked down and killed on one of her after-work runs.

I had not felt much in a long time, but suddenly I now felt everything all at once. Cheated. Confused. Relieved. Angry. Grateful. Maybe Amelia now would not face justice, but perhaps she never would have anyway. And this way I would not have to worry about convincing Afferson to arrest her, or somehow safeguarding her patients here in Zambia.

As the preacher finished speaking, a torrential rain began to fall, but nobody ran for shelter. Instead six strong men got up and hoisted the muddy white coffin on their shoulders, and the rest of us followed them. They led us behind the hospital buildings and over the small brook that ran by it. There we found ourselves in a green field that turned to red mud even as we walked across it.

Small wooden crosses littered the earth as we made our way to the hole that had only recently been dug, but was already rapidly filling with water; the men did not wait for the preacher, but quickly lowered the coffin in to get ahead of it. The crowd then took turns to throw handfuls of red dirt atop the white coffin, and when my moment came I did my best to remember the good things Amelia had done along with the bad. Jacob threw a handful of earth in too, and when it was all done he patted me on the back and told me it was okay. I appreciated it, but I was even more grateful when he agreed to hang around that night before taking me back to the airport in the morning.

When I introduced myself, the chief nurse of Mbala offered her condolences about Amelia, and then insisted on giving me a tour of her hospital.

The large tent turned out to be the waiting room. It contained so many patients that a clinic consisted of asking everybody who had a cough to raise their hands, then treating them all for tuberculosis. Likewise, anybody with a fever and a raised hand got treated for malaria. When I asked the chief nurse about the patients who were inevitably misdiagnosed, she said, "They come back, or they die."

The thought struck me then that, for all our tests and our scans, it was not so different from what we did at St. Luke's: patch them up, send them out, and see if they come back. Perhaps I inadvertently frowned at this, because the chief nurse hurried to tell me that she hoped I would not consider the care they provided at Mbala lacking. I replied, truthfully, that I had no idea how they managed any of it.

She then proudly took me through the wards and the X-ray room. She apologized profusely that the ICU was currently closed due to rainy-season flooding, and it was only finally as our tour entered the laboratory—little more than a cupboard with a microscope—that I was able to summon up the courage to ask the chief nurse what Amelia had been like as a doctor here.

"She was the best doctor we have ever had!" she said.

I wanted to ask her more, of course. I wanted to ask her whether there had been incidents, but I already knew the answer: if there were, nobody had noticed them. How could they possibly have, when everyone with a cough got treated for tuberculosis, and everyone with a fever got treated for malaria? Anyway, the chief nurse had already begun to imply that I might like to be Dr. Amelia's replacement, so I made a point of saying that I was not half the doctor she had been. The chief nurse did not question this.

That evening there was a kind of wake for Dr. Amelia. It was very informal: curried goat and maize porridge, local beer and endless talk about her. Everybody had a story about Dr. Amelia making a difficult diagnosis and saving some patient or other's life; if I had not witnessed the very same things myself, I would not have believed the half of them. At one point they even asked me what kind of doctor Amelia had been in London, and I told them the truth: she had been an extraordinary one.

Perhaps, I told myself that night, Amelia really had done no harm here. Maybe George's death had changed her, and she had even come to Zambia for redemption. How many lives do you need to save to make up for deliberately taking one. One? Ten? A hundred? A thousand? It was all academic now. Amelia was dead and, with the single exception of Louise Fisher, the book could be closed forever.

Before we left the next morning, Jacob took me aside and said that the chief nurse had asked him to persuade me to stay, as the people of Mbala desperately needed a doctor. I apologized and told him I could not. For one thing, I wasn't good enough, or at least not nearly as good as Amelia. For another, I already had a job, and the conditions still on my practice would anyway render it impossible. Then there were the opioids I needed, and also the fact that I simply did not want to spend a year in the red mud. Jacob said he entirely understood, but we nonetheless spent much of the next two days driving back south in silence.

Dr. Harold Shipman worked as a general practitioner in a small town in the north of England. He was known as a skilled and dedicated physician who would always go the extra mile for his patients, many of whom knew him as the Good Doctor.

Dr. Shipman's kindly facade belied a dark secret: he was murdering his patients, particularly elderly women. He would give them lethal doses of diamorphine, and then alter medical records to indicate they had required the drug due to poor health or addiction. As a GP, he could then write the death certificate that would obviate any need for a postmortem.

Dr. Shipman's downfall only began when he forged the will of one of his victims. The family called in the police, who exhumed the victim's body and found traces of diamorphine. Dr. Shipman claimed the deceased woman had been an opioid addict, but digital forensic examination showed that he had added this information to her medical records only after she had died. When news of his arrest broke, hundreds more people came forward with concerns about the Good Doctor's interactions with their late relatives.

Dr. Shipman killed himself in prison before he could be tried, but a public inquiry subsequently found him responsible for at least two hundred and fifty deaths. The report did not assign a motive to him, but—the single forged will aside—Shipman appears not to have been motivated by money. Likewise, "power" seems unlikely to be the answer: Dr. Shipman's victims were usually frail and vulnerable, and many of them may have had months rather than years left to live. And yet Shipman's motive certainly could not have been mercy, for the vast majority of his patients were not acutely sick.

The most intriguing explanation may relate to Dr. Shipman's own mother. She died of lung cancer when he was seventeen years old, and during her decline the young Harold Shipman would reportedly watch with morbid fascination as her pain was relieved by morphine injections provided by the family doctor. Is it then possible that two hundred and fifty people lost their lives due to some psychodrama playing out in the good doctor's head? It seems as likely as any other explanation, and yet it shows only how unfathomably fragile and utterly random all human life is: a single cell divided erroneously in Mrs. Shipman's lungs, and decades later her son murdered hundreds.

CHAPTER 45

Back in London, I still had a few days of my annual leave left, and I went and found Afferson in the British Library. He came downstairs to talk to me in the tearoom where I had once run into Collette. When I told him about my trip to Zambia, he was furious. He told me there was an active murder investigation and I may very well have jeopardized it. I was fairly sure he had not actually done anything about what I had told him, and so I assumed his anger was mostly performative. Still, Afferson made a good show of it: What if Amelia now ran, he wanted to know? What would happen then?

"She won't run," I told him.

"And how do you know that?" Afferson asked me. "How do you know that?"

"Because she's dead."

And then I told him the whole thing: the funeral in the rain that we had happened upon, the gaudy coffin I had watched lowered into the ground, and how much they had all loved her.

Afferson stirred his coffee, looked around the room, and then sighed.

"Well, I suppose that's that, then," he said. "Nothing more to be done, is there?"

When I pointed out that Louise Fisher was still in Durham Prison, Afferson shrugged.

"And what is Nurse Fisher in prison for?" he asked.

"Murder."

"Whose?"

I stopped. As far as Afferson was concerned, Louise had been convicted of the murder of a patient she had indeed killed, and he saw no reason whatsoever to challenge that. The fact that he had become wealthy and famous based upon that conviction was, he seemed to want me to believe, simply incidental.

"Of course, if you could find me Mr. Athole's drug chart," Afferson said, "then we'd be in business."

We both knew the drug chart was long gone. I stood up and left.

I went to Scotland later that spring, and did stop off in Durham again on the way. Louise Fisher seemed happier even than she had been the last time I visited, and proudly informed me that she had become "a kind of advanced nurse practitioner for the prisoners." The prison doctor, Louise whispered, wasn't very competent, and the girls on the wings trusted her clinical expertise far more. She said she had even been helping out some of the staff with their own medical problems.

Eventually, Louise asked me about the information in my letter, and I told her the full story. She listened quietly and intently, but when I was finished she simply told me a version of the same thing that Afferson had said: one way or another, she had killed Mr. Athole, so really she was in the place she deserved to be, at least for the time being. She promised me she would mention what I had told her to her lawyer, but as she understood it, her appeals were mostly exhausted. She seemed to actually smile as she said this.

I left utterly bemused, but on the train north I saw that it all made a horrible kind of sense. In prison, Louise was considered the esteemed professional she had always dreamed of being. She was a celebrity, she had respect, and even a degree of power. More than anything, people listened to her and gave her the attention she craved. It was just about everything she had ever wanted, even since those bygone days.

All the same, for the first few months I kept thinking I would hear again from Louise or her lawyer, but I never did.

CHAPTER 46

These events were all two decades ago now. Louise Fisher will be eligible for parole next year, and a few of the newspapers have already been running their annual story about how the Angel of Death has become a model prisoner. It doesn't matter, of course, because the current Home Secretary is far more likely to bring back hanging than ever set Louise Fisher free.

But none of that is what prompted me to set all this down. A month ago, I was watching the ten o'clock news when a report came on from a war-torn hospital somewhere in the Middle East. It was a scene so familiar I barely paid attention: a harried young doctor tended to the bandaged and bleeding victims of a drone strike, explaining to the camera as she worked that without antibiotics, or morphine or even simply clean water, she was more or less powerless to help any of them.

But then they cut to a wider shot of the crowded emergency department itself. And there, in the background, using her stethoscope to listen to the heart of a man who appeared to be dying, was Amelia. I glimpsed her only for a second, and she had aged the same twenty years we all have, but it was unmistakably her. In that moment, I immediately understood what had happened on those hot days in Mbala all those years ago.

Amelia had known I was coming to Zambia. I had written and told her about the photograph I had found, and she was smart enough to know that I would eventually put it all together. And so she had been waiting for me. It would not have been hard for her to do: maybe somebody at the clinic knew someone at the airline, or perhaps one of the taxi drivers who declined to take me to Mbala had been somebody's cousin. It'd only have taken a single phone call to set the whole thing in motion. Jacob had no doubt been in on it too, because his willingness to take me and his prolonged bathroom break at the roadside restaurant fifteen miles from Mbala suddenly now made sense.

It would have been easy enough for Dr. Amelia to get the chief nurse on side, but I wondered what she had told them: that I was a crazed ex-boyfriend, or a stalker, or a violent former colleague with a grudge. Whatever it was, they no doubt all already loved her so much they would have done just about anything for her. Throwing a pretend funeral and wake would have been the smallest of asks, and the guilt trip the chief nurse laid on me was simply the coup de grâce. For a brief moment I wondered if Amelia had actually been there that day, watching me from within the ICU. I did not wonder about this for long, because the answer was as obvious as all the rest of it: of course Amelia had been there watching me that day. She was a doctor, and loved to be proved right as much as the rest of us.

I searched online for information about the news report I had seen, and found the clip again. The website said it had been filmed somewhere in the northwest of Syria, but for security reasons they would not specify where. I tried to call Afferson, but he has long since retired from police work; his website told me that he was in America consulting on a police show for cable television. Eventually, I tracked down Newington, who was now an Assistant Chief Constable in charge of some kind of internal policy review department. It took her a moment to place me, and when I finally explained what I was calling about, she said that if I sent her the information she would look into it.

Three days later, Newington called me back and said that they had confirmed with the relevant aid organization that the doctor in the footage was not Amelia. I did not believe her, and I don't think she even expected me to. I say this because she went on to explain that the world was not perfect, and that Louise Fisher was up for parole this year, and her lawyers would not want any unnecessary noise, so why not just let sleeping dogs lie? She said, too, the quiet part out loud: that even if Amelia had been responsible for what happened at St. Luke's, maybe the good she was doing now offset it. It was true, more even than it had once been in Zambia, that nobody wanted to go and work in Syria, and so Amelia's patients there would be lucky to have her. At least, some of them would be.

CHAPTER 47

A nd so here we now are.

For twenty years, anytime I have been unable to sleep the old question has returned to nag at me. It is the question we never ask in medicine, because we all know it has no answer. And yet in this particular case, the word still whispers itself to me each time the blood pulses in my ears on those sleepless nights: Why? Why? Why?

No doubt the experts would say that Amelia was a psychopath, and then argue among themselves about whether or not she also fulfilled the diagnostic criteria for Munchausen syndrome by proxy. Just as Afferson had once done in his book about Louise Fisher, they would search for a magical combination of nature and nurture that might somehow explain it all: a childhood illness, a sick parent, a history of abuse or neglect, a head injury. And yet when that part of the conversation was over, they would anyway sigh and shrug, and declare that the bottom line was that

Amelia was simply hardwired wrong. Nothing anyone could do. Barely even worth studying. Throw away the key.

Maybe they'd even be right. I have read endless lurid paper-back books about medical killers, and every academic paper that has ever been published on the subject, and the only consistent conclusion I can draw is that we all must pray we never suf-fer the misfortune to fall under the care of such an individual.

Still, on those nights when I lie awake, I find myself return-ing to a hypothesis of my own. Long before I had ever heard of St. Luke's, I had wondered if spending so many days and nights wandering the corridors between life and death meant that some of us eventually begin to see things differently: no God, no redemption, no salvation. Only: some bodies that get lucky amid the carnage, and many that do not. Medicine is a dark and a terrible knowledge, and sometimes it can even be a lethal one. The junior doctors found in parking lots and walking out onto bridges at night, the consultants who dis-appear on their solo hiking trips. People say it is the stress of the job that kills us, but I do not think that it is. I think it is the knowledge.

As the small hours tick by, I wonder if it was this knowledge that changed Amelia. Not the knowledge that we dutifully learn by rote in the library, but the kind we come by harder on the wards, and at the bedside. The knowledge that nobody is com-ing to save us, that any one of us could drop dead at any time and—beyond the grief of those few nearest to us—it would merit no more than a raised eyebrow, a hurried postmortem, and some lines on a piece of paper that ultimately explain nothing.

We each seek our solace from that terrible truth wherever we can. For some of us, it is family, children, or a parallel ca-reer as an opera singer. For myself and many others, our solace too often ends up coming in a bottle or a needle; twice a day, I still measure out five mililiters of the red liquid, and will do so now for the rest of my life. Perhaps, I decide in those sleepless hours, Amelia simply sought and found her solace somewhere infinitely worse still.

Why? Why? Why? I have watched human babies born and cannot believe such perfect creatures could ever be hardwired wrong. Maybe, then, Amelia too had her tonsils removed in those bygone days, and the sight of the nurses in their starched uniforms planted a seed that was finally watered to fruit years later. Maybe she had a sickly parent. Perhaps in her first year of university she found herself dissecting a body while her classmates chatted about their plans for a skiing trip. Or maybe the incident at Cambridge truly was an accident, and the random misfortune of her stupendous fall from grace fractured her mind forever.

None of those feels quite like a correct diagnosis, and there is no blood test that could ever elucidate her motivation, no X-ray of the heart that could confirm it. I suspect that even Amelia herself—brilliant diagnostician though she always was—could not tell you the reason for the things that she has done. But on each night that I find myself turning this all over, I inevitably finally return to the sole idea that seems at once simple and correct enough to allow me to drift toward my uneasy dreams: for the rest of us there is a satisfaction in curing disease; perhaps, when you are as gifted at that as Amelia, there is simply a darker satisfaction in causing it.

And maybe, I conclude as I slip off, it does not matter much in the end anyway. A cell divides unconscionably, a blood vessel clots itself off, a piece of food lodges in the trachea, a heart slips into a rhythm it should not, and eventually the green line on the monitor turns forever flat. We are all no more than bodies, and sometimes people die.

★ ★ ★ ★ ★